PRAISE FOR

YOUNG-HA KIM's

I HAVE THE RIGHT TO DESTROY MYSELF

"Think of it as Korean noir."
—LOS ANGELES TIMES

"Stylish . . . This book is anything but predictable."
—NEWARK STAR LEDGER

"Mesmerizing."
—BOOKLIST

"A stylish, inventive writer . . . Noir with a piquant exotic twist."
—KIRKUS REVIEWS

"Kim's tantalizing debut novel . . . is a self-conscious literary exploration
of truth, death, desire and identity."
—PUBLISHERS WEEKLY

"Mr. Kim's writing is tense, elemental, tangy. Like Georges Simenon, his keen
engagement with human perversity yields an abundance of thrills as well as chills
(and for good measure, a couple of memorable laughs). This is a real find."
— Han Ong, author of FIXER CHAO

YOUR REPUBLIC IS
CALLING YOU

BOOKS BY YOUNG-HA KIM

I Have the Right to Destroy Myself
Your Republic Is Calling You

YOUR
REPUBLIC

IS CALLING
YOU

YOUNG-HA KIM

Translated from the Korean by Chi-Young Kim

A Mariner Original > Mariner Books > Houghton Mifflin Harcourt
Boston   New York

For information about permission to reproduce
selections from this book, write to Permissions,
Houghton Mifflin Harcourt Publishing Company,
215 Park Avenue South, New York, New York 10003.

www.hmhbooks.com

Library of Congress Cataloging-in-Publication Data
Kim, Young-ha, date.
  [Pitui cheguk. English]
  Your republic is calling you / Young-ha Kim ; translated
from the Korean by Chi-Young Kim.
      p. cm.
  "A Mariner Original"
  ISBN 978-0-15-101545-0
  1. Kim, Young-ha, date—Translations into English. I. Kim,
Chi-Young. II. Title.
  PL992.415.Y5863P5813 2010
  895.7'34—dc22   2010002432

Book design by Melissa Lotfy

Printed in the United States of America

DOC 10 9 8 7 6 5 4 3

*The translation of this book was funded in part by the
Daesan Foundation.*

To Eunsoo

YOUR REPUBLIC IS
CALLING YOU

SPEAK UP

H<small>E OPENS HIS EYES.</small> He feels heavy and his breath stinks. Slowly, his brain whirs into activity, and a word gradually reveals itself, like a stranger emerging from fog. Headache. He has never in his entire life suffered from a headache, but he would have to agree if someone pronounced that what he feels is indeed a headache. He thinks it odd that such an insidious, unfamiliar throbbing could be expressed in one bland word—"headache." This intricate amalgam of physical pain and psychic irritation started last night; it triggered an ominous feeling about everything that would soon unfold in the world beyond his bed. He feels a passing disgust at his own body. It's as if his soul, having lain dormant in his body, woke up, discovered the heavy and authoritative being trapping it, and began pounding on it loudly in protest.

Lying still, he thinks about his headache, his agony growing worse. A small needle is stabbing the back of his head. He doesn't know how to deal with it. He resolves to think of this mysterious pain as a temporary visitor, which makes it easier to tolerate. He stretches out to caress his wife's hip. She moves away, mumbling nasally. He pushes his hand deep into her panties and strokes the hair sprouting all the way up to her belly button, but she doesn't react. He slides his hand out of her underwear and rubs his eyes.

She asks, still half asleep, "Aren't you going to work?"

"Huh?"

"Aren't you going to work?"

"What about you?"

"Feed the cat." She buries her face into her pillow.

Ki-yong pushes the covers off and gets out of bed slowly. The cat comes over and rubs her head on his feet as she does each morning, demanding food. He measures out some cat food with a stainless steel scoop and pours it into her bowl. The cat, whose mottled brown, black, and white fur creates a map of the world on her body, contentedly chomps on her kibble. He gently strokes her neck, then goes into the bathroom, takes out his night guard, and places it in a cup.

Last winter, his dentist warned: "If you don't do something about that teeth grinding, you're going to need dentures soon."

Ki-yong unscrews the cap of the mouthwash bottle and pours the blue liquid into the cup holding his custom-made mouthpiece. He squeezes toothpaste onto his toothbrush, his thoughts wandering to the small needle poking his brain. The more he tries to forget about the needle, the more insistent it becomes. Now it attacks one spot persistently, like a wire jabbing at a clogged pipe. He taps the back of his head with his hand but it doesn't help.

"Dad."

He looks into the mirror at his daughter with the toothbrush still in his mouth.

"Are you feeling okay?" she asks.

"Iffwoffing." He wants to say "It's nothing," but his toothbrush is in the way. Hyon-mi pokes him in the back, her lips dancing as she tries to hide her smile. Wearing pink Mickey Mouse pajamas, the fifteen-year-old drags herself to the dining table. She pours Kellogg's cereal into a bowl, opens the fridge, and takes out the milk carton. The cereal crackles as the milk fills the bowl. She crunches on her breakfast. The cat wanders by, rubbing against Hyon-mi's foot. It feels like a slinking snake to Hyon-mi.

"Meooowwwr," the cat protests, as if she knows what the girl is thinking.

After rinsing, Ki-yong comes out of the bathroom and picks up the cat. Only at that point does his wife, Ma-ri, step out of the bedroom, in her underwear. She isn't wearing a bra and the blue veins threading past her nipples make her look cold. She scratches her stomach with her left hand, encased in a cast, while covering a yawn with the other. Approaching the table, she tousles Hyon-mi's hair with her injured hand.

"Did you sleep well?" Ma-ri asks her daughter.

Hyon-mi shakes her head. Hyon-mi hates that her mother walks around the house half naked, so she won't even glance at Ma-ri when she isn't wearing anything. Ki-yong presses his fingers against his temple and offers, "My head hurts."

"You never get headaches," Ma-ri says.

"Well, I guess I do now."

"What's wrong with you?" Ma-ri throws back, heading into the bathroom.

"What's that supposed to mean?"

"Sorry, I meant to say something else. Is it a migraine? Is it only on one side?"

"It feels like a needle is sticking into my brain. When does your cast come off?"

His question is buried under the flow of water. "What?" she asks, frowning.

"The cast on your arm."

"Oh, they told me to come by next week. It's so itchy, it feels like ants are crawling around in there."

"Maybe they are."

Ma-ri closes the bathroom door. She broke her wrist two weeks ago, when a department store escalator lurched to a stop and she fell, unable to stay on her feet against the crush of people behind her.

"You should listen to Yuki Kuramoto," Hyon-mi instructs Ki-yong as she places her bowl in the sink.

"Yuki who?"

"He's a Japanese pianist. He's supposed to be good for headaches."

"You're kidding."

"Dad, you're not one of those people who think kids only say stupid things, are you?" asks Hyon-mi, shooting him a look.

"No."

"So give it a try, okay?"

Hyon-mi is already holding out a Yuki Kuramoto CD. He takes it and slides it in his briefcase. For a split second, Ki-yong feels as if he were floating. It's a joyous feeling, a sensation of his heels lifting slightly off the ground. The mere act of holding the CD is alleviating his pain. Or is it the solace of his daughter's worried expression?

Feeling buoyant, he tells Hyon-mi, "I think it's working already."

"See, told you." Hyon-mi heads into her room to change.

Ki-yong hears Ma-ri flush. He goes into the master bathroom, washes his face, and starts to shave. The water is warm and the suds are soft on his face. He wipes his face with a towel and reviews his schedule for the day. He doesn't think he will be that busy. He has to settle the accounts with a theater in the afternoon, but since it's only a formality, a phone call will do.

He picks out a brand-new shirt and a bluish gray silk tie. He puts on a navy jacket, and he's ready for work. Briefcase in hand, he knocks on the bathroom door.

"Are you going to be late tonight?" he asks Ma-ri.

"What?" Ma-ri opens the door and pokes her head out. "What did you say?"

"Are you going to be late tonight?"

Ma-ri thinks for a second and shakes her head. "I'm not sure. What about you?"

"I don't have any plans, but I'm not sure either."

Hyon-mi comes out of her room, fastening the blouse buttons of her school uniform. She pushes her feet into her Pumas and yanks open the front door. Ki-yong follows her.

"Then everyone's on their own for dinner," Ma-ri says.

"Okay, see you later," Ki-yong tells Ma-ri.

"Yeah, okay," Ma-ri says, following them to the front door. "Hyon-mi, you're coming home straight from school, right?"

"What for? Nobody's going to be here anyway."

"Where are you going to be, then?"

"I don't know." Hyon-mi slams the door behind her.

Ma-ri reopens it a crack and admonishes her daughter, her face solemn. "You have to understand that we're busy with work. You don't even go to cram schools. Where do you think you're going to go?"

"I'm not going anywhere!" Hyon-mi shoots back.

This time, Ma-ri closes the door without a word. Ki-yong and Hyon-mi stand in silence in front of the elevator. The doors open and they get on.

"Dad."

"Yeah?"

"You guys are really weird sometimes. It's like you're expecting me to get in trouble. You really don't trust me?"

"No, it's just that scary things happen."

"Well, you don't have to worry about me," Hyon-mi says, and pouts. The elevator arrives at the first floor. They exit, one after the other. "See you later, Dad," Hyon-mi calls out as Ki-yong heads toward the underground garage.

"See you later."

Walking down to the garage, Ki-yong's head starts to pound again. The needles, having multiplied, swim slowly in his brain.

HYON-MI WALKS DOWN the winding path through the apartment complex and stops in front of Building 104. She takes out her cell phone to check the time. 7:42 A.M. She frowns a little, but then feels a hand on her shoulder. As she turns her head, a finger pokes her cheek.

"What the hell?"

It's A-yong. "I get you every time!" she crows.

"You're dead!" Hyon-mi says, aiming a gentle kick to A-yong's calf.

Like a cartoon character, A-yong raises both arms and cries, "Oww!" The two girls, who are the same height and have identical hairstyles, start toward school.

A-yong asks, "Did you do the homework?"

"Which class?"

"Viper's?"

"Math? Oops, no."

"What are you going to do?"

"I can do it when I get to school." Giggling, they walk out of the apartment complex and down a street lined with cherry trees.

At a crosswalk in front of a convenience store, Hyon-mi asks, "A-yong, can you keep a secret?"

"What?"

"It really is a secret. You can't tell anyone."

"Okay, okay. What is it?"

Hyon-mi assumes a grave expression. "My mom is really my stepmother."

"What?"

"Really, she's my stepmother."

"That's crazy."

"It's true!"

"Sure," A-yong says, smirking.

"I don't care that she is. It's actually better this way," Hyon-mi says.

"How did you find out?"

The light turns green and they cross the street.

"I found out a while ago."

"But your maternal grandmother likes you the best."

"She does it to hide that Mom's not my real mom. It's all just an act." Hyon-mi stops and looks into A-yong's eyes. "You don't believe me, do you?"

"No, I believe you."

"I don't think you do."

"Hey, I said I do."

The two girls amble across another crosswalk. Students from their school walk along the street, headed to class. A-yong slips her arm through Hyon-mi's.

Hyon-mi asks, "A-yong, what's the meaning of life?"

"What's wrong with you?"

"Do you think it makes sense for people to live meaningless lives and then die?"

"I guess not."

"Right? I'm going to be a nun," Hyon-mi says.

"You think you're Mother Teresa?" A-yong teases.

"How'd you know I read her biography yesterday? You're psychic, A-yong!"

"She's the only nun I know. She was on our test, remember? You read way too much. Last week you said you wanted to be Madame Curie!"

"Who says nuns can't do physics? Sister Lee Hae-in writes poetry," Hyon-mi retorts.

"That doesn't make any sense. You think physics is the same thing as poetry?"

"Well, anyway I'm going to try to figure out the meaning of life," Hyon-mi concludes.

"Good luck."

"Just stop laughing at me," Hyon-mi says.

"Fine."

Hyon-mi sighs. "I think having a family is so pointless. Women are always trapped by their families, don't you think?"

A-yong slides her arm away from Hyon-mi's and changes the subject. "So have you given up completely on playing Go?"

"I can't compete with the guys. They're machines. When I'm next to them I feel like they're emotionless robots or something."

"But you can make a ton of money if you do well."

"Not a lot of people can do that well. Hey, you're all about the money, aren't you?"

"Nah, I don't care about money. Still. I wish I were you. I could play Go and drop out of school. Why aren't I good at anything?"

They see more students as they near the school gates. Girls, chattering like birds, trot quickly through the gates toward the classrooms. The boys look like oddly drawn figures, their adolescent bodies disproportionate, off kilter. A few boys shoot A-yong a funny glance.

"Are they still making a big deal out of that?" Hyon-mi glares at them.

A-yong noticeably withdraws into herself as they enter the gates. She mumbles under her breath, "Whatever. I don't care. They'll do it until they croak."

Hyon-mi walks in front of A-yong, as if to protect her. "Jesus, those assholes. Don't they have anything better to do?" she spits out loudly.

A-yong averts her eyes from the hostile looks. Last fall, when A-yong was video chatting with her boyfriend, she flashed him. Her boyfriend captured the image and instant messaged it around. The incident wasn't forgotten. Everyone in school, from the principal to the security guard, knows A-yong as "The Chest." She's the girl who flashed a boy, and that is all she will ever be to them. Other mean-spirited rumors bubbled up as well. If A-yong weren't best friends with cool Hyon-mi, it would be difficult for her to deal with the fallout. But everyone is in awe of Hyon-mi, a girl famous for having played Go and then being a stellar student after she quit competing. Hyon-mi's tough streak commands attention, although she is more popular among the girls than the boys.

Like the other kids, Hyon-mi first assumed A-yong would transfer. She even wrote her a farewell card. But A-yong's parents didn't choose that route. They had a unique worldview. They believed that human beings would soon achieve eternal life thanks to the development of bioengineering and cloning techniques, following a scheme developed by extraterrestrials who'd come to Earth a long time ago. Because A-yong's parents believed such things, they didn't understand their daughter's humiliation at the hands of her peers. They figured she could go through a little degradation for a while, since she would become immortal anyway. Given eternal life, the three years of middle school were a mere blip. Following rules was the most important factor in achieving eternal life, not maintaining friendships. "That's not what's important in life" was A-yong's mother's favorite saying. Her parents had a number of quirks. They consumed only unprocessed food, like raw vegetables, never ate meat, and didn't have a car. They spent almost every day in church. So A-yong frequently ate alone, fixing instant noodles for dinner.

A-yong's least favorite period was gym, where she had to be active and run. She felt that everyone stared at her chest when she ran, which was not entirely false. She always asked the gym teacher if she could stay behind in the classroom; he leered and let her stay without asking why, acting like he was doing her a big favor.

Entering their classroom, A-yong lets out a sigh and heads to her seat near the back of the room. Hyon-mi, walking to her desk by the window, glances back at A-yong. She still can't believe that a girl as shy and introverted as A-yong exposed her breasts on camera. That event was a glimpse into the dark and sinister underbelly of life, one that Hyon-mi wasn't supposed to know about. She wonders if there is some mysterious element inside her, too, waiting like an alien for the right moment to emerge.

Hyon-mi glances at her watch. 7:50 A.M. She should be able to get her math homework done before class. She takes out a notebook from her backpack but doesn't feel like opening it. Her chin cupped in one hand, she wonders what kind of woman A-yong will grow up to be.

A RED LIGHT. Ki-yong gently applies the brake. His headache had subsided a bit, possibly thanks to Yuki Kuramoto.

He switches CDs, inserting the *Buena Vista Social Club* sound-track. Upbeat Cuban melodies fill the air. The piano, guitar, trumpet, and vocals are a little too exuberant for the sound system in his car. Ki-yong sings along. *Oompah, oompah, oompah, oompah, tralalala.* Life is worth living again. The sun is rising in the distance, his car zooms powerfully up the hill when he steps on the gas, and the band sings joyously. As his headache disappears, a feeling of ecstasy washes over him, as if a shot of morphine were injected into his arm. This is as good a start to a day as any; he woke up at the same time as always, his bright daughter adores him, business is going well. He's healthy and he doesn't even need reading glasses yet.

As soon as the light turns green, the motorcycle messengers idling next to him gun through the intersection. A 125cc Honda motorcycle pulls up beside Ki-yong's window. He glances at the helmeted driver, who turns toward him. For a split second, their eyes meet. With a boom, the motorcycle bolts past Ki-yong's car. Ki-yong turns up the stereo, forcing the old Cuban men to blow on the brass with all their might. He speeds up, changes lanes, and passes four cars.

AFTER HER HUSBAND and daughter leave, Ma-ri finishes up in the bathroom. She's now wide awake. She takes out her cell phone from her purse and her thumb blurs over the keypad, tapping out a text message.

—Lunch?

A little later, an answer pops up on her screen.

—OK. Where?

Her thumb flies.

—Napoli. 12?

—OK!

She tosses her phone back in her bag. Sitting in front of

the vanity, she starts blow-drying her hair. Men who are curious about what women are like when they think nobody is watching should try to catch a woman as she gets ready in the morning. Ma-ri is one of those women who blows out her hair and applies makeup like a cyborg, mechanically patting on foundation and slicking on eyeliner. She stands up and puts on the clothes she laid out the night before, pausing to yawn. She pulls on stockings, tosses her makeup bag in her purse, and walks to the front door. The cat follows her, meowing. Ma-ri steps around her, concerned that cat hair will get on her black skirt. She slips on her shoes.

"Bye, kitty, Mommy's leaving," she says, opening the front door. The cat stares back.

STILL LYING IN BED, Park Chol-su stretches his hand out slowly and picks up his wallet from the bedside table. Three hundred thousand won. He lays it back on the table and clicks the remote, turning on the TV. The clock on the top right-hand corner of the screen reads 7:47 A.M. He sits up, using only his abs and keeping his lower half completely immobile. His body is taut, ready for action. There isn't an ounce of fat on him, from his head to his toes. He looks at the TV. A sleek black horse gallops along North Riverside Road. Four horses have escaped from a trailer heading for the Wondang racetrack during rush hour, and cars are stuck on the road, unable to move. Emergency crews are trying to get close enough to the horses to grab their bridles. A smile flickering on his face, Chol-su watches the commotion that has erupted in the middle of the city. The frightened horses dwarf the drivers in their cars, who instinctively shrink away when the horses leap by, their large penises jiggling at eye level.

When the news moves on to another item, Chol-su heads into the musty bathroom to pee. He flushes. He plugs the sink, letting the water pool, and washes his face carefully, making sure not to splash outside the sink, and pats his face dry with a towel. He starts singing "Speak Up" by Crying Nut. *Speak up, speak up, speak uuuup.*

DREAMING JARS OF OCTOPUS

MA-RI OPENS her Volkswagen Golf and gets in. Rain from the day before has made the fabric damp and the seat sticks to her legs. She rolls down the window to let in some air. Waiting for the engine to heat up, she lowers the visor and looks into the mirror. In the darkness, the crow's-feet around her eyes appear more defined. She flips the visor up and releases the parking brake, her plastered hand hovering between her chest and the wheel. With a metallic clank, the car jerks forward.

She has to drive more carefully than usual because of her useless left hand. It brings her back to the days when she was a novice. *When did I first get behind the wheel?* It was the summer of 1994, during a heat wave. The driving-school car had no air conditioning. She remembers beads of sweat rolling down her face, stinging her eyes.

She begins to reminisce about all the firsts in her life. The first time she rode a bike was during the summer after third grade. Boys biked away from the neighborhood en masse, like a desert caravan. She didn't know how to ride, so she perched on the back of the biggest kid's bike. Near the creek, the boy who'd given her a lift taught her to ride. She wobbled and weaved. After half an hour, she was able to manage this two-wheeled monster, which had a mind of its own. When she could finally pedal along the narrow road next to the creek by herself, the boys whistled and clapped from a distance. She returned to the starting point, breathing hard from the excitement, and the boy who had been running alongside, holding on to the back of the bike, handed her a cigarette.

Really? she asks herself. *Did kids that young get together to smoke?* She is suspicious of her own recollections; memories can become distorted. But that scene is clear and vivid in her mind. She remembers coughing before she even inhaled, not because she was choking on smoke, but because she thought that was what she was supposed to do. The boys, giggling, took one last deep drag, threw the butts into the dirty creek, and then climbed back on their bikes and headed home.

Ma-ri suddenly craves a cigarette. She opens the glove compartment, hoping for a stroke of good luck, but there are no cigarettes inside. She wishes there were just one. She wishes she bought a pack earlier.

The brake lights of the car in front shine crimson. Traffic starts to thicken. She cranes her neck, looking for the reason for the delay, and sees a car on the shoulder, its bumper damaged, several tow trucks and a police car flocked around it. The car appears to have swerved off the road and smashed into the guardrail lining the side of the riverside road.

Switching on her hazards, she pulls up behind the police car. She gets out and approaches the cop, who is on one knee, measuring the length of the skid marks. The cop struggles to stand up, his midsection as round as a tire.

"Which insurance company are you from? That was fast."

"Did someone die?" she asks.

The cop stares at her, then fixes his gaze on her cast. He seems to have realized that she isn't from an insurance company. A man in a worn leather jacket comes over and stands between her and the cop. He is flushed and limping a little—the driver of the car.

"Nobody died. Who are you? Who are you with?" the man asks.

Ma-ri turns away. "Never mind. I'm no one."

"Are you with the insurance company?"

"No."

The man turns red, like a scolded child. "Then who are you?"

"It doesn't matter." She addresses the rotund cop who is about to kneel again, "Can I bum a cigarette from you?"

Surprisingly without hesitation, the cop slips out a pack of cigarettes from his pocket and holds it out to her. Salems. She starts to pull out two, then pauses to smile beguilingly at the cop to ask for permission. He nods lightly, and, leering, says, "Like it minty, huh?"

"Thank you," Ma-ri replies.

The cop holds out a lighter but she politely declines. Back in her car, she uses its lighter and takes a leisurely drag. If her left hand weren't injured, she would drive off as she smoked. Her brain is reacting to the nicotine before it even reaches her lungs. She relaxes; the world is somewhat brighter. She exhales and opens her eyes. The cop and the driver are staring at the small, round glow of Ma-ri's cigarette through the tinted windows of her car. Smoke snakes out through the sunroof like strands of noodles.

She starts thinking about her firsts again. How old was she when she realized that people died? She remembers a single white chrysanthemum lying across a lone empty desk.

The elderly teacher pressing a handkerchief to her reddened nose and her classmates sniffling. Sitting right behind the desk with the chrysanthemum, Ma-ri felt the eyes of the teacher and kids on her, watching to see how sad she was. All the kids were stealing glances at her, because she was the only one not crying. So she covered her face with her hands but thought it was unfair. The girl wearing a pink dress, the one who sat next to her, told her what happened. The occupant of the empty desk was tricked and kidnapped by a bad man, then was discovered a few days later in an abandoned suitcase in front of a dry cleaner. Ma-ri didn't understand what kidnapping was. But the face of the girl found dead inside the suitcase was etched in Ma-ri's mind. Why did she have to go inside the suitcase and make everyone so sad? Was she playing a game of hide-and-seek? Why did she have to go to such lengths for a stupid game? She glared at the empty desk overtaken by the solitary chrysanthemum. Despite the vacant seat, the girl's absence was oppressive. Nobody noticed her when she was alive, but her disappearance made her unforgettable. Was she really never coming back? Ma-ri didn't fully understand the finality of death. But the girl never returned. For a while the class monitor brought a new flower every morning, but the ritual eventually petered out.

So then Ma-ri had a working definition for death. It consisted first of a disappearance, then controlling everyone's emotions even after you were gone. That sounded pretty neat. She decided to pretend she was dead. When she got home from school, she took her shoes in hand and snuck into her grandmother's closet. At first nobody realized she was gone. She was bored but waited patiently. She even dozed off. Since the kidnapped girl wasn't discovered for a few days, she had to be patient, too. She fell asleep. When she woke up, the house had erupted into chaos, just like she had wanted. It even smelled different. Through a crack in the closet, she saw dark blue police uniforms. They were the same uniforms that appeared at school. She glimpsed her grandfather, his expression grave. Someone was already weeping, probably her youngest aunt. This ruckus continued for a while. Her grandmother called Ma-ri's mother, who was in Seoul at the time. Ma-ri was gone for only a few hours, but the place was in an uproar because of the earlier kidnapping case. The commotion created by her small joke so surprised her that she wished she were actually dead. It would have been much better if she really died and could float above everyone's heads, invisible like an angel. Then she wouldn't have to disappoint her grandmother, aunt, or mother. Their grief had to be easier to witness than their disappointment. She tried to strangle herself with her hands. She couldn't breathe. While she was trying to kill herself, her leg jerked and kicked the closet door. Then her grandmother's beloved chihuahua—was his name Jerry?—started barking furiously at the closet. Springing up, her grandmother flung open the closet door. Her grandmother, who was 5'7" and quite strong, grabbed her by the hair and yanked her out. Ma-ri rolled out onto the floor, along with a mound of blankets. She was lucky she didn't break anything.

HER VOLKSWAGEN ROLLS gently into the company's parking garage. The security guard, his uniform wrinkled, comes running out when he sees her. He stands in front of the car, blocking her way. She brakes. The guard moves over to the driver's side and opens the door.

"What are you trying to do with that broken wrist? Here, get out."

She gets out, feigning reluctance. The guard gets in and

slides the car into the lift in one fluid move. She thanks him, smoothes her clothes, and enters the showroom. Inside, sparkling new automobiles are displayed like dinosaur skeletons in a natural history museum. She walks through the showroom to the office, bows with a bright smile to the branch manager, and sits at her desk. She revels in this moment, when she glances across her neat and tidy desk, opens the large drawer to the right, and places her purse inside. She also loves the hard marble under her heels when she walks into the showroom. Compared to work, home is an uncontrollable monster. There are always odd things in her kitchen cabinets—sauces she doesn't remember buying and mysterious herbal teas taking up space indefinitely because they never expire. The fridge is in such disorder that she can't get herself to clean it out. Her daughter's room is always a mess. She has a husband she still can't read and a daughter who becomes more adept at avoiding her as she grows up. Nothing at home has a clear-cut solution. Her head hurts just thinking about it all.

Her computer finishes booting up. An IM springs open. It's the manager. He often IM's her even though he sits directly behind her.

—Please report your morning schedule.

She types back:

—A customer's coming for a test drive this morning. In the afternoon I'm working on the mail merge for the motor show invitation list.

She looks behind her. The manager is studying his screen. He starts typing. Soon his message pops up on her screen.

—Ms. Jang, didn't you say you quit smoking?

She sneaks a sniff of her sleeve. She smells like mint and stale cigarettes. She takes out a fabric deodorizer spray from a drawer and heads to the bathroom. The manager, curly-haired and sporting horn-rimmed glasses, never looks up from his screen but knows everything that goes on in the showroom. *Nagging me for smoking when he used to be a druggie!* Ma-ri knows that's why he is so sensitive to the smell of smoke. He used to sell Gucci, Ferragamo, and marijuana at the imported clothing boutique he set up with money from his nouveau riche father. He waited impatiently for the arrival of the inventory not only because he was concerned about the success of his boutique but also to satisfy his own consumption. When actors, singers, and the young moneyed set heard he was a source for weed, his shop became a destination. He spent his twenties smoking marijuana and snorting coke, partying at various hotels. He never got caught, even when the singers and actors were arrested, one after the other. He avoided jail time by providing the police with the names of his well-known customers.

What Ma-ri can't understand is that the singers, actors, and other customers continued their relationships with him after serving their sentences. Is addiction that powerful? Or does he have a special charm that attracts people to him? To Ma-ri, he looks like an average middle-aged man. He is fairly short and not all that handsome. Sure, he knows how to select the right shoes to go with his nice clothes, befitting his former occupation as a clothier, but that isn't enough to overcome the limitation of his plain looks. It's been five years that Ma-ri has worked with him but she hasn't yet detected an ounce of masculine charm. Perhaps he possesses some hidden charisma that is invisible to her. After all, his second wife is a former model and he enjoys a continuous supply of women.

The network he created as a dealer is still intact. Sometimes, hoarse, has-been rockers come to the showroom and take test drives with him. They all swear publicly that they have given up drugs, but it isn't clear if they really have. It does seem that the manager has truly quit. He says he was able to quit by turning to Christianity. When he was suffering from withdrawal symptoms, he bumped into a friend from middle school. The friend mentioned church, something he had neglected for a long time. He remembered the glorious state of transcendence he'd achieved as a teenager by speaking in tongues. Returning to church, he realized that he could transcend his current existence and achieve ecstasy without getting high. He goes to church every Wednesday and Sunday and has even stopped smoking cigarettes. He says he believes in Jesus Christ as his savior but it isn't clear to Ma-ri whether his faith stems from his belief in God or his addiction to that feeling of ecstasy.

KI-YONG ARRIVES AT work earlier than usual. 8:30 A.M. His sole employee, Wi Song-gon, is already there. He's in his early thirties but almost completely bald, having begun to lose his hair in his early twenties. After college he went to work at a steel company in Pohang, then quit and attended several film schools. He dreamed of directing but ended up in Ki-yong's office, after trying his hand at different projects. Song-gon had acted as a guarantor for his father, who dabbled in inventions and had terrible credit, and ended up ruining his credit, too. To avoid having the bank garnish his salary, Ki-yong pays him in cash.

"Hello, sir, you're here early," Song-gon greets him.

"Yeah, I am. Hey, Song-gon, do you eat breakfast?" Ki-yong asks.

"Well, I know I should."

"I heard on the radio that eating breakfast makes your brain work better."

"That's what they always say. Do you eat breakfast?"

"No."

Song-gon checks his computer screen and reports loudly, "Oh, they say it's going to be difficult for *The Green Shade*."

"Yeah? Then we shouldn't go ahead with it. It was expensive anyway. What about Bergman's film?"

"I think we'll be able to get our hands on a print, but there aren't that many places that'll show it."

"Well, find out where we can," Ki-yong directs.

"Sure."

"How's the other stuff?"

"Everything else is going well. Do you have anything important scheduled today?"

"No, I don't think so." Ki-yong sits at his desk in the corner and turns on his computer. Song-gon turns back to his computer and starts typing.

When he first started working for Ki-yong, Song-gon's screen was positioned so that Ki-yong could see it, but at some point, Song-gon turned it away. Now all Ki-yong can see is the back of the monitor. Anyone spending a few days with Song-gon will quickly realize that he has an incurable porn addiction. Ki-yong hired female employees a couple of times, but when they found out that Song-gon was surfing the Net for porn, they quit. Song-gon was never lewd with the women, but they made their decisions quickly, almost harshly. A bald porn addict with lousy credit, Song-gon possesses all the qualities a modern young woman abhors.

"People collect knives or watch bizarre movies, so what's wrong with my liking porn?" he protested once to Ki-yong, who could only agree.

But Ki-yong really wanted to say something more: "Your problem is your lack of charisma. If you were overflowing with charm, watching porn wouldn't be an issue. People will overlook anything if someone's got charm. Even if he's immoral, lies, does evil things—all of that is fine. But they can't forgive a bald loser with a lame job who watches porn."

Ki-yong tears his eyes away from Song-gon and carefully opens a drawer. Three empty 35-mm film canisters are rolling around inside. Someone's gone through his desk. Placing empty film canisters upright in his drawer is his preferred method of booby-trapping. He glances at Song-gon. It's possible, but he doesn't think he could be the culprit. Ki-yong absentmindedly plays with the film canisters. This is already the second time. The CIA, working out of the American embassy in Moscow, once created a set of protocols called the Moscow Rules. There is one rule in particular that he recalls: "Once is an accident. Twice is coincidence. Three times is an enemy action." That means there is one more break-in to go.

Ki-yong presses his temple with his fingers. His headache is starting up again. Who rummaged through his drawer overnight? He doesn't keep anything important in there. Only files and pens and pieces of paper that would be in any movie importer's desk. Should he install a surveillance camera? He might be able to prevent a random infiltration but he wouldn't be able to detect the traces of someone targeting him. A professional wouldn't enter a room equipped with a surveillance camera, and there is no need to go to such lengths to apprehend a novice. He could also install a hidden camera but they would be able to figure out its existence with an electromagnetic detector. He senses something ominous brewing.

The phone rings. Song-gon picks up. "It's for you."

Ki-yong takes the phone.

"Is this Mr. Kim Ki-yong?"

"Yes?"

"I sent you an e-mail but you haven't opened it."

"Who's this?"

The man pauses for a moment. "I'm a friend of Ansong Uncle. I started a new loan company. If you ever need quick money for your business please give me a call."

"I'm sorry? Who?"

The caller hangs up.

"Hello? Hello?" Ki-yong returns the receiver to its cradle, his brow furrowed.

He bites his fingernail, unsettled. He swivels his head, taps his desk lightly with his fist. Hesitating, he places his mouse over the Outlook Express icon. He doesn't know what will leap out of the tiny icon. He pauses once more before double clicking. With a whir of the hard drive, the e-mail program pops up. He selects his inbox and enlarges the window. One e-mail announces the imminent arrival at customs of a print of an Iranian movie he licensed last fall at the Pusan International Film Festival. There are messages about his college class holding a charity event and an agent telling him about a few movies with affordable licensing fees. The rest are spam. But he reads each title carefully and deletes them one by one, rather than selecting and deleting them all at once. His cursor pauses at a subject line that reads: "(Ad) Instant Loan Without Collateral for Office Workers and Civil Servants."

He glances around him surreptitiously. Song-gon, about to get up from his seat, catches his eye.

"Oh, do you need something?" Song-gon asks.

"No, I'm fine."

"Do you want some coffee?"

"Do we have any made?"

"No, but I can make some."

"Thanks. I'd love a cup."

As Song-gon makes coffee, humming, Ki-yong clicks on the e-mail. The words in the body of the e-mail disappear in a series of flashy effects. He reads the e-mail carefully. He clicks on the red "here" in "Please click here if you want an estimate of a loan." A new window pops up. When he clicks on another word, another window pops up. He goes through a couple more of these. When he reaches the end of the process, he pauses again and looks around. The coffeemaker is hissing steam. Song-gon brings over the carafe and a mug. Ki-yong quickly changes the open window to Google.

"Here you go," Song-gon says, pouring the coffee.

"Thanks. That Iranian movie is going to go through customs soon."

"Oh, good. I guess we'll get busy again when it gets here."
"Yeah."

Ki-yong opens Outlook again only after Song-gon is settled in his seat. He closes all the pop-ups and opens the last window. Finally the last message appears.

The jars of octopus—
brief dreams
under the summer moon

Ki-yong swallows, his mouth is dry. It feels as though he's swallowing the sentence, syllable by syllable. He gulps down the coffee cooling next to his mouse. If memory serves him right, this haiku signals Order 4. He turns and selects from the bookcase volume 53 of the *World Poetry Collection* published by Minumsa. That haiku, written by Matsuo Basho, is printed on page 67. Ki-yong feels his hands get clammy. He tries to relax by balling his fists and opening them repeatedly. He subtracts 63, the last two digits of his birth year, from 67. Four. The order he's never received. He can't deny that it has arrived.

This haiku has a prelude, "One night in Akashi." Akashi is a Japanese town famous for its octopus. The fishermen, taking advantage of the octopus's tendency to hide in small spaces, toss clay jars into the sea at night. In the morning they pull up the jars and capture the octopi. The octopi dream their last dreams in hiding.

Ki-yong flips through the book. In the 1980s, Lee Sang-hyok of Office No. 35 rediscovered the benefit of transmitting codes through poetry and books. You didn't have to fumble with a table of random numbers or shortwave radios. All you needed were a few books and a good memory. Order 4 could be given through several different poems. Pablo Neruda's sonnets and Khalil Gibran's aphorisms and maxims. The seventeenth-century monk's haiku that has planted itself in Ki-yong's lap is starved of its literary significance, much like a camel that loses weight after passing through a vast desert. Ripe nuances disappear and only one meaning remains: "Liquidate everything and return immediately. This order will not be revoked." Basho's haiku, like the order itself, hints at the end of dreams.

He believed the order would never come. No—he believed that all orders, not only this one, were forever on hold. But here it is, resting in his inbox. He can't tell who sent it, or why it was sent now. Drumming his fingers on his desk, he tries to gather his thoughts. Since the purge of Lee Sang-hyok, ten years has passed without a single order. The agents sent south by Lee Sang-hyok were cut off from the north and from one another, and they focused on their own survival, unaware of—no, turning a blind eye to—one another's existence.

Is this a cruel joke? Or a mistake, delivered to him but meant for someone else? Or maybe it was supposed to be sent later but was accidentally transmitted now. No. The person on the phone definitely said his name. Did Lee Sang-hyok return to Liaison Office 130? Is he restoring the lines of communication he established years ago? Ki-yong sinks into the murky depths of confusion. It's as if he's awoken from a dream only to discover that it has become reality, all the while refusing to admit to himself that he had the dream. He has to go through several more steps in the e-mail to learn the details of where, when, and how to return, but he stands up. On his way out, he trips over a plastic wastepaper basket, toppling it with a crash. It has been rooted to the same spot for several years and he's never bumped into it. Paper cups and Kleenex are strewn all over.

Song-gon leaps up. "Are you okay, sir?"

"Yeah, I'm fine." Ki-yong turns the basket upright and starts to gather the trash, but cuts his right thumb on the tab of an orange juice can. Frowning, he bounds to his feet and delivers a vicious kick to the basket. It flies across the room and crashes into Song-gon's desk.

"Fuck, what the hell is this shit?" Ki-yong mutters.

Shocked, Song-gon runs toward him. "Did you hurt yourself?"

Ki-yong, breathing hard, sucks on his cut thumb. "Sorry, Song-gon."

"Don't worry, I'll take care of it." Song-gon, looking at him warily, retrieves the garbage can and cleans up the mess. Ki-yong stands in place silently, watching Song-gon. His head is pounding. He can't think of what to do. Song-gon returns the wastepaper basket to its place and goes back to his desk. Ki-yong, forgetting that he was on his way out, picks up the phone and dials. He gets an automated message requesting the caller to try again because the phone is turned off. Ki-yong thinks for a moment and heads out of the office. He dials on his cell phone this time.

"Hello? Is this the teachers' office? Can I speak with Ms. So Ji-hyon, please? Oh, I see, she's in class. When does she get out? Yes, I'm a parent. I wanted to talk to her about my daughter. Okay, please give her the message that Kim Hyon-mi's father called. Yes, yes, please tell her I'll be there at ten. Thank you."

Ki-yong checks his watch and tugs at his disheveled clothes. He feels dizzy with each step but soon regains his composure. He hears a siren in the distance.

IN THE BATHROOM, Ma-ri fights the urge to rip off the cast and scratch away at the skin underneath until she draws blood. But that isn't something a reasonable adult would do. She spritzes deodorizer on her clothes. The smell of mint mingles with the ammonia. She opens the window. Ashes are scattered on the windowsill, remnants of the smoking habits of the building's female employees. She knows that three women meet here to smoke. They work for different companies but gather like old friends, smoke together, and gossip.

She washes her hands and returns to her desk. The manager isn't at his. At this moment, she has no idea how this day is going to turn out. She just hopes to sell a car to the customer who is coming for a test drive. She checks her schedule again, to make sure she isn't forgetting anything. Her calendar reminds her that the anniversary of her father's death is coming up in two days. She feels guilty—it has been only two years but she has completely forgotten about it.

Her father, Jang Ik-dok, was born on November 14, 1925, on the same day as the legendary Korean-Japanese pro wrestler Rikidozan. Lee O-dok, the Korean language activist, was also born on that date, but her father wasn't interested in promoting the Korean language. Rather, he was obsessed with Rikidozan's fate, the fate of a man he had never met. Once, he even went over to Japan and for a hefty sum bought a towel with which Rikidozan supposedly wiped

his forehead; some Korean-Japanese businessman sold it to
him. On December 15, 1963, two days before General Park
Chung Hee, the mastermind of the coup d'état, was sworn
in as president of the Third Republic, thirty-nine-year-old
liquor wholesaler Ik-dok was drinking with his friends on
Kwangju's Chungjangno when he felt a sharp pain in his
lower abdomen. When the big man collapsed, cold sweat
running down his face, the bar owner and Ik-dok's friends
rushed him to the hospital.

It was acute appendicitis. In the emergency room, he was
examined by the on-call doctor. Next to Ik-dok's bed was a
family of five who'd tried to kill themselves by eating blow-
fish soup. One was already dead and the rest were in critical condition. That family was the talk of the emergency
room. Ik-dok, suffering merely from appendicitis, was an af-
terthought. After a long time he was wheeled into the op-
erating room. Cold sweat covered Ik-dok's forehead. The
surgeon and nurses were preparing for the surgery. He was
feeling light-headed because of the severe pain in his abdomen, but he could still hear the radio. Sitting in the corner
of the room, it had stopped broadcasting music to transmit
breaking news. The surgeon was coming toward him with a
needle. Despite the enormous wave of pain lapping at him,
Ik-dok raised his hand to stop him. The surgeon flicked the
needle with his thumb and forefinger. Ik-dok paused his
moaning and pointed at the radio. The brand-new model
transistor radio reported that Rikidozan, who had been
stabbed by a Yakuza's knife a week ago, was dead.

"Rikidozan, the giant of Japanese pro wrestling, died on
the fifteenth at 10:00 P.M. while being treated at Sanno Hospital in Tokyo for a wound that developed into peritonitis,"
Kyodo News reported. "Rikidozan was stabbed in the abdomen in a cabaret fight with a gang member named Murata

Katsuji on the eighth and has been in the hospital since then."

Tears rolled down Ik-dok's face, but a sharp pain attacked his lower abdomen. The sorrow of losing his spiritual brother, Rikidozan, transformed his pain into something else. Later he bragged about the appendicitis, considering it to be a unique pact of solidarity in sickness with the dying Rikidozan. The surgeon, who didn't think highly of pro wrestling, turned off the radio and inserted the needle in Ik-dok's arm. Ik-dok lost consciousness, tears rolling down his face, and the operation began.

At that moment, Ik-dok claimed, he dreamt that Rikidozan came to him, dressed in a sharp suit. As soon as Ik-dok woke up, he looked at his family clustered around his bed and uttered in Japanese: "You have to live just like you sing a song." He insisted that this sentence was Rikidozan's last words. His family was shocked, and rightly so, since it was the first time he'd spoken Japanese in the eighteen years since liberation from Japanese occupation.

After that day, Ik-dok repeated that phrase as often as the French say "C'est la vie." So much so that, at his deathbed, the family waited for him to make that pronouncement. Not because they liked it, but because it was a perfect phrase for the moment of his death, like a familiar slogan in an ad campaign.

But Ik-dok didn't open his mouth. He blinked his sleep-filled eyes like a cow and turned his head with difficulty. They knew the end was near. He called over his second eldest son, In-sok, who was standing by his feet. In-sok shuffled nearer to his father but couldn't advance farther than Ik-dok's waist because his mother was standing by the old man's head. Ik-dok nodded for him to come closer. In-sok was finally able to lean over his father's mouth after pushing past his mother, who reluctantly let him take her spot. Ik-dok left his last words to his son in an inaudible voice, moving his dry mouth slowly. In-sok listened, nodding, with a heavy and dark expression. A short while later, just as in a TV drama, Ik-dok's heart stopped beating. But the family members didn't throw themselves on his body, sobbing, as it was a death they'd been expecting. The new widow asked her son, "What did your father say?"

In-sok looked uncomfortable and didn't want to say anything.

"It's okay. He's gone," his mother encouraged.

"I'll tell you later. It's nothing important."

The more he declined to tell, the more curious everyone became, including Ma-ri.

"What did he say?" Ma-ri asked.

"Well . . ."

"Spit it out," their mother urged. Outside, the nurses were getting ready to move the body. Ik-dok's stomach, which had ballooned to a great size because of his illness, started to smell like wet socks.

Finally, In-sok opened his mouth. "Be wary of taxes." It was In-sok's mouth that was moving, but as if by a feat of ventriloquism, his voice sounded like Ik-dok's.

"Taxes?"

"Yes, he said to be mindful of taxes."

It was a fitting end for a liquor wholesaler. Taxes were his arch nemesis; he had been fighting them his entire life. Even though everyone understood this, each thought wistfully of the legendary pro wrestler.

PREMATURE NOSTALGIA

THE NOISE WITHIN the classroom subsides when Soji opens the door. She tosses the roll call book onto the lectern. The kids call her Soji, not by her full name, So Ji-hyon. She's used to the nickname. When she was in school, there was a girl named Maeng Ji-son, and their friends referred to her as Maengji, while she was called Soji. She often thinks that Soji is preferable to such a common name like Ji-hyon.

The kids scurry back to their seats. If it were nice outside, everyone would frown at the thick dust floating around the classroom, but it isn't visible in this weather. Soji glances out the window. It is overcast and possibly drizzling. The class president, Hyon-mi, stands up and leads the class in greeting Soji in a powerful voice, unusual for a girl. Soji looks at Hyon-mi. When their gazes meet, Hyon-mi widens her eyes. She isn't really pretty, but there is something attractive about her. Hyon-mi was in Soji's seventh grade Korean class, and her reading comprehension and language skills were excellent. There are many different kinds of students, as many as there are different types of lovers. Some you want to take out for a nice meal, and others you want to converse with, meandering together through an art museum. Hyon-mi is the kind of kid who would be a perfect partner for playing board games. She smiles a lot and is considerate of others, and even gives you the feeling that you're getting smarter just by sitting across from her. Overcome with emotion all of a sudden, Soji closes her eyes and takes a deep breath. She opens her eyes and flips open the roll call book.

"What day is it today?" she asks.

"Tuesday," the kids shout in unison, their voices ringing metallically.

"And what's the date?"

"March fifteenth."

She jots down the date in the roll call book. She looks around the class, but it seems like everyone is present. She starts the class. She thumbs through the textbook, questions the kids, wakes up the dozing ones, and assigns homework. Korean is the hardest subject to convince kids to take seriously. They don't understand why they have to learn more Korean when they all speak it fluently.

When the bell rings Soji leaves the room with the roll call book and textbook tucked under her arm. A few kids greet her as they walk past. She clacks toward the teachers' office and stops short. She stands in place blankly, like an unwound windup toy. A few students pause to say hello but, noticing her blank stare, continue on, looking uncomfortable. A minute passes. Two boys laugh, one saying, "Hey, look who's zonked out again. I bet she won't even notice if we hit her."

"Do it, I dare you. I'll give you a thousand won if you do."

"Okay, I'll do it. You better mean it."

"Fucker, I bet you can't."

"So it's a bet?"

"Do it. Chicken."

The boy with spiky hair approaches Soji in large, exaggerated steps. But she comes to her senses right before he is about to take a swipe. She blinks a few times and shakes her head, and starts to walk forward.

"Hey, the light came on," the boys snicker, and walk off.

Soji goes into the teachers' office. From far away, she hears "Für Elise," the chime indicating the start of the second period.

THE SCHOOL IS on top of a steep hill. Ki-yong's car drives over the yellow speed bumps embedded tenaciously on parts of the slope. On the shoulder of the winding two-lane road, dogs with bald patches are lying around, scratching their necks with their hind legs. Stationery stores that were swamped in the morning gear up for afternoon traffic. It's such a typical school scene that it's almost surreal. Two boys too young for school are bent over a small video game machine in front of a stationery store like old men playing chess.

Ki-yong's car glides through the front gates of the school. The sprinkling of rain that dampened the windshield has stopped. The aging security guard squints and stares at Ki-yong, but soon loses interest and turns back to his sports daily. Ki-yong parks in the empty lot in front of the school building and pockets the car keys. He closes the door and watches girls in gym clothes playing volleyball.

One girl throws the ball in the air with both hands, and the girl standing in front of the net sets it up for a spike. The girls running up to the net follow rehearsed steps, jump up, their stomachs sticking out like frogs, and try to spike the ball. Most hit it below the net and some miss altogether.

The ball lands in various parts of the net. The teacher, sitting in the referee's chair with a whistle in his mouth, looks down at the kids with a world-weary expression. The girls are overweight. They run up to the net uncomfortably and just barely manage to hit the ball. Then they return to the starting line to wait their turn. On their way back to the line or while waiting, the girls surreptitiously pull the edge of their underwear down, which has become wedged between their buttocks. Throw the ball, run up to the net, wait, spike the ball, pull down the underwear. Ki-yong feels like he's watching Charlie Chaplin's *Modern Times*. The kids do what they have to when their turns come, then go back to their places.

Ki-yong stands by his car for a while, watching them. A sadness wells from within. If he could label every feeling, this would be "premature nostalgia." Ki-yong, now that he has received the return order, is experiencing everything in a different light—as is to be expected. It's akin to the way a traveler preparing for a long journey packs his bags. Mentally, he is already at his destination, so that he can think of the things he will need when he arrives. Just as such travelers gather shampoo and underwear, eye masks and nail clippers, Ki-yong is collecting and storing images, noises, and smells from this world; ingredients necessary for later use, for that extravagant treat called nostalgia.

"Taegukkgi is waving in the wind," he hums as he walks past the flagpole. He learned this song when he was twenty years old, an immigrant belatedly learning something that even babies knew. He passes the flowerbeds enclosed by a privet hedge and salvia flowers and the hallway lined with monument-like trophies and plaques, and walks into the teachers' office. Teachers returning from classes enter the room. A few chat with one another, coffee cups cradled in their hands. As is his old habit, he notes the number of people and their positions in the room. Thirteen teachers are there, four men and nine women.

"I'm here to see Ms. So Ji-hyon," Ki-yong announces to a teacher wearing a black cardigan.

Before that teacher can respond, someone says behind him, "Are you Hyon-mi's father?"

Soji and Ki-yong look at each other for a moment. Soji bows and Ki-yong follows suit.

Soji breaks the silence. "Please, come with me to the conference room."

She leads the way. The conference room is at the end of the hall, about 150 feet away from the teachers' office. When he steps into the hall, he feels a chill typical of a concrete building. There isn't much inside the conference room; it resembles an interrogation room. Like many spaces without a designated owner, it doesn't feel welcoming. Just a long table, a three-person couch starting to look shabby, and a few metal chairs. On the wall hang student poems that were once submitted in an exhibition.

"I wasn't expecting you." Soji drags a metal chair to the table, making a terrible scraping noise, and sits down. Ki-yong settles in comfortably. Soji props her chin up with one hand and looks at him. "Is something wrong? I was surprised to get your message."

"I didn't want to say on the phone," Ki-yong explains.

Soji smiles and narrows her eyes at him. "What, did you and Ma-ri get into a fight?"

"No."

"So I hear you said you were the parent of one of my students, even though I'm not a homeroom teacher. That was bold."

"Well, I am a student's parent. You're Hyon-mi's Korean teacher."

"If Hyon-mi's homeroom teacher finds out he's going to think it's odd."

"Well, let him."

"So what's going on?"

Ki-yong pulls his chair closer to the table. His collar starts to choke him. The needle in his head that was wriggling earlier is starting up again. His mind flits back to Order 4. Glancing up, he catches her staring at him.

"I don't have much time. I have another class," Soji comments.

Ki-yong rubs his face and looks away. "You know the thing I asked you to keep for me?"

"What?"

"You know. The thing I asked you to keep for me a long time ago."

Soji squints. "Oh, yeah. What about it?"

"I need it."

"It's at home."

"It's not far from here," Ki-yong says.

"I don't have time to go home and come back right now. Do you need it today? Can't I messenger it over tomorrow?"

"I'm going to need it today."

"You came all the way here just to say that? You could have called me."

"I just stopped by. I was in the neighborhood."

"What's in that thing, anyway? Can't you tell me?"

Ki-yong looks up at the clock on the wall. The red digital numbers read 9:21. Soji notices him checking the time. "I guess you're pressed for time. How about this? When I get off work at four, I'll run home and get it. Where should we meet?"

"Can it be earlier?" Ki-yong tries.

"I'm really sorry, but I have a lot of classes today so I don't think I can before then." She studies him carefully.

"Then can you make it at six?"

"Of course."

"You do have it at home, right?"

Soji seems a little unsure. "Well, I know I saw it when I moved. It should be in my closet if nobody touched it."

"Okay, good." In his head, Ki-yong goes over the steps he needs to take. It would work even if he gets it at 6:00 P.M. He wants to rush back to the office for the details of Order 4. Whether he decides to go back or not, he should know more about it. A wave of regret washes over him. He should have read the e-mail before he left. Why did he avoid it? This isn't the proper behavior of someone who used to be a member of Liaison Office 130.

"Okay, well, I should go. See you later," Ki-yong says, getting up. Soji's expression doesn't change. She looks like she's blaming him for something but she's oddly detached.

"Okay? Soji?" Ki-yong peers closely into her face. Even when he moves his head, her gaze doesn't follow. He waves his hand in front of her eyes, then settles in to wait until she comes to. A little later, her eyes regain their sparkle. She rubs her cheeks with her hands.

"Oh, I did it again, didn't I?"

"Yeah. Does it happen often these days?" Ki-yong asks tentatively.

"It's gotten more frequent. I'm pulling all-nighters to work on that novel I told you about. I think it gets worse when I'm tired. Whatever, it's fine. I come back quickly enough. How long have I been out?"

"Maybe three minutes. Do you really lose consciousness?"

"No, it's not like that. Like I told you before, I can hear everything. I just can't react. It's a kind of epilepsy."

"You know what it was like? It felt like being on the phone even after the other person already hung up, but you keep talking because you don't realize it's happened."

"You were saying you were busy?"

"So you did hear me."

"Well, you should get going."

"No, I don't have to right away." Ki-yong forces himself to relax a little.

"Then can you stay a little longer? How about some coffee?"

"Sure."

Soji opens the door and goes outside. He hears coins clanking and paper cups being dispensed. She returns with two cups of coffee from the machine.

"I'm addicted to this stuff. I drink this even at home." She offers one to Ki-yong, who takes a gulp. Sweet but otherwise tasteless. "Hey, I was at home last weekend and that movie was on OCN. Remember *Swordsman II*?"

One day in April 1992, Soji and Ki-yong saw *Swordsman II*, starring Brigitte Lin and Jet Li, in a theater in Chongno. Brigitte Lin starred as an invincible martial artist who became more of a woman the more she trained in martial arts. They'd felt a little uncomfortable because of the homoerotic scenes.

Ki-yong closes his eyes at the memory. "You didn't trust anyone. You made yourself that way. Who's still standing next to you now?"

"What?" Soji widens her eyes at Ki-yong's gibberish.

"That's what Jet Li said to Brigitte Lin. In *Swordsman II*."

"Really? You still remember the dialogue? Are you sure it's right?"

"I don't know, I just remembered it. You don't remember? You saw it last week!"

That day, after the movie, they went for a bite on the first floor of the Nagwon Arcade. On TV the L.A. riots were being broadcast as breaking news. They watched as black men stormed into stores and grabbed electronics. The image of Rodney King, driving along in his Hyundai Excel, then beaten by cops, repeated on a loop. Gunfights and arson ensued. The City of Angels became a city of lawlessness, and Korean immigrants guarded their shops and streets with guns.

"Remember, it was the day of the L.A. riots," Ki-yong says.

"Yeah. But the name of the martial arts manual was . . ."

The Sacred Flower Scroll.

"Wow, you really do remember everything. And I'm the one who saw it last week!" The thought that Ki-yong might remember everything makes Soji a little uncomfortable. She sweeps up her hair with a tired flick of her wrist. "So you remember what I told you back then, too?"

Ki-yong nods slowly. That night in 1992, on April 30, Soji confessed something after getting drunk at the blood sausage soup joint, something she'd never told anyone. Sex followed, as if it had been some kind of transaction. As if it were required because a secret was revealed. She tore down Ki-yong's hesitancy with deep, passionate kisses. That day, college students swarmed into the National Tax Service, demanding a widescale reinvestigation of conglomerate tax evasion tactics. While she was sleeping with Ki-yong, Soji's father, who worked for the National Tax Service, was clucking as he read the propaganda leafleted by students at the National Tax Service building in Susong-dong, Chongno.

As a child, she had thought working for the government was the most lucrative job in the world, as her father's assets grew miraculously. Top-quality imported liquor was stacked everywhere and bundles of American dollars were wrapped in plastic and laid below racks of short ribs in the freezer. Only when she was in high school did she discover the secret to her father's amazing accumulation of wealth. She disapproved. The ethical standards she learned in school were different from those followed at home. Her father would often utter vague pronouncements: "Things are done because they can be done." It was the kind of theory paraded around by imperialists who colonized and murdered natives. "That we can do this means that we are allowed to do it, that it was approved by God." By the time she got to college, she was ashamed of her father; she couldn't even eat at the same table. He embodied society's evils and the corrupt dictatorship. She threw away Byron and Wordsworth and picked up Marx and Engels. She separated from her father emotionally and economically. In those days, nobody thought twice about it; others had done the same thing. Some of her friends were a little jealous of her. She did have the emotional luxury that students from poorer families didn't—the luxury of casting off rich, immoral parents. The poorer kids instinctively knew that the rich parents, as long as they were parents, would use that wealth and power to protect their children. Everyone around her understood this.

A few months earlier, in January, she had been asleep in her friend's apartment when detectives from the Seoul Police Department burst in and took her away. There was already a warrant out for her. In the police van on the way to jail, she had only one thought in her head. She just didn't want her father to find out. She wasn't the ringleader of the student movement, so she wouldn't have to serve a stringent sentence. She couldn't stand to see her father use his connections to get her out, then lecture her arrogantly. She regretted that she hadn't violated the National Security Law; even her father couldn't rescue her from something that serious. But the police already knew who she was and there was no reason not to notify her parents right away.

But a small miracle happened as she awaited her fate in the interrogation room with her head bowed. One of the higher-ups of the Seoul Police Department recognized her as he passed the room. He walked in slowly. The detectives stood up and saluted.

"Hey, aren't you Ji-hyon?"

Soji looked up. He casually flipped through a file that was being compiled by a young detective. He was from the same hometown and had attended the same high school as her father, so she had called him Uncle since childhood. He was one of the people her father kept up with regularly, sending him liquor and money in the days leading up to the holidays. Sometimes when he came over to her house and played Go with her father, Uncle would leave with a plain unmarked plastic bag.

Soji screwed her eyes shut and said, "Please don't tell my parents. I'm not a minor anymore."

Uncle stared down at her, placing the file on the desk. "You're all grown up," he said, and grinned.

She detected servility in that smile. It was an expression you would expect from someone who was entering a bank first thing in the morning to get an emergency loan. Uncle told the detectives to bring him the file when it was completed, and reassured her, "I'm not going to tell your father, so don't worry."

He left the room without even unleashing a standard lecture about how she shouldn't go around protesting. The detectives' attitudes changed visibly. They became polite and gentler. Hot coffee and cigarettes were provided. When evening came, they brought her to Uncle. Perched on a fluffy couch, she smoked a cigarette he offered her.

"We can't undo a violation that's already happened. You'll probably get a stay or be paroled. You didn't throw a Molotov cocktail and you didn't violate the National Security Law, so it isn't going to be a big problem. The prosecutor will summon you a couple of times. You do need to go to those. Okay?"

Soji smoked quietly. When she finished her cigarette, Uncle took her out to dinner. In a fancy restaurant with private rooms, she tasted fermented skate, a delicacy, for the first time. Uncle kindly told her the names of the dishes and offered them to her. She was tired, but ate too much and drank a couple of beers, which caused her face to flush.

Uncle said, "Everyone has dreams, right?"

Soji agreed.

"When you're my age, dreams vanish and, how should I say this, desire grows in you. You know what I mean?"

Soji glared at him, understanding what he was trying to say.

He bit his nails anxiously. "I'm not talking about sex. Just, you know, everyone wants something different. But if you can't get it, it stores up inside you and turns into a sickness. Do you know what I mean?"

"No," she retorted.

"I did what you wanted. I hope you'll do something for your uncle, too. People want different things, and exchanging these things to mutual benefit is what capitalism is all about. Even if you don't like it immediately, it becomes beneficial for everyone. That's what's missing from socialism. Socialism doesn't take into consideration that people want different things." Uncle avoided her gaze and picked up his glass.

Soji didn't say anything. But a little later, they ended up in a shabby hotel downtown. He took off his clothes and lay down on the bathroom floor. Trembling, he closed his eyes. Soji, standing upright, pissed on his face. Her hot urine splashed the face of the senior superintendent for public security and dripped to the floor, into the drain. It felt like all the beer she'd consumed at the restaurant was gushing out. When she finished, he opened his eyes. Smiling in a servile manner, he closed his eyes again. She spat in his face. It made him happier. To climax before all of that wonderful piss ran off his face, he masturbated hurriedly. Crying, Soji left the bathroom and wiped herself with a towel. But she couldn't deny the primal pleasure she experienced from pissing on the face of a high-level police official, the ultimate symbol of the state. She felt a theatrical thrill. The man with power and influence acted like a naked child, while the defendant humiliated him, standing above him like a goddess. She was the actor, and at the same time, the viewer. Soji felt relieved. Uncle would keep his promise and her incident would be hushed up. She felt like a young thug being initiated into a mob family. She figured that now she was a grown-up, getting a sense of how the world worked—a place where different powers struggled against each other, where one act was exchanged for another.

Uncle, after he finished, showered, wiped the bathroom floor, and came out to get dressed.

"Thanks," he said.

She didn't doubt that their secret would remain between them. She went back to jail and was freed the next day; the prosecutor dropped the charges. The day L.A. burned up, she told Ki-yong the whole story, and afterward they went to a motel as naturally as if they were old lovers. Ki-yong wondered for a second whether he was going to have to lie down on the bathroom floor in Uncle's place, whether that was what she secretly liked. But it wasn't. She just needed someone who would listen. Her lust was born from the excitement of confession, and Ki-yong happened to be there when she broke her silence.

"After that, Uncle sometimes came over to our house. I only saw him a few times, but it was like I had the upper hand. He wouldn't look at me. I felt sorry for my father whenever I thought about his ignorance. Like it was some kind of payback."

"Yeah, you told me that."

"Oh, I did?"

"Yeah." Ki-yong nods.

"But there's something I didn't tell you."

"What?"

"Uncle died."

"How?"

"An airplane crash in Mokpo."

"Oh, the Asiana flight headed to Seoul."

"Amazing. You sure I didn't tell you about it? Good memory. I was in the U.S. at the time and my mom called me with the news that a plane crashed in Mokpo. At first I thought my father died. But the night before she called, I dreamt that Uncle was sitting at the foot of my bed, grinning, dressed in mourning whites."

"I don't think he would be resting in a nice place," Ki-yong comments after a moment.

"Clearly." Soji pushes her hair back, and they smile listlessly at each other. "But is everything okay? You don't look too good."

"Really?"

"Yeah."

"I have a headache."

"You never get headaches."

"Yeah, but I got one this morning. I guess now I get head-aches. Things change as we get older."

"Yeah, it's true. Where do you want to meet later?"

Ki-yong thinks for a minute. "How about the Japanese restaurant at the Westin Chosun?"

Soji squints at him. "Now I'm getting more suspicious. What's in that bag of yours? Drugs?"

"I'm craving their sushi."

"Is that place any good?"

"I never took you? They do a good steamed cod head, too."

"You only took me to cheap places," Soji says.

"My treat, okay? It's really good."

"Thanks. So let's meet in the lobby at six."

"Okay. I'd better get going now." Ki-yong pauses at the door. "So we'll meet there at six, and if something comes up I'll call."

The hallway outside the conference room is quiet. Ki-yong bows. Soji returns his bow. Ki-yong walks toward the main entrance, where daylight is filtering through. A beat later, Soji follows. The music signaling the end of the period re-verberates through the speakers; Schubert's "Trout Quintet." With that signal, the giant monster of a school starts to come alive. Like a small earthquake, the floors thunder and the high voices of students coagulate, sticky like mucus, grow-ing slowly in intensity. The vibration and the noise, erupt-ing from the higher floors, slither down to the first floor. Ki-yong goes back through the dark hall lined with trophies and plaques and emerges from the building. He feels sluggish. The kids who had gym brush past him and run up the stairs, chattering. The pungent, not unpleasant smell of sweat and body odor trickles into his nostrils. Ki-yong regains his energy. He might not have that much time, but he doesn't want to lie obediently on the butcher block awaiting his fate. He starts the car. Soji stands at the entrance of the school building, watching him disappear beyond the front gates.

HYON-MI ISN'T ONE of those kids who race around during breaks. She prefers to remain by herself, resting her chin on her hand, and look down at the grounds from the window. Some impatient boys who have gym next period run out to play basketball before the kids who just finished gym even get back to the classroom. Near the basketball court, a middle-aged man with a familiar gait and demeanor walks briskly toward the parking lot. Hyon-mi cranes her neck to get a good look. Dad! Why is he here, and not Mom? Did he meet with her homeroom teacher? But her teacher would have told her. Hyon-mi wonders if she should open the window and call out to him, but ends up just looking at his retreating figure. It's the first time she's seen her dad from above. Maybe because of the angle and the distance, he looks unusually small and dispirited. That morning, at home, he was larger than life, but the guy walking across the school grounds is a different man. He's one of many suits driving a Sonata, no different from her asshole physics teacher. Her father looks back at the school building—where kids emerge, hunched against the early spring chill—and gets into his car. A woman stands at a distance from her dad. Soji, her Korean teacher. She has short spiky hair like a Japanese career woman, so she's distinguishable from the other female teachers. It's clear that Soji walked her dad out. Why Soji, not her homeroom teacher? Her father's car glides through the front gates and turns down the steep road.

A-yong comes over and sits next to her. "Whatcha looking at?"

"Nothing."

A-yong rolls her small eyes in a knowing way and asks, "Are you going later?"

"Where?" Hyon-mi averts her eyes, pretending to fiddle with something.

A-yong whispers, "Jin-guk's house. Are you going?"

"Oh . . ."

A-yong narrows her eyes. "Stop pretending like you don't want to."

"I should go, right?"

"You mean you want to go, don't you?"

Hyon-mi, starting to get annoyed, gnaws on her nails. "You know, I don't get him."

"Who cares? You like him, and that's all that counts."

"I don't know. That's the thing I'm not sure about."

"It's his birthday. You should at least go to the party."

"Are you going, too?"

"Should I? Won't I be the clueless third wheel if I go with you?"

"No way. I'm not going by myself."

"Is it true that his parents are divorced?" A-yong asks.

"I don't think so. I don't really know."

"I heard people talking. You haven't been to his house, have you?"

"No."

A-yong snickers and starts doodling a cartoon figure of a girl with long legs and big eyes on Hyon-mi's notebook. "Or you can go alone. I'm not going."

"Why not?"

"It doesn't matter. Do whatever you want." A-yong goes back to her seat, grinning mischievously.

Students are returning from the cafeteria or from hanging out with their friends in other classrooms. Hyon-mi glances at Jin-guk, who is coming in the back door. When their eyes meet, Jin-guk looks away. Hyon-mi stares down at her desk. Doodling in her notebook, she wonders why she's suddenly attracted to this guy. She didn't even know he existed at the beginning of the semester but then, just in the past two weeks, she's become obsessed with him. He isn't that good in school or noticeably popular. At the beginning of the semester, their math teacher, nicknamed King Kong, said, "I don't know if you guys know, but a long time ago, there was something called ham radio. Amateur wireless communications . . ." A few kids looked at Jin-guk, murmuring, "They're still around." That was when she became conscious of his existence. Visibly excited, King Kong approached Jin-guk, but Jin-guk only mumbled, "My dad did it, so . . ." But King Kong dug deeper, and found out that Jin-guk had a third-level amateur wireless communication license.

Hyon-mi is fascinated that, in an age of instant messaging and chatting, Jin-guk knows Morse code. He has his own call signature, something unique and different from an instant messaging ID, which anyone can have. Hyon-mi feels close to Jin-guk. A former Go champion and a wireless communication aficionado: they're both holdouts from a bygone era.

THE MAN WHO made the appointment to test drive the Passat comes into the showroom just minutes before 10:00. Through the large showroom window glass, Ma-ri sizes up the car he arrived in, the way shoe salesmen judge people by their shoes. It's a 2003 silver Hyundai Grandeur, the kind of car driven by someone who doesn't depend on a monthly wage, a ride for a man who owns his own business even if it's small, who wants to hear that he has style but doesn't have an adventurous streak. A good candidate for a Volkswagen. Volkswagen customers are different from people who buy other German cars, like Mercedes or BMWs. They tend to be organized entrepreneurs who dislike showing off. Never gangsters or swindlers, they exude less masculinity. And they're the kind of people who think they are extremely knowledgeable about cars.

The man walks toward Ma-ri, his steps precise and confident. Like a man who hasn't ever been punched in his entire life. Economical and neat, he doesn't make unnecessary movements. He's taut, from head to toe. His pinstriped navy blue suit isn't cut from the best cloth but it's stylish, with a little nip at the waist.

Ma-ri smiles and stands up. "Are you . . . ?" she trails off.

"Yes, I made an appointment yesterday. My name is Park Chol-su."

"Yes, hello." Ma-ri hurriedly takes out a business card from its case on her desk. She fumbles a little and the cover of the case starts to fall. The man, who is observing her every movement, snatches the falling cover swiftly and hands it to Ma-ri.

"Thank you."

They exchange business cards.

"Is the car ready?" Chol-su asks.

"Yes, it's right outside."

Chol-su looks down at Ma-ri's arm. "How did that happen?"

"Oh, it's nothing." Ma-ri smiles brightly, as if she had known him for a long time. After bowing to the manager, Ma-ri leaves the showroom with Chol-su.

THE WEIGHT OF ENNUI

Cʜᴏʟ-sᴜ ɢᴇᴛs in the driver's side of the car as Ma-ri buckles up in the passenger seat. He checks the gauges, the parking brake, and the rearview mirror. After carefully glancing around the car, he tentatively starts the engine. Ma-ri offers some tips from the passenger seat, but he doesn't seem to need much help. The Passat passes Yangjae Highway and merges onto the highway toward Pundang. Chol-su abruptly guns the engine to test the car's reaction time and weaves in and out of the lanes, leaving other cars behind. His expression doesn't change but he has melded with the car, breathing with it. Ma-ri can almost feel the adrenaline pumping from his brain—a man, restrained but agile, calm but giving in to an intense energy, is sitting next to her. Unconsciously, Ma-ri moves away from him and leans against the window.

A test drive is dangerous in many ways. Drivers are encountering a particular car for the first time, so they are basically beginners. They usually can't locate what they need quickly and panic. Since they aren't yet used to the feel of the brakes and have trouble reining in their excitement, the car jerks or swerves. And they floor it without an ounce of hesitation, something they don't do in their own cars. The rpm gauge dances beyond the red line and their bodies are plastered to the seats, as if someone is pulling them from behind. A few times, Ma-ri has actually wondered whether men were aroused by the smell of a new car. As soon as their feet touch the accelerator, their breathing grows irregular and excited. Their upper bodies lean forward, in attack mode, and their aftershave mixes with their sweat, emitting musk. The scent of virile males. Forgetting that Ma-ri is sitting next to them, they swear and revert to a state of boyhood. In this tight space, their shoulders brushing against each other, a peculiar tension grows between the test drivers and Ma-ri. The men become attracted to her, a chick who understands cars, and Ma-ri sometimes feels a burning heat, sitting next to these boylike men. But as soon as they return to the showroom and the men hand over the keys, they revert to being nice, polite middle-aged men. They leave quickly, looking a little embarrassed. They bluff a little, acting as if they might buy the car right away, quickly going over their financial situations in their heads, then get back into their own cars, feeling a little shriveled.

Chol-su switches into manual mode and shifts gears. The car jolts forward.

"Powerful engine," he comments.

"It has good horsepower, but the torque is what sets this car apart."

He glances into his rearview mirror and switches into the passing lane. "When I was young my family had a Mark V. Have you heard of it?"

"No."

"Ford and Hyundai collaborated on it. It was our first car. When my father washed the car in the parking lot of our apartment complex, the kids would come out to watch."

"There weren't many cars back then," Ma-ri agrees.

"It wasn't because of the car; it was because of my father, who was a comedian. The kids would swarm over and imitate him. But he was different in real life, quiet and introverted. When he didn't react, the kids would taunt him with his stage name."

"Did he do anything?"

"Sorry?"

"Your father. Did he do anything about it?"

He smiles. "He would say that kids throw rocks at monkeys in a zoo and bang on windows of a pet store because they want to communicate. Because the animals don't respond to them, the kids try to talk to them the only way they know how."

Ma-ri nods. The rpm needle shoots past 2,500.

"If they kept calling out to him, he would put the rag on the hood of the car, turn around, and do his signature silly dance, grinning. The kids would laugh and copy him, and the whole neighborhood would be filled with dancing kids. Then he would turn around, finish washing the car, and come back home. He would put Karajan on the record player, lie on the sofa, and listen to it without speaking. Watching him, I understood that being a comedian was harder than it looked."

"Ah . . ."

"The next day, my father would be back on TV, joking and dancing his trademark dance. Oh, how did I get to this? Sorry about that."

"No, no, it's a funny story."

His eyes harden. "You think that's funny?"

Ma-ri starts to apologize. "No, that's not what I meant. I meant . . ."

The corners of his mouth lift a little. "No, it's fine. Other people's stories are always funny."

A short silence ensues.

"The speed limit is fifty miles per hour here," she warns, pointing to a sign. A silver camera reveals itself with a flash, the sunlight refracting off its surface. Chol-su slides his foot over to the brake.

Ki-yong parks his car in the lot in front of his office. He looks into his car one last time as he shuts the door. The thought that he may never drive it again flits through his head. He glances around and takes the stairs to his office. Song-gon, who was watching Japanese porn with his earphones on, hurriedly closes his browser window.

"Hello, sir, you're back already?"

"What do you mean 'already'?"

Song-gon glances at the clock. "Oh, I lost track of time."

"Did you find out about the screens?"

"They're supposed to call me back."

"I'm sorry to ask you this, Song-gon, but can you go buy me a keyboard? Something's wrong with mine. Some keys work and some don't. I forgot to pick one up on my way in."

"Sure, I know how frustrating it is even if one key doesn't work. Is it urgent? It's going to take a little time."

"That's fine. Why don't you take your lunch break while you're out?"

"Okay."

Ki-yong takes out a few ten-thousand-won bills from his wallet and hands them to Song-gon, who heads out. As soon as Song-gon leaves, Ki-yong opens Song-gon's desk drawer and rummages through messy files, a rainbow of Post-its, earphones, a stapler, a stack of business cards, wires, a promotional paperweight, and packing tape. He studies everything carefully but nothing arouses his suspicions. Ki-yong replaces the items in the reverse order he took them out and goes to his own desk. His monitor is blinking slowly like the eyes of a cow, lulled into energy-saving mode. When Ki-yong taps on some keys, the computer comes alive, awaiting orders. He clicks on the e-mail that indicated Order 4 and follows each step, collecting strange metaphors. Finally, he reaches the end: "March 16th, 0300 hours. Rendezvous at 3674828."

Ki-yong looks at his watch. He has less than twenty-four hours. He takes out a map and finds the coordinates. Taean Peninsula on the west coast. He digs his fingernails into his temple. An agent of Ki-yong's stature can easily go back through China, so why was this dangerous course chosen? Two possibilities pop into his head. Either his identity has been leaked and the South's intelligence agency has barred his leaving the country, or it's a test of Ki-yong's loyalty. Either way, it's a problem.

Ki-yong opens the body of the computer with a Phillips screwdriver. Big balls of dust roll around inside. He carefully removes the hard drive. He takes it to the bathroom, places it in the sink, and turns on the tap. Sinking to the bottom, the hard drive emits a few errant air bubbles. Only bubbles, despite all the hours they spent together—it feels as if he were watching a part of his brain being sliced out. When the bubbling stops, he picks up the hard drive, shakes the water out, and brings it back to the office. Now it would be safe to throw it away in a trash can in a subway station bathroom. Ki-yong reassembles the computer. He then takes out his desk drawers, one by one. Business cards, pens, paper clips, a stapler, and glue sticks fall on the rubber pad protecting his desk. He sifts through the stack of business cards; some names he remembers, others he doesn't. They would soon be whispering about that movie importer who suddenly disappeared. He puts the cards back in the drawer so that anyone looking through it could find them easily, and sweeps the rest of the items back in his desk.

He walks up to the bookshelves. Like a man about to go on his summer vacation, he deliberately runs his hand over the spine of each book. Which books should he take? Will he have time to read? And if he follows Order 4 and goes back, could he even read these books? Probably not. He will have to go from an existence surrounded by books to one made up of walls. He selects Simon Singh's *Fermat's Enigma*. Since it is a mathematics book, neither the South nor the North would have an issue with it. He picks out the poetry volume necessary to crack codes in case he gets another order. He hesitates, then puts in his bag Oloikov's *Death of a Soldier*, a novel he has always meant to read.

Ki-yong also grabs his iPod, on which he has more than two thousand songs. How many songs will he be able to listen to in the future? It has taken so long to collect this many. At first, when he got to the South, he listened to cassettes. He was intimidated by the walls of CDs and tapes stacked in music stores without space for even a toothpick between them. He couldn't believe that all these different kinds of music could coexist in the world. He had grown up in a country of marching songs. His countrymen didn't enjoy music in private, but sang in unison to tunes blared from speakers in the streets. The first electronic gadget he bought when he got here was a Sony Walkman. He listened to the South's pop stars, especially Cho Yong-pil and Lee Mun-se, and the Beatles. The Beatles in particular shook his soul to its core.

He listened to "Hey Jude" or "Michelle" alone in his room through the headphones of his Walkman, savoring the forbidden. These songs opened a door to a new kind of happiness, one he'd never experienced in Pyongyang. Later, when he found a more permanent place to live, the first thing he did was set up a small stereo system and a CD player. As time passed and sound quality and fidelity improved, his tastes gravitated toward classical and jazz. And then, before he realized it, the era of the CD had passed and everyone listened to music in the form of audio files. He was diligent about ripping a CD, converting it to MP3s, and storing them in his iPod, but these days he never surrendered himself to music quite as passionately as he did during his first few years in the South.

It isn't only Ki-yong who changed. The world around him has transformed as well. He came south before personal computers became widely available—he learned how to use one alongside South Koreans. He learned FORTRAN and BASIC, and entered the world of word processing through programs like Posokgul. And he transitioned from the world of MS-DOS to Windows, from the Bulletin Board System to the Internet. He actually adapted quicker to this new world than the average forty-year-old South Korean. As a transplant in South Korean society, his whole mission was to adapt. He didn't have the confidence or the courage to resist or reject change. That was a privilege of only the natives.

He unfastens his watch. He takes out a Sunnto scuba diving watch from the drawer and swaps it with the watch he was wearing, which was a part of his wife's dowry. Plated with 14k gold, it's unfashionable now. Unfashionable—it feels foreign to judge aesthetics so fluidly. In his former world, judging beauty and ugliness according to individual standards was one of the most dangerous adventures one could undertake. Ki-yong's eyes, heart, and hard drive have been completely rewired to become a product of this current world, like a refurbished cyborg. As if someone drugged him, rendered him unconscious, and switched everything out. His old hard drive was thrown into a pool of water and bubbled to its demise.

He was born in 1963 in Pyongyang. But when he came south, he was given the name and identity of Kim Ki-yong, a man born in 1967. The real Kim Ki-yong, an orphan, was born in Seoul. When he was seventeen years old, he left the orphanage and disappeared, and his identity records were expunged. What happened to Kim Ki-yong, the man who lent him this shell? Sometimes he dreamed that the real Ki-yong came back. A man with an erased face stood at the head of his bed. Even though he never said anything, he could tell that this was the real Ki-yong.

In the spring of 1985, he went to a government office in Yongsan and renewed Kim Ki-yong's expired identity card, got fingerprinted, and received a brand-new card, assuming the identity of a man he'd never met. The North Korean mole stationed at the office was a dejected middle-aged man, not the young man impassioned with revolutionary fervor Ki-yong had expected. After the conclusion of their official business, they drank coffee in the hallway. The man addressed him in a nonchalant tone, "So you made it. I thought they had forgotten about me." He didn't seem all that pleased with Ki-yong appearing out of the blue. His tone was curt and rude.

"What do you mean 'forgot'?"

"It's been a while since a customer came by." The man glanced at Ki-yong. He stubbed out his cigarette in the sand on top of the trash can. "I've been meaning to go up but haven't had the chance."

"Do you still have someone over there?"

"Yeah."

"Who?"

"My mother lives near Sunan district in Pyongyang and my uncle is probably in Chongjin."

"I hope you'll be able to visit one day."

The man hawked and spat into the ash can. "If I go now, after all of this, will I be able to live happily? Is that possible?"

"What?"

The man's mouth twisted and he smiled as if to say, What does a kid like you know? He sighed. "Nothing. Good luck." He crushed the paper cup in his hand and tossed it in the trash can, then headed back into the office. He looked like a man who had seen all of his dreams and hopes sputter and managed only to survive, powered by the few drops of cynicism left in the bottom of his fuel can. Ennui dripped down his pant legs with his every step.

For Ki-yong, who had just graduated from the Operations Class of Kim Jong Il University of Political and Military Science, commonly called Liaison Office 130, the man's defeatist attitude was surprising. How could he live in enemy territory without being alert? How could he let go of his animosity toward the South, where the great enemy Chun Doo Hwan massacred thousands of people in Kwangju in broad daylight? Later, he realized the South specialized in lifelessness and defeatism. Indiscriminate weariness was prevalent. Ki-yong knew what ennui was, but this was the first time he personally observed it. At home, it was an abstract idea batted about when criticizing capitalism. Of course, there was ennui back home, too. But in a socialist society it was closer to boredom. And it was really a matter of inadequate motivation; a bit of stimulation could change the feeling of boredom. But the prototypical capitalist ennui Ki-yong encountered for the first time in the South was heavy and voluminous. Like poisonous gas, it suffocated and suppressed life. Mere exposure to it prompted the growth of fear. Sometimes you encountered people who inspired in you an immediate primal caution, something that made you say, I don't want to live like that. That civil servant in the office had this effect on Ki-yong. He represented depression, emptiness, cynicism. Unattractive and dressed shabbily, the man triggered a feeling of discomfort in Ki-yong even though they spent only a few minutes together.

Ki-yong ended up seeing him again years later, in a completely different situation. It was the summer of 1999. A man wearing a red cape stood on a small wooden box in Chongnyangni station, screaming. The cape was embroidered with a black cross with a gold border, which made it look like a college cheerleading uniform from far away. Sweat trickled down his face and black flies buzzed around his head. Ki-yong stood in place, staring at him for a long time. The man had changed immensely. He was thinner and his eyes were glowing. In a reverberating voice, he boomed that the end of the world was near. How did the spy steeped in ennui become an eschatologist? Had he really become one? Frozen in the square, which was crisscrossed by prostitutes, cops, college students, and laborers, Ki-yong gawked at the former spy turned religious fanatic. But the man didn't recognize him. When Ki-yong approached him, he was handed a pamphlet describing the end of the world. It was crudely laid out, studded with excerpts from the book of Revelation.

Ki-yong asked, "Don't you recognize me?"

The man glared at him. Without answering, he turned away to preach to another person. Ki-yong tugged at his arm. He looked back at Ki-yong, annoyed, and tossed back, "What? You think I'm crazy?"

"No, I met you once in Tongbu Ichon-dong."

The man's face tightened slightly. "What's the use? None of it matters. Read the pamphlet. We will soon be beamed up. That day will come soon."

Feeling a little abandoned, Ki-yong started to leave the square. The man got off his box and trotted after Ki-yong. "I do know who you are."

Ki-yong stopped.

"But it doesn't matter. I discovered the secret of the universe. Before, I was just frustrated with life. But I knew, as soon as I received the Holy Spirit, that everything about this life was useless. I was fooled. Look at the faces around you. See any happy faces? They're all kicking and struggling and living each day like pigs. Why? Because they don't know why the world exists. That's why they keep walking on aimlessly. If they knew why, they wouldn't have to wander. You just have to walk the path pointed out by our Lord."

His harangue wasn't coming to an end anytime soon. Ki-yong interjected, "So you're saying that before this year is over, people will be beamed up to the sky from their cars and their empty vehicles will fall off the overpasses and the people left behind will want to be dead, howling in pain?"

"They'll regret being born as a human."

"How do you know that before you even experience it?"

The man pointed at his ear, small and ugly like an unshapely gourd. "Do you only believe in things you see? I heard with this ear here. The Lord told me. Listen hard. Our Lord speaks only to those who listen." He climbed back on his box and cleared his throat.

The end of that year was not met with bodies being lifted to heaven. The New Year began with thirty-three citizens ringing the bell in the Bosin Pavilion, just like every previous year. Despite the millennium bug, planes didn't plummet to the ground and trains didn't derail. Nuclear power plants didn't break down and satellites didn't malfunction or accidentally launch nuclear missiles. Ki-yong thought of the red-cloaked man when he saw on the news that an assembly of 166 churches was to take place, for the devout to pray as the world ended. What happened to the man betrayed both by the revolution and Armageddon? And to all the people who congregated in the 166 churches? Why didn't they take their own lives when it became clear that the world was not coming to an end? Could Armageddon be held at bay that easily? But soon, everyone quickly forgot the large signs saying PERFECT PREPARATION FOR Y2K that hung on tall buildings in Kwanghwamun. Nobody thought twice about the millions of people around the world who barricaded themselves at home with generators and basic necessities. Of course, some people reaped profit from fear. One trillion won was spent in South Korea alone; even more was spent in the United States and in Europe.

Fear and greed propelled people to act at the end of the century. It was trepidation of the unknown, not of war or disease or riots. It sounded scientific that a four-digit number starting with a 2 would shove the world into chaos, but shamanism was at its core. Ki-yong wasn't affected at all by the anxiety that reigned in those days. Maybe it was because a stranger's identity cloaked him and his world was tangled with codes. Or maybe because he grew up ignorant of the Christian worldview. In any case, he didn't think a god of catastrophe and destruction, if one existed, would appear in that way. Why would he come at a predetermined date? A true disaster would march forth from the unknown, like

Burnham Wood attacking Macbeth's castle. The way Basho's haiku popped up on his screen this morning.

Ki-yong sweeps the items on his desk into his black Samsonite briefcase. Song-gon isn't back yet. He stands up and strides out of the office. With an electronic whir, the door locks automatically behind him. He looks back. A small green light blinks above the keypad. Next to it is a well-known security company's logo of a fine mesh web, connected in sharp angles. He heads to the subway station. Dark clouds billow between buildings, wending along the wrinkles of the city. His car, crouched and still, observes him walking away. Ki-yong encounters more people the closer he gets to the subway station but nobody looks at him. He isn't a man who stands out. Lee Sang-hyok at Liaison Office 130 instructed, "Erase yourself until your alias becomes your second nature. Become someone who is seen, but doesn't leave an impression. You need to be boring, not charming. Always be polite and don't ever argue with anyone, especially about religion and politics. That kind of conversation always creates enemies. You'll slowly fade. From time to time, you'll feel your personality straining to get out from within you. You'll ask yourself, Why should I let myself disappear? Practice and practice again so this question will never present itself in your mind." According to Lee Sang-hyok, repetitive and conscious training, similar to that followed by a Zen monk in eliminating egocentric images, would allow one to reach a point where one could fully erase oneself. It was similar to working on one's golf swing. By relaxing the shoulders and eliminating unnecessary movement, one can swing more gently and efficiently. A spy's mindset and actions can be modified, too. In that sense, Ki-yong was the descendant of Pavlov and Skinner.

"Why do people remember you? Because you annoy them. If you're partial to a loud tie or unusual accessories or have exaggerated gestures, people notice you. Seasoned spies aren't easily caught. Even neighbors who lived next to them for years don't remember them when the police come knocking on their doors. A police sketch becomes a faint outline of an average face. Good spies are like ghosts. People don't notice even if they tap-dance in the street or do the butterfly stroke in the pool."

Ki-yong knows that people have warped ideas about what a spy is—Mata Hari, sex appeal, infiltration and escape tactics, extremely tiny cameras, bribery and appeasement, threats. In truth, all the information gathered by spies is already out in the open. Spying is similar to clipping newspaper articles. The quality of the information culled by spies isn't any better or worse than that. Information covers the sky in a black mass, like migratory birds in early winter. No, Ki-yong thinks, that is too menacing an image. It is more like a flood during rainy seasons, sweeping away objects in its path—a cow trying to swim, a chest door inlaid with mother-of-pearl, a pregnant Berkshire sow, red dirt-filled water bubbling up, timber from a pine tree, the corpse of an impatient hiker, Styrofoam buoys. Ki-yong and his colleagues' assignment was to pull out meaningful information from this flow of facts, then analyze it. Because they read endlessly and organize what they learn, they are as academic as any scholar. It was no accident that the spy Chung Su-il, also known as Khansu, became one of the most renowned scholars on the history of exchanges among civilizations.

The most important asset for a spy isn't the ability to infiltrate or disguise oneself, but to possess an acute sensitivity, an ability to discern the crux of the information from the common barrage of words. Near the end of World War II, a famous spy received an order from the KGB to report on the German army's deployment. He went to a blanket factory near the Austrian border and asked them all kinds of questions, posing as a blanket seller. By figuring out where the blankets were going, he could piece together the positions held by the German army. The German army's movements were as clear to him as if he were looking at tropical fish in a tank. Most information is not stored in steel safes deep in cloistered rooms, protected by infrared detectors. All the words coming out of someone's mouth and all the written phrases in public documents—these are the crucial clues.

Ki-yong goes down the subway stairs. A beggar is prostrated on the steps, his forehead resting on the floor and his hands outstretched. He holds a sign made of a cardboard ramen box, the letters written forcefully in black marker. The pen strokes, strong and desperately drawn, shriek in sorrow: I GOT NO LEGS. Ki-yong passes him by, but then doubles back and drops a 500-won coin in his cup. Unable to lower his head any farther, the beggar bends his back and sticks his rear up in the air in gratitude. It is the first time Ki-yong has ever been charitable. From the entrance above, a strong wind pushes into the subterranean tunnel. A sour smell hits his nose, wafting from the beggar and his dirty cloth backpack. Ki-yong runs down the stairs.

BART SIMPSON
AND CHE GUEVARA

NDER CHOL-SU'S direction, the Passat gently hops the sidewalk, turns elegantly, and backs into the parking space in front of the showroom. Ma-ri likes guys who can park gracefully. Good drivers tend to show off, but a man who knows how to park has a delicacy about him and an ability to concentrate.

Chol-su bids Ma-ri goodbye as he gets out of the car. "It's a nice car. I'll give you a call."

"Please do. Bye."

He gets into his Grandeur and turns on the engine. Ma-ri enters the office. The manager nods in greeting as Ma-ri says, "I'm back."

Another dealer, Kim I-yop, who started working there a year after Ma-ri, smiles brightly and greets her. "How'd it go?"

"I didn't see you this morning," Ma-ri comments.

"Tong-il was sick."

"Oh . . . So how is he?" Ma-ri regrets her question as soon as it escapes her lips. There is a brief silence.

"Oh, you know. Same as usual." I-yop smiles. His son has malignant lymphoma. Once, I-yop brought him to work, and the kid grinned from ear to ear, so excited to see all the sparkling cars in the showroom. I-yop placed his son in the driver's seat of a car worth more than 100 million won, and the boy happily honked the horn. The year the boy was diagnosed with malignant lymphoma, he was shuttled around to take all sorts of tests. One day, his wife's car barged over the center divider, crashing into a one-ton truck. The airbag didn't deploy and she died instantly. But emergency personnel found the two-year-old fastened in his car seat, smiling, without a single scratch. The insurance company refused to pay out in full because her car had breached the divider, and I-yop sued. The company apparently thought his wife was trying to commit suicide and that she'd purposefully shot over to the other side of the street. It was a plausible theory but nobody knew for sure. When I-yop was at work, his wife's unmarried older sister looked after the boy. Once, he confessed that he would be taken aback at the sight of her when he got home, thinking for a second that his wife was standing there. Well aware of his situation, his colleagues sometimes give him credit for their contracts, which he doesn't refuse. Judging only from his cheery surface, one can't begin to guess at the depths of misfortune that sprang on his family. At times, his cheer feels a little creepy, like the optimistic beginning of a horror movie. If someone came up to her one day and exclaimed, "Kim I-yop hanged himself last night," Ma-ri wouldn't be all that surprised.

Back at her desk, Ma-ri takes out her cell phone and double-checks the text message she received earlier that morning. Her body starts to burn up, the way it does when she soaks in the tub. Heat travels up in waves from deep within her. She will see him in one hour. They will eat together and she will stare at his lips moving delicately as he chews. Ma-ri touches her face with her hands. Her hands are cool on her hot cheeks. *I'm almost forty. What am I doing?*

KI-YONG BUYS A ticket and pushes through the turnstiles. Although his credit card doubles as a public transportation card, he consciously chose to purchase a single ticket. A while ago, Ki-yong bumped into a *JoongAng Ilbo* film critic at a movie screening. He told Ki-yong that he'd gone to some screening at Seoul Theater in Chongno. When the critic returned to his office, his phone rang. The person on the line identified himself as an employee of a messenger company, and asked him where they should deliver a package.

"Do you know where Hoam Art Hall is? *JoongAng Ilbo?* Come to the lobby and call up," the critic said.

"Wait, are you a reporter there?"

"Yes, why?"

"Do you know Park Hyong-sok?"

"I'll give you his number. You can call him directly."

"No, it's okay. I'm actually with the Namdaemun Police Department."

"What?"

"This is Detective Hong, Namdaemun Police Department Crime Division. Park's on this beat."

"What's this about?"

"We just want to ask you a few questions. Were you at Chongno sam-ga today around 4:00 P.M.?"

"Yes."

"Did you see anything out of the ordinary?"

"I don't know, I just went to a film screening."

"Oh, I see. Which movie was it?"

"Why do you need to know that?"

"Oh, never mind. Thank you."

"What's this about?"

"There was a murder right near there today. We're just asking around, so you don't need to be alarmed. Thanks for your cooperation. We should go grab a drink with Park one of these days," the detective said politely, and hung up.

The critic started wondering how the detective knew he had been in Chongno at that time, how he found his phone number, how he knew where to reach him but didn't know anything else about him. He had frequented police stations when he covered metro, so he was pretty familiar with the way the department worked, but he couldn't wrap his mind around this mystery.

He told Ki-yong, tentatively, "It's probably from some surveillance camera footage or something. They're on every subway platform these days."

Ki-yong carefully pointed out the obvious. "How would they find your phone number from a blurry image? And if they knew who you were from the image, they wouldn't have called you like that."

"What do you think happened?" the critic asked, his expression serious. Even a native of capitalism wasn't sure what to make of a situation that could have been written by George Orwell. He was as shocked as Cain hearing God's voice.

"I don't know," Ki-yong replied, but he did know. It was probably the credit cards that doubled as public transportation cards. The police would have narrowed their search to men in their twenties and thirties and questioned all the men fitting the profile who went through the Chongno sam-ga station around that time. Once they even caught a murderer on the loose at 3:00 A.M. by analyzing the footage of a speed-monitoring camera on Olympic Highway. Detectives of the Kangnam Police Department surmised that a murderer would have adrenaline pumping through his veins right after committing a crime, that he would be more likely to speed, and their hunch had proven correct.

Ki-yong pretends to drop his ticket on the ground and glances quickly behind him. He feels his gut fold over his belt as he bends down. Once upon a time, he boasted a taut physique with hard muscles, envied by members of the combat team. The very fact that he spent time with the combat agents, professional assassins who specialized in infiltration and escape, meant he was in good shape. But that was a long time ago. He is becoming an average middle-aged South Korean man, his belly round, his chest puny, and his arms jiggly. People relax when they look at his belly. They assume that someone like him can't be a mugger. It's safest to be a man who is uninteresting, neither too old nor young. Someone living a settled life. The kind of man who supports his family but is ignored by them. These ordinary men sometimes take part in risky transactions when the opportunity presents itself, their hearts racing, trying to believe they're safe because everyone does it. They can become mired in a bog of corruption, perhaps in the form of kickbacks, bribery, or slush funds, and they don't foolishly dream that they can wade out of it. Nothing has changed since their college days when they clandestinely studied Kim Il Sung's Juche Idea. Some men say that being involved in politics is like balancing on prison walls—morally precarious. But Ki-yong believes that this is the common fate of all men. Those men who were once bewitched by illegal ideology in college are probably leading the same mundane life as Ki-yong. They would have realized the harsh reality that is capitalism and quickly given their all to the world into which they were born.

Wading through the most dangerous moment of his life, Ki-yong knows nothing, other than that an order was issued. *I want to know more. I want to know more. I want to know more.* Ki-yong thirsts to know—not what is going on, but whether he is the only target. He needs to know whether the others are aware of what is going on. Why was he given Order 4? Was his identity revealed or did he inadvertently leak something? The two possibilities sound like the same thing, but they are actually very different. If it is the former, the authorities are recalling him for his protection; the latter, to punish him. But there is no way to know which it is until he returns. During the Cold War, the KGB had overseas spies return to Moscow under the pretext of holding an important discussion, then killed them. A furnace waited for the moles who aided the enemy. The shamed spies were slowly slid into the smelter's melting iron, surrounded by their colleagues, like the Terminator. Of course, sometimes there really was a discussion, and afterward they would be sent back out again. *I don't know. I don't know. I don't know. I don't know a thing.* Ki-yong has no idea what is happening. He has been living as a forgotten spy since Lee Sang-hyok was purged. As he hasn't engaged in very many activities there hasn't been much chance to be discovered. But you never know. It is possible that he unwittingly made a fatal error, or it could always be a misunderstanding. Anyway, he has less than a day. He has to find something out, anything, before the deadline. There has to be a clue somewhere. *I'm sure there was some kind of sign but I just didn't notice it. What happened to me in the past few days? Was there an odd phone call or a stranger following me? If there had been, wouldn't I have noticed it?* No, his senses could have been dulled because he's been living complacently for so long.

By now, he is standing on the subway platform. He hears the announcement that the train is about to arrive. He draws in a deep breath, inhaling it all, like he is going to cherish these scents forever—minute dust particles, the smell of car lubricant, liquor on the breath of an old drunk, the perfume of a young, sexy woman. He holds his breath, then exhales slowly through his nose. Right then, the subway train rattles past him and slows. The people on the platform wait patiently for the doors to open, standing docilely on the footprints on the floor, pasted behind the yellow line to encourage queuing. *Will I have to go back? Will I be safe if I go? Will I even be able to decide whether to go or not? Why would I go back? No, I can't. I can't. I can't go back.* He places a hand on his forehead and steps back. The doors open and people rush out of the car and the quicker ones push in and find seats. Ki-yong continues to waver as he takes in the scene inside the car—the announcement that the car will leave soon, the automatic door vibrating, impatient and ready to shut at any moment, the black-hatted conductor sticking his head out to check the platform, the provocative jeans ad on the side of the car, the model's sexy ass sticking out like a duck's, the seagull-shaped stitching on the pockets emphasizing the curve of her behind, the dirty floor covered in black splotches of spat-out chewing gum, the calm gazes of passengers sitting inside. He can't decide whether to get on or not. Finally, the car doors bang shut, as if yelling, Get out of here! He feels as if a door were slammed in his face, or as if his innermost secrets have been revealed. The people sitting in the subway car leaving the station look at him as if they could see the dark, murky waters churning in his heart. They smile conspiratorially and look back at him standing immobile on the platform. *Asshole! Know your place. Act your age and status. We all learned what we can and can't do under this system. Don't you know it's a crime not to follow those rules? Go back to the empire of strong red paint strokes, the country where children, blowing on their frozen hands to keep them warm, turn their cards in unison to create an ever-changing backdrop in the stadium during the Mass Games, where people scorn women in other countries for wearing jeans. Your republic is calling you.* Everyone seems to be yelling at him from inside the subway car, their hands cupped around their mouths. He imagines plugging his ears with his hands, but that wouldn't drown anything out. The subway car, headed toward Ponghwasan, leaves behind a sharp metallic screech, as if refusing to hear Ki-yong's reply, and resolutely disappears into the dark tunnel.

He is the only one left standing on the platform. He is overcome with emotion. There is something sweet about these cheap sentiments. His eyes closed, Ki-yong revels in his memories. He wants to wriggle deeper into his own wet insides, into the warm darkness, like a snail thrown on the ground. He wants to close his eyes and ears and stay somewhere safe and forget about the order. Isn't it possible that someone will call him tomorrow and tell him it is all a joke?

At that moment, someone bumps into him. His eyes fly open. It's a young man with spiky burgundy hair, wearing ripped, baggy pants. The young man stops, pulls off his earphones, and bows politely. "I'm sorry." He seems sincere, although his appearance would suggest otherwise.

Ki-yong tells him it's okay and goes to sit on a bench. The young man plugs his earphones back in and perches on the edge of a bench, bopping along to his music. His hairstyle and face remind Ki-yong of Bart Simpson, and his loose red T-shirt is emblazoned with Che Guevara's face. He is prob-

ably listening to Rage Against the Machine, or some similar band. The most capitalist country in the world produced
these far-left lyrics, and on the CD—filled with the imagery
of a Vietnamese monk sitting cross-legged while engulfed in
fire, young Seoulites throwing Molotov cocktails—the singers swear, scream, and yell that we have to smash the system. It's fitting music for the kid in the Che Guevara shirt. If
Stalin and Lenin were alive to hear this music, what would
they think? Would they feel the urge to send the band to the
Siberian archipelago?

Five laborers, wearing dirty pants and carrying a red flag,
pass Bart and Ki-yong, following the yellow line drawn on
the floor. There must be a large workers' rally in the afternoon. They are talking among themselves—they're uninterested in Che Guevara. They concentrate on their own problems: the rise in part-time positions, the once-trusted leftist
government's anti-labor policies, and the asshole employer
who keeps evading collective bargaining negotiations.

Now that he has one day left in this world, every clichéd
image in front of his eyes comes to life. He greedily absorbs
everything that the world scribbles at him, his entire being having turned into a dried-up, brittle piece of recycled
paper. Like an amateur poet burning with creativity, like a
young boy who experiences his first kiss, everything around
him becomes poetry. He notices things that form a contrasting resonance, like Bart Simpson and Che Guevara, or
irony, like the jeans model and the shabby workers bearing
a red flag. People seem to be actors who suddenly appear to
awaken his sensitivity toward capitalist society.

As if to remind him that he isn't observing a scene in a
play, another train clatters into the station. When the doors
slide open, Ki-yong enters the subway car, brushing past a
Sikh in a turban. Cheap perfume assaults his nose, then dis-

sipates. He looks for an empty seat and sits down. Right before the door is about to shut, someone runs up and sticks his foot in the gap. The door reopens and he gets on. Ki-yong's senses spring to attention. Is this man following him? Did he wait until the last moment because he was worried Ki-yong wouldn't get on or that he would get off as soon as he got on? The man, wearing a black jacket and overly shiny shoes, walks slowly toward Ki-yong and sits next to him. He has a free newspaper in his hand. The car isn't empty, but there are open seats other than the one next to him. As soon as the man sits down, he starts reading his newspaper, but Ki-yong feels that the whole thing is unnatural. If he's a tail, which side is he on? If the man is the agent in charge of supervising Ki-yong's return, it would be smarter not to go back north. If they trust him, he won't be followed. This means he probably did something wrong, and that's why they're bringing him back. But if the man is with the South's National Intelligence Service, it would be better for Ki-yong to follow the order and return obediently. Then Order 4 would have been sent to ensure his safety, to ward off the arrest, torture, and the possibility that he would, in a state of hallucination and desperation coming from the injection of narcotics and lack of sleep, blow the others' identities, putting them in jeopardy.

All he has to do is figure out which side this suspicious man is working for. His newfound poetic sensibility disappears in a flash, and he assumes the armor of prose, of detachment. He glances at the paper the man is reading. No hints are forthcoming. Ki-yong takes out his cell phone, pretends to look for a text message, and flips his phone open and shut several times. Finally, Ki-yong makes up his mind and stares into the man's face, as if he just discovered that someone was sitting next to him. He sees that the man is starting to look unsure. Ki-yong opens his mouth. "Do you believe in eternal life?"

Ki-yong unfastens his briefcase, as if he's about to take out some pamphlets. But he doesn't let down his guard. If the man takes out a pair of handcuffs or a pistol, he's ready to jab his elbow into his side and grab the emergency hammer from its glass box above his head. If he could get to the hammer, he would smash it down on the guy's head without hesitation, the way he was trained a long time ago. The man's skull would fracture, probably requiring brain surgery. The man would give the sign if he is the agent in charge of guiding Ki-yong back north. But he doesn't. The man stands and turns toward Ki-yong—since Ki-yong is sitting down, he's at a disadvantage. But Ki-yong resolves not to be defeated easily, and tenses his thighs and calves. The man continues to look down at him, his eyes narrowed. He doesn't look surprised or even suspicious, just annoyed. If he thought Ki-yong was an evangelist, he could have just waved him off, so why did he stand up like that? The man and Ki-yong glare at each other, sizing the other up. But the man looks away first. He walks to the front of the car toward an empty seat between two women. The train brakes suddenly, and the car lurches, but the man doesn't lose his balance or even sway, quickly sliding in between the two women. He glances at Ki-yong and goes back to his newspaper. Is he not a tail? Does he merely dislike evangelists? Ki-yong waits for the doors to open. People get off and on. The announcement blares that the car will leave the station shortly. Ki-yong bounds out of his seat right before the doors close and runs onto the platform. The man doesn't look at him, immersed as he is in the newspaper. No harm in being careful. Maybe he succeeded in getting the man off his tail. Standing on the quiet platform, recovering his calm, he mutters to himself, *Do you believe in eternal life?*

MA-RI STANDS UP and looks at the clock. The manager throws her a sidelong glance, as he always does.

"I have a lunch meeting . . ."

The manager asks quietly, without raising his head, "Is it regarding a sale?"

Even though he's a car salesman, he has a way with words. A former French literature major who revered Albert Camus, he always throws her off. It's annoying, the way his words carry a tone of attack, something she can't openly complain about.

"No."

"Okay."

She acknowledges Kim I-yop with her eyes and leaves the showroom. She stands in front of the crosswalk. Napoli is about one thousand feet to the left, on the other side of the twelve-lane road. The chilly air soothes the itch on her left arm that has been bothering her all morning. She thinks about the lobe in the brain that governs the sensation of itching, the lobe whose name she doesn't know. An itch isn't pure pain or pleasure, but a commingled sensation, one that makes her feel like she is going to go crazy if she doesn't scratch it. It coaxes her to revel in instant, sweet gratification. An itch is like sexual desire. She thinks that's why, on the night she lost her virginity, she lay in bed feeling ticklish where the boy's hands touched her skin.

The light at the crosswalk turns green but a couple of cars run the red and zoom through. Everyone starts walking across the street at once. Ma-ri steps off the curb.

HARMONICA APARTMENTS

K<small>I-YONG LIKES</small> going to Seoul Art Cinema, where the old Hollywood Theater used to stand. The theater shows the works of filmmaking titans of times past, relying on government funding to finance its operations. He feels safe and cozy, sitting inside a dark, empty theater. He sometimes relaxes so much that he falls asleep. Here, he doesn't feel like an outsider. People come to see old films and they don't care who else is watching. These moviegoers are capitalist snobs, who put on a show of being hip and ironic to conceal their snobbery. Large cities breed anonymity precisely because of this attitude, this pretension of sophistication. Everyone can live together, each person's real self hidden away. Homosexuals, criminals, prostitutes, and illegal immigrants like Ki-yong. But he's not sure if his analysis of his fellow movie-goers is correct. He would probably never be able to understand these young Seoulites. They may be pretentious, they may not be. Maybe, because they grew up watching all kinds of movies from all over the world and got tired of Hollywood's current predictable fare, they have gone back to the origin of all the copies. Maybe they have ended up sincerely loving Luchino Visconti and Ozu Yasujiro.

Ki-yong didn't live the cultural experiences the others take for granted. He spent his childhood ignorant about King Kong and Mazinger Z, Bruce Lee and Jackie Chan, Donald Duck and Woody Woodpecker, Superman and Spiderman. Instead, he had to study Steve McQueen's *Papillon* and *The Great Escape,* movies that played on TV during every holiday in the South, and experienced *Gone With the Wind* and *Ben-Hur* on cable. He didn't know about the time the soccer titan Cha Bum-Kun was a Bundesliga star. He couldn't say, like the others, that he remembered the huge pop phenomena Kim Chooja and Na Hoon-Ah. At Liaison Office 130, he memorized and rememorized cultural facts and took quizzes on a weekly basis, but he learned his cultural history only intellectually. He could answer the questions but couldn't feel what the answers meant, and this made him think of himself as a human made of circuits and microchips. He knew more facts about Cho Yong-pil and Aster and Seo Tae-ji than anyone else, and could rattle off the history of professional baseball or the student movement of the 1980s, but this knowledge didn't fill the emptiness. He remembered the shockwaves created by Lee Mun-se's second album and the Korean baseball series of '86 and '87 when Sun Dong-yul's Haitai beat the reigning champs, Samsung, but that memory could never be a substitute for his emotional citizenship.

The tedium exuded by these movie buffs intimidated Ki-yong. Everything that elicited the disinterested comment "This is so lame" was unknown, or at least new, to him. He devoted energy and time figuring out which parts were boring to others. It was the life of a transplant, having to give his all just to understand the mundane.

At the Anguk-dong Rotary, he walks toward Nagwon Arcade. Old men are clustered in front of the Seniors' Welfare Foundation, selling magnifying glasses and black-market cigarettes. Others, wearing wool caps, wander among the peddlers, trying to amuse themselves. Ki-yong weaves through the cigarette smoke billowing from the groups of old men, passes the rice cake stores displaying special prices for weddings, and goes up the stairs of Nagwon Arcade. Nagwon— *Paradise*. The normally ordinary word feels unfamiliar to him all of a sudden. When he was young, he went around referring to socialist paradise this and socialist paradise that. At the time he never doubted that the phrase referred to Pyongyang and North Korea. But now he thinks it is a brazen slogan. Paradise? Was it Hitler who said that the masses are fooled by big lies?

The first time Ki-yong felt doubt about the slogan was at Lotte World. Right after he came to the South, the "This is Lotte World" ad was always playing on TV. Fireworks burst above a lake while actors danced around in Snow White and raccoon costumes. He didn't understand why South Korean children were so fond of raccoons. Only later did he find out the raccoon was the mascot for Lotte World. He bought an all-day pass. A ticket that got you into all the rides—this was a concept similar to the logic of his world.

But when he actually entered the theme park, it wasn't the brilliant shows or the heart-stopping rides that shocked him. He was amazed that so many people patiently lined up for popular rides without fighting. Everyone waited for their turn, their faces elated with expectation. Nobody cut in line and even if someone did, nobody got angry. Everyone had to line up like that in Pyongyang, too, for the boat to cross Tae-dong River or to enter the School Children's Palace. There were always people who cut in line. Young soldiers doing ten years of service did it for the long years they would sacrifice for their country, the Party members did so out of a sense of privilege, and some did just because they knew someone up ahead. So tension mounted as the lines got longer. People became irritable and were poised to explode at the littlest thing. Cutting in line wasn't the only problem. Sometimes, without notice, people were turned away, for the simple reason that all the items were gone, or because of unforeseen circumstances. Then the line that had been building for hours would just melt away.

Of course, he wasn't a wide-eyed hick who confused Lotte World with paradise. But sometimes, riding the subway past Chamsil station, the stop for Lotte World, he felt a little off balance—a wave of gentle nausea. He remembered the frightening thought that flitted through his mind while he was at Lotte World—that a socialist paradise might be a lie and Lotte World might be the true paradise. Shocked by his audacity, he tried to repress it by scrambling onto an inane raft ride with no line and bouncing down a darkened tunnel.

He passes stores selling musical instruments that line the second floor. A pimply-faced kid stands next to the pony-tailed owner of one store with a covetous look on his face as the owner plays Gary Moore on an electric guitar. Ki-yong stops in front of a store selling harmonicas. He looks at the harmonica's double set of reeds, capable of producing two layers of sound.

The apartment building where he was born and grew up had a long, dark hallway, with faint light coming in through each end. Doors lined the hall on each side, opening into small apartments. People called these harmonica apartments. If looked at from above, the layout would have resembled harmonica reeds. There wasn't any privacy. The walls were thin, and you opened your front door practically into the apartment across from yours. There were few light bulbs hanging from the ceiling, and even those were low-watt bulbs, so it was always dark in the middle of the hall, and the corners that never saw sunlight smelled like mildew. Ki-yong's home was near the middle of the harmonica. It faced west, so in the evening the waning sun lengthened into the apartment. Sometimes wind blew in from one end of the hall and dashed through the window on the opposite side, and the apartment building would wheeze. The wind, breezing through the narrow hallway, would sound a higher note and retreat when encountering open doors or objects. Sometimes it would slam doors shut and hum toward the end of the hallway and the sunlight, lowering its tone. Only when someone in the apartment at the very end of the hall came out and closed the window did the harmonica ever stop sighing.

Ki-yong's father enjoyed fishing and often took his son to Taedong River. Father and son would sit quietly, their fishing poles drawn. They would dump the fish they caught in a bin and walk home. His father was an engineer who constructed dams. He designed the dams at Yalu River and Imjin River and was respected as the foremost expert in the industry. Hydropower plants were a very important resource for North Korea, which suffered from a dearth of electricity. The locations of dams and hydropower plants were shrouded carefully to guard against American bombing operations, so his father lived under layers of surveillance, so much so that when he went to Moscow to study, briefly in the 1970s, he wasn't given much freedom. He had to report everything that happened on a daily basis to the security agent.

Not long after Ki-yong came south, he realized that all such security measures were useless. America knew exactly what North Korea was up to. The higher-ups in the North probably knew this too. The spying was not protection from America, but an exercise of habitual bureaucratic routine. Up north, anything could be classified as top secret. Even the quality of the river water was confidential information. Without any sanitation facilities, factory discharge laced with heavy metals and daily sewage poured into the river. But any language that chipped away at the legend of the socialist paradise was prohibited. Even uttering something that was legal, depending on who said it and in what way, could be considered taboo, and innocent acts sometimes led to being branded as a spy for American imperialists.

"Are you cold? Do you want the heat pouch?" Ki-yong's father offered.

"No, I don't need it."

His father slid the hook out of the fish gills and tossed the catch in the bin. The fish was a decent size. "Look. It flaps around because it's out of the water."

"Is there a fish that doesn't?" Ki-yong asked.

His father tossed his line back into the river. The fish flopped around in the dry bucket. "No. If there is no water, fish open their gills and flap around, then die. When you're building a dam, you sometimes erect beams and pump water out through a tunnel, so that you can pour in concrete. The fish that don't manage to get out are left dying at the bottom. Comrades are happy to gather them up and make stew, but there are so many you can't eat them all. So they rot. And smell. It's quite disgusting; it makes you want to vomit. So listen carefully to what I am saying. Don't be a fish; be a frog. Swim in the water and jump when you hit ground. Do you understand me?"

That was the last time they went fishing together, right before Ki-yong was selected as an operative trainee of Liaison Office 130. His father sensed what his son's future would hold. His father's advice to become a frog was prescient. Ki-yong adapted well to this chaotic South Korean society, able to survive on his own even after Lee Sang-hyok was purged in a factional struggle.

That day, holding the fish bin with his father, Ki-yong silently padded down the hallway of the harmonica apartment building. It was right after sunset so the hallway was darker than usual. The smell of cooking wafted from each apartment, mingling in the hallway. Some families were making soup seasoned with soybean paste, and others were boiling vegetables. His stepmother, who had been waiting for them, took their bucket. Water was already boiling on the stove.

"Did you two go visit with the King of the Ocean?" his stepmother teased them about their long absence.

His father laughed and started to peel off his jacket. "We had to catch at least one to save face around here, didn't we?"

His stepmother expertly slit the fish's belly and scooped out its guts. She cleaned and scaled it, cut it into three or four chunks, and dropped them into the boiling water seasoned with red pepper paste. Ki-yong's younger brothers gathered around the pot, their spoons already in their mouths. His stepmother scolded them, glancing at his father and Ki-yong. It was before food became scarce, though there was always more food available in Pyongyang than in other regions.

His stepmother was a middle school teacher. Sometimes parents would bring her rare gifts to ask for favors, so their family was better off than other households. Though his stepmother worked the same hours as his father, she had more duties since she had to keep house, too. His younger brothers' pockets always jangled with nails. They picked them up from construction sites and played a variant of marbles with their friends. They would try to throw a nail and hit another, and if one were pushed out beyond the line, the striker would take that nail. Their pants always had holes in them, ripped by these sharp nails, but their stepmother mended the pockets under a dim light without complaining, even though they weren't her own children. "You can't carry such sharp things in soft material," their stepmother once said, and the youngest one retorted, "Mother, there's a Chinese saying that a gimlet in a pouch pokes its way out!"

"Children, that's not what that means!" Father interjected, looking up from the paper and shaking his head. Though he studied water and dirt, he was knowledgeable about Chinese classics. He explained, "It means a talented man commands attention without trying."

The younger children giggled and wrestled around in the tiny room, and it was hard to tell whether they understood the point. By now, they probably finished their mandatory ten years in the army and were assigned to jobs, and his stepmother would still be leading her life somewhere.

Unlike his stepmother, Ki-yong's birth mother came from a very good family. She was from Chaeryong in Hwanghae Province. A right-wing faction murdered her father, so the family was given the respect due to a family of a political murder victim. Most members from such families ended up in key positions in the Party and the People's Army.

His father's background wasn't as illustrious. He was a Communist prisoner of war who chose to return to the North after spending time at the camp on Koje Island in the South. The returned prisoners of war weren't welcome anywhere. Only a tiny minority was given any opportunity for education and work, to showcase the generosity of the Great Leader Kim Il Sung. Ki-yong's father was one of the lucky ones. He studied hydraulics in Moscow and returned to Pyongyang in 1959, immediately becoming a functionary in the hydropower department of the Pyongyang Electric Power Design Office.

Ki-yong's father, a returned POW, and his mother, a member of the Workers Party of Korea, were a most unlikely pair. Ki-yong never heard the story of how they met. Nobody spoke of it. In any case, they met and married. Their relationship didn't seem to have been forced on them. If his father's status had been higher, that might have been a possibility. This unlikely couple was assigned a newlywed apartment typical of Pyongyang—a living room and one bedroom, narrow and long—and held a simple wedding ceremony at the groom's workplace. Nobody forecast a terrible ending. They were on good terms and didn't seem to have any problems. In the photograph taken that day, Ki-yong's young, shy mother linked arms with his father, looking happy.

They had Ki-yong a year after the wedding and two more boys after him. Ki-yong's first memory is of Father standing in front of a bright window with a big, mischievous smile, kissing his mother on the nose. His mother frowned, saying it tickled, but her expression frightened Ki-yong. After that, he would burst into tears whenever she frowned, and when he got older he would turn and run away. The adults thought it was funny and would ask his mother to frown, dissolving into laughter when Ki-yong got scared. But later, after his mother met her tragic end, people said that Ki-yong must have seen something ominous that only a young child could detect.

His mother went crazy, very slowly. She worked at the Party External Commercial Management Office. She usually dealt with transactions having to do with China, Hong Kong, or Macau, focusing on numbers and money. She would sometimes go to Beijing on long business trips. Her job, dealing with foreign currency and traveling abroad, was coveted by other families of political murder victims. But it proved to be a post that overwhelmed his mother, who had frail nerves.

Ki-yong never found out what really happened. People said that she had been sacrificed by the inner politics of the Party External Commercial Management Office, or that she had been falsely incriminated by other families vying for that job, or that she had been involved in a very serious fraud and received a severe reprimand from her supervisor. Ki-yong didn't want to know which it was. Anyway, his mother left that job, and after taking some time off, she became the manager at a foreign currency shop, which catered to people who bought foreign goods with foreign currency acquired through various channels.

If one took her background into consideration, it was an assignment that was almost shameful, but she went to work every day without revealing her true feelings. She did receive a good salary, and there were quite a number of people who slipped her an extra something to get certain items. But she didn't allow exceptions or give anyone special treatment. She didn't forgive herself if the numbers didn't match up. She stayed at the shop long into the night until the numbers matched, working the abacus over and over. Since there wasn't any corruption and it looked like she was working hard, nobody thought she had such a serious problem. They would just cluck, saying, Comrade Yu Myong-suk is so conscientious.

The store was on the way to Oesong Middle School. On his way home from school, Ki-yong sometimes stopped by to say hello. His mother would whisper that someone at the back of the line was criticizing her. "Listen carefully. Those women always say negative things about me behind my back."

Ki-yong listened in on the women's conversation; it wasn't true. They were just chatting about their lives. They were happy, exuberant because they were buying expensive items with foreign currency—but to his mother, everything was a secretive plot.

"Mother, they are not talking about you," Ki-yong would say, but his mother would frown and shake her head.

"I can read lips. I learned to do that in the People's Army. But it doesn't matter if they talk behind my back. The Great Leader and the Party support me."

Even then, Ki-yong didn't think she was suffering from a disease. He didn't think much of it, really, since he expected her to hear all sorts of complaints on the job, having to face people and their demands on a daily basis. She was normal at home, waking up before the 7:00 A.M. siren, efficiently cooking breakfast for the family, eating with them, and leaving for work with Father.

When Ki-yong turned fifteen, his mother grew suspicious of his father. Or it may have been that she had been suspicious of him for a long time. A note she found in his pocket triggered her doubts. A pretty feminine script looped across the paper, "A flower blooming, hidden on an unknown road. Do you know this nameless flower? Please know my feelings when you smell this flower as you walk along a bumpy road." Father explained that it was the lyrics of the song "We Will Go with the Song of Happiness in Our Arms." While Mother knew the song as well, she believed it was a love letter, that a tramp in love with her husband had written the note under the guise of a song. Father told her that he had heard it on the radio and liked it, and asked one of the workers under his supervision to jot down the lyrics for him, but Mother's suspicions weren't dispelled. One day, when Ki-yong and

Father were fishing at Taedong River, Father slid a cigarette between his lips and said, "I'm worried about your mother."

Since their home was a two-room apartment, no secret could be kept from the children. The layout forced them to grow up quickly. Ki-yong realized that Father was not asserting his innocence. Instead of saying he was hurt by her suspicions, he was saying he was worried about Mother. Ki-yong understood vaguely what that signified but didn't show it on his face.

Mother also lamented about her situation to Ki-yong. "Since you are the eldest son, you have to take my side no matter what happens. Your father was always popular with women. His nose is always in a book, so when women chase after him he doesn't know what to do and just ends up going along with them." Mother stopped and lowered her voice, looking around. "Shh. They're listening in next door, those sneaky rats."

"Mother, please stop!" Ki-yong spat out.

Mother looked bewildered, then sank into a deep despair. "You don't believe me either!" she accused.

Ki-yong looked away. It would have been preferable to deal with some other problem. He wouldn't have minded if Father had really cheated on her, he hadn't been a party member, or he had committed a more serious offense. For a moment, Ki-yong wished he had a different mother. He wanted his mother to be a comforting, warm, unsuspicious, mature woman.

She shot at him, "I knew it. You're on his side because you're a boy."

Mother threatened Father that she would complain to the Party and to his bosses. Father ignored her. One weekend, leaving Mother alone at home, Father took the three boys to the ice skating rink. The two younger ones glided on the frozen pond, blissfully ignorant of the situation at home. The large thermometer hanging at the rink indicated a temperature of fourteen degrees. Little kids rode on sleds while the older ones skated, and when they got hungry they gnawed on corn on the cob they had stashed in their pockets. Ki-yong had put on Father's skates; they were a little too roomy. To this day, he remembers clearly what Father said to him at the rink. "What is Juche Ideology?"

Ki-yong hesitated, then reeled off what he'd learned in school. "It is a revolutionary ideology putting forth that humans have creativity, consciousness, and independence, and decide their own fate."

Father looked tired. He squinted as the low-hanging winter sun shone on his face. "Do you really believe humans are that mighty?"

Ki-yong couldn't believe his ears. This was forbidden talk, something that was near impossible to hear at school. "Pardon?"

Father lit a cigarette. The spark from the match jumped to the cigarette paper and flared brightly before it extinguished.

"The ancient Greeks believed that the world was composed of four elements."

"We learned that at school."

"What are they?"

"Water, fire, air, and earth. Greek philosophy soon became dialectic materialism . . ."

Father cut him off. "That is right. As you know, I make dams to capture water. Of those four elements, I studied water and earth. I don't know much about the rest. I was never interested in how humans did what. Juche Ideology . . . well, it is probably right. It's a good thing for a human to create his own destiny through creativity, consciousness, and independence. But remember when there was a flood in Hwanghae Province two years ago? If the dam floods over and bursts, humans are the same as dogs or pigs. They're just swept away."

"Isn't that why people like you put theory into practice and build dams to control nature?"

"That's only a temporary solution. The last war was all about fire. Pyongyang went back to the stone age because of American bombs. After that was the era of earth. We picked up our shovels and erected cities. Through the Chollima Movement, we built a republic as good as any other. Now it's the era of water. Water appears placid from the outside but there's actually a very powerful energy within it. That's why we have to control water. We're doing that now, but nobody knows what will happen. Soon it will become the era of air. It may be the most painful era, more than the periods of fire, earth, and water. You can't see air but without it, people can't breathe."

At the time, Ki-yong didn't know what Father was trying to tell him. But soon, he understood that Father was deriding the pointless self-centered worldview of Juche Ideology, and was accurately prophesying North Korea's future. Years later, in the early 1990s, after a series of floods, the so-called arduous march began. It was the era of starvation, where the only available food was grass and bark and dirt. Stomachs went empty. The era of air. People said, *If this is how it is, let's fight with anyone, be it South Korea or America. Let's go all the way until the very end.*

Father changed the subject. "Your mother is a child of the earth. She's from a farming family. But as you know, I'm a child of water."

Ki-yong's grandfather was a boatman on Taedong River.

He remained one even when the Japanese built a railway bridge over the river and luminaries like Natsume Soseki, Yi Kwangsu, and Na Hye-sok traversed it by train. When Ki-yong's father came back from Koje Island, his own father was waiting for him in a hut on a riverbank dense with weeping willows. Like the willows, a few of whose branches were always dipped in water, Father had a damp and dark side to him. Even his preference of talking frankly, instead of beating around the bush, was more characteristic of water than of earth or fire. Ki-yong, who was quick to catch on to nuances and possessed a good ear for language, understood that waterlike Father was telling him that he was being trapped by Mother, the earth, and that at some point the water would breach the earthen walls and go where it wanted. But this knowledge made Ki-yong feel uncomfortable. Why were they getting him involved in their arguments?

Ki-yong was a good skater. Even in ill-fitting skates, he turned corners faster than anyone and stopped precisely, with a spray of ice. Ki-yong bent low and shot forward, his legs stretching and lengthening. He went around counterclockwise on the outer edge of the pond as the beginners in the inner circle slowly wobbled around in the other direction. The chilly wind slapped his cheeks, but it wasn't painful. The smoke from a small fire of weeds, kindled to ward off the cold, billowed, aromatic and sulfurous. Ki-yong glided faster and completed a loop. He straightened and placed his feet parallel to each other, braking to a stop with a flourish, sending up a shower of ice chips.

That day was the first time he spoke with Jong-hee, a girl who lived on the same floor as Ki-yong's family, at the southern end of the hall. Her cheeks were red and her small nose was pert. At 7:20 A.M., when all the students gathered at the meeting place and marched to school together, grouped by

class, their eyes met. It happened again at the skating rink.
Jong-hee smiled, a red knitted scarf looped around her neck,
and Ki-yong slid past her, missing his chance to reciprocate.
Fifteen-year-old Ki-yong didn't have the courage to double back to say hello. But as he rested by the wooden post,
watching his breath turn white, she came over to him, her
long limbs moving elegantly.

"You're a very good skater."

Ki-yong was self-conscious about the gaze of his father,
who was probably observing this from somewhere, and that
of his school friends. He felt a little proud, too, but didn't
know how to express this pride, and so it was a sort of pointless emotion.

"Are they your skates?" Jong-hee asked finally, when
Ki-yong didn't say anything.

"No, my father's."

"So you can speak!" Jong-hee flashed him a smile and
pushed off toward the inner circle. It was an embarrassingly
unsophisticated conversation, but it was Pyongyang in the
mid-1970s. Openly dating symbolized one's ideological laxity
and was the subject of severe criticism. Nobody knew what
to do or say to a girl at the ice rink; it wasn't only Ki-yong
who was terribly inept. Dating was a clear taboo. Their in-
teraction that day wouldn't have been that strained had he
known that he would soon vomit on her, and twenty years
later, would unexpectedly bump into her.

Jong-hee was well known in school. From the age of
eleven, she was chosen to represent their school in large-
scale Mass Games with children from all around the country,
to celebrate the founding anniversary of the Workers Party
or the War Victory Anniversary. More than eighty thousand
children were divided into ten teams, and each came out
and performed awe-inspiring, circuslike aerobics routines.

Jong-hee was tall and good enough to be in the front row of her team. The performances went on for twenty days and all the schoolchildren in Pyongyang went to watch. Everyone dressed up—students in uniforms, men in suits, and women in blue or red hanbok. The crowd walked between the large columns and gathered in the Main Theater.

The aerobics routines were composed of scenes from revolutionary history, such as the armed anti-Japanese struggle. Ki-yong and the rest of the boys tracked Jong-hee's movements with their eyes, proud of their school representative. She leaned back, picked up a small ball and threw it high in the sky, did a running start like a doe, and launched into a somersault, catching the falling ball with her legs. More than one hundred girls threw the balls high above their heads and caught them with their legs in unison, and not a single one dropped the ball. Jong-hee looked more mature than her age because of her vivid eye makeup and red lipstick. Ki-yong and his friends watched Jong-hee's leaps and turns with their mouths agape, envious of the children who lifted her up and marched away.

Why would someone like that talk to him? Ki-yong couldn't believe it. A little later, when he looked for her, she was already gone. His brothers grew tired of sledding and the sun was dropping behind Moran Peak. They gathered their skates and sleds and went home.

A few days after their skating excursion, Father went to check on a Yalu River dam and power plant. A fissure had been discovered in the dam, which was built during the Japanese occupation, so a drove of functionaries from Pyongyang had to go to Sinuiju. That day happened to be Ki-yong's sixteenth birthday. Everything was symbolic: there was a fissure in the dam, Father wasn't home, Pyongyang was experiencing a blackout, and his two brothers were chosen as school representatives to go on a trip to Myohyang Mountain. Ki-yong felt an inexplicable dread for having to spend his birthday with only Mother.

"Mother will cook chicken stew for you. I'll bring you a present from Sinuiju. What would you like?" Father asked.

"A foreign-made ballpoint pen, please." Ki-yong actually wanted a good pair of shoes. But he ended up asking for a ballpoint pen made in a foreign country. Father ruffled his hair and left for work.

Father took the 6:00 P.M. train from Pyongyang station. As soon as it left, Pyongyang tumbled into darkness, as if someone had flicked off the light switch. Nobody knew if the blackout involved a problem with the hydropower plant or the electricity line coming into Pyongyang. Nobody in the North had any inkling about what was going on. The paper and television didn't mention it at all, leaving rumors to fill the void. In darkened Pyongyang, nothing out of the ordinary happened. Blackouts were routine. Or it could be a blackout drill to prepare for an air attack. But there was no siren that indicated the onset of a drill. Ki-yong walked home from the subway station. The December sun set early; it was already dark. Ki-yong stopped by his mother's foreign currency store. The unlit store was closed. Ki-yong shook the steel shutters a few times, but when nobody came out, he headed home. He climbed the stairs of the harmonica apartment building and approached his unit, the savory smell of chicken stew greeting him.

"Mother, I'm home!"

No answer. It was dark inside the apartment and the gas burner was on, casting a bluish glow. Ki-yong turned it off and went into the master bedroom. Mother wasn't there either. Did she go somewhere to borrow a candle? Ki-yong went out to the hall and looked around, peeking into a few apartments with open doors, but she wasn't to be found. Instead, he bumped into Jong-hee, who was coming home from practice. Even under the faint candlelight, he could tell that she was smiling at him. She bounced down the hall, her steps lighthearted and airy, revealing her talent for gymnastics. Ki-yong went back inside and tossed his book bag under his desk. The aroma of the chicken stew wasn't quite as strong anymore. He went into the bathroom, scooped some cold water they had saved in the tub into a big bucket and thoroughly washed his hands, face, and neck. It was dark in the bathroom, so dark that he couldn't even see his face in the mirror. Ki-yong searched like a blind man for a towel, but then slipped and fell. He tried to get up but fell again. The floor was slippery, coated with something wet. Ki-yong, sitting on the bathroom floor rubbing his aching tailbone, realized that there was someone else sitting on the floor, next to him. He reached out and felt clothes and then a brassiere under the clothes. He patted the face and the waist, then started to scream. It was a body, crumpled.

Ki-yong bolted out into the hall and sprinted toward the end of the hallway, where faint light was coming through. He panted, leaning against the railing. He could hear his breath and found himself feeling inhuman, like an animal, a wild hog cornered during a hunt. Jong-hee ran out of her apartment, candle in hand. Ki-yong was covered in blood, but it looked like dirt in the dim light. His neighbors rushed out, surprised by his screams. Jong-hee boldly embraced Ki-yong and led him toward the narrow balcony hanging at the end of the hallway, where people couldn't see them. The westerly wind from the Yellow Sea battered them. Ki-yong, on his knees, in Jong-hee's arms, drew in ragged breaths, then vomited warm, sour liquid onto her chest.

"What's wrong? What's going on?"

He didn't answer. Jong-hee drew Ki-yong's face deeper into her stomach, holding him. His face was buried in his vomit on her school uniform, the blood from his hands dyeing her clothes.

"It's not my fault. It's really not my fault."

"Okay, okay. What's wrong?"

"Mother. I think Mother is dead." Ki-yong's speech was garbled, so Jong-hee didn't catch "is dead." But she did hear "Mother." Dancing candlelight illuminated the apartment windows across the way.

"It's all right, it's all right. It's all right now," Jong-hee soothed. She led him back slowly to the hallway. Perhaps she was worried that he would jump from the railing. People were still gathered in the dark hallway, murmuring. Like ghosts wandering around subterranean cemeteries, their faces and candles floated in the air.

"What's going on? Hey, aren't you . . . ?" The man who lived across the way from Jong-hee pushed a candle in Ki-yong's face and his eyes widened in shock as they registered the dark blood covering the boy. He took a step back. All the candles rushed toward Ki-yong, like a horde of moths. Ki-yong's bloody body and face glowed in the darkness, as if he were a Caravaggio painting.

Ki-yong tried to say "in the bathroom," but it came out "uhhhaahhhuhh." He pointed weakly toward his home. As soon as they heard the women scream, the men rushed into Ki-yong's apartment without bothering to take off their shoes. Candles paraded into his apartment. The hall was dark again. Jong-hee was still holding Ki-yong's hand, but nobody noticed.

Only later was Ki-yong overcome by an intense anger —after agents from the Ministry of People's Security came by, took the body, and sent telegrams to Myohyang Mountain and Sinuiju, and after Ki-yong changed into clean clothes provided by the neighbors. Why did she have to cut her wrists on his sixteenth birthday? Did she hate him that much? Why did she have to do it on the one day Father wasn't around? Ki-yong wanted to ask her these questions. After some time passed, a clinging guilt tempered his anger. If he had listened more attentively to Mother's complaints, if he had come home a little earlier instead of playing basketball with his friends, no, if he had never been born . . . Uneasy thoughts dogged him, tormented him.

Father was brought back to Pyongyang and underwent an investigation conducted by the Ministry of People's Security, and the records kept in Mother's store were searched. But nobody found anything. It was the kind of situation that rendered Communists helpless. Suicide meant you left the socialist paradise of your own free will, for no good reason. Officially, their society didn't have suicides; without known statistics, nobody knew what the suicide rate was. In the end, the Ministry of People's Security found evidence of Mother's insanity. In a cabinet in the store, they found meaningless statistics and accounting books that she had been compiling in the few months before her death. The records didn't match the items in the storeroom or other records held by agencies that provided the goods. Transactions that existed solely in Mother's head filled more than twenty books. Nonexistent people bought made-up items in great quantities, and these imaginary transactions were meticulously recorded. Nobody had thought twice about her, a hardworking woman who never made a mistake, because so many books were created in such a short time and there was no problem in the actual circulation of items.

Later, when he arrived in Seoul, Ki-yong saw Stanley Kubrick's *The Shining*. Watching Jack Nicholson go crazy in a cabin in the snow-covered Rockies, he remembered his mother, which he hadn't done in a long time. As Jack Nicholson typed, "All work and no play makes Jack a dull boy," over and over on several hundred pages, he imagined Mother, sitting alone in her store, tittering like an idiot. He couldn't finish watching the movie. From then on, Ki-yong kept a safe distance from *The Shining* and chicken stew. But now, almost thirty years later, he wondered if she would have killed herself if there hadn't been a power outage and she could have continued to write in the books like she did every day. Maybe Father's business trip, the sudden blackout, and his birthday—three unusual events—merged and broke her rhythm, unfastening the safety latch located somewhere in her brain.

Ki-yong saw Jong-hee again in 2001, in Seoul. He was sitting in a subway car, on the northbound Line 3, crossing the Han River. A woman was staring at him, sitting across the aisle. He glanced at her too, but couldn't place her. He tried to remember. Who was she? She was wearing a neat slate-colored skirt that came to her knees, and looked to be in her late thirties. Although she had faint lines around her eyes and on her neck, she was a beauty, with symmetrical features. Her hair was tied back, secured with pins and an elastic band. Her wrists were thin, and she had narrow shoulders. There was something old-fashioned about her makeup. Her eyebrows were thin and drawn in, her lips were red, and she wasn't wearing mascara. She was gripping the handle of her purse as if her life depended on it, looking frightened out of her mind, or maybe sad. It was an expression he couldn't decipher. He looked away, and she looked down at her lap hastily. But soon, they were staring at each other again.

A subway car is laid out awkwardly, forcing people to stare at each other from across the way. The aisle's too wide to say hello, but it's too narrow to just ignore someone, so it's always difficult to decide where to look. Ki-yong squinted and studied her face again. The more he looked at her, the more it convinced him that he knew her. But he couldn't remember where he'd seen her. She wasn't someone in the movie business, and she didn't seem like someone he went to school with. If it had been someone who did publicity for movies, she wouldn't have stared at him like that, making him uncomfortable. He wanted to ask, Who are you? But if he had gotten up from his seat and walked over, people would have stared. He couldn't go up to a woman whose name he didn't know and ask, "Excuse me, who are you and why do you keep staring at me?"

Her gaze was testing Ki-yong's patience. The train was still clattering across the Han River. She twisted her lips into a wry smile. There was something unnatural about her expression, revealing a tragic plea. That's when he realized who it was. He never imagined that he would see her in Seoul. Jong-hee. He whispered her name to himself, but his voice was so low that the sound evaporated as soon as it escaped his mouth. But she was reading his lips. Her expression stiffened, and when the car stopped at Yaksu station, she bolted up and hastily left the car. Ki-yong followed her out. She was walking briskly toward the transfer station, toward Line 6. He dodged the sea of people coming toward him and followed her. She kept looking behind her, frightened. Finally, stumbling like she would fall over, she started running. Ki-yong started running too. Why was she here? And why was she so desperately running away from him?

Finally, he caught up to her, close enough that he could grab and stop her. She backed up against a wall and her breath came out in rasps, her shoulders tense. People walked by, glancing at them. She was crying. "Please, please."

"Jong-hee, what's going on? You're Jong-hee, right? Right?" Ki-yong asked.

She kept repeating the same words. "Please, please," she said, seeking his generosity, hands clasped and bowing her head in supplication.

"All right, I'm sorry. I won't do anything. I'm going to go, so you can get up, okay?" He tried to help her up, as she was sliding down the wall, but she shrank away as if she had touched a snake.

Ki-yong raised his hands, palms open, and stepped back.

She got up with difficulty. "Thank you. Thank you."

Ki-yong turned toward Line 3. Only after she saw him leave did she start walking toward Line 6, with cautious steps. Ki-yong looked back after a while, but she was already gone.

A while later, he learned that she and her husband had escaped the North via Macau and Bangkok. He looked it up online, which revealed their route and reasons for escaping. In the twenty-first century, leaving North Korea had become a nonevent, something that wasn't all that shocking. People he used to know in Pyongyang might be living in Seoul, and he might even bump into them on the street.

Jong-hee was the last person he saw before he was selected to go into Liaison Office 130. She was a member of the most renowned dance troupe in the North, Mansudae Art Troupe. He told her they wouldn't be able to see each other for a long time. She knew exactly what Liaison Office 130 and Office No. 35 entailed, and that he would be sent down south as an agent. He realized why she had looked so terrified when she saw him on the subway. She must have thought he had orders to kill her. It wasn't a ridiculous thought. In 1997, Lee Han-yong, a nephew of Kim Jong Il's wife, was shot to death in front of his South Korean apartment by the Operation Department assassination squad, which then went back north, evading capture.

Ki-yong heard later that Jong-hee's husband, who had managed North Korea's overseas slush fund in Macau, opened a restaurant in Seoul, specializing in North Korean cold noodles. Jong-hee, who used to be the best dancer in North Korea, made a living serving cold noodles with her husband. He did want to go say hello, but he never went. He didn't want to scare them when they had finally managed to lead a peaceful life. It was also possible that, if he appeared, they would call the policeman helping them settle in South Korean society. But he sometimes thought of her, and remembered the warmth of her belly, where he had briefly rested his head.

KI-YONG ORDERS AN Americano at the café at the theater and sits down in a black metal chair that resembles the body of an ant. A few people from the Film Forum office greet him. How are you? Did you come to see a movie? What movie are you importing next? A torrent of polite words pours onto him. All the men are wearing the same hip uniform of black, horn-rimmed glasses. Ki-yong takes out his cell phone and presses a speed dial number, but he doesn't hear a ring. A recorded voice tells him that the subscriber is unavailable. He enters the phone number manually.

"Hello?"

"Hi, is Mr. Han there?"

Silence. The woman raises her tone a little. "Who's speaking?"

"I'm a friend."

"Mr. Han is abroad on business?"

Ki-yong recognizes her voice. Whenever he goes to Jong-hun's office, she sits there, typing away on IM. She always ends her sentences with a question mark. He decides to pretend not to know who she is.

Ki-yong asks, "Abroad? Where? That's sudden."

"I don't know. I'm not sure either?"

Ki-yong swallows. He's never heard of an owner of an automobile parts franchise leaving for business overseas this urgently. After a moment of silence, the woman on the other end asks, clearly annoyed, "Hello? Who is this? Are you really a friend?"

"Okay, thank you." Ki-yong is about to hang up without answering her question when she says, quickly, "Is this Mr. Kim?"

"Yes, you recognize my voice."

"Of course."

Ki-yong is surprised; he thought she had only been focused on her instant messenger.

"I actually don't know where Mr. Han is. Two days ago he ran in, took some things, and left right away. And there were so many phone calls today. Mrs. Han came by, too. She was worried out of her mind; she said he hadn't come home in two days. Do you have any idea where he might be?"

"Has he ever done this before?"

Her voice grows louder, indignant. "No. I've been here four years, and he's never even been late!"

"Was he in debt? Did he get calls from creditors?"

"Debt? You're asking the same things as the cops. We have no debt."

"The cops came by?"

"I think Mrs. Han filed a missing persons report. They came by a while ago and turned the office upside down."

Ki-yong knows he has to hang up. "I'll ask around, too, but I'm sure he's fine."

"If you find him, can you call Mrs. Han?"

"Sure." Ki-yong hangs up. Something is definitely happening. Maybe he just didn't notice the signs of change in the past few days.

Ki-yong and Han Jong-hun entered Liaison Office 130 the same year, both stationed under Lee Sang-hyok. Lee Sang-hyok groomed them and sent them south, along with two others. When Lee Sang-hyok was purged, the four of them were the only agents who were stranded in the South. When it became clear that the lines of communication were severed, one agent left Seoul to study in Seattle. He received a PhD and became a professor, and later became an American citizen. Ki-yong doesn't know what happened to the fourth. He kept in touch with only Jong-hun. But they didn't rely on each other or maintain a close friendship. When the power that united them disappeared they reverted to their true natures. They were like astronauts who were once connected in outer space, but returned to their separate lives back on Earth. Ki-yong and Jong-hun had to survive on their own in South Korea, where they didn't know another soul, and support their newly forming families. They met up sometimes for a drink, but their conversations were as mundane as the small talk at any South Korean high school reunion. How are you? Do you think Roh Moo Hyun will become president? Will the economy fare better next year? How's the wife? I can't believe I have this potbelly. Sometimes they stopped by a karaoke bar to sing along to pop superstars Kim Gun Mo and Shin Seung Hun. They never talked about the possibility of receiving Order 4. Fear always circled them, making it difficult for them to fully enjoy their time together. Afraid that voicing the unmentionable would make it come true, they stuck to dull topics. But now, the very thing they dreaded has become reality.

In 2002, Ki-yong bought a forty-inch television. It was

right before the World Cup, but that was just a coincidence—he didn't buy it for the games. Ki-yong invited Jong-
hun to his apartment for the group qualifier match between
South Korea and Portugal; he probably had the tiniest unconscious urge to show off his new TV and apartment. Jong-
hun was still living in a twenty-pyong rental, but Ki-yong
was the proud owner of a thirty-pyong condo.

"Nice place," Jong-hun said, handing Ki-yong a six-pack
of beer.

"Oh, right, you haven't been here since we moved in."

"It's nice and big, perfect for a family of three."

"I took out a loan," Ki-yong said, embarrassed. His embarrassment was part of a complicated mix of emotions. Ki-
yong achieved a dream that people born and raised in Seoul
were often unable to attain, and now he was bragging about
it. He wondered if Jong-hun, his oldest friend in the South,
who knew where he'd come from, could detect the snobbery
deep within him.

"I'm sure," Jong-hun replied. "Nobody buys a home with
cash. So where's the missus and Hyon-mi?"

"Ma-ri's going to be late and Hyon-mi went downtown to
cheer on the Korean team with her friends."

"Oh, the kids are going to yell, Goooo Korea," Jong-hun
laughed, imitating the popular cheers. "It's been a long time
since it was just the two of us." They sat side by side on the
sofa and drank beer, snacking on dried squid and seaweed.

Jong-hun ventured, "I still don't really care for seaweed,
since we never ate it growing up."

"Yeah, you're right—they didn't grow it in the North. But
when you get used to it you really end up liking it. Do you
want something else?"

"Do you have dried fish or something like that?"

Ki-yong brought out dried pollack. The South Korean

team, led by Coach Hiddink, was giving the Portuguese a run for their money.

"Remember the 1966 World Cup?" Jong-hun asked.

"The one in London?"

Every single person north of the demilitarized zone knew about this famous game. It was North Korea's best performance in an international setting.

"Choson beat Italy and went up against Portugal in the quarterfinals, remember?"

Choson—the North Koreans' name for their country —was so unfamiliar to Ki-yong's ears after all this time that he was rendered speechless for a minute. "I watched that game over and over when I was a kid," he replied.

"You remember Pak Sung Jin, that player for Chollima Soccer Team? The man who scored in the forty-second minute in the second half against Chile and who scored one against Portugal . . ."

"Oh, yeah, him."

"He's my uncle."

"Really?" Ki-yong sat up, surprised. Pak Sung Jin, along with Pak Doo Ik, was a North Korean sports hero. "Why didn't you ever tell me?"

Jong-hun smiled bitterly. "I was afraid people would want me to show them my soccer skills. I'm terrible at sports but if I tell people about my uncle, everyone wants to see how well I play."

"I bet."

"When my uncle came to visit us when I was young, all the kids in the neighborhood came over. My uncle would line them up and toss the ball to each kid, telling them to head it. The kids would bump it with their heads and go back to the line to wait for their next turn."

"Do you think they're watching this game up north?"

"I doubt it. Maybe it will be recorded and shown later."

As the game neared its end, their bodies jerked and tensed with every move on the field. Every time a player took control of the ball, they moaned. Then, when Park Ji-Sung fired a volley into the back of the net they both sprang up from the couch and cheered. But Jong-hun's elation subsided when Park Ji-Sung ran over to the benches and leaped into Guus Hiddink's waiting arms. He sat back down and downed some beer. "I still don't understand it. Why do they need a foreign coach? The players dye their hair and the coaches are foreigners; how can anyone say this team is representing our nation?"

Ki-yong didn't agree with this sentiment, but he didn't refute it either. Nationalism was the backbone of politics, especially in the North. Although the religious worship of Kim Il Sung and Kim Jong Il could be dismantled somehow, nationalism would live on for much longer. Ki-yong's belief solidified every time he saw Jong-hun. Jong-hun might no longer trust or be loyal to the northern government. The childish delusion that everyone in the world revered the Juche Ideology and its creator, Kim Il Sung, must have been shattered soon after he reached the South. But he resisted changing certain values instilled in him from childhood. Jong-hun didn't cede an inch of his belief that the Korean people were superior. In his mind, the Korean people shared a pure, unique bloodline—this belief went far beyond nationalism.

Ma-ri wasn't home even after the South Korean team beat Portugal and cemented its ascent to the top of Group 1. The two friends switched to hard liquor and drank some more. Jong-hun, trying to sound casual but revealing a hidden desperation, blurted: "Do you dream at night? What kind of dreams do you have?"

Ki-yong doesn't remember what he replied. But he does remember being cautious, on guard, knowing it was a dangerous question.

But where did Jong-hun go? Ki-yong tosses his coffee cup in the trash can and starts down the stairs of the Nagwon Arcade.

Ko song-uk plucks his copy of Edgar Snow's *Red Star Over China* from his bag and lays it on the table. He thinks the cover of the book, which faintly depicts Mao's chubby face by a convergence of a million little dots on a red background, looks good against the white tablecloth. He leafs through the book to the page he was reading on the subway, the scene where Snow, who followed Mao and the Red Army as he covered the Long March, attended the Red Theater in Pao An. Snow described several one-acts about the resistance against Japan but the part that grabbed Song-uk's attention was something called the Dance of the Red Machines. "By sound and gesture, by an interplay and interlocking of arms, legs, and heads, the little dancers ingeniously imitated the thrust and drive of pistons, the turn of cogs and wheels, the hum of dynamos—and visions of a machine-age China of the future," Snow wrote in 1938. Young dancers miming machines—Song-uk imagines it to be quite a powerful image, and wishes he could have seen it in person.

Song-uk likes the vibe of communism, revolution, the color red, and machinery. These four things go well together. Mao's and Stalin's ideologies seem cooler than Bakunin's anarchism. Song-uk feels mildly turned on when he watches a proud parade of endless gray uniforms marching across a vast square like *Star Wars* clones, flanked by grand architecture, amid the rippling red flags, like a well-oiled, fast-spinning machine—error-free. It's similar to having a fetish for and collecting Third Reich SS uniforms. But he doesn't really want to march across a square with the sun blazing down on him, raising his straightened legs high. He just likes watching the footage on cable documentary channels. It's like discovering 1970s art rock bands that nobody knows about. If he talks about Mao, Stalin, and Hitler, everyone becomes quiet, as if they don't know what to say in response. Song-uk mistakes this silence as awe for his esoteric taste. This is understandable; he is, after all, only twenty years old.

When he glances up, Ma-ri is standing by the table. He lets his eyes linger over her voluptuous chest. He grins at her in greeting. She sits down across from him.

"Have you been waiting long?" Ma-ri asks, putting her purse down.

Song-uk whispers, "You have beautiful breasts."

"Oh, come on," Ma-ri says, narrowing her eyes, but she doesn't seem displeased.

"Still have the cast, huh?"

"Yeah, they're taking it off this weekend."

"It's gotta be so annoying."

"Yeah, it's so itchy!" Ma-ri acts babyish despite herself.

The waitress, wearing a white apron, comes over with the menus. Ma-ri glances through it, then pushes it to the side and looks at Song-uk's copy of *Red Star Over China* sitting on the table.

"*Red Star Over China*?"

"You know this book?" Song-uk asks, surprised.

Ma-ri wonders what she should say. *I know you think I'm a middle-aged woman, but at one point I used to pass a human wall of cops on my way to school, scared, with that book in my bag. And at that time I never even dreamed that this book could be left out in the open at an Italian restaurant one day.* But of course Ma-ri doesn't say this. She regrets even acknowledging knowing what it is. But it's too late.

"Isn't it about Mo Taek-dong's Long March?"

"You have to call him Mao Tse-tung these days, the Chinese way."

"Same thing."

"You must read a lot."

Ma-ri smiles. "I used to. Not anymore. What are you getting?"

"I'm going to have the seafood risotto. What about you?"

"I don't know. Um . . . I . . . Oh, this one, the tomato and mozzarella salad."

"You don't want anything else?"

"No, I'm not that hungry." Ma-ri turns her head, and the waitress catches her eye and comes over. She takes out her notepad. It doesn't escape Ma-ri's attention that the waitress is chilly toward her but smiles warmly at Song-uk.

"Can we get a seafood risotto and a tomato and mozzarella salad?" Song-uk asks.

Ma-ri waves Song-uk off. "No, actually, I'll have spaghetti vongole."

"You changed your mind?" Song-uk asks.

The waitress crosses out what she wrote and scribbles the new order with a cool expression.

Ma-ri addresses the waitress. "Hold on, please."

"Yes?"

"I'll just have the first thing I ordered."

"The first thing?" The waitress sounds annoyed.

"The tomato and mozzarella salad."

The waitress jots it down and asks, as if by rote: "Would you like anything else?"

"Want a Coke?" Ma-ri asks Song-uk. He nods.

"A Coke and some warm water, please," Ma-ri requests.

The waitress nods and leaves their table.

"She smiled at you," Ma-ri says, glancing back at the waitress.

Song-uk laughs good-naturedly. "What, are you jealous?"

"I wonder what she thinks we are?"

"I thought we said we wouldn't talk about things like that. I don't like chicks like her; she has no taste or class."

"You don't prefer girls your own age?"

"Nah. Why do you let our age difference bother you so much? I'm not your average guy."

Ma-ri feels outdated, like a record player or an ABBA LP. This sort of affair would be impossible were it not for a twenty-year-old law student's not-so-average tastes.

"Have you thought about it?" Song-uk asks.

"About what?"

"The thing I asked you about before," he says innocently, like a little boy asking for a cookie.

Ma-ri laughs awkwardly. She can't get angry at Song-uk, but she can't pretend that everything is fine. "I don't think so."

"It's really not that complicated. Think about it really simply."

"All I need is you." Ma-ri completely believes in what she's saying as soon as the words leave her mouth.

But the young man sitting across from her isn't interested in her conviction. "You're already wet, right?" Song-uk's foot starts pushing its way under Ma-ri's skirt. He slides his tongue out mischievously.

Ma-ri closes her eyes. "Stop. I'm not going to change my mind just because you do this."

Song-uk's foot moves away, his face sullen. "You're acting like my mom!"

"What?" Ma-ri can't speak. She feels as if dry cotton is being shoved down her throat. She calms herself and says, slowly: "Are you really going to be like this?"

"We love each other. Why can't we do this?"

"Love is supposed to be exclusive. I love you and you love me. If I love you and love someone else, that's breaking the rules."

"If you loved me you would do what I wanted." Song-uk presses his lips together stubbornly and glares at her.

"And what if I don't?"

"Then you don't love me," Song-uk says forcefully.

"You . . . really . . . think . . . so?" Ma-ri shapes her mouth around the words; uttering them pains her. Her words float toward Song-uk but fall limply to the floor—he is a fortress.

"Yes."

"So if I don't do what you want, you're going to leave me?" Ma-ri asks, but she is retreating, bit by bit, and he knows this, too. He pursues relentlessly.

"If there's something I want to do I have to do it," Song-uk says, then stops talking, obstinate.

I suppose you can say something like that if you grow up hearing what a gifted child you are, study at the best undergraduate law department in the nation, tutor high school kids for fun to buy yourself the newest tablet notebook, and hang out with friends who want to become judges, prosecutors, diplomats, or politicians. I'm sure if you say something like this, everyone usually feels guilty and says they're sorry and lets you do whatever you want. I'm different. I know what kind of person you are. I think you expect me to be maternal with you, but that's not part of the deal. I'm a woman, not your mother. Ma-ri drinks some water. The waitress comes over, puts down a Coke, and tops off her glass.

After she leaves, Song-uk whines like a child: "I won't ask

you to do something like this again, really. Just this once. I can't sleep at night because I keep thinking about it. I can't study because I can't concentrate."

"You're so stubborn."

"No, Ma-ri, you're too old-fashioned. Why is everything else okay but not that? We're not even married."

"Aren't you worried that you might lose me?"

"Yeah, but I know that you'll be fine with it in the end."

Where does he get this confidence? She's starting to realize that it isn't going to be easy to make his desire wane.

"I have to go to the bathroom. I'll be back." Ma-ri takes her purse into the bathroom and stands in front of the mirror. Crow's-feet adorn her eyes and her hair is losing its luster. Through the door that is slightly ajar, she glimpses Song-uk's confident face. *He's young, and he'll be young for a while. And I'm getting older.* It's the bare truth. A kid on a student's budget, with bad fashion sense, is controlling a woman with money and a good job. *Other than his youth, what does he have that I don't?* She feels the way she does when she uses one of her credit cards, knowing full well that she's nearing the limit, hoping against her better judgment, telling the clerk, "This one will probably go through." She can sense defeat looming, but she doesn't want to acknowledge it just yet.

A woman enters the bathroom, taking a lighter out of her purse.

"Can I bum a cigarette?" Ma-ri asks.

The woman, whose hair is in a short, straight bob, hands her a Marlboro Light. The woman stands by the window, while Ma-ri smokes in front of the mirror. She feels calmer. *Fine. I'll do it. He wants it so badly. I'll do it. But not too easily, no. I'm going to make him regret asking me to do that, make it so that he'll be too embarrassed to talk about it to his friends. No, what am I thinking? I can't do it. Of course I can't do it. No means no.* Ma-ri takes one last drag, snuffs out the cigarette, and washes her hands.

She goes back to the table. The waitress is serving their food and doesn't move out of the way, although she knows Ma-ri is waiting to get past her. Ma-ri sits down after the waitress finally leaves. Song-uk frowns as he picks up his fork. "Did you smoke again?"

"Yeah, I was feeling nauseated. Does it smell really strong?"

"You promised you were going to quit."

"I did, but . . ."

"You know I hate it."

"Sorry, I'll really quit."

"Promise?"

"Yeah. Come on, eat." She cuts a small piece of tomato and cheese. "So," she says.

He looks up. "Yes?"

"Why do you hate it when women smoke? I'm curious."

"I don't mind women smoking in general. I just don't want my woman to smoke."

"Why not?"

"What?" Song-uk, unable to answer this unexpected question, sinks deep into thought. Why doesn't he like for his woman to smoke? It's an interesting question. Sometimes he thinks the girls who smoke on the benches in front of school look cool. He likes the way women wearing evening gowns in films noirs smoke long, thin cigarettes. So why does it bother him when Ma-ri smokes? "I don't know. I just thought of this, but maybe it's that I don't like the expression a woman makes when she smokes."

"What about it?"

"It's like she's complacent or something, when she's leisurely blowing smoke. It makes me feel like they're pushing me, or guys like me, away. You know what I mean?"

"No, not really."

"Um, well, in high school, the girls would always be talking and giggling in groups. Guys feel uncomfortable when that happens. It's like they're laughing at us. They're definitely laughing, as if to say, 'Look, we don't need you, you guys are stupid. You're always checking us out, even though you pretend that you're not.' You know, something like that. And that's what it's like with smoking. They're always closing their eyes to better enjoy it. When they do that I feel small."

"You're jealous."

"Yeah, I think so. I think women really understand pleasure." He lowers his voice. "Like, you come so many times. A guy comes once and that's it. And we don't scream or faint when we're coming. Sometimes I wish I were a woman."

Hearing those words, a switch somewhere inside her flicks on, unleashing an intense surge of lust. She wants to leave right now and roll around naked on a white-sheeted bed. She wants to practically beg: *I won't smoke anymore. I'll do whatever you want. Just get up and let's go to the nearest hotel right now.* Suddenly, the kid sitting across from her looks like a powerful sultan.

"Am I boring you?" Song-uk asks.

"No, it's interesting. I think that makes sense."

"There's a book called *War and Violence,* and it says that soldiers rape and kill women when they're at war because they want to get back at them for having been oppressed by them. During peacetime women ignore soldiers, snickering at them when they walk by and refusing to have anything to do with them."

"You think so too? You think women ignore you?"

"Well, not really, but I feel like sometimes they're teasing me."

"When?"

"You do it too, Ma-ri."

"Me?"

"Like now, when you know how much I want it and all you do is tease me for months."

"But . . ."

"Don't make excuses, you know it's true."

"I still have a cast," she says, her tone already apologetic.

"I like it better with the cast. It's sexier. When will I ever be able to do it with a woman in a cast?"

His seafood risotto is getting cold. She keeps thinking that his food shouldn't get any colder, not food that will go into her young lover's mouth. She looks anxiously at the risotto. Her fingertips are trembling, and a faint shudder of disgust shoots up from her shoulders to her chin.

She blurts out, "Fine."

"What?"

She cuts the remaining mozzarella in half. "I'll do it."

"Do what?" he teases.

"Forget it then." She watches as his mouth stretches into a grin.

"Really?" He's so thrilled, truly, with all his heart. His eyes sparkle.

Forgetting for an instant exactly what is making him so happy, she is simply happy that she can make him that elated.

"Thank you, thank you," he says.

She slides another piece of cold cheese onto her tongue. She can't taste anything. "But I don't want it to be with someone you don't know. I want it to be someone you know well, someone who can keep it a secret."

"Okay, I know someone who's perfect for this. He's in my class in school. He's one of my best friends from childhood. He even passed the first round of the bar exam, and basically he's an awesome guy."

"So passing the first round of the bar exam makes him awesome?"

"Well, that's not what I meant. I mean . . ."

She holds up her hand. "Stop, I don't have to know everything. It's fine if you're really that close."

"How's tonight?"

"Isn't that too soon?"

"Too soon? I've been waiting for months!"

She's actually relieved. She can't believe she refused for so long, when he's this giddy. She feels a little guilty. "You're really excited about this, aren't you?"

"I'm so proud of you is all. How about seven?"

"Okay."

"Dinner's on me."

"It's fine. You're a student, I know you have a tight budget. It will be my treat," Ma-ri offers.

"Are we going to go somewhere good?"

"What do you want to eat?"

"He likes barbecued pork belly. What about that restaurant with the wine-marinated pork belly?"

"Sure, I'll see you there."

Trembling slightly from all the excitement, Song-uk shovels the remaining seafood risotto into his mouth, checking his phone as he eats. When it buzzes with the arrival of a new text, he switches his fork over to his left hand and starts typing with his right thumb. She figures he must be texting his law school friend. What is he writing? Is he already telling him about her? She gulps down the lukewarm water. The waitress comes by and fills her empty glass. She feels deserted, like she's abandoned in a vast open space, even though she's sitting in the middle of a bustling restaurant. She takes out her cell phone. There are two texts, one from Ki-yong.

—Might be late tonight.

She wonders what's come up. The next text is from Hyon-mi.

—B-day party after school. Will eat dinner there. Don't worry.

She feels unsettled that nobody will be home for dinner. It's as if her family is conspiring to push her toward Song-uk. She sends a message to Hyon-mi that she will be late, too, but just types "OK" to Ki-yong. When she glances up, she catches Song-uk looking at her. Thin veins are crisscrossing the whites of his eyes. For some reason she thinks of a lump of fish roe in a pot of overboiled stew.

HYON-MI CHECKS THE text message that has just arrived in her inbox. She returns her lunch tray to the front of the room and heads down to the snack bar with A-yong for some banana milk. Hyon-mi's addicted to banana milk; she craves it even after she drinks three or four cartons. Milk in hand, the girls walk toward the bench near the flower bed outside. A gaggle of girls pass by them, and Jin-guk appears close behind.

"Hey," A-yong calls.

Jin-guk only notices them then.

"Hi," A-yong says again.

"Hi," Jin-guk replies, blushing slightly. A couple of boys passing by glance at them.

"So who's coming later?" A-yong asks.

Jin-guk looks around. "You guys and two of my friends."

Hyon-mi interjects: "Do we know these guys?"

"No, probably not."

"Oh, they don't go here?"

"No, they don't go to school."

"They don't go to school?" A-yong asks, surprised.

"Yeah, why, does that matter?" Jin-guk's expression reveals that he was expecting such a reaction. "But they're not the kind of guys you think they are."

"Oh, so what kind of guys do we think they are?"

"You don't have to come if you don't want to," Jin-guk retorts.

Hyon-mi and A-yong exchange glances.

Jin-guk, fidgeting uncomfortably, scratches his head and adds, "But I hope you do come."

Hyon-mi and A-yong look unconvinced. A-yong speaks for them both: "Well, we'll think about it."

Jin-guk's cheeks grow redder. "Okay, text me later."

"Have fun, even if we don't come."

"Aw, no, you guys really should come," Jin-guk tries once more, then leaves for the snack bar.

Hyon-mi tosses the empty banana milk carton into the trash can. They trip along the flower bed toward the flagpole. A group of boys, squeezing in a game of basketball during the lunch hour, run around with their hands outstretched, like apes.

"Jin-guk's kinda weird, huh?" A-yong comments.

Hyon-mi nods. "Yeah, don't you think his friends would be weird too?"

"Yeah, but I like that."

"What do you mean?"

"I don't like the kids at our school." A shadow falls across A-yong's features.

Hyon-mi squeezes her friend's hand. They burst into giggles and break into a run. They stop abruptly, breathing hard.

"My mom's working late today," Hyon-mi remembers.

"Yeah?" A-yong welcomes this piece of news. "Then we can go home a little late."

"What about your cram school?"

"Whatever, it's just one day. I wish I didn't have to go, like you."

"I wish I could go, but my stepmother won't give me the money."

A-yong laughs and playfully punches her on the shoulder. Hyon-mi yelps an exaggerated "Hey!" and bolts into the building, A-yong on her heels. The music indicating the end of lunch follows their footsteps and echoes through the campus.

THE HILTON HOTEL IN PYONGYANG

K I-YONG WALKS west from Chongno sam-ga, weaving through the crowd, reading the signs. He sees these signs every single day, but today they seem brand-new. Familiar sights meld with the unfamiliar, creating a jarring harmony. To Ki-yong, everything in Chongno is at once familiar and foreign. It's the one place that didn't feel alien to him when he first reached Seoul, but in the twenty years since, it's never grown more familiar. Although it's in the center of Seoul, it always seems like a street on the fringes of the city. At the same time, it feels the most authentically Seoul.

ONE DAY, back when he was a member of Liaison Office 130, Ki-yong and his comrades filed onto a bus with boarded-up windows. Lit only by faint dome lights, everyone looked washed out. The bus drove all around Pyongyang, making it hard to figure out where they were being taken. Suddenly, they started to go downhill, as if sinking, and after a long while the bus jerked to a stop. Everyone raised their heads to look through the windshield and saw barricades, the kind often set up at checkpoints. Just beyond the barricades stood a concrete structure that looked like a bomb shelter, its igloolike entrance covered in camouflage. There was also a metal gate just wide enough for a bus to squeeze through. The gate opened and the bus entered the darkness. This building was well concealed from American satellite patrols, so secure that it was probably even safe against atomic bombs. The bus kept moving for a while before it finally stopped. They disembarked. Following the guide's orders, they marched, single file, toward a squat gray building.

They were led into the changing room and were ordered to place their clothes in a basket on a shelf. They received new clothes, socks, and shoes. Are we in a correctional facility? someone whispered in Ki-yong's ear. It wasn't an outlandish thought. Ki-yong had seen a film about Auschwitz when he was in high school. He had thought it was interesting that the beginning of one's stint in a concentration camp was identical to that of being inducted into the military. Both required the new arrivals to take off their clothes and change into uniforms, their heads were shaved and they were ordered to bathe. But this time they weren't shaved or ordered to bathe. Ki-yong was quietly relieved.

The group left the changing room through a different door, and immediately let out a yell of surprise. They were standing in the darkened streets of Chongno in Seoul. People wearing South Korean clothes milled about on sidewalks of plum-colored bricks, neon signs flashing above their heads. Mounds of fruit lay piled in bins in a grocery store, next to a bar selling OB beer on tap. The grocery store and a night-club flanked the police station. Though none of them had been to Seoul, that didn't seem quite right. But everything else appeared to be very authentic. There was even a beggar, prostrate on the street with his palms outstretched, a rubber mat covering his legs, just like in the South.

The store clerks, hotel employees, and cops were people who had been kidnapped from South Korea or who came up north voluntarily. They spoke with perfect South Korean accents and came to work each morning to this mini-Seoul, re-creating the life they had once known. In the grocery store, the owner swatted at flies settling on apples while a woman who seemed to be his wife worked on the books, but it was impossible to know whether they were really a couple.

Lee Sang-hyok strode out through the revolving doors of the Hilton Hotel, a surreal sight for Ki-yong and his comrades, who had rarely had the chance to lay eyes on him. Grinning like a movie star, he came down the stairs and stood before the agent candidates.

"Hello, everyone!" His speech would have normally started with "Comrades!" but this was the Seoul style. Ki-yong and his fellow candidates answered like Seoulites, too: "Hello!"

Lee Sang-hyok swept his arm toward the street. "So, what do you think? Amazing, isn't it?"

"Yes!"

"Don't answer in unison. Nobody answers a question in chorus in Seoul. Do you understand?"

Nobody answered.

"The Republic's film functionaries completed this street to the best of their ability, under the guidance of our beloved leader, Comrade Kim Jong Il. Here, you must behave as if you were actually in Seoul."

Ki-yong's field adaptation training had taken place right before Shin Sang-ok, one of South Korea's top directors, and his wife, the popular actress Choi Eun-hee—who had been kidnapped years earlier under Kim Jong Il's orders—escaped and returned to the South. Shin Sang-ok and Choi Eun-hee evaded their North Korean handlers in Vienna and escaped via the American embassy. The media coverage following their escape revealed the mysterious Northern leader's love for movies, which went beyond the usual film buff's appreciation.

Kim Jong Il kidnapped his favorite director and actress and ordered them to make movies in North Korea. He appeared on set, revised the script at his whim, and even directed the actors. So it was only a matter of time until the dictator came up with the idea of using elements of film production to improve the training of South-bound agents. An ardent fan of movies and the opera, Kim Jong Il eventually transformed all of North Korean society into theater. Eighty thousand people gathered in a stadium to conduct the Mass Games. Youths waving red flags marched through the streets in time to war songs. A couple of lead actors and hundreds of thousands of extras created gigantic epics.

There was no such thing as an individual in the North. According to the Juche Ideology, which dictated that societal life was more important than biological life, every person had to belong to a group. A person's identity was represented by the Socialist Working Youth League, the Democratic Korean Women's Union, or the Workers Party of Korea. Every group met daily or at least a couple of times a week for critique sessions, living in a prison of watchful eyes. In a society where everyone submitted their inadvertent mistakes to their comrades for judgment, nobody could evade the gazes. Like actors on set, North Koreans went about their days, conscious of the eyes of the "director" and "cast." And an actor couldn't only be careful of his own mistakes; he also had to be vigilant about the others' transgressions. Any error would stop the cameras and invite the director's wrath.

Strangely, the Seoul set didn't feel foreign to the trainees. It was still fundamentally Northern in character, despite attempting to replicate Seoul exactly. The real Chongno wasn't beautiful, no matter how you looked at it. Chongno was a jumble of dirty, unwholesome elements and flashy, sophisticated ones, but it was above all organic. Chongno had a naturalness about it, like the way a dandelion seed lands on a yellow squash blossom sprouting from an old tile roof. The set in Pyongyang, though clean and orderly, felt fake, illuminated by high-wattage artificial lights instead of the sun—it was too different from what it was trying to be. Obviously, the architect of the set saw a different aesthetic value. For Kim Jong Il, it must have been like his own private, miniature theme park. In five minutes, he could go from Chongno to London's Piccadilly Circus. It was rumored that there were other pseudocities beyond the streets of fake Seoul, where the Dutch, British, and French lived—a world where an aging American deserter of the Korean War who had married a Thai woman kidnapped from Macau could drink Sri Lankan tea with a French woman tricked into coming to Pyongyang under the guise of a job opportunity. In certain respects, they weren't any different from the foreigners who moved to Tokyo or Seoul to teach English at private institutes, since it was their job to teach foreign languages to agents to be dispatched to the South. The only difference was that the foreigners in North Korea could never leave.

In a book called *Film Art Theory*, Kim Jong Il wrote, "Film literature, a Juche-oriented study of human beings, was born by reflecting on the need of an independent era. It puts forth human beings as the owners of the universe and their own destinies and contributes to helping them fulfill their responsibilities and roles as such. It illuminates both the true nature of autonomy and the human issues arising from it." Although Ki-yong knew that paragraph word for word, not a single person he met on that strange set was the owner of his own destiny. If purgatory existed, as the Christians believed, the set embodied it. People there lived a life without urgency, in a twilight zone, neither a part of the world they were in nor a part of the world beyond. Time stood still, and mass unemployment, contagious diseases, and great depressions didn't exist.

Lee Sang-hyok pointed at the three-story Hilton. "You will all go into the hotel and settle in. In your room, you will each find a card describing your mission. You must act according to those orders. Pedestrians and officials in the stores will be observing you. If you speak in our accent or make a mistake because you don't know how to act like a South Korean, you will be arrested. You have to understand that South Koreans are vigilant about reporting suspicious people. As you know, once the Korean Central Intelligence Agency or police officers capture an agent, they conduct vicious torture. You must overcome even that torture." He grinned again.

The punishment implemented on the set would probably be harsher than its model, even though it was supposedly a replica of Southern torture. Ki-yong was given a bundle containing three million won, issued by the South's Bank of Korea, and entered the hotel. The bored clerk at the front desk handed him a form. Ki-yong wrote down his name, address, and phone number. The clerk took the paper back and asked whether he smoked and which room he preferred. Even though Ki-yong had been practicing, it was still awkward to respond to this capitalist way of questioning, to voice his personal preferences. Ki-yong replied as calmly as he could and succeeded in receiving the key. He entered his room and placed his luggage next to the closet. First things first. He opened the card containing his mission. He was supposed to purchase a couple of basic necessities from the supermarket, open a bank account and make a deposit, and buy lingerie for his wife at the department store.

Jong-hun, his roommate, had a different mission—to order beer at the nightclub and buy a novel at the bookstore.

"Will they really torture us?" Ki-yong wondered.

"I think so. We were tortured before in the mountains, remember?" Jong-hun was referring to their infiltration training. Agents disguised as the South's special action team captured them, strung them upside down from a tree, and poured water spiked with red pepper powder into their nostrils. Ki-yong didn't want to experience that ever again.

Ki-yong went over his lines again and again, as if he were learning a foreign language. "I'm not sure what my wife's size is, could you help me? I'm not sure what my wife's size is, could you help me? I'm not sure what my wife's size is, could you help me?"

"You have a great accent. I can see how you got into Pyongyang University of Foreign Studies," Jong-hun exclaimed at Ki-yong's authentic Southern intonation.

His accent was the one thing that gave Ki-yong confidence. Even his diction teacher at the Liaison Office 130 had praised his intonation. His teacher was a Southerner from Puan, in North Cholla Province, and one day, after they had become friends, he blurted out: "If you do go down South, please don't bring back an innocent kid playing on the beach." Ki-yong saw the naïve vulnerability of such a boy shimmering quickly over his teacher's face like a hologram.

Ki-yong exited the Hilton. It felt like everyone he encountered on the street was glancing at him surreptitiously.

A lot of what Lee Sang-hyok had said was probably true. He was certain that there were undercover officials, grading his every move and utterance to announce at the critique later. He walked through the doors of the supermarket. In the North, customers paid for their items first, then received the goods from the clerk, who would take them out of the display case. He wasn't used to first picking out the groceries himself then paying for them. He selected a couple of apples and put them in a plastic bag. A bored clerk, who was leaning against one of the fruit displays, weighed them and stickered the price on the bag. Ki-yong added a can of Dongwon tuna and four bags of Samyang ramen into his basket and headed to the checkout. The cashier was staring at him. He fumbled through his pockets and tried to hand her the cash. She looked at his basket, pointedly. *Ah!* He quickly put the basket on the counter. He was grateful that she had helped him, preventing him from being dragged off to the torture chambers, but couldn't thank her—someone else was waiting behind him. She handed him a large plastic bag containing his purchases. He headed out. The clerk called after him: "Thank you." Hearing that, he hesitated at the doors, caught off guard because no clerk in any store in Pyongyang thanked a customer. *What is she thankful for? I'm the one who bought the food.*

Ki-yong went into the bank, about sixty feet away. There was a single teller at the window.

"How can I help you?"

"I would like to open an account, please."

"Please fill this out," the clerk said, pushing an application toward him. It was a South Korean form, used by Chohung Bank. He filled it out, using the name, address, and citizen ID number that he had memorized.

"Your seal, please."

When he gave her his seal, she stamped it in three different places on the form.

"How much would you like to deposit today?"

He gave her a million won from his wallet. She put it in a drawer and recorded it in a booklet. As he reached out for the booklet, Ki-yong's eyes met the teller's. Her eyes were saying something to him, like the checkout clerk in the supermarket. He opened the booklet. On one of the pages, there was something written in pencil, a seven-digit phone number in the South and someone's name. Under the name she had written, "Please tell them I'm doing fine. Thank you." He looked up at the teller again, but she avoided his gaze and started rummaging around in her desk. "Thank you for coming in," she said.

Ki-yong was confused. Maybe she really was asking him to send a message on her behalf to her family in the South, but it was possible that this was merely a ploy to test the strength of Ki-yong's ideology. He hesitated, and that moment's pause weakened his ideological resolve. He turned around and left. On the street, he stopped and looked around.

Don't ever stand around purposelessly in the South. It's the most visible thing you do. Just keep moving, Lee Sang-hyok would often remind them. Ki-yong walked toward the department store at an even pace. Inside, he found the bathroom. As he lowered his zipper and urinated, he slid the booklet out from his pocket and looked at it again. "Please tell them I'm doing fine. Thank you." With his thumb, he rubbed the words forcefully, erasing one woman's desperation. But the ominous dark mark wasn't completely gone. He ripped the page into shreds, put it in his mouth, and chewed. The paper bits were as tough as dried anchovies. He worked his teeth and tongue, macerating the paper with all his might. After a long while the wad finally yielded, becoming soft and mushy. On the count of three, he gulped down the gob of pulp, made pliable with spit.

TWENTY YEARS LATER, he's standing in the middle of the real Seoul. *What happened to all the people who were on that set? They were living my life, the one I will be forced into when I return. Will I have to work there until the day I die? Will North Korea exist long enough for me to work on the set?*

Ki-yong passes a street lined with jewelry stores and pauses in front of a Lotteria. He's thirsty. He goes in and orders: "Coke. A small. Light on the ice."

"A small Coke. One thousand won, please. Thank you."

He orders fluidly, like water flowing along in a creek. But immediately after he came south, ordering food at a Lotteria was very intimidating. In that dark tunnel beneath Pyongyang, there weren't any fast food joints like McDonald's or Burger King. In 1986, even in the South, these restaurants were a brand-new form of eatery that had been around only for a few years. The first time he went to a Lotteria, Ki-yong paced outside, trying to figure out what the word "self-service" meant. It was stamped on a poster hanging on the wall inside. Some people walked toward the cashier, while others headed over to a row of trash cans with their trays, threw out whatever was on them, and left without paying. Everyone, even junior high school students, acted as if everything came naturally. Nobody hesitated, as if they had all received mass instruction on what to do at a fast food restaurant. He couldn't ask anyone what he was supposed to do. Finally, he went inside and sat down at a table. Even though he sat there for a while, nobody came to his table. Only after he remained there for a long time, watching people ordering at the counter, did he finally understand what "self-service" meant. How could you call that service, when the customers did the ordering, fetched the food, and threw it out after they were done? But he got used to it. And there were many other things that he had to absorb, things he hadn't learned on the underground set in Pyongyang.

MA-RI AMBLES DOWN the street. Although she isn't one to agonize over important issues in her life, this is different. Sometimes, she wants to shout "Time!" like in a basketball game, and this is that kind of moment. She isn't losing the game yet. She's still in the lead by a good margin, but her opponent is pursuing her doggedly, and she can feel the whole thing tilting in his favor. If it continues like this, the lead will undoubtedly flip and it could be hard to get back on top.

Where did it go wrong? Every time she updates her résumé to apply for a new job, she tries to pinpoint the exact moment her life started to veer off track. She wonders if her problem isn't her unexciting professional experience, but her family issues, and her thoughts naturally flow to her mother.

Ma-ri's mother suffered from depression starting in her late twenties. She didn't know it was a disease until the end of the 1980s. Once she discovered it was an illness, she started taking medication, but it never did much to make her better. Her depression pressed down on her entire family like a thick blanket. Ma-ri's father's heart grew heavy every time he thought of his wife lying immobile in their room, dark behind closed curtains. Like many people suffering from depression, Ma-ri's mother tossed and turned night after night, lying awake, consumed by increasingly negative thoughts, which made it even more difficult to fall asleep. It was a vicious cycle. Ik-dok went to church to seek advice from a Catholic priest and only then realized that his wife was suffering from an illness, but this newfound knowledge didn't really change anything. Although a graduate of a college in Seoul, he'd gone back home to Kwangju and worked in the family's wholesale liquor business. He was immersed in an environment that made it difficult for him to understand silly illnesses like depression. He could only compare it to the melancholy that washed over him during a post-binge hangover. Such drinking was to be expected to a certain degree, since he dealt with lazy bums and tough guys as a liquor wholesaler. Though he himself wasn't a lazy good-for-nothing, he always maintained good relations with them, something he had to do to thrive in that world.

Ik-dok always ranted: "You know how people pour some liquor on the ground to ward off evil spirits when they're out drinking? That's basically what taxes are—whatever's left after you pour some out for the evil spirits. Why can't they just collect all of it when you sell the alcohol, instead of slapping on the VAT?" It wasn't an exaggeration to say that his entire life was a battle against taxes. If you had to find one phrase that described Jang Ik-dok's life philosophy, it would be "No documentation." He didn't believe in receipts or accounting books, and instead had his own system, a notebook filled with a code of letters and numbers and a personal network of business contacts and friends. Even though knives and personal contacts took the place of modern contractual relationships, it was, in its own way, an efficient and rational system.

"The government's like a bandit. It's better for you if you don't bump into it," Ik-dok once said to his daughter after he slipped a couple of folded ten-thousand-won bills to a cop, who had stopped him for a traffic violation. "Every time you do, you find yourself out of cash."

"The fine would be thirty thousand won. Do you really

need to do this? Why don't you just pay the ticket when you get it in the mail?" Ma-ri asked.

He stared at his daughter, baffled. "But then I'll be in their records!"

Neither Ma-ri nor anyone else could change his mind. If they tried to correct him, they endured an entire day of his bandit theories. His long-winded speech would go: "Let's say a bandit is ruling a village for a week, okay? Before the day's gone, he's going to take everything. But if he's in power for a year, he'll wait until fall harvest to steal things and will probably let the villagers live. If he rules for ten years, he'll even make plans—feeding the villagers because you can't have them all die of hunger, giving them clothes and other things. If he's there for thirty years, then he's going to be meddling in your business, telling you to have children or whatnot. What I'm telling you is that the government is the bandit that rules for thirty years."

"So if we're going to live under a bandit anyway, it's better to be under one that's going to be in power for a long time?" Ma-ri would ask.

Her father would grin and reply, like a riddler, "No, it's just an example. And don't go around saying that your dad said so."

Logic wasn't important to him. Ma-ri thinks he latched on to any old rhetoric to evade taxes. Back then, with the National Security Law in full force, you could be taken in and interrogated for that kind of talk.

In some ways, he was like a ghost, the way he went out of his way to avoid the government in any shape or form. For several years, he earned hundreds of millions of won a year, but he always kept his business slotted in the simple VAT taxation bracket, the category for the smallest businesses.

He would just register several businesses and disperse his earnings. But he did not forget the tax officials' hard work, and visited them with monetary gifts at holidays. He was able to avoid taxes by employing all sorts of shady tactics, but even he couldn't do anything about his wife's depression. He felt powerless when he came home to his wife lying in their darkened bedroom, curtains drawn. He dragged her out and forced her to go on walks and take Chinese herbal medicine, but none of it worked.

He wondered, guiltily, if it was his fault, since he was the one who brought her to this place, away from Seoul where she had been happily attending college. A native Seoulite, his wife would never have imagined that she would follow her husband down to Kwangju and live the life of a liquor wholesaler's wife. When he grew frustrated and angry at the whole situation, he wanted to give up and get a divorce. But what was done was done. Deep down, Ik-dok knew he was not the reason she was depressed, but he didn't feel any better about it.

They had children despite it all. Ma-ri, the baby of the family, earned good grades. Ik-dok bragged about his smart daughter, who was often at the top of her class. Soon, Ma-ri was admitted to a college in Seoul and left home. Their eldest son, Jong-sok, suffered a brain injury when he was five, when he ran after a fire engine and was hit by another fire truck following close behind. Despite several bouts of neurosurgery, he was diagnosed with serious developmental delay. The second son, In-sok, was a quiet, somber child who liked to read and play alone. He would always find a hiding place in the storage room stacked with soju crates and snuggle into a nook for a whole day. He knew the storage room so well that nobody, except for their dog, could find him when he went off inside by himself. In-sok was fairly com-

petent in school, but he didn't go to Seoul for his education.
Instead, he went to a public university nearby so he could
remain with his parents. But Ma-ri had always been different. She wasn't at all like her mother; rather, she inherited
her father's preternatural optimism. She was a happy, outgo-
ing girl who liked to show off and brag and had a competi-
tive streak.

But her mother's depression affected her severely. She
dreaded coming home and seeing her mother lying in bed,
pulling the covers over her head instead of acknowledging
her children's hellos. Seeing the shape of her mother under the covers, Ma-ri would worry that she had died, but a
secret part of her wished that her mother was lying quietly
dead in her bed. She didn't think there was any hope for her
mother. Turning away from her, Ma-ri would bump into her
eldest brother, grinning idiotically at her. There was nothing malicious about him, but sometimes he would mastur-
bate in his room without realizing that the door was open,
so she thought of him more as a giant orangutan than a human being. He gained weight steadily, reaching 330 pounds
by the time she left home. After that nobody knew how
much he weighed. He detested getting on the scale, and nobody could force his huge bulk onto it. He even had his own
bathroom—ordinary ceramic toilets would shatter under
his weight, so they ended up installing a custom-made toilet
constructed of strengthened plastic. Ma-ri always thought
he wouldn't have gotten so obese if their mother hadn't been
depressed.

Ma-ri never admitted it to anyone, but her dream had always been to leave and go as far away as she possibly could,
and she knew that the only way to achieve her goal was to be
a star student. Once she got to college, away from her mother's weighty shadows, her natural optimism was reborn.

Even if she encountered problems, she'd mumble to herself, "It'll all work out somehow. It's not a big deal." In her diaries, she would scribble things like, "Words are crucial. If one's words change, one's behavior changes, and that will lead to the transformation of one's fate."

The university bared its true self the day after the admission ceremony in early March, when the campus was chaotic with people selling cotton candy and film and photographers offering to take pictures. Composed of a few grand brick buildings erected during the Japanese colonization and hastily built, cheap, cracked concrete ones funded by Western aid, the campus awaited her. The azaleas and magnolias that would eventually disguise the ugly architecture had yet to bloom, and the wind blowing over the small hill to the north of the school raced through the empty quad and out the front gates. The statue of the founder stood forlornly, and the plaza in front of the library was covered with asphalt instead of bricks, to discourage students from prying pieces loose and hurling them at the riot police. It was the beginning of 1986, with the newly formed New Democratic Party pushing for the reform of the electoral process to institute direct elections. The current of change would culminate only a few months later on May 3 with the student riots at Inchon, but Ma-ri, a freshman, wasn't aware of this volatile situation. Large posters flapping in the wind against the library walls hinted at the looming political turmoil. All around town, cinemas were playing a Japanese documentary about the 1980 Kwangju massacre, in which the government murdered students and civilians. But none of this was new or shocking for a native of Kwangju.

On the first day of school, eighteen-year-old Ma-ri's attention was drawn to a "charming walk" workshop, hosted by Esquire, the shoe company. The ad in the newspaper asked her: "Does your walk have the seven essential marks of beauty?

1. When you walk, the toe of your shoe touches the ground first.
2. You walk with straight legs.
3. Your knees brush against each other when you walk.
4. Your steps are buoyant and you walk in a straight line.
5. You walk tall.
6. Your arms swing out to 15 degrees.
7. You face forward, your head up.

"How is your walk? People judge your personality, sophistication, and intelligence from the way you walk. Comfortable shoes and a good posture are the foundation of a beautiful walk."

Reading this ad, Ma-ri suddenly became embarrassed. None of the seven essential marks described her walk. It was the first time she realized that there was more to a walk than transporting herself from one point to another. According to the ad, it was really a language that expressed one's personality, sophistication, and intelligence. She had to get rid of her Nikes and get herself a pair of cute heels. She went to Myongdong to buy a pair of Esquires and received a ticket to attend the charming walk workshop, taught by a top model. There were two sessions, one at 2:00 P.M. and another at 7:30 P.M., in Apgujong-dong, and she decided to go to the later one. Wearing her brand-new, shiny, pointy black heels, Ma-ri boarded the bus to Apgujong-dong. The bus crossed Hannam Bridge, passed Sinsa-dong, and raced toward Apgujong-dong. New buildings were rising all around the

Kangnam district, which was just beginning to be developed, creating a sparse and uneven landscape like the mouth of a child who has started to lose teeth. On every new building hung a huge banner that said FOR LEASE. Some criticized Kangnam, with its many buildings and little greenery, calling it overdeveloped and likening it to a gigantic brickyard, but the fact that these neighborhoods didn't have any patches of green made them cooler to Ma-ri. Green was dated—gray was in. Kangnam instantly captivated her; a chic world lit by bright signs and inhabited by fashionable women driving along wide boulevards.

Ma-ri got off the bus in front of Hanyang Department Store and walked to her destination, looking around like a tourist at the McDonald's, Pizza Hut, and other American franchises. The new shoes didn't fit very well and her heels were starting to chafe. Just when she was wondering how in the world she was going to learn to walk elegantly in this condition, one of her heels caught in the space between two bricks in the sidewalk and she twisted her ankle. The tiniest shocks had always hurt her joints easily, as they would throughout her life. If she'd plopped down right there and massaged her ankle, soothing her injured muscle and ligament, she probably would have been fine, but she kept walking through the pain, embarrassed, feeling as if all the people at the bus stop and those standing in front of the McDonald's were staring at her. She had to stop a few steps later, collapsing on the border of a flower bed. Ma-ri, more upset about missing the charm workshop than hurting her ankle, shed a few tears. Her ankle was now throbbing so painfully that she couldn't put any weight on it, and her inquiring touch confirmed that it was already swollen. She perched on the edge of the flower bed for a long time, trying hard to look nonchalant, pretending she was waiting for a friend. But as the sun set it got colder and colder, and Ma-ri was wearing a short skirt. This city, where she didn't know anyone she could call for help, started to frighten her.

Kangnam, which had won her over just a few hours earlier, was a cold and uncaring concrete monster. Nobody approached her to help. Concluding that she was going to end up freezing to death if she didn't take action, Ma-ri boldly slipped off her shoes and tucked them into her bag. She limped down the frigid street. She was wearing stockings, but she might as well have been barefoot, the iciness from the sidewalk traveling to her heart and chilling it. The stylish residents of Apgujong-dong didn't pay any attention to this shoeless girl. This aloof, uncaring attitude of city dwellers was shocking to her. If a girl had been hobbling barefoot down Chungjangno in Kwangju, someone would have already given her a piggyback ride or put her in a taxi. But nobody even glanced at her in Apgujong-dong. Limping, she crossed the street and waited for the bus, holding on to a newly planted gingko tree, but the bus didn't appear for a long time. Finally, it arrived and she managed to get on and make it back to her boardinghouse in Sinchon.

What would have happened to her if she hadn't sprained her ankle? If she had been able to attend the workshop and learn how to walk gracefully? If she had kept her first impression of Kangnam as a wonderful place? If she hadn't sprained her ankle, she wouldn't have had to spend a few days lying in her room. She wouldn't have been brought to the hospital by an acquaintance from back home. She wouldn't have joined or even heard of the group of politically active students of which the acquaintance was a member. At the time, she felt rejected from Kangnam and Seoul, and she was happy to hang out with the people who'd come forward to help her, hometown people whose words were heavy with the same accent as hers.

She also wonders how her life would have turned out if she had never become pregnant with Hyon-mi. If her mother hadn't been depressed. If she hadn't met Ki-yong. If she hadn't decided to go to college in Seoul. Where did things start going awry? That might be a stupid question. What would her life have been if she'd made different choices? She idles in front of the crosswalk, lost in thought. She's shocked at how quickly the alternatives pop into her head. She wouldn't have been a student activist. She would have learned English, played tennis on the weekends, and gone camping during the summer with the guys in the yacht club. She would have dated a rich guy slated to go abroad for additional degrees, then chosen to marry an even richer guy, who would have been jealous of the first one. She would have earned her degree in sociology or psychology, returned to Korea and would be teaching at a university by now. She wouldn't be nearing forty without anything to show for it, with only a history of going from job to job like a nomad. She's never been particularly good at what she was doing, whether it was when she was an insurance saleswoman, a leftist student activist supporting Kim Il Sung, or even now, as a car saleswoman. She's never excelled at anything. Why is she only ordinary, when she was always at the top of her class in high school and was respected by all of her teachers? Was this some conspiracy? She can't accept the conclusion that it's the result of her poor choices. It must be because of someone's persistent evil intentions, some invisible hand that secretly twisted her life and derailed it from success. Otherwise, how could her promising life have turned out this way?

Beeeep beeeep. The sound alerting pedestrians that the

light has turned green wakes Ma-ri from her reverie, and she unthinkingly steps off the curb. She takes four steps and an SUV screams by in front of her—really only a few inches from her nose—without slowing down. She sees a brief darkness in front of her, and the forceful backwind makes her falter. Her heart in her mouth, she turns to her right to glare at the car that almost careened over her, and spots a policeman. He lumbers onto the road, waves at the SUV to slow down, and motions for it to pull over.

A cop pulling over a driver is just like a bear hunting for food; he looks lethargic but zeroes in on his target with great precision. The driver's window slides down as the cop approaches. Ma-ri draws in a deep breath and heads toward the car. *And I bummed a cigarette off a cop this morning,* she thinks, amused. If the driver argues that he didn't do anything wrong, she's going to make sure that he doesn't get away with it. She's going to tell the policeman that the car most definitely ran a red light. At this point, she's still confident. The cop glances at Ma-ri and the driver's head pokes out, to see what's going on. Ma-ri expects a young, muscular, and virile man, but the driver is a woman in her twenties wearing a stylish dark suit with a deep V-neck, probably Prada, her carefully styled layered hair shimmering gently around her small, cute face.

Shooting Ma-ri a look of disdain, she flirts with the cop. "Oh, I'm so sorry, I have to be somewhere and I'm late. I only got my license a few weeks ago, too. See?" She gives him a coy glance and hands him her license. Even then, she doesn't lower her guard toward Ma-ri. The cop, unable to continuously ignore Ma-ri's chilly presence, finally asks, "Can I help you?"

She tries as hard as she can to remain calm, and enunciates clearly, "This car almost ran me over in the crosswalk."

The policeman looks at her cast-bound arm, then her face. "So are you hurt?"

"No, I wasn't hurt, but I almost died," Ma-ri says, becoming indignant.

The girl in Prada interjects. "Look, lady, that's because you jumped out when the light wasn't even green, you should wait before . . ."

As those words reach Ma-ri's ears, an uncontrollable rage overtakes her. It's the kind of anger that the average person experiences at most a couple of times in her life. Like a poisonous snake darting away from the foot that has stepped on its tail, her hand shoots into the window and grips the girl's mane. The girl starts shrieking. Undeterred, Ma-ri shakes the fistful of hair back and forth as she yells, pointing to the crosswalk splayed across the twelve-lane road: "You're the one who ran the red! What the fuck's wrong with you? Can't you even say you're sorry?"

If the cop didn't yank her off, she would have pulled out a handful of that silky hair. Ma-ri loosens her grip unwillingly. The girl, her hair covering her face, is shocked into silence. The cop warns Ma-ri gravely, like a soccer umpire, "What are you doing? If you keep at it, I'm going to arrest you for assault."

Ma-ri's eyes swim. Everything is so unfair. She's the one who almost died, but the cop is taking the side of the hot young girl. She feels attacked and criticized, like the whole world is against her, even the cop treating her as though she's falsely accusing the girl. The cop blocks the Prada girl from getting out of her car, telling her, "Look, I'm not going to give you a ticket, so just leave."

The girl smoothes her hair and puts her hand on the steering wheel. She jerks the gear into D, glares at Ma-ri, and spits, "What a psycho." She doesn't forget to smile at the cop, calling, "Thank you! Have a good day!" as the SUV jets off, leaving behind a roar and fumes.

"Why did you let her go?" Ma-ri demands.

The cop stares at her. "Lady, give me your ID."

"My ID? What for? What the hell did I do?" she screams.

"Just hand it over."

"You have no right to do this! You think being a cop gives you all the power?" It's been a long time since she felt this crackle of electricity coursing through her, making her hair stand on end, but it isn't satisfying. Her enemy has disappeared and now she's fighting with the wrong person, a witness.

"Excuse me, what's going on?" someone asks, approaching them.

Even before she turns around, she knows it's the branch manager. He stands behind them, concerned. "Can I help? She works for me," the manager explains in a gentle but firm tone, a tone only successful men possess.

The cop's attitude changes completely, and he asks deferentially: "Are you her supervisor? Please take her with you." The cop goes on to explain that Ma-ri was interfering with his duties, and the manager listens silently. Ma-ri gives up defending herself and follows the manager across the street.

"Ms. Jang," the manager starts.

"Yes?"

"Is everything okay with you these days?"

Ma-ri's newfound calm dissipates and her blood starts roiling. It's unfair that people assume that a woman's anger is abnormal and that something emotional is lurking beneath her wrath. That damn girl in the SUV is the one who violated traffic laws, not her. And the cop ignored a citizen's righteous complaint and let the violator go free. That's the only thing she's angry about. There's nothing deeper or emotional. She wants to turn to the manager and unleash everything on her mind, but stops herself. It's not worth it. And, well, it's true that things aren't exactly okay with her these days.

"I'm fine. I'm just really angry, that's all."

"Ms. Jang, as members of the service industry, we wrangle with emotions. You have to know how to stay calm. If you get overwhelmed by your anger, how are you going to control other situations?"

Everything he says is true, but her fury is about to reach the breaking point. She wants to ask, sarcastically, *Then why, if you can control yourself so well all the time, did you have to take drugs?*, but she manages to keep her mouth closed. The pair walks silently past the showroom and go to their desks in the office. Ma-ri's dying for a smoke but doesn't want to push the manager. She takes a series of deep breaths and succeeds in staying in her seat. With great effort, she conjures a memory of Song-uk—his body, his scent, the way his skin feels against hers, the way he moves his limbs. Her anger shrivels bit by bit; perhaps her brain understands her intentions and is emitting dopamine. She begins to think of Song-uk's suggestion, which she considered impossible only yesterday, as her revenge on the world.

CHOL-SU STUBS HIS cigarette out in front of the adults-only game room and, out of habit, looks around surreptitiously. He goes up the stairs. Three young men are leaving the pool hall on the second floor, laughing. One of them has a bit of dark sauce around his mouth, remnants of the black bean noodles people order while they're playing pool. Chol-su bypasses the pool hall and continues up to the third, through a metal gate. The sign on the door on the third floor says, TAEDONG TNC. He presses his right index finger on a black strip under the sign. With a beep, it recognizes his prints, and the door automatically opens and slides shut behind him.

"I'm back," Chol-su announces.

"Did you eat?" asks his superior, Supervisor Jong.

"Yes."

"What'd you eat?"

"Spaghetti."

"By yourself?"

"Well, yes, I often do."

"How can you eat something like spaghetti by yourself?" Jong asks.

"There's a place I go all the time," Chol-su explains, leaning on his desk.

"Do you cook it at home, too?"

"Sometimes."

Jong shakes his head, as if he can't understand Chol-su, and changes the subject. "How is she?"

"I don't think she's figured anything out," Chol-su reports.

"Really?"

"Well, unless she's pretending she doesn't know anything."

"You really think his own wife, who sleeps in the same bed, wouldn't know?" Jong asks.

"I think it might be possible. How's Kim Ki-yong today?"

"I think the son of a bitch figured it out. He went to his kid's school today and stayed there for an hour."

"You think he went to talk to his daughter?"

"I don't know what he did inside." Jong probes his ear with a cotton swab, a habit he acquired after his stomach cancer surgery. After they cut out half of his stomach the inside of his ear was always itchy. He eats seven small meals a day and digs around his ears with cotton swabs hundreds of times. It's as if his life's purpose is to eat and clean out his ears.

"Where is he now?" asks Chol-su.

"Oh, he parked his car near his office, then brought some stuff out and got on the subway."

"Then what happened?"

"Then I lost him. He used his cell in Chongno and then after that, nothing." Jong switches the cotton swab to his left hand and starts going at his other ear. "But this Kim Ki-yong is a really bizarre guy. It looks like he hasn't been active for the past ten years. How's that possible? He just imports movies that make you fall sleep, and that's it! Crazy son of a bitch. Why is Pyongyang leaving him alone?"

"Maybe they have some secret mission for him."

"You mean like that hag Lee Son-sil? That was amazing, coming down here in nineteen eighty and doing nothing until nineteen ninety-one."

"She was ranked twenty-two in the Workers Party of Korea, right?"

"Yeah. Rank twenty-two means she was at a premier level. A high-ranking spy comes down and for ten years she's befriending housewives, haggling over the price of bean sprouts, and participating in informal cash pools. She never gets caught, then she ends up going back north on the midget submarine that docked at Kanghwa Island, like nothing happened. She was a hugely talented agent, a natural. Just the fact that she was able to do nothing for ten years . . ."

"Do you think Kim Ki-yong is a bigwig like her?" Chol-su asks, straightening up and heading toward the coffeemaker.

"I don't think so. He's a little young for that. Now that he's on the move, we'll keep an eye on him for a few days. He'll run someplace, now that we've shaken him up a bit. It's also possible that he's just going to confess everything. These assholes are like grasshoppers, they all jump when one guy does."

Chol-su pours himself some coffee and sits down at his desk. Jong starts flipping through a newspaper. Chol-su's thoughts wander not to Kim Ki-yong, but to Ma-ri. Her youthful cheeks that lead to her graceful neck and then finally to her full, still perky chest. Her ivory blouse and contrasting brown eye shadow seem to reflect her conflicted self-perception, in limbo between youth and middle age. Her sophisticated makeup hides fine lines and dark circles but still reveals the fact that she's aging, demonstrating her resolve not to give up on her looks. Every pore on her body is bursting with this contradiction. Maybe that's why he felt suffocated sitting next to her in that small car. Even though it was only for a brief time, he felt ambushed by the strong womanly scent rolling off her in waves. It wasn't perfume; it was something different. Frankly, she wasn't that beautiful a woman. But something about her made her glow, enhancing her attractiveness. Everything about the test drive was different from Chol-su's everyday life—Ma-ri, wearing a sleek suit, the car worth over forty million won, the fancy showroom. Chol-su suddenly wishes—no, he craves—that he were rich. He's sick of his government employee life. On the same day every month, he uses his entire paycheck to pay his credit card bill. No matter what happens at work, he's trapped into staying, imprisoned by the pension he would receive upon retirement. Would he be able to grab the attention of someone like Ma-ri? What would happen to Ma-ri if Ki-yong were caught or went back north? She'd be shaken, the foundation of her life would crumble. Would it be possible then? Would he be able to be with her?

. . .

THE MUSIC CHIMES, signifying the end of fifth period. Like a radio whose frequency is suddenly jumbled, the classroom fills up instantly with various kinds of noise. Kids shoot out of their seats and wander around the classroom, gabbing. Hyon-mi thinks this must be what life is like for molecules when water reaches its boiling point. Her desk starts buzzing and her pencil rolls off onto the floor. She takes out her cell.

"Come to the teachers' office."

It's a text from her homeroom teacher. She gets up and tells A-yong, "Our homeroom teacher wants me to come see him at the teachers' office. Can you tell Viper if I'm late?"

"Sure."

Hyon-mi pushes past her classmates and heads to the door. When her homeroom teacher sees her come through the doors of the teachers' office, he smiles and pulls a swiveling chair toward him. These days he's obsessed with the Book of Changes. He spends every available moment determining the fate of his students. "Sit, sit," he offers.

"It's okay."

"No, it's for me, so my neck won't hurt looking up at you."

Hyon-mi perches on the chair, which is padded with a flowery cushion.

"What's going on with the school beautification project?" her teacher asks.

"I'm going to do it with Jae-gyong and Tae-su, from the art club."

"Will two be enough?"

"I think so."

"What about Han-saem, too?"

"Han-saem?" Hyon-mi hesitates; she isn't fond of Han-saem.

"Get her to do it, too," he instructs.

Hyon-mi nods. "All right, I will."

"Okay, that's it. See you later."

Hyon-mi stands up, bows, and bumps into Soji at the door.

"Hi, Ms. So," Hyon-mi says.

"Hey, Hyon-mi." Soji reaches out to stroke the girl's hair. "Want to sit?" she asks, going to her desk. "How's your mom?"

"She's fine."

"You're looking more like her the older you get."

Hyon-mi purses her lips, unhappy. "No, everyone says I look like Dad."

"Hmm. Ma-ri used to be really smart and cool."

"Really?"

"Of course. There were a lot of cool girls back then, and your mom was one of them."

"I don't believe it."

"Why not?"

"Mom's just, I don't know. I don't know." Hyon-mi shakes her head. She has never once thought that her mom was smart or intelligent. She thinks those words describe students like her. Of course, once upon a time her mom was a student, but it's still an odd way to think of her.

Soji asks, "By the way, what do you want to be when you grow up?"

"I don't know. Well, I think . . . uh, you're not going to laugh at me, right?"

"Of course not."

"I think I want to be a judge."

"Yeah?"

Hyon-mi studies Soji's expression. "You're already making fun of me. You're like, Oh, you're so predictable."

"No, no. Why do you want to be a judge?"

Hyon-mi answers gravely, "I think the law is the most important thing in society. If there weren't laws, people would be exposed to the violence of the majority and wouldn't be able to defend themselves. You know what happened with A-yong, right? Without laws, kids like A-yong wouldn't get any protection. I think the law is able to give at least some power to the weak."

Hyon-mi's determination reminds Soji of Ma-ri, back when she believed that good and evil divided the world, that people knew how to tell them apart, that the world would become utopian if everyone just followed her conscience, that to achieve a utopia it was necessary to overthrow the oppressive government and eliminate those who profited from it. Ma-ri had looked just like Hyon-mi when she believed that could be easily achieved. Soji wonders if the passion shared by mother and daughter is the product of genetic makeup.

"You look at the law in a very interesting way," Soji comments. "It seems to me that other kids look at the law as a means to punish those who commit crimes."

"Well, of course there's that too. But the real purpose of the law is to protect the weak. It was only because of the law that they were able to get those kids who streamed that footage of A-yong, and that's why they were able to stop it before it got out of hand." Hyon-mi's voice grows louder and more impassioned.

Soji is starting to feel self-conscious in front of the other teachers. "That's true, actually," she concedes.

"Everyone laughed and made fun of her but the law was the only thing that was on her side."

Soji nods, taking in Hyon-mi's smooth forehead, and wonders what the girl will look like when she grows up. Hyon-mi is on the brink of becoming an adult. She's a little surprised that Hyon-mi is praising the purity of the law and the system without any reservation. "You don't think there can be bad laws?"

Hyon-mi tilts her head. "What do you think is a bad law?"

Soji can't think of anything, and realizes that she hasn't pondered that kind of question in a long time. Students usually ask such basic questions, the kind adults have ceased thinking about.

Hyon-mi seems to understand Soji's embarrassment. "That's why we have a legislature, so that bad laws can be changed. They'll change them gradually."

"You sound so mature, Hyon-mi. Do you have a boyfriend?"

Hyon-mi, turning pink, starts stuttering. "No. I mean, well, not really. Uh, I'm only in eighth grade."

"Apparently even elementary school kids have boyfriends these days."

"Oh, well, that's just little kid stuff. What do they know about life?"

"Oh, so you know about life?" Soji covers her mouth, unable to suppress her laughter. The music comes on the loudspeakers. Hyon-mi leans forward to say something else, but Soji points at the ceiling, as if the music is playing from there. "The music, Hyon-mi, you should get to class."

"Okay, see you later," Hyon-mi says, bowing to her teacher, and runs off.

THREE COUNTRIES

K I-YONG ENTERED COLLEGE in the South in 1986. During the previous year, he had taken a prep course in Noryangjin, studying for the high school equivalency exam and college aptitude test. Though he didn't graduate, he majored in English at Pyongyang University of Foreign Studies, and he always liked math, so those subjects weren't much of a problem. He did have a harder time with the other subjects. With his inadequate South Korean vocabulary, it would have been difficult to pass if the exams hadn't been all multiple choice. Compared to the four brutal years he had spent as an agent trainee, studying in a warm library was like heaven. Also, subjects like politics, economics, and citizen ethics helped him adapt to southern society. Citizen ethics, which taught him about the importance of putting the state and societal morals before anything else, was familiar. It all made sense if he replaced "state" and "nation" with "Leader" and "Party." Like the prince and the pauper in Mark Twain's classic, the ethics of the South and the North were similar enough that when they ran into each other, each recognized something in the other.

In those days, he didn't have a woman to distract him or even a drinking buddy. He studied hard, and, that winter, he was able to gain admission into the math department of the prestigious Yonsei University. On a cold day, with the damp wind freezing his ears, he crossed the large field at Yonsei, dotted with patches of snow and ice, to read the list of accepted students posted on the bulletin board. Eighteen-year-old students, who had confirmed their admission over the phone but still came out to personally find their exam numbers on the list, were chatting in groups around him. Ki-yong knew why he, who had been at the top of his class at the University of Foreign Studies, had been selected to be sent south by Liaison Office 130. They needed agents who could get into the South's prestigious universities.

Ki-yong's mission was an audacious attempt. Pyongyang was observing with interest the South's rapidly growing leftist student activist movement. At the time, in 1986, with Kim Yong-hwan of Seoul National University leading the way, Juche Ideology was at the cusp of popularity, poised to spread across college campuses nationwide. The North Korean leaders believed they needed a new process to create better agents. Before, they used undercover agents disguised as immigrants, as well as homegrown communists. Pyongyang's new, ambitious plan was to get a well-trained agent to infiltrate a college freshman class in the South and have him mature and develop with budding student activists.

For Ki-yong, college life in Seoul was amazing. At the end of March, forsythia began to bloom, competing fiercely with the busily flowering azaleas. The freshmen took one group picture after another in front of the primary-colored flowers. The flowers were so brilliant that even eighteen-year-old youth paled next to them. April was even more gorgeous. Magnolias broke off branches and fluttered to the ground at the lightest sprinkling of rain. From the back gate of the women's university beyond the small hill, the intense scent of lilacs drifted with the southern wind. Ki-yong often sat on what was known as Turgenev's Hill behind the medical school and read the Russian greats of the nineteenth century and Korean classics of the 1970s, borrowed from the library. He was amazed that nobody ever looked for him. In Pyong-yang, happiness at school meant he could promptly respond when his name was called, then relax until he was called again. But in Seoul, the time outside of lectures was all his, and no one cared if he didn't go to class. He wasn't required to attend nightly critiques and he wasn't forced to find fault with himself and confess his failings to his peers.

In May, a menacing mood permeated the campus. The smell of tear gas hung heavily in the air. Protests to amend the constitution to provide for direct presidential elections started in Inchon and spread to other cities. A hurricane of change was approaching. Young activists, armed with passion and ideology, breathed in the revolutionary energy, but Ki-yong was oblivious to these changes. All he could see were cherry blossoms covering the hills and girls around him in short skirts. It was to be expected, since he didn't know what South Korean colleges had been like before 1984. He'd never lived through the days when a government-controlled students' national defense corps represented students instead of the student government, riot police ate side by side with students on campus, and a few die-hard activists were arrested for breaking large windows of the library and distributing literature, roped together. In movies, characters who travel through time often go back to important moments in history. They arrive just as the fire that will kill Joan of Arc is being kindled, or as Napoleon is marching toward Waterloo. In some ways, Ki-yong was just like them, having been dropped into the making of history. The only difference was that he didn't know what would happen next.

On a hot June day, after the flowers had given way to greenery, he knocked on the door of the Political Economic Research Society, which was housed in the student union. Four young men and one young woman greeted him in the smoke-filled room. That sole young woman was Ma-ri.

One of the older students told them, grinning, "You two should be friends since you're both freshmen. But don't fall in love or anything." Later, when they got together, Ki-yong and Ma-ri remembered this half-joking prediction of their destiny almost at the same time and, like many couples, used it to paint the story of their love as a product of fate.

That day in June, Ki-yong sat on a creaky wooden chair and chatted with them about his interests. The room was musty and stagnant from cigarette smoke; a portable butane burner lay next to a nickel pot with strands of old ramen stuck to the bottom. The room was furnished with an old sofa, one side of which had been chewed up by rats. A rolled-up khaki sleeping bag and a guitar had been flung on the sofa, and a reproduction of O Yun's wood carving of a masked dancer and Sin Dong-yop's poem "Kumgang" were hanging on the wall, side by side. They asked him where he was from and why he wanted to join the group. A junior explained that they studied politics and economics, which weren't dead disciplines, as the group focused on putting the theories into practice in the real world. Ki-yong replied that he had always been fascinated by the contradictions inherent in society, but because he hadn't been able to figure out the fundamental reason for such contradictions, he wanted to find like-minded people with whom to discuss these problems. The upperclassmen, who had been trying to recruit freshmen, liked his answer. They took Ki-yong to a bar near the school and drank fermented rice wine together. A few months later, he participated in his first protest with one of the upperclassmen.

"Hey, you're a really fast runner!" the upperclassman commented, in awe of Ki-yong's speedy retreat from tear gas. After that, Ki-yong remembered to slow down and put less force in his arm when throwing rocks. When winter vacation approached, an upperclassman from Mokpo approached him. "I think you're ready for intensive study."

"Oh, do you really think so?"

"You can't change the world with only passion and a sense of justice. You need to be immersed in revolutionary ideology so that you can lead the masses and arm the workers."

Ki-yong followed him into an empty lecture hall, where a group had gathered: members of other student organizations he'd encountered at protests as well as unfamiliar faces. A deeply tanned guy came up and offered his hand, saying, "Nice to meet you. I'm Lee Tok-su."

Tok-su first advised them of the secretive nature of the gathering. "This meeting is top secret, even from other members of your organizations. You must realize that you are the driving force of the revolution, and you should be proud of this. As a member of the vanguard, you should be as strong as steel, be the best you can be, and be a model for the masses."

But in Ki-yong's eyes, Tok-su was far from a steely revolutionary vanguard. His gaze was forceful, but he was really only a frightened twenty-two-year-old kid. "Our pressing goal is to adopt the ideology of Kim Il Sung as our revolutionary coda and complete South Korea's revolution, driving American imperialists from our land." Tok-su then taught them the secret lingo. Kim Il Sung was KIS, Kim Jong Il was DLCK for Dear Leader Comrade Kim Jong Il, Juche Ideology was JI or Sub, North Korea was NK. Ki-yong quietly memorized the secret code, but the exaggerated seriousness of the meeting in the empty lecture hall made it seem like a farce. Were these really the revolutionary vanguards who would overthrow the South Korean regime? These young kids, with peach fuzz still on their faces? Would they be able to survive the KCIA's notorious torture and go on to overthrow the oppressive state? Ki-yong had a hard time believing it. The revolutionaries he had been used to seeing in the North were old men in their seventies, like Oh Jin-woo and Kim Il Sung. Of course, Kim Il Sung started the revolution when he was in his twenties, but that never felt real to him, since he associated the revolution only with what he saw in the North's propagandist operas like *Bloodbath*. Despite his reservations, Ki-yong became an activist of the NL camp at this meeting.

Scholarly pursuits in the name of the revolution occurred in the dead of night. During the day, the members participated in legitimate organizations, like the student government or other groups, but at night, they met with the education cell and learned about Juche Ideology. Fearful and hesitant, they met clandestinely and learned about Kim Il Sung's days as a freedom fighter against the Japanese occupation, exchanging looks of awe and referring to Kim Il Sung as Dear Leader and Kim Jong Il as General. For Southern youths in their early twenties, having been indoctrinated in anti-Communist education in schools, speaking this way felt vulgar, much like hearing a prim woman referring to a penis as a cock. At first, it was difficult for them to refer to the two heads of state as Dear Leader or the General, but once they did, they shivered with the excitement that came with breaking the law.

Of course, it was different for Ki-yong. He had to hide the ideological tattoo that was inked into his soul. Since he didn't grow up in a place where people had to refer to Kim Il Sung and Kim Jong Il in code, he sometimes slipped and uttered their names together with their titles, and received warnings from the upperclassmen who were vigilant about security. He quickly learned to appear hesitant as he shut his eyes tightly and recited in a low voice, "Long live the great general Kim Il Sung," just like the others. Like gangsters who took turns stabbing their brothers who had betrayed them, they ensured their safety by becoming accomplices to the same crime. Saying those words was definitely a violation of the law. And this surreptitious vocalization might have been the most important initiation rite, more so than learning about the forbidden Northern ideology. Perhaps Juche Ideology spread so quickly precisely because it was so dangerous.

The group thought Ki-yong was a not too bright but dedicated, circumspect activist, which was the kind of person everyone sought to recruit. People who asked too many questions or bragged that they were official members of the group were not welcome. Ki-yong wasn't like that, not that he could be even if he wanted to. He just periodically asked whether Juche Ideology really was the greatest ideology in the history of philosophy. He'd cautiously ask: "When all things and ideologies are supposed to change and develop in a dialectical manner, how can all processes stop when it comes to Juche Ideology?" But the others had a ready answer for this question because it was one that everyone asked, and laughed off his comments. Ki-yong listened to their impassioned but ultimately unpersuasive answers and nodded along. Their blind belief in Juche Ideology actually started to chip away at his own ideological certainty. How could they believe all of it without harboring any doubts, after reading only a couple of thin pamphlets and incomplete broadcast transcripts of the National Democratic Front of South Korea? A few members even argued that Juche Ideology was so powerful precisely because it was easy to understand. Unlike difficult and confusing bourgeois philosophies, this was a new idea that workers could adopt as their own, created with their comprehension in mind by the generous leader. Ki-yong's few questions, which he posed only to ensure a perfect disguise, boomeranged back at his soul.

After he became a member of the Juche Ideology faction in compliance with his initial orders, the Party didn't send down orders for a while. He lay in the dark in his room at the boardinghouse and wondered what Pyongyang ultimately wanted from him. He didn't fully comprehend the meaning behind the order—why he, a member of the Workers Party of Korea, had to pretend to learn about Juche Ideology instead of leading these students. Only after a long time did he come to the conclusion that Lee Sang-hyok and other power players in Pyongyang wanted him not to lead the South's student activism, but to assume a persona formed by authentic experiences. Liaison Office 130 might have wanted him to obtain a criminal record by breaking a group demonstration law. It was crucial that he copy everything the Southerners did—if he wanted to be exactly like them—without circumventing the scars they received in the process.

But fortunately—or unfortunately—he was never arrested. It was partly because he had been trained to evade arrest, but it was also because he didn't stand out in a crowd. He was often skipped over when the group, at a bar, counted how many people were there. Sometimes a bunch of them would be talking among themselves and suddenly notice Ki-yong sitting next to them and ask, surprised, when he got there. But a couple of members always remembered and in-

cluded him, in spite of his invisibility. The young Juche Ideology faction members, though they attended rallies, defi-
antly handing out leaflets and throwing Molotov cocktails at
cops, were really only boys who had grown up too quickly,
whose faces were covered with acne scars. They went out for
spicy rice cakes, talked about girls they had crushes on, and
obsessed over Hong Kong movies like *A Better Tomorrow*. On
New Year's, knowing Ki-yong didn't have family, they would
bring him home with them and share a bowl of rice cake
soup.

One summer day, three of them—a disheveled guy who
went by the nickname Magpie, another who answered to
Snout, and Ki-yong, who was known as Hammer—visited
Wolmi Island near Inchon. Magpie, drunk off soju and the
marine wind, lay across a bench on the beach and asked:
"Do you guys think the revolution will come?"

Magpie's older brother was a loyal activist and a central theorist of a minority group known as PD. As someone
who had given everything to the student movement, he op-
posed Magpie going to college. *What's the point of going to
college when it will only make you a servant of the bourgeoi-
sie? You might as well go straight into the factories and organize
the workers. Learn from my mistakes. I'm always regretting that
it took me so long to quit college to organize the factories. You
should become a worker as soon as you can and throw yourself
into class struggle, so you can live without guilt like I do.* Having always been close to his older brother, growing up together in a single-room house without space for even a desk,
Magpie had a difficult time dealing with this pressure. Magpie's brother even confiscated his books and threw out the
apple crate he was using as a desk. *Oh, so you don't want me
to go to college when you got to go? At least you got to go to college in the first place.* Magpie, feeling rebellious, studied hard,

hiding it from his brother, and got into Yonsei. But just like his brother, he became deeply involved in the student movement as soon as he stepped foot on campus and he never went near a lecture hall. The only difference was that he chose a different group from his brother and became an NL, accepting Juche Ideology as the fundamental truth.

Snout replied: "Don't you think it will happen at some point?"

"Actually," Magpie said, carefully, "I'm afraid that it will happen."

"What do you mean?"

"If the revolution happens, I won't be able to go rent comic books or play video games."

Snout nodded, although he would have sat up straight and rebutted that sentiment if he hadn't been so drunk, saying, "Yeah, you wouldn't be able to do any of that."

"I mean, even if we ousted America and overturned the dictatorship and smashed the imperialist, feudal system and the world became the kind of place where every man was the master of his destiny . . . then what? What would we do? Wouldn't we be bored?"

Ki-yong quietly listened to their conversation, thinking that they really had no idea what it was like to live in a world where everyone got up at the same time when the morning siren went off at seven, went to work at the same time, got a Sunday off only when the Central Committee of the Party mandated it, and came together with the whole community every night to rehash and criticize the day's mistakes. Of course, you could be happy in a society like that. You could play badminton or a pick-up game of soccer, or ice-skate. But you wouldn't be able to sit by yourself in a dark room watching porn, listen to the Eagles through your earphones, or read violent Japanese manga.

Snout, noticing Ki-yong's silence, nudged him. "What do you think?"

"I don't know. You probably wouldn't be able to do any of that. I'm sure it'll be a little boring, like Magpie says. But couldn't it be fun in its own way?" Ki-yong replied.

Years later, Ki-yong often recalled the conversation they had that day at Wolmi Island. They worried about the quality of life after the revolution that would never come, sitting on a beach strewn with young lovers and drunk, singing soldiers on leave, smelling whiffs of salty marine wind. Instead of revolution, the International Monetary Fund came in and completely restructured South Korea, like the American military did in 1945.

In the 1980s, when Ki-yong was in college, South Korea was closer to North Korea than it was to today's South. Jobs were guaranteed for life and college students never worried about their futures. The banks and conglomerates, with their lobbies of imported marble, seemed indestructible. Adult children took care of their parents and respected them. The president was chosen by a huge margin, through indirect election, and the opposition party existed only in name. Most people weren't too interested in the world beyond South Korea's borders. The North's motto, "Let's Live Our Way," described South Korea during the 1980s. In redistributing resources, the government's whim was more powerful than market principles, so government employees were severely corrupted by rampant bribes and fraudulent dealings, just like in the North. All students, whether they were in high school or college, were in the government-controlled students' national defense corps, heading to school a few times a week in drill uniforms. And once a month the entire citizenry would participate in civil defense drills. The capitals of both countries would turn pitch black once every few months for the mandatory blackout drills, initiated to better prepare for possible air raids.

The South today is nothing like the South of the 1980s. Today's South is actually a completely different country, one that morphed organically into something different from the North. Now it's probably more like Singapore or France. Married couples don't feel the need to have children, the per capita income is around twenty thousand dollars, the futures of banks and large conglomerates aren't set in stone, tens of thousands of foreigners arrive every year to marry Koreans and to obtain jobs, and elementary school students fly out of Inchon International Airport daily to study English abroad. Russian guns are sold in Pusan, sex partners are found online, people watch live broadcasts of the Winter Olympics on their cell phones, San Franciscan Ecstasy is transported in FedEx boxes, and half the Korean population invests in mutual funds. The president, humorless and unable to laugh off satire, is the target of jeers, and a party representing the workers was elected to the National Assembly for the first time after liberation from the Japanese occupation. If Ki-yong had predicted that the South would change like this in twenty years, he would have been treated like he was crazy.

Sitting on a red plastic Lotteria chair in Chongno o-ga, Ki-yong thinks about the three countries he's lived in—North Korea, the South of the 1980s and 1990s, and the South of the twenty-first century. One is already a relic of history. He is standing at a fork in the road of his life. Which should he choose, the North or the South? For the first time in his life, he wants to kneel in front of someone and ask: What would you do? No, he would just ask, What do you think I should do? For the past twenty years, he believed that he was working a job that was a little more dangerous than your average one. In a world filled with large-scale layoffs and series of bankruptcies, collapses of department stores and bridges and fires in the subways, he didn't think that his life as a forgotten spy was that perilous. But he forgot about his destiny, which hadn't forgotten about him, just like Paul Bourget's poem that stated, One must live the way one thinks or end up thinking the way one has lived.

Ki-yong's cell vibrates. It's Song-gon. He presses the talk button.

"Hello, sir, it's me."

"Hi, Song-gon."

"I just got back from buying the keyboard, and I was wondering where you were."

"Oh, sorry. Something came up. I don't know if I'll be back in the office today."

There's a brief silence. Normally, he wouldn't think twice about it. But with his nerves on edge, he feels this silence to be very unnatural.

"But . . . where are you?"

"Why, did someone ask for me?" he says, calmly.

"No, but I was wondering what I should tell people if they ask for you?"

"Just tell them to call back tomorrow."

"Sure, sure. Oh, and—"

Ki-yong cuts him off. "Sorry, I have to go. I'm talking to someone."

"Okay, got it—" Song-gon is speaking too slowly.

Ki-yong hangs up on him and powers off his phone. He's unsettled. He has a nagging thought that he shouldn't have trusted his own employee. It's a feeling he experienced as he was coming South on the midget submarine from Haeju. The vessel descended slowly, after filling up its oxygen tanks. He'd been excited at the prospect of embarking on a voyage into the vast ocean but at the same time had felt a little claustrophobic from being shut up in the small submarine. He'd given in to a feeling of intense but temporary resignation. There wasn't anything he could do, at least not while they were underwater. Especially for Communists, who aren't able to depend on God or prayer for everything, there was nothing to do other than to consciously surrender to the situation. This sensation is what Ki-yong recalls right at this moment.

He enters a cell phone store. The employee greets him cheerfully. Ki-yong smiles, a little embarrassed, and asks, "Do you have any prepaid phones?"

The clerk, who has punkish hair sculpted with wax, squints at him. "Prepaid phones? What kind are you looking for?"

Ki-yong scratches his head, sheepish. "I can't really open an account under my name because I have bad credit . . ."

The clerk understands quickly. He takes out an old cell phone from a drawer, covered in scratches and nicks.

"How much is it?" Ki-yong asks. He adds an extra bill on top of what the clerk tells him. The clerk, his face expressionless, tells him that he doesn't know in whose name the phone is registered, and that Ki-yong doesn't have to know either. Pressing several buttons, he shows Ki-yong how to use the phone. Ki-yong thanks him and leaves.

IF HE CONCENTRATES, Chol-su can hear the billiard balls, faintly, hitting against one another downstairs. He closes his eyes once in a while to listen to their clicks. They sound like heavy snow breaking branches in the dark of the night. *Crack. Clack.* That kind of snow, heavy with moisture, falls quietly onto branches struggling to remain whole. Tree branches are groomed to reach for the sky, stretching higher than the other branches in order to obtain more sunlight. With too much snow piled on it, any branch will break.

When his father's earnings as a comedian weren't sufficient, Chol-su was sent to his grandparents' house in Hoeng-gye, in the foothills of Taegwallyong in Kangwon Province, two thousand feet above sea level. Potato fields surrounded Chol-su's grandparents' house. Their roof was built low to the ground to withstand strong winter winds, and it was secured at the ends with rocks. A stroke had left Chol-su's grandfather with a limp, and his grandmother was mentally disabled. Despite his pronounced handicap, Grandfather was able to do everything. Their small storage room was filled to the brim with firewood, and they had more than enough potatoes, corn, and rice. During the last week of October, Grandfather would pick up a hoe and dig holes, where he would bury pots of kimchi for the winter. Grandmother was slow, but she wasn't dumb or crazy. She was consistent, a warm and quiet being who loved Chol-su more than anyone else, and was capable of expressing every ounce of that love. Chol-su's gentle, sweet grandmother was a rare soul amid the stoic grandmothers who populated the hills of Kangwon Province. She wasn't good with numbers—in fact, she knew basically nothing about them, as she had a hard time understanding any number beyond five—and didn't know how to read, but she didn't have any problem understanding what people said. When young Chol-su read his children's books out loud for her, Grandmother would lie on her stomach like a kid, immersed in the stories.

"Oh, this is fun. Like snowmen," she'd say. Or sometimes she commented: "The draft is blowing on a whistle," an idiom of her own creation. She sobbed when Chol-su read sad scenes and clapped when something joyous happened. Even though she loved stories, she never had much interest in TV dramas, frowning and becoming agitated when they came on. She preferred being read to, even if it was the same book over and over again, rather than watching a show where scenes changed constantly and new characters appeared. Grandmother's favorite stories were Oscar Wilde's *The Happy Prince* and Frances Hodgson Burnett's *A Little Princess*. For others, it might have been strange to see his grandmother, living in an isolated cottage in the hills of Kangwon Province, listening intently to *A Little Princess*, but that was just everyday life for Chol-su. He thought his friends' normal grandmothers were the odd ones, since they always looked so mean and scary, as if they would bare their teeth at any second and growl, unleashing their coarse, dirty breaths.

One very snowy day, so snowy that the branches outside snapped under their burden, the old couple made love, quietly.

"Stop moving around so much," Grandfather whispered, and Chol-su could hear his healthy right hand raising Grandmother's skirts under the covers. Her muslin slip rustled. The lovemaking ended quickly, with a grunt from Grandfather. Afterward, the old couple whispered and giggled like children under the covers.

On another winter day, Grandfather left the house, limping through the snow-covered fields to get some medicine from the village head for Grandmother, whose cold had worsened. But he didn't come back. Chol-su slept fitfully as his grandmother paced the room. The faraway cry of a pheasant reverberated in the hills. The next morning, the villagers retraced Grandfather's footprints, which headed toward the mountain. He hadn't even started out toward the village head's house. The right prints were clear, but the left were rubbed out, since he dragged that foot along the ground.

The footprints vanished in front of the conglomerate dairy farm, as if he had ascended to heaven. The surrounding area was an open field, without a single tree. In the winter, the dairy farm and its gentle, curved hills resembled a ski slope. Where did Grandfather go? The villagers were befuddled. He had limped four miles away from home, then disappeared without a trace. He must have walked at least two hours in the dark. Since the town was close to the DMZ and a quick-moving person could reach North Korea in a day by taking the Taebaek mountain range, the police came out to investigate whether this was a case of a Southerner going up north illegally. They knew that Grandfather was from the North, from Wonsan in South Hamgyong Province. But it didn't make sense that an old man would leave his beloved wife behind, tromp through ankle-deep snow drifts, and, limping, get beyond the DMZ where tens of thousands of soldiers were standing guard, all just to visit his childhood hometown.

Grandmother knew intuitively what had happened when she received many visitors and Grandfather was nowhere to be seen. In some sense, Grandmother's intuition was far superior to other people's. Instead of relying on language, she picked up the core idea from tone and inflection. In this way, she was a lot like a dog. She huddled in the corner of the room and cried, heartbroken. "I'm sad with the cicadas. I'm sad with the cicadas."

Until then, Chol-su had always thought that she had been afraid of cicadas, but he wondered if she actually pitied them. Her grammar was incorrect, and maybe because of its awkwardness, Grandmother's acute sorrow was delivered directly to Chol-su's heart. It was too intense to be called sadness. It was an emotion so powerful that Chol-su could feel its heavy weight on his back and shoulders, pressing him down like a sack of potatoes. He fell asleep, praying that his father would hurry up and come and take him away.

His father finally appeared, two days after Grandfather went missing. He embraced Grandmother and didn't say anything for a long time. Grandmother cried like a young girl in his arms. Chol-su's father, whose job was to make people laugh, didn't laugh once while he was there.

It had always been a mystery to Chol-su how his verbose father had been born from his silent grandfather, whose yearly tally of uttered words was fewer than those in the Charter of Citizens' Education, and his grandmother, who didn't know how to string together a proper sentence. Perhaps his father felt pressure to prove his eloquence from childhood. He probably believed that it was the best way to break the perception that he was a stupid child. He became famous by dancing jigs and jabbering rat-tat-tat like a quick-fire gun. One TV program even counted how many words he could utter in one minute. Even a tale long enough for a novel could be told in two minutes if his father had a go at it. His father talked nonstop; people couldn't ask him questions because they were so busy listening. Chol-su's father's most popular shtick was to repeat whatever the other guy was saying, and then tack on what he wanted to say. So he'd often start: "Oh, so you think such and such? Well, I think . . ."

Chol-su didn't know what words were exchanged between Father and Grandmother. One day, when he came back to the house after venturing into the village to eat dried persimmons, he found Father packing their things. Grandmother had refused to come with them. She had already figured out how to live with her sorrow—she would set the table for her husband and herself, and during meals she would talk with him as if he were sitting there. If a normal person had done this, she would have been sent to the mental hospital, but since it was Grandmother, nobody thought anything of it.

Father and Chol-su went back to Seoul.

"What about Grandmother?" Chol-su inquired.

"The neighbors said they would take care of her."

Three years later, a ginseng hunter discovered Grandfather, covered by a blanket of rotten leaves, in a ravine about three miles away from where his footsteps had vanished. It remained unsolved how he got there and why, but that didn't change the fact that there he was, lying in the depths of the mountains. Not long after Grandfather's burial, Grandmother died in her sleep. Chol-su's father, who was very busy at the time because of a gig hosting a TV show, returned to his hometown to bury his mother. He seemed annoyed and reproachful, as if he were saying, "It would have been easier if you'd both passed away at the same time!"

The cracking of the billiards downstairs drifts up to Chol-su's ears again.

Jong, who's been nodding off, opens his eyes, feeling Chol-su looking at him. "What?"

"Nothing." Chol-su shifts his gaze.

"You should keep tailing the woman. I hear she's pretty?"

"Yeah, but even if she's pretty, she's still the wife. He's lived with her for over ten years."

"Yeah, but I'm sure he'll go see her. Just follow her."

Chol-su gets up from his seat, taking his time.

Jong advises, "Keep your eyes open, 'cause she could be one of them too."

Chol-su nods and is about to head toward the door when Jong's cell rings. "Yeah, uh-huh, uh-huh, okay," he says, glancing at Chol-su, who decides to wait.

Jong hangs up. "So it turns out that she's not one of them," he informs Chol-su, as he scribbles something on a piece of paper and hands it to him.

"Should I go arrest him?"

"No, just follow him. This asshole's starting to panic."

"Okay."

"If you lose him, follow the wife, okay?"

Chol-su nods and leaves the office.

THE NOOK BETWEEN
HER COLLARBONES

I NEED CHOCOLATE. Ma-ri hangs her head so that her chin nestles in the nook between her collarbones. If she hung her head any further, she would look like a marionette with broken strings. I wish I had some dark chocolate, she thinks, rummaging through her desk. But all she finds are crumpled pieces of silver paper, smudged with chocolate on one side. She's so desperate she almost smoothes out the paper and licks it.

On her desk is a heap of motor show invitations she needs to send to her customers. The invitations are more than a pile of thick paper; they signify the emotions she will soon experience. Her customers will come to the motor show, find her, expect her to smile and welcome them, then go back home without buying a single car. The manager will give her a hard time. So every time she looks at the pile she wishes she had a piece of chocolate. But she doesn't have any.

Last month, when her waistline ballooned to nearly twenty-nine inches, she quit cold turkey. But her waist didn't return to its normal size. Song-uk told her he liked the slight pouch on her belly and her fleshier waist, but she didn't believe him. "You're just saying that to make me feel better. I know I'm getting old."

"No, really, I like it like this."

This conversation repeated itself several times, like codes shared between soldiers at guard posts. Song-uk admired Ma-ri's midsection, stroking it, Ma-ri was unbelieving, and Song-uk reiterated his love for it.

One day, he said, "Girls my age just have all of the negative aspects of women."

"What do you mean?"

"They're critical and picky and self-conscious and they want so many things, like kids. But they don't even know what they really want. You're different, because you have only the good parts of a woman. You're warm, you're a good listener, and you're confident. You're ready to accept what life gives you."

You have no idea, do you? You will never know, and you never should. I'm not that woman, it's just that I'm in love.

She tried to smile like Raphael's Virgin Mary, but she couldn't help smirking. Her young lover didn't notice and they kissed instead of speaking. His tongue burrowed in her mouth, attacking, as if it were a knife about to slice off her tongue. *You're really confident about life. You probably think you can do whatever you want with the older woman in front of you. I used to think I could change the world, but now I realize that I can't even control my urge to eat something sweet.*

Ma-ri hangs her head again. She feels a masochistic pleasure in having an affair with a twenty-year-old guy. As if she were hanging naked from the ceiling, revealing her private parts to the whole world. As if her sensitivity to criticism were becoming more and more acute, leaving her so self-conscious at meeting people's gazes that she's forced to look away, punishing herself even as she sinks deeper into the relationship.

BOWLING AND MURDER

A LMOND PISTACHIO for me."

"Green tea, please."

Ki-yong pays for both. The acne-covered clerk sinks his silver scoop into the ice cream containers, carves out balls of ice cream, and deposits them into paper cups for the two men. They docilely pick up plastic spoons and go find seats. Ki-yong glances out the floor-to-ceiling windows, watching the hundreds of people walking hurriedly by, scurrying like ants in the mazelike underground tunnels of the Coex building.

"It's been a long time," Ki-yong starts.

"Yes, it really has."

The Baskin-Robbins is nearly empty. In the store are three girls, probably in their early teens, but they're immersed in their own conversation. The two men start eating their ice cream.

"These days I find myself preferring cold food," Ki-yong's companion says, making small talk.

"Really? Usually the older you get, the less you like cold food."

"I think I feel hotter these days."

"That's not necessarily a bad thing, I guess."

"Well, I can get very sweaty. In the summer it's a little too much."

Ki-yong contemplates the man across from him. He didn't think he could find him so easily, as they weren't that close during their days at Liaison Office 130. Lee Sang-hyok managed each of them in completely separate lines of command.

"I thought I had forgotten your name," Ki-yong offers.

His companion isn't amused. His eyes betray a strong suspicion. "It's been a long time. I'm surprised you found me," he replies, edgy.

"I was walking down Chongno and for some reason your name came to me, like a revelation. Like it was written on an electronic signboard," Ki-yong explains.

The man snorts. His skin is dark, perhaps an indication of the vast quantities of alcohol that have wrecked his liver. Overall, his body isn't alert. Ki-yong finds himself frowning at the man's state, and is shocked at himself. He's surveying the man like a reviewer from Pyongyang who's come to verify the man's ideology. Maybe this man sitting across from him is looking at Ki-yong the same way, too. This thought makes him a little uncomfortable.

"So you called me up out of the blue because you remembered my name and thought, 'Oh, I should look him up'?" the man asks, still suspicious.

"No, that's not exactly it." Ki-yong pauses for another bite of ice cream. The sweet creamy spoonful slides down his throat. He raises his head. "Mr. Lee Pil," he calls.

"What?" The man slowly removes his spoon from his mouth, his eyes a conflicting mix of fear and annoyance.

"Did anything out of the ordinary happen today or yesterday?" Ki-yong asks carefully. His leg starts to tremble, shaking the table. Ki-yong presses his elbow on the table in an effort to stop the vibration.

"What's going on?" Pil demands, looking around a little wild-eyed.

"Was there nothing out of the ordinary?"

Pil turns his head and scans the outside of the store.

"There's no tail. I checked on my way here," Ki-yong reassures him.

"Look," Pil says.

"Yes?"

Pil lowers his head and whispers, "My kid is sick."

"What?"

"He has cerebral palsy. I'm divorced and if I'm not here, there's nobody to look after him. I'm barely making ends meet, running a cell phone store. I'm sure you know this. I don't have anything left over after I pay the bill for my kid's special education school." Pil starts to tear up.

Ki-yong feels trapped. "Mr. Lee, why are you telling me this?"

Pil straightens in his seat, wincing every time he moves; it seems as if he's injured his back. "Please take pity on me."

Ki-yong is rendered mute.

"Please take pity on me!"

Ki-yong looks around and grabs Pil's wrist. He has to calm him down. "Look, Comrade Lee, I know what you're thinking. Don't worry, I'm not here to take you back."

Pil tilts his head to the right, uncertain. He doesn't seem to trust Ki-yong completely yet. "Really?"

"Of course. Why would I ask you to meet me here, if that were the case?"

Pil looks around again, his body relaxing a little. "I guess that's true."

"I understand why you're concerned."

"Wouldn't you be? You turned up out of the clear blue sky for the first time in ten years and dragged me here."

"Well, I didn't drag you," Ki-yong corrects.

Annoyed, Pil spoons up more ice cream but then stabs his spoon into his cup, as if he has lost his appetite. "So what do you want from me?"

Ki-yong studies his face. Dark circles and deep wrinkles shadow his eyes. He has gained weight in the past decade and seems to be in a general state of exhaustion. Ki-yong is reminded of Dalí's melting clocks. He pulls his chair closer to Pil. "I think Secretary Lee has come back."

Pil furrows his brow, looking nervous, as if he just woke up from a nightmare. His face is a dark question mark. "What? Lee Sang-hyok? I thought he was purged years ago."

"That's what I thought, too. I thought after that one thing we did, he"—Ki-yong twitches his right cheek and lifts his chin to one side, to signify something had flown far away— "was tossed out."

Pil nods in agreement. A hint of supplication lurks in his gesture of affirmation. "Is Lee Sang-hyok . . . Is he here? In Seoul?"

"I'm not sure about that yet."

"And?"

"I don't really know myself. All I do know is that some-one's found out about us."

Pil's breathing grows ragged, agitated. "But we were cut off so long ago!"

"This morning, I received"—Ki-yong holds up four fingers—"the order."

Pil looks even more worried.

"Someone called and told me to check my e-mail. I did, and it was definitely Order Four," Ki-yong explains.

"The return time?"

"Tomorrow at dawn."

"Shit," Pil spits, visibly shaken. "I mean, we were both Lee Sang-hyok's line. They wouldn't have just found you. No. No way. What the hell am I going to do about my son? He'd never be able to survive up there. He won't be able to deal with the change. It was so hard with this new school, too. At first I put him in regular school but he couldn't fit in. Those asshole kids. Having palsy doesn't mean you're stupid but the little fuckers stuffed dirty tissues into his mouth and kicked him around. Children, they're devils. These Seoul kids, these sons-of-bitches spawns of capitalism, they don't know what the hell living in a community means. They have no clue as to how to help one another. All they know is how to be selfish. And it's not even their fault, it's what their parents teach them."

"Calm down," Ki-yong orders.

Pil glares at him, his eyes burning. "You," he accuses.

"What?" Ki-yong tenses automatically.

"You, what are you, a fucking rat?"

Ki-yong scowls.

"The KCIA, no, now they're called National Intelligence Service. Did you go over to their side? You fucking asshole . . ."

"Hey, watch what you say," Ki-yong warns. Though he lowers his tone, every syllable is gnarled and harsh.

"Let's be honest with each other, okay? Let's put all our

cards on the table." Pil's rage brings out their regional Pyongan accent. That stops Ki-yong cold. He draws in a deep breath. *Calm down. Calm down. I can't get into this. I won't be pushed around by anything.*

"I don't blame you for thinking this, but let me tell you once and for all that I'm not an informant," Ki-yong replies evenly.

Pil squints at him. He stands up, comes around the small plastic table, and all of a sudden, he tackles Ki-yong, like a kid goofing around. He swiftly pats him down, in a way that is hard to believe of a man who was sitting across from Ki-yong just a minute before, crumpled and unfit. He's looking for handcuffs or a gun. Ki-yong grabs Pil's shoulders and shoots up from his seat. They wrestle, entangled like boxers in a clinch. A plastic chair falls over with a clatter. The young clerk screams, "Stop!"

"Come on, you asshole, let's do this outside," Pil says to Ki-yong, rudely. They don't loosen their grips.

"Fine," Ki-yong says, nodding. They let go of each other but don't stop glaring. They raise the chair upright, apologize to the clerk, throw out their paper cups, and leave. The girls in the shop are still gabbing away, unaware of what has just happened.

Outside, Ki-yong raises his arms. "Search me."

"I did already." Pil looks around. "Sorry, but you would've done the same."

"Okay, so now we're fine?"

Pil shakes his head. "Not yet."

"What else do you need?"

"Are you trying to buy me? If it's about money, shit, I have no problem bowing down before money. I'm serious." Pil tries to gauge Ki-yong's reaction.

Ki-yong doesn't say anything but points to a small bar

across the way. It's still early for it to be crowded inside. It's the kind of bar that people going to see a movie at the multiplex visit to kill time with a few beers. They go inside, and the stale stench of old beer assaults their noses. It's dark and the employees are cleaning up.

"You open?"

As their eyes get used to the dark, they see silhouettes of young people drinking beer. An unfriendly bow-tied waiter shows them to a table. As they sit down, Ki-yong orders a Heineken and Pil asks for a Guinness.

"I hear a glass or two of beer a day is good for you," Pil says, as if the wrestling match they just engaged in happened a long time ago.

Today has been a shitty day for both of them. They were wrenched from their lives, which they were living in peace, one day at a time. Sure, there were some hard days, but they never encountered anything of this magnitude. They wait for their beer in silence. The waiter rushes over with two beers and bowls of tortilla chips and salsa. The waiter puts the Heineken in front of Pil and the Guinness in front of Ki-yong. They trade. Ki-yong gulps down the cold beer.

Pil opens his mouth first. "So? What are you going to do? Are you going back?"

Ki-yong eats a chip. "Remember Han Jong-hun?"

"Who?"

"From Liaison Office 130. Remember, the three of us . . ."

Pil frowns. "Oh yeah, him."

"He's gone. Yesterday he told his secretary that he was going abroad for business and they haven't heard from him since. His wife doesn't know where he is either."

"So what happened to him?"

Ki-yong glares at Pil. "Why do you keep hounding me? I don't know a thing. What the hell would I possibly know?

It's been a long time since our line's been cut, and I've been busy making a life, just like you."

"How would I know that's true?" Pil retorts, smiling sardonically. "How the hell am I supposed to know what you're up to? I really have no idea why you're telling me all of this."

Ki-yong tries to breathe evenly. His former comrade is even more nervous than he. It's no surprise that he's on edge and guarded, but Ki-yong wants to be able to complain too, and be reassured. "Look, for what it's worth, we're in the same boat. I don't know if Han Jong-hun went back or is in hiding. But we have to believe that since I got an order, you're going to get one too."

"How would you know that?" Pil asks aggressively, but he appears less enraged.

Ki-yong doesn't reply.

"Lee Sang-hyok was thrown out. The guy after him wouldn't touch our line with a ten-foot pole; he couldn't trust us. The guy after that probably didn't even know we existed. After a couple more guys, there would have been a real nitpicky guy, and he would have found you and Han as he was going through files. It's possible that they haven't found me yet, and it's not a given that they will. It's a mess up there, you know."

"I wish that were true," Ki-yong says.

"That's what I think—I think I'm safe. Nothing's happened yet."

Ki-yong sighs. "Fine, it sounds like you really know nothing. Don't worry. I'll take care of my problem myself."

Pil leans back, relaxing a bit. "Are you going to go up?"

"Maybe."

Pil leans forward. "You won't talk about me if you do?" Raising his glass to his mouth, he glances at Ki-yong in a conciliatory way.

"I don't know."

"I have a disabled son, like I was telling you," reminds Pil.

"I have a wife and daughter."

"I know. She was a baby then. What was her name . . ."

"When?"

"You know, then."

He knows what Pil means by "then." But he doesn't want to talk about that. He doesn't want to talk about Hyon-mi in that context, afraid that something nefarious will happen to her if he does. "Let's not talk about it."

Pil rubs his face, which crinkles under his hands like a mask. "Sometimes I dream that I'm bowling."

"Bowling?"

"I'm standing at a lane by myself, in an empty bowling alley. I know people are looking at me, but I don't know where they are. I stand at the line, feeling tremendous pressure to do well. I stick my fingers in the ball, get ready, and run forward," Pil explains.

"And?"

"I throw that ball as hard as I can, but the bowling alley's gone and all that's left is a smashed head—"

"Stop," Ki-yong interrupts, holding out his palm.

Pil doesn't listen. "I keep thinking it's a bowling ball and I try to catch it, but I can't. The head tells me that bowling isn't as easy a sport as you might think."

"What does that mean?" Ki-yong asks despite himself.

"How do I know, it's a dream. Anyway, he just keeps saying that. Bowling's not an easy sport. You need to control your mind. I don't know the exact words but it's all the same idea, and it gets really scary because, you know, it's a smashed head saying it. I slide my fingers in the dark eye sockets and pick it up like it's a ball. Sometimes the sockets are so slippery that the head keeps falling out of my hands."

Ten years ago, the final order—though back then they didn't know it would be the last—came down to Pil, Ki-yong, and Jong-hun. Their target was a mole with the code name North Star. They didn't know why he had to be eliminated, but the order was urgent, so urgent that it was conveyed to them without having been translated into code. Assassination wasn't their expertise, but they all understood that it wasn't the time to question the order. None of the three had ever killed a man. But they knew they had to do it and they didn't discuss their lack of experience.

Jong-hun was the decoy, entrusted to lure North Star to the designated place, and the assassination itself would be done by Ki-yong and Pil. Jong-hun met North Star in the dark underground parking garage of an apartment building, carrying a bag that was supposed to contain cash. Hidden behind a pole, North Star received the bag from Jong-hun with his left hand. He hoisted it up a couple of times to gauge its weight. Jong-hun got into his car first and drove out, and North Star went to his car leisurely, probably relieved that the deal went down smoothly. North Star got into his car and placed the bag on the passenger seat. He fastened his seat belt. He seemed calm. Watching him, Ki-yong felt as if a sprinkler were whipping around in his head, spinning and spraying adrenaline. When North Star settled in, Ki-yong walked toward the car, his jacket hiding a Colt .45 outfitted with a silencer. He rapped lightly on the window with his knuckles. The dark tinted window slid down, revealing the target's face.

North Star, looking surprised, smiled at him. "Hey, Ki-yong! Aren't you Ki-yong?"

He couldn't smile back. Could this be? Was this the famous mole North Star? In a split second, a million thoughts exploded and raced through his mind, so fast they nearly paralyzed him. In contrast his words came out pedestrian and calm. "Hi, Ji-hun. Yeah, it's me, Ki-yong."

He slid the gun out of his pocket and pointed it at Ji-hun's head. Well, no, it wasn't as fluid as that. The sight caught in the lining of his jacket and he ended up having to tug it out, ripping his jacket in the process. It must have looked ridiculous, but his bumbling actually lent more gravity to the situation.

"Ki-yong, what are you doing?" North Star's smile faded. He didn't say anything clichéd, like "stop joking around." He could probably read Ki-yong's resolve from his violently trembling fingers.

"I'm sorry, Ji-hun, I didn't know it was you until now. I'm sorry. I can't do anything about it," Ki-yong said.

Pil, standing on the other side of the car, was taking out his gun in case Ki-yong missed. Ki-yong shot three times; two of them hit the target. North Star's chest jumped up violently and sank, as if he had been electrocuted. Ki-yong saw, very clearly, how his half-open mouth grew stiff. Pil opened the passenger side door and took the bag out. Before he shut the door, he glanced at the wound in North Star's cranium, pierced by the spiraling bullet, dark blood and brain matter gushing out like a newly dug oil field. Pil couldn't have known that the half second of death he witnessed would jolt him awake night after night for the next ten years, when he wasn't even the one who had pulled the trigger.

The nightmares Pil recounts to Ki-yong are intensely vivid and personal. There is something about assassination that is indeed similar to bowling, in that you focus, glare at the target, and slowly rush toward it with all your might. Ki-yong knows that this is what Pil wants to talk about. About that night ten years ago, when they hopped into their respective cars and drove out of the garage. They haven't seen each other again until now, but they need each other to talk about this, since they are the only ones who went through this event.

"That guy, North Star," Ki-yong starts.

Pil empties his glass. The brown foam slides slowly down the side of the glass, like mud.

"We used to know each other in college," Ki-yong continues.

"Right, I forgot you went to college," Pil comments.

"Yeah, that's probably why I'm better off than you or Jong-hun," Ki-yong says frankly.

Pil smiles bitterly. "And that's what capitalism is all about. Polarization, academic elitism, succession of wealth, the Pareto principle."

"Since when did you become such a lefty?" Ki-yong jokes.

Pil doesn't get it. "What?"

"Never mind, it's nothing."

"What did you say?" Pil insists.

"I asked since when did you become a Marxist."

Pil still doesn't realize that Ki-yong was joking. "What's that supposed to mean?"

"It's just a joke."

"What kind of joke is that?"

Ki-yong scratches his head apologetically. But, still annoyed, Pil isn't looking at him.

"Sorry, I'm sorry. That's not what I wanted to say. What I meant to say is, well, I just wonder why it had to be me. I had to shoot a smiling friend in the face. How do you think I felt?" Ki-yong explains.

"That's what we were trained to do," Pil blurts. Even he seems to be a little taken aback at the cold words that burst out of his mouth. "I know how you felt," Pil tries to reassure him.

Ki-yong shakes his head. "No, probably not."

Coldly, as if he doesn't want to sink into sentimentality, Pil says, "It was fair. We were the ones who decided who was going to pull the trigger. We pulled straws, remember?"

Ki-yong understands that Pil is trying to console him. "Yeah, but I keep thinking that even our pulling straws was somehow a ruse. I feel like they had it planned from the beginning, my shooting him," Ki-yong muses.

"That doesn't make any sense."

"I know. But I can't help thinking that." Ki-yong knows he's being unreasonable. He glances at his watch. He shouldn't linger anywhere for too long. If Pil knows nothing, he has to find someone who does. Who could that be?

"Look," Ki-yong says, picking up the bill, "I won't be able to keep a secret if torture's involved. I mean, if I get tortured, I won't be able to hide the fact that you're here—I don't think I'll be that strong. But in any other situation, like if I get a deal or something like that, I'll keep it a secret. Can you do the same?"

Pil nods.

Ki-yong stands up. "I'll take care of the tab."

Pil doesn't try to stop him. They pat each other on the back with professional equanimity, like businessmen who have successfully completed a merger. They part outside the bar. It became even more crowded while they were inside. Ki-yong walks toward the subway station, his every nerve at attention. He suddenly wonders how Pil could have not received the order. Even he was able to find Pil easily, though they hadn't talked in ten years. How is it possible that they didn't get to him? A bad feeling gnaws at him. He starts walking faster. He stalks through the underground maze of the Coex building, changing directions constantly. Every time he turns a corner, every time there's a mirror or a window, he checks for a tail. He discovers at least two people speeding up and slowing down when he does, matching his tempo. The men on his tail are tense, too. Following someone is a very difficult mission. Tailing someone is the most important element of a spy war. Being shadowed always gives the advantage to the person being chased. Once he realizes he's being followed, it's the person being followed who dominates the game. In some ways, the whole game of being shadowed is similar to solving a riddle when you already know the answer. Ki-yong slips into Bandi & Luni's, knowing that large bookstores always have a separate entrance for employees and book shipments. Without bothering to pretend that he doesn't know he's being tailed and flipping through a book, he makes a beeline toward a metal door that says Employees Only. Nobody stops him. In the dark corridor, uniformed clerks walk past him, uninterested in why he's there. He walks on confidently, trusting that there will be an exit somewhere. He finds a fire exit. The door opens easily, into an empty space filled with boxes. The elevator there would take him to the underground parking lot. He presses the button, and the freight elevator starts moving, clanking. Ki-yong doesn't wait for the elevator but goes through the emergency exit and takes the stairs.

The parking lot is crowded with cars. If he were starring in a movie, he would swiftly break into a car, play with some wires in the glove compartment to turn it on, and go on to participate in a lengthy car chase. But Ki-yong was never taught that kind of skill, and never even thought it was really possible. He walks quickly down the rows of cars. The thick walls and poles installed to support the weight of the skyscraper create many blind spots. He goes toward the Inter-Continental Hotel but at the last minute turns toward City Air Terminal, where there will be a line of taxis waiting for customers. His back is damp with cold sweat. He's perspiring so much today—usually he barely breaks a sweat. Wishing he could change out of his damp shirt, he briefly thinks how terrible it would be if he were dragged off without being able to put on clean clothes. Cinching his tie as if to bolster his weakening resolve, he quickens his pace.

CHOL-SU PERCHES ON a folding chair the bookstore set out for customers. Lee Pil's tip was spot on—just a minute ago, Ki-yong was right in front of him, darting away into this underground city. Now he's nowhere to be found. He clearly isn't an amateur, having picked this confusing complex as a meeting place; it houses a hotel, the Korea World Trade Center, an airport terminal, a multiplex, a subway station, and a convention center. He must know Seoul like the back of his hand.

Chol-su hates being assigned to shadow someone. It's like doing penance. Once the target is determined, one's whole being has to be fixated on the target, and the target becomes the master. He doesn't like being dominated, or being servile. The target can choose where to go, wander wherever he wants. All Chol-su can do is follow him. It's up to the target to decide whether to go into a café or take the subway. He has to wait for his master to move, patiently, like a loyal hunting dog. He has to focus all of his attention on the target, listening carefully and quickly processing all of the visual stimuli that fill a city. He has to read the signs on the street, watch out for the motorcycle roaring close behind him, and at the same time, match the speed of the target. All of this makes him feel anxious. The most important thing, the first commandment of tailing, is not to lose the target walking in front of you.

But he lost his target. He feels like shit. Once he compares his situation to that of a servile dog, he can't get it out of his head. Is this what stray dogs feel like? This Coex Center would be the ideal place to abandon a dog. He raises his nose, sniffing like one. For a canine, this has to be the worst place in the world to get lost, with no chance of finding its owner in this sea of smells.

His cell vibrates. He picks it up. "Yes, hello. No, I made a reservation, but it looks like it's been canceled. Okay. I'll keep you updated." He hangs up and sticks his cell phone in his pocket.

There are a lot of people in the bookstore. He gets up and goes toward the exit. Just as he's about to leave the bookstore, two men in navy suits stop him. "Could you please come with us?" one of them asks politely.

"Why?" Chol-su frowns.

"It'll only be a minute."

People are starting to steal glances at him. He hesitates. Should he show them his government ID, or should he let them search him? He doesn't want to make a scene, so he follows the men through a door marked Employees Only, which leads to a long corridor. He guesses this is how Ki-yong disappeared so quickly.

They accompany him to a small room and ask him to open his bag.

"Where does that corridor lead?" Chol-su asks.

"Why do you want to know?" the smaller of the men inquires.

Instead of opening his bag, Chol-su takes out his wallet and shows them his fancy ID, issued by the National Intelligence Service. "I'm undercover . . . Actually, I'm in the middle of pursuing a suspect," he explains.

The men aren't impressed. The taller one takes his ID and

studies it, but doesn't hand it back. They look at each other and smirk. "Do you have a citizen ID?"

Chol-su takes it out and gives it to them. They study it. "Please open your bag."

Chol-su is offended. There is no way he's going to open the bag. "You don't seem to understand. I'm following a spy, okay? You don't know who you're dealing with. If you aren't going to help me get this guy, just stay out of my way, okay?" He starts to move toward the door.

The tall one blocks his way. "All you need to do is show us what's in the bag."

The smaller one asks, "Sir, if you have nothing to hide, why can't you show it to us?"

"You have no right to search me. This is a violation of my privacy."

"No right?"

"That's right, you guys can't search me. You have a warrant?"

"If we suspect theft, we can search you with your consent," one of them explains.

Chol-su laughs. "Only the police have that right."

The two men grin, and as if they rehearsed it, they draw out their badges at the same time. "We're the police, okay? Now show us what's in your bag."

Their badges identify them as detectives with the Kangnam police station. He can't believe his eyes. Why are they searching him? What's going on? He opens his bag and shows its contents to them. They take out the small Toshiba walkie-talkie, study it, and put it on the table. Because they are so focused on searching through his belongings, Chol-su starts to doubt himself. He even wonders if it's possible that there's something in his bag that proves he's not who he says he is.

"Look, you have my ID number. Call your situation room, and you'll find out whatever you need!" he says unpleasantly, raising his voice. But they continue to go through all the pockets in his bag. The short one looks at the tall one and shakes his head. The tall one takes out his PDA and types in Chol-su's ID number and date of issue, sending the information to their situation room.

"What's going on?" Chol-su protests.

Soon, the results of the ID check come through on the PDA. The tall cop holds Chol-su's ID out. The instant Chol-su sticks out his hand to take it, the small cop grabs his arm and twists it: the *waki gatame* move, barred in modern judo. Immobilized, he can't fight back.

"Are you sure this is your ID?" the small cop barks.

"What the hell are you talking about?" Chol-su yells, in pain, his face shoved into the desk.

The small cop cuffs him. "The date of issue isn't correct. This ID was lost a long time ago."

Chol-su finally figures out what's going on. "Oh, that. Look, I can explain. I lost my ID for a while, so I got a new one. I accidentally took my old one this morning."

They don't seem to believe him. One of them grabs him by the arms and pulls him upright. His hands cuffed behind his back, he stands in front of the two detectives, defeated. Instead of rage, he feels humiliated. "Call the Company, they'll explain it to you," Chol-su says, a little more politely. "My business card is in my wallet."

The shorter detective goes through his wallet again. He finds the business card and holds it up in front of Chol-su's eyes. Chol-su nods. The short one leaves the room. Chol-su never even imagined that someone would want to check his citizen ID; the Company's ID has always been sufficient.

The short one yells something from outside the room, and the taller cop answers. He sits Chol-su in a chair and goes outside. Left alone, Chol-su looks around. He doesn't know what to do. He doesn't want to be dragged out like this, to be humiliated in public. But there's no way to get out of it. His mind is racing. He wonders if they are agents of the North, delaying him in the name of some bullshit interrogation to protect Ki-yong. Or they could be petty thieves, disguised as policemen. It might be their con to pretend they're cops and steal his wallet. The more he thinks about it, the more suspicious he becomes. But then again, they were able to find out that his ID issue date was incorrect, so maybe they are legitimate. He gets up and walks to the door. He manages to pry open the door despite his cuffs. The two detectives are standing outside. His eyes meet theirs, and somehow he gets the feeling that they are less intent on arresting him. As he's wondering why, he hears footsteps approaching them. He turns around. It's Potato, a fellow officer at the Company who is stationed at a different location. They know each other from counterintelligence workshops, and they are pretty friendly because they are around the same age. Potato sees him in cuffs and grins, amused. Four officers are behind him. Potato goes over to the detectives and whispers something, and the detectives hurriedly find the key and uncuff Chol-su, returning his wallet and ID. The detectives step back, contrite. Chol-su slides his wallet into his back pocket, turns around, and kicks the tall cop across the shins, yelling, "You asshole!"

The tall cop bends over and falls to the ground. The second kick, aimed at the small cop, doesn't meet its target, because he's bolted away, abandoning his partner. Potato and his men rush over and hold Chol-su back. "Stop!"

Unable to let it go, Chol-su keeps trying to get at the small cop. In the meantime, the tall cop manages to get up and run away after his partner, limping.

"Okay, that's enough," Potato says.

"Those assholes . . ."

"Calm down," Potato counsels. "They were dispatched here because they got a tip about suspicious activity. They're just doing their job, you know."

Chol-su rubs his wrists, imprinted with cuff marks. "How were you able to find out and come get me?"

"Our situation room caught your ID being checked. We were nearby for an undercover operation. Apparently Supervisor Jong called our supervisor for a favor."

"So you guys were stationed around this place too?"

"We received an intelligence tip." Potato brushes the dust from his jacket, avoiding Chol-su's eyes.

"Right, like I'm going to believe that you really got an intelligence tip. You sure you didn't speed over here because you caught the inquiry about my ID and you were curious?"

"Could be. Believe whatever you want. You're not hurt, though, are you?" Potato grins.

Chol-su is positive that people at the Company won't easily forget this incident. He realizes that he makes an unbelievably pathetic figure, apprehended and cuffed by the police like an idiot. "Did you catch those assholes' names?"

"Why do you want to know? You want to file a public grievance with the Office of the President? You're not exactly completely innocent, either. Wasn't that ID of yours supposedly lost?"

Chol-su draws in a deep breath. He turns around and stalks down the hall, in the direction the cops ran off. The bookstore employees, poking their heads out of the doorway and peeking at him, shut the door when their eyes meet. Potato and his men are still rooted in place, deliberating over something. Chol-su opens the door at the end of the corridor and leaves the bookstore. He sees an emergency exit and a freight elevator. Now he's certain that he discovered Ki-yong's escape route. Potato follows Chol-su, and they exchange goodbyes. Chol-su takes the stairs to P2 for his car. He rummages through his pockets for his parking ticket.

HYON-MI'S FAVORITE TIME of day is the late afternoon, after the classroom is cleaned. Sometimes she stays behind after class and writes in her journal or catches up on some homework. During that time of day, the sun creeps through the west windows of the classroom, slanting all the way to the third row of desks. If she looked outside, she would see boys stripped to their undershirts, sweating on the basketball court in the corner of the field. Everything else would be resting in such peace. But today, she isn't alone—three students lean on desks, facing her.

"We have to go to our cram schools," Jae-gyong says, trying to get things going.

"Okay, Jae-gyong. We can start now that everyone's here," Hyon-mi reassures her. She looks around the small group. "So you heard what our teacher said, right? About the classroom beautification project? I'd love it if you guys could help out."

"Really, help out? Don't you mean we're going to have to do everything?" smirks Han-saem, who scored the second highest after Hyon-mi in the previous month's exams.

"No, no, of course I'm going to work on it too," Hyon-mi explains. "But I need your help, 'cause, well, you guys know how bad I am at this artsy stuff."

"It's not like you need artistic talent for this," Han-saem interrupts.

Tae-su, the only boy in the group, interjects: "Why don't we just get it over with and go home? Hyon-mi, what do you want me to do?"

It's an open secret that Tae-su has a crush on Jae-gyong. Had it not been for that, Hyon-mi doesn't think he would have volunteered for a beautification project, which would just make the other boys poke fun at him. But it doesn't matter what his motive is. Hyon-mi is just grateful that he intervened.

"Okay, let's just decide what we're going to do with the back wall and the bulletin board and the windows, and then starting tomorrow we'll stay after class every day, just for a little while, until it's done," Hyon-mi directs.

They push together several desks, take out a notebook, and brainstorm. Once the meeting starts, everyone becomes involved, even Jae-gyong and Han-saem. Tae-su glances at Jae-gyong periodically, but she ignores him. Hyon-mi doesn't dominate the discussion, and soon Han-saem takes charge and suggests several options, getting louder and bossier the more she gets into it. Everything is going well. Near the end of their brainstorming session, Jae-gyong nudges Hyon-mi.

"Hey, Hyon-mi, need to go to the bathroom?"

Hyon-mi doesn't really have to, but she readily follows Jae-gyong out. As soon as they are inside the bathroom, Jae-gyong turns to her and blurts, "I really, really don't like Tae-su, Hyon-mi."

"Why not? I think he likes you."

"Whatever. I don't care. I really can't stand him."

"Why?"

"Do I have to have a reason for not liking him?"

"Like, you don't even want to look at him?"

"Exactly," Jae-gyong agrees.

Hyon-mi studies her in a serious manner.

"I want to quit," Jae-gyong announces.

"You can't! What're we going to do without you? Who's going to do all the drawings?"

"What do I care? I don't do art so that I can beautify the classroom." Jae-gyong pouts.

"What did Tae-su ever do to you?"

"Nothing, but he keeps looking at me. Ew. He totally grosses me out."

"Want me to tell him to stop?"

"No, don't do that. Don't even talk to him about it."

"I don't mind," Hyon-mi offers.

"No, if you do he's going to think that I like him."

"Fine," Hyon-mi decides, "then can't we just make Tae-su do other stuff while you do the drawings? We can make him hammer things and lug planters and stuff like that so he's not around. Come on, you won't have to work with him. You know how hard it is to get guys to do this."

"You don't get it, do you? If we do this beautification project together, he's going to, like, cherish this memory like it's some stupid trophy. I don't want him to think about me at all, it's so freaking disgusting. Get it?" Jae-gyong insists.

Hyon-mi doesn't think Tae-su is the kind of kid who deserves to be that vilified. Tae-su is a very ordinary boy, a little shorter than average, around the top 10 percent of the class. He's crazy about manga and J-Pop. He's the kind of kid who puts on earphones during breaks and reads. Sure, he's a little obsessed with manga and anime, but it isn't like he's in anyone's way. Hyon-mi is a little surprised that someone could hate a guy like that for no reason.

Jae-gyong takes some tissue from her pocket and wipes the corners of her eyes, having worked herself up a little. Hyon-mi hugs her with one arm to reassure her, although she isn't quite sure why she's trying to make her feel better.

It seems to her that Tae-su is the one who should be reassured, but it really isn't the kind of situation where she can do what is fair.

"I'm going to have to quit. I came today for our teacher's sake but I really can't do this with Tae-su here. Tell the teacher for me, okay?" Jae-gyong asks Hyon-mi.

They go back to the classroom. Han-saem squints at them suspiciously, as if she detected what is going on. Hyon-mi hurriedly wraps things up. "Let's meet for a little bit after classes tomorrow, too."

Jae-gyong leaves first without a word, slinging her backpack across her shoulders. Tae-su follows her out, but goes off in the opposite direction.

"What's up with Jae-gyong?" Han-saem stops Hyon-mi, who is getting ready to leave.

"What?"

"Why's she all mad?"

"She's not mad." Hyon-mi walks down the corridor toward the stairs.

Han-saem tags after her. "So I hear you're going to Jin-guk's today."

"What?" Hyon-mi whips around and glares at her.

Han-saem grins triumphantly. "Why're you so shocked? So you're not going?" Han-saem probes.

"Who told you?"

"So are you going or not?"

"Why do you care?"

"Oh, so I can't even ask?"

Hyon-mi starts walking forward. "I'm not going."

"Really? I heard it was Jin-guk's birthday."

"So?" Hyon-mi retorts.

"You didn't get invited?" Han-saem pursues.

Hyon-mi is stuck between a rock and a hard place. There's nothing wrong with being invited to a friend's birthday party, but she knows how catty girls can be. She knows that tomorrow everyone at school will know, and soon all the teachers will know too, and eventually all sorts of sordid rumors will be circulating. She doesn't know how to get out of this. But then a thought materializes in her head, like a message from God, transforming into words and leaking out of her mouth, as if it were just waiting to be said out loud. "Oh, I'm not the one who was invited, it was A-yong."

"Really?" Han-saem's eyes grow wide at this new piece of information. "Oh, I get it." She nods. "I thought you were dating him."

"Well, he's really going out with A-yong, but you know how it is with her. So I talk to him for her, and—"

Han-saem cuts her off. "Oh, it all makes sense. No wonder."

"A-yong wants me to go with her."

"She's so weird! Are you going?"

"I don't know yet." Hyon-mi feels guilty that Han-saem believes all of her spontaneous lies, but she also feels superior, like an artist. She's made something out of nothing, and the usefulness of her creation instantly becomes clear. She's controlling the situation now, although she was cornered only a minute ago.

She goes one step further. "Oh, and Jae-gyong? She told me she hated Tae-su, and so she's going to quit the beautification project."

"Really?" Han-saem says, her eyes glittering. "Bitch. There's nothing wrong with Tae-su."

"I know, right?" Hyon-mi agrees.

Han-saem links arms with Hyon-mi. Hyon-mi has never

liked how girls she isn't close with link their arms through hers, but this time she doesn't slide her arm out. Instead, she grins at Han-saem, who tightens her grip.

ON THE WAY home from work, Soji can't stop thinking about Ki-yong. Although she has known him for a long time, she's never seen him act like this. She realizes that she doesn't really know him all that well. An orphan with nobody to rely on, he always seems to have a shadow cast across his face. He doesn't know how to joke and doesn't seem like the type who could ever hurt anyone. He never gives the impression that he's mean or cowardly. But sometimes she thinks he has lost his passion for life. Other times she thinks he purposely wears his sorrow on his sleeve to trigger women's maternal instincts. But Soji has always thought of him as the kind of guy who wouldn't put his feelings before other matters. He assumes a shell of hardened detachment common to men who have led difficult lives. Her thoughts only confirm that she doesn't know anything about him.

Today, he was completely different from his usual self. He looked hounded, as if he had just shot a man dead. Soji was reminded of something on the news recently, a government employee who killed his wife before going to work. He ran around all day in a frenzy—even calling the police to file a missing person report, saying that his wife wasn't picking up the phone—until he finally confessed that he was the one who'd killed her.

Ever since Ki-yong asked her to keep something safe for him five years ago, she has been curious about what was inside. She met up with him after a long hiatus, near the end of the IT boom, when all kinds of websites became popular, and you could make billions of won if you created a good one, and he handed her a small bag.

"Can you keep this for me?" Ki-yong asked.

"What is it?"

The bag was secured with a small gold lock with a three-numbered code. It bulged a little.

"I've become interested in writing, so I wrote a novel, but I'm embarrassed to keep it at home. My diaries are in there too. I'm not going to tell Ma-ri for a while yet."

Soji was surprised. She never dreamed that he would write a novel. She knew he enjoyed reading books and watching movies, but she had no idea that he would be interested in writing or doing something creative. At the time, having recently made her debut as a fiction writer, Soji was working on her first full-length novel, *Otter*, about a man fighting to save his house. She thought it was odd that, in a country filled with men who devoted their lives to amassing resources to purchase a home, nobody had written a novel about buying and keeping one's house.

Ki-yong, after listening to Soji's idea for her novel, commented, "That reminds me of one of Sam Peckinpah's films. What's it called? Oh, *Straw Dogs*. Dustin Hoffman is a mathematician who escapes the violent city and goes to live in the countryside, in his wife's hometown. And his wife's ex-boyfriends start building a garage that encroaches on his property."

"I've never heard of that movie."

"Dustin Hoffman can't get out of a hunting trip his wife's ex-boyfriends invite him to, but suddenly he realizes that he's left alone at the hunting site. Meanwhile the guys in the neighborhood are raping his wife. So the Dustin Hoffman character, who's a cowardly and fearful man, grabs a shotgun and other weapons to defend his home."

"I should see that movie," Soji said.

"I don't know if it'll have anything to do with your novel.

I always thought the movie was really about the violent instinct of men, not about the struggle to protect your house."

"But that's the same thing! When do you think this violent instinct comes into play? When you talk about protecting your home, it obviously means that you're protecting your woman and child, too."

Ki-yong conceded her point.

Soji kept talking. "I don't know why that's never addressed in Korean novels, I mean the story of the man who's desperately defending his house. Especially since so many people's houses and families are taken away from them. In this era of bad credit, so many men just look on as their houses, something they've worked to have their whole lives, are handed over to other people, all because of a small amount of debt. Why isn't anyone going after them with weapons? Where are the sit-ins and self-immolations? When we were in college, people would rally around a cause and protest, all because some stranger somewhere got tortured. All the people who protested back then make up the core of society today, the heads of families, and I wonder why they just let the loan sharks and banks take their homes."

"Do you really want me to answer?" Ki-yong asked.

"Who else would I be talking to?"

"I don't know."

Soji, taking a sip of beer, continued. "That story is always the subject of American Westerns, you know. If someone comes to take your house and farm, you resist to the death. And if that doesn't work, you go get your revenge. Why don't we have a culture of revenge? When people suffer such terrible things, why don't they get revenge? Have you ever read any Korean novel dealing with the theme of revenge?"

"Now that I think of it, I don't think so. I feel like there's always talk of forgiveness instead," Ki-yong thought out loud.

"Right? I don't think we care as much about good and evil as the Westerners do. And since we don't think about the world in those terms, there's no reason for revenge. We're always saying, Oh, but those people have hit hard times too, or something like that."

"Yeah, we do say that."

"But even if we don't care about good and evil, I don't think anyone can really just stay calm and not be outraged if someone comes and takes their home."

"Are you trying to make your readers mad?"

"No, but I do want to get at the rage that's hiding inside. You know how they say a great novel is one that makes you realize there was nothing like it before? You know what I mean?"

There was a short and awkward silence.

"You're going to be a great novelist," Ki-yong said.

Soji grew embarrassed. "You shouldn't say things you don't believe."

Ki-yong laughed. "I have to say it's kind of hard to believe, actually."

She patted the bag he had handed her. "So what's your novel about?"

"Oh, nothing."

"No, tell me," Soji pressed.

Ki-yong hesitated, then said, "It's just, you know, stuff about the 1980s. Stuff about college . . ."

She cut him off. "No, don't write about that stuff yet. It's everywhere right now."

"You think so?"

"Yeah. There are way too many novels about that time."

"Yeah, I guess you're right."

If she had known what he had really written about, she wouldn't have said that so glibly. Since he came down, Ki-yong has been a prolific chronicler of the boundary between life and death, except he never puts it down on paper. For over ten years after he arrived in Seoul in 1984, he'd been in charge of facilitating agents' entry into South Korea. Hundreds of agents used him as the entry point to disperse all over the country. He assigned them appropriate names and jobs, something only an agent who had survived for that long in the dizzying sea of words in the South could do. This wasn't something Office No. 35 could do from up north, with access only to indirect information culled from books and magazines. There was always something inauthentic about life stories created by agents in Pyongyang. As the years went by, language grew outdated as new words were coined, older phrases coming to mean something different or disappearing entirely. An agent needed more than the language learned through books and TV dramas. Ki-yong's job was to arm them with the most current vocabulary and a life story that wouldn't draw suspicion.

Lee Sang-hyok thought Ki-yong was perfect for that job, and Ki-yong enjoyed it too. He didn't have to cock a gun at someone, or be stuck in the cabin of a midget submarine, breathing in the limited supply of oxygen, wearing a damp scuba suit, chewing on uncooked ramen noodles, fighting motion sickness. Instead, Ki-yong read Korean literature and religiously watched the documentary TV series *The Human Era*, which showed a week in the life of an ordinary person. He studied subtitles on videos and memorized entire sentences. He had to know how all the different classes lived in the South. On weekends, he would go out to the markets and talk to people, or take a tour bus from Kwanghwamun all the way to the mountains in Kangwon Province. The people on the bus for a weekend hike told him their life stories, without suspecting a thing. They spilled their stories by springs at Buddhist temples, on helipads at the top of a mountain, in frost-covered eulalia fields.

In a way, he was like a playwright working in-house at a theater production company. When the roles were cast, his job was to create the character. The agents committed to memory stories of a construction worker from Ulsan, a student from the Philippines, or a retired teacher, and went on to complete their missions. He didn't have to be the director. Directing and acting were the agents' responsibilities. He had to come up with countless new stories. Most agents took the roles he created and assigned them, went out, successfully completed their missions, and returned north, but there were some who didn't make it. He was saddened each time he heard of a failed mission, but it wasn't clear whether his depression was caused by empathy for another human's misfortune or his displeasure with his creations' imperfections.

"Are you going to show me your manuscript when you're done with it?" Soji asked.

"Just keep it safe, okay?"

"Don't worry. Let me know if you start writing again."

"I was thinking about renting a desk in a study hall somewhere. But I don't know if I'll have time to really write."

"You have to make time," Soji counseled. "You can't wait for it to come to you."

Soji remembers their conversation ended around that point. She gets off at her stop and walks up the street toward home. She's renting a single-story house in Ahyon-dong, in a neighborhood slated for redevelopment. The redevelopment plan, which was supposed to be underway already, has been delayed again. This delay has allowed her to continue to pay low rent for the past few years, and she's fortunate to live in a house with a backyard dotted with apple and magnolia trees. Her neighborhood is an old one, one without skyscrapers, one that still retains its winding alleys. Hanging between telephone poles, ragged placards wave forlornly in the wind, printed with the words "Congratulations! Redevelopment Committee Formed." It's the kind of place where neighbors greet one another in the street and the corner store sells items on credit. Of course, you can't even dream of bringing a man home with you, but it's an interesting neighborhood from Soji's perspective as a novelist. If she opens her window, she becomes a live witness to a half-naked man and his wife screaming at each other, and sometimes her eyes meet those of a woman who is stealing some red pepper paste from a neighbor's jar. People call her Teacher So and they refer to her house as Teacher So's house. Some people even think she owns the house.

She unlocks the gate by swiping her electronic card key along the lock. She enters the house and the door shuts behind her with a digital beep. She takes off her shoes, tosses her purse onto the couch, and goes into her office, which is always dark and damp because it faces north. Venetian blinds block the tiny bit of light that shines through the window, so she can't see anything if she doesn't turn on the lights. She flicks on the light switch and tries to remember where she hid Ki-yong's bag. She has no idea. She must have put it somewhere safe because it was important, but she can't figure out where that might be.

She opens the wardrobe and rummages between the folded blankets, but it isn't there. She drags over the chair from the vanity and climbs on it to check the top of the wardrobe, but it isn't there either. She discovers only heaps of dust, someone's PhD dissertation, and books she brought back from America. She hops down and searches near the bookcase. Since it's a bag, she wouldn't have put it on the bookcase, nor would she have been able to fit it in a drawer. She peeks under the sink and even digs around in the shoe cabinet. She casts a sweeping look under the couch and ventures out on the balcony. Nothing. She wouldn't have ripped up the floor or the ceiling of the bathroom to bury it, since the bag didn't contain anything illegal, like a gun or drugs. Then again, Soji thinks, maybe the bag did contain something illegal. That bag could contain a part of Ki-yong she is completely unaware of.

She checks the time. It's almost 5:00 P.M. She starts to get a little anxious, and at the same time, her curiosity as to what is in the bag grows so that she can't stand it. She finally begins to empty out every drawer and rifle through every nook. All she unearths are random odds and ends. Finally, her gaze falls on the large red suitcase standing next to the desk. The suitcase is made of polypropylene, hard and stubborn.

She tugs it toward her and lays it on its side. It falls to the floor with a bang, but she can't wrench it open because of the number lock. She tries 783, which are the first three digits of her phone number; 417 doesn't work either. It isn't 531, her birthday, or 000, which she tries as a random guess. She wrestles with the code in the middle of the messy room, which by now looks like someone broke in. Sweat dots her forehead and her mussed bangs stick to her skin. She wanted to fix her hair and freshen up her makeup before she goes to meet Ki-yong, but now she won't have time. Her underarms are getting sweaty, so she peels off her blouse and attacks the suitcase in her bra. It isn't working. She's going to have to start guessing the code systematically, from 000, then 001, 002, 003. She starts twirling the numbers, but it isn't easy to rotate each key separately; sometimes two numbers move at the same time, so after 010 she gets to 021, and when she tries to correct it, it becomes not 011 but 010. She looks at the clock again. It's already twenty past five. She's only at 183. The more time passes, the more she becomes convinced that Ki-yong's bag is inside the suitcase. She gets up, goes to the foyer, and takes out her tool kit from the shoe cabinet. A wrench falls out, hits her on the head, and tumbles to the ground, narrowly missing her foot. The kit must have been unzipped. She grabs a hammer, takes a deep breath, and approaches the damn suitcase. She rights it, spitting out, "Get up, you bitch."

Those words remind her of a guy she dated in the States, who would grab her by the hair and drag her around the house. She would be lurched out of bed, half asleep, unable to wrap her mind or body around what was happening, and be thrown around the room, reduced to tears, forced to stare at the floor. He immigrated to America with his family when he was ten, earned his MBA at NYU, and worked at a Japanese investment bank in the World Trade Center. His parents divorced shortly after immigrating, and he grew up with his father, a radiologist who settled in quickly but was an alcoholic. As a student, she needed a man with a house, a job, and medical insurance. New York was an expensive town and she didn't want to have to depend on the dirty money her father sent her.

On September 11, 2001, she was back in Korea, lying around this very house, watching an old Ingrid Bergman movie on cable. Suddenly, a caption popped up at the bottom of the screen: "Private Airplane Crashes Into New York World Trade Center." She didn't pay much attention to it. But when the caption changed from "private airplane" to "commercial aircraft," she switched to CNN. People were falling off the tall buildings like flower petals drifting away in the wind. Soon, the south tower fell. The screen, focused on the fleeing crowd, was shaking; the cameraman was running too. She heard screams in English, Arabic, Chinese, Spanish, Korean, Japanese, and countless other languages. She wondered, Was he dead? He would have gone to work early, as always, wearing a crisp shirt, a silk tie, and a well-tailored gray suit. He would have smiled at the fat woman at reception. Even though her ex-boyfriend worked in an office on the ninety-second floor of the south tower, the one United 175 crashed into, Soji didn't think he would have been killed. Even though the plane slammed into the building near the eightieth floor, and more people on the higher floors perished than survived.

The next day, her former New York roommate called her. Her roommate had quit school and was working at a beauty parlor in Brooklyn. She told Soji that her ex survived, miraculously. She repeated the word "miracle" several times, but Soji didn't think it was a miracle. He was too selfish to die like that. It turned out that he left his office as soon as he found out about the American Airlines plane crashing into the adjacent tower, without waiting for any announcement or assistance, and took the elevator all the way down to the ground floor. Many Americans waited in their offices for the firefighters to arrive, as they had been taught from childhood to await further instructions, but he wasn't the sort to rely on the generosity of that system. The security guard on the ground floor advised him to go back and wait, that there was no need to evacuate, but he ignored him, in fact pushed him away, and darted down the stairs toward the underground concourse. As soon as he set foot in the concourse, he heard a powerful blast. A second plane had smashed into his building. He was safe by the time the burning remnants of the collision hurtled to the ground like hail: chunks of aluminum alloy from the tail of the plane, concrete blocks, the toner of a Xerox machine, an Hermès bag, paper clips, a Benetton suitcase, shards of reinforced glass, an audio system, a small safe, bent steel, a piece of a banister. Soon he was standing just north of the site, on West Street, looking at the two buildings billowing fire. By the time Soji heard that he was safe, she no longer had any feelings for him. It was astonishing to her that this man cared only about survival and control. He didn't have any inner depth, he didn't have an interest in God or another supernatural existence, he didn't believe in the next life.

Soji aims the hammer at the dial. Hesitating, she lays it down and tries 184, 185, 186. None of them work. She picks up the hammer again and strikes down at the lock. The strong urethane of the suitcase forces the hammer to rebound violently, causing her to nearly hit herself in the head. She hammers again, once, twice, three times. Eventually, she succeeds in smashing the lock, which is now so wrecked that it's impossible to read the numbers. But the suitcase still refuses to open. If she had a saw, she would use it to hack at the suitcase. She finds a kitchen knife and slides the blade in the gap of the closure. She tries twisting it. She can hear the sharp steel and the knife grating against each other. The noise is unbearable, but she doesn't stop. She decides to try cutting the lock. All she does is create a loud screech. Feeling impatient, she wishes again that she had a saw. She goes to the kitchen, takes the wooden doorstop that is propping open the kitchen door, and sticks it into the crack. She starts banging on the doorstop with the hammer. The crack gets wider and wider, and finally the fortress-like lock falls off. The suitcase opens up powerlessly, its jaws agape. But nothing is inside. She lies on the floor, her arms spread open in defeat. Then, she sees a clay jar she hasn't used in a while, with a film of dust on it. Her mother gave it to her so she could keep rice in it, telling her that it would keep the rice fresh, but she's never put rice in it. She raises her body and crawls over to the jar. When she touches the lid, it slides off, as if it were just waiting to fall off. Clay shards fly all around her. Blood drips from her hand.

5:00 P.M.

WOLF HUNT

CHOL-SU STOPS the car and rolls down his window. The wind, heavy with moisture, chills him slightly. He can see the Volkswagen showroom across the road. Since it is dusk, the inside of the showroom is brighter than the outside, making it look like a space station in a sci-fi flick. He sees a woman, whom he assumes to be Ma-ri, working at her desk. She gets up a couple of times to talk to the man sitting behind her.

He tries to imagine what Ki-yong would do. Now that it's clear he's being pursued, would he come to see his wife? He gives Supervisor Jong a call to see what he thinks. Jong sounds like he's eating something. "Hey Chol-su, you think people weigh their options before they act? No, no, we live by instinct. Do you know how the Yankees used to hunt wolves? They'd tie a dog in heat on a pole. Then a wolf smells her and comes by. The thing about these members of the dog family is that, once the male gets going, the head of its penis swells up and it's hard to pull it out. You know what I mean? You know the anchors you use when you're hammering stuff in walls? It's kind of like that. So anyway, when they're stuck together like that, they'd creep up—bam, and they'd beat him over the head with a bat."

"What about the bitch?"

"The bitch? Oh, the dog in heat? All you need to do is pet it and praise it, and it's happy. Then it sits there, still in heat, waiting for the next wolf." Jong starts chewing again, making a lot of noise. "Just you wait. You'll see. He'll come to her. Males are hardwired to go to their bitches."

Jong tells Chol-su that the wiretapping team was deployed, so if Ki-yong calls his wife, they can hone in on the signal of his phone. They hang up. Chol-su leans back in his seat, more relaxed. He's dead tired. Perhaps the humiliation he suffered in the hands of the detectives at the Coex mall sapped whatever energy he had. He's never been arrested before. For the first time in his life, he considers the feelings of criminals who are caught, the defeated state they must be in, dealing with people who toy with their fate. He closes his eyes and recalls Jong's words. He pictures a nineteenth-century forest, dark even at midday, the wolf's howl ripping through the frigid air, the bitch tied to a pole, whining, ruddy Anglo-Saxon hunters armed with sticks and guns, waiting for the wolf, and the wolf itself, circling in the vicinity, torn between lust and fear. That wolf had to be low in the hierarchy of the pack, or maybe he was a wanderer that was kicked out of the pack. Otherwise why would he risk his life on this adventure? Chol-su imagines the wolf approaching the bitch, faltering, placing his front legs on the bitch's back, and pushing into her swollen genitals—but then he dozes off.

By the time Chol-su jolts awake, the world hasn't changed much. How long was he asleep, as far away from consciousness as death? Reality dawns on him, rising slowly into his consciousness like water filling a tub. He looks over at the showroom, which is even brighter than before; it has gotten darker. Thankfully, Ma-ri hasn't left yet. She's tidying up around her workstation, readying to leave. He checks his watch. It's just past 5:50.

KI-YONG AVOIDS SAMSUNG station, the subway stop nearest to the Coex Center, and goes on to the next station, Sollung, to catch Line 2. He gets off at Seoul National University of Education to transfer onto Line 3. He walks through the underground tunnels briskly, remaining alert to the people behind him. What is he running away from? Does he have to evade the tail so desperately, going to such extremes?

The subway car is fairly empty. He takes a seat. His thoughts are in a jumble. A lot of people get on when the train stops at the express bus terminal, one of those hubs always crowded with throngs of people. He studies the men closely but doesn't detect anything out of the ordinary. He closes his eyes. He's tired, but his mind is alert. The woman sitting next to him is gabbing on her cell. "I know, I know. Look, I know exactly what you mean."

What is it that she knows? Ki-yong wonders.

"I mean, yeah, I mean . . . yeah, yeah."

Every time the person on the other end says something, she repeats, "I mean . . ."

"I know. Yeah, that's what I mean . . . She's always like that. She's so annoying . . . That's exactly what I mean . . ." Her call is suddenly dropped, but, undeterred, she calls out "Hello? Hello?" into the phone. She finally dials her friend back. During the brief minute she stops talking to redial, the car regains silence.

While she's trying to get through to her friend, the man across from Ki-yong receives a call. "Oh, me?" he says into his phone. He swivels around. "Oh, I'm just passing Yaksu station. I'm almost there."

A blatant lie. They are only passing Sinsa station, and Yaksu is five stops away. As he hangs up, looking a bit embarrassed, the woman's conversation starts again.

"Why'd you hang up on me? You didn't? Oh, okay. I thought you did. Anyway, what were we talking about? Oh, yeah, yeah. Yeah. I mean . . . I know, I mean . . ." She gets off at Apgujong station, her phone glued to her ear.

Ki-yong smiles to himself, realizing that he won't be subjected to other people's private conversations if he goes back to Pyongyang. The subway leaves Apgujong and moves on to Tongho Bridge. Clanking, they cross the Han River. The setting sun, opening its red mouth wide, is swallowing the river from far away.

A-YONG IS WAITING for Hyon-mi in front of a game console at the stationery store.

"Were you waiting for a long time?" Hyon-mi asks apologetically.

"What took you so long?" grumbles A-yong.

Hyon-mi doesn't answer, so A-yong starts guessing. "Were they a pain? Did something happen?"

"No, not really. We were just talking about ideas and what to do, and it took longer than I thought."

"Oh, okay then."

They head home, both sensing a little awkwardness.

"Are you going to Jin-guk's?" A-yong asks.

Hyon-mi changes the subject, a little coldly. "You really don't have to go to cram school?"

A-yong stops in her tracks. Hyon-mi keeps going, but when A-yong doesn't come after her, she whips around and snaps, "What, are you in love with Jin-guk or something?"

"What?" A-yong says loudly in disbelief.

"Why else would you keep bugging me about it? I told you I'm not going."

"When'd you say that?"

"Earlier!" Hyon-mi shoots back.

"You're acting really weird," A-yong comments, glaring at her.

"What's that supposed to mean?"

"Never mind," A-yong says, tearing up.

Hyon-mi gets even angrier. "Now what are you crying for?"

"Who's crying?" A-yong retorts, wiping her eyes with the back of her hand. She stalks away.

"Where're you going?"

"I hope you're happy!" A-yong tosses back.

Hyon-mi calls out to her friend, but A-yong refuses to look back and breaks into a run. Hyon-mi doesn't chase after her, but she does call her name a few more times. She gives up when A-yong is too far away to hear her. Loneliness washes over her. She takes out her cell but puts it away. She feels even more alone. She kicks at a rock as hard as she can, causing it to roll into the sewer. *What do you think you're doing, Hyon-mi?* she chastises herself. *A-yong thought you were her friend and trusted you. You betrayed her and made her cry. She's vulnerable and you know she needs your help.*

She starts after A-yong. Maybe she's waiting for her on the bench at the playground, where they often hang out. Maybe she's sitting there, having thought up some corny saying to toss at her, like, If you laugh right after you cry, you're going to grow horns on your butt! Hyon-mi trots along faster, her heart pounding. She feels anxious and rushed, as in a bad dream. When she glimpses the apartment complex they live in, she breaks into a sprint. But she doesn't see A-yong anywhere. She enters the side gate between the tennis court and the complex. Three high school boys are standing around smoking, glancing at her as she dashes by. She runs past a rose-covered arch, benches under wreaths of wisteria, and a small fountain that has been broken for a while. She can hardly breathe by the time she reaches the playground. She stops near the jungle gym and looks around. All she can see is a woman and her baby, just learning to toddle. The mother steals a suspicious glance at her, a girl who dashed in suddenly, gasping for breath. The woman cranes her neck to look behind Hyon-mi, trying to figure out if someone is following her. She swings her baby out of the sandbox and buckles him in the stroller. Hyon-mi collapses on the concrete bench, which is sculpted to look like a log. It's cold. The woman leaves, pushing the stroller ahead of her. Now she's the only one here. The damp wind brushes against her bare legs.

Why do I feel so bad? I'm the one who made A-yong go away, but why do I feel like I'm the one who was left behind? Hyon-mi takes out her cell and scrolls through the texts. The only message in her inbox is from her mom, from earlier that afternoon, telling her that she's going to be late that night. She deletes it. *Should I just go home and make ramen for dinner? Or should I go to the comic book rental store and borrow some books?* While she weighs her options, a bell chimes, alerting her to a new text.

"where r u. bored. ☺" It's from Jin-guk.

Her fingers fly over the number pad. "where r u? ☺"

Jin-guk's reply comes immediately. "coming? cool. ☺"

As she hesitates, a new text arrives, with his address. She doesn't send a reply, but she's already standing up, her feet striding toward Jin-guk's apartment. For the first time in her life, she understands that there must be some kind of automatic nerve system linking her mind and body, something different in character from the automatic nerve system she learned about in biology. That system isn't regulated by reason and has nothing to do with physical desire. But right now, her body and heart are following the dictate of this unknown nerve. It's almost as if an alien had entered her body and were controlling her mind, making her do questionable things. She isn't hallucinating, she isn't hypnotized. But she's staring down at herself and the choices she's making in a detached manner, as if she were hovering outside her body.

6:00 P.M.

THOSE WERE THE DAYS

I T'S SIX, BUT Ma-ri doesn't grab her purse to leave, even though her coworkers are starting to head home, one by one. Finally, the last person to leave, the manager, comes up to her, briefcase in hand. "Aren't you going home, Ms. Jang?"

She purses her lips. "Go ahead, I'm going to . . ."

"Okay, see you tomorrow." He slowly heads out of the showroom, as if he's reluctant to leave. Or maybe he's conscious of the fact that Ma-ri is watching him walk away.

She's now alone in the showroom. Her eyes fixed on the manager walking away from the building, she wonders, out of the blue, about the model he's living with. Are they happy? Once, when they all went out for drinks after work, Ma-ri, coming back from the bathroom, overheard the manager whispering to the male employees that "skinny chicks aren't that great in bed. You end up getting bruises on your pelvis." Did they really do it so violently that their pelvic bones butted against each other? Well, maybe, at least in the beginning. But she can't believe that they would go at it so intensely even now, after all that time together. She grabs a pen and doodles on a piece of paper. She draws a triangle on top of a triangle, creating a six-pointed star, like the Star of David. She scrawls another triangle, and then another. The scribbling morphs into a circular mess. She writes "pelvis" next to it, and also "bruised pelvis." She draws another triangle on top of it, and writes "pelvis" in an empty space amid the doodles. She keeps scrawling "pelvis" and "bruised," over and over again. The words soon lose their meaning, looking like just any other symbol, like the triangles. She takes out another piece of paper and starts the whole process over again, drawing triangles and jotting down "bruised pelvis."

"What are you doing, Ms. Jang?"

Startled, Ma-ri whips around. I-yop is standing behind her. She slides her arm over the paper but it's too late. "What are you doing here?" she asks.

"My car's dead. The tow truck's going to get here in thirty minutes."

Unlike the manager, Kim I-yop parks in the pay lot behind the building. He isn't allowed to park in front of the showroom because he doesn't drive a Volkswagen.

"I was just killing time, because I have to be somewhere at seven," Ma-ri explains, though he didn't ask.

They stand in awkward silence. I-yop snuck over to startle her, but since the paper he glanced at had the phrase "bruised pelvis" written all over it, that image is the only thing swimming around in his head.

"So what's wrong with your car?" she asks.

"I don't know. It won't budge. I didn't want to get dirty so I didn't even pop the hood. I'm sure my insurance company is going to take care of it."

"Can you get it to start?"

"No."

"Maybe the battery's dead," suggests Ma-ri.

"Yeah, I think that might be what it is. My sister-in-law's going to be pissed that I'm late."

"Oh, right, she's looking after your son?"

"Yeah. I think she's got a new boyfriend or something. These days, she gets really annoyed even when I'm only a few minutes late."

"I have jumper cables," Ma-ri offers. She means it to come off as casual, to let him know that he can borrow them, but as she says it she feels cheap. It feels as if she's trying to seduce a man walking down the street. She wonders if it's because of her tone, or because of the offer itself.

"Wow, you have them in your car?"

"Of course," she says, getting up confidently.

He follows her outside, surprise etched on his face. The security guard runs over, hands her the keys, and says excitedly, "Oh, hi, I already pulled out your car."

Her Golf, which was parked underground, is already outside, waiting for her. For a while, the guard has been encroaching into her territory, little by little, without bothering to ask if it was okay.

"Thank you," she tells him, and gets in her car. I-yop gets in the passenger side. She turns on the engine and idles, warming it. She catches the annoyed look on the guard's face through the rearview mirror. *What the hell, is he jealous?* She shakes her head. *What's wrong with me today? Why am I thinking that every expression and tone means something? Have I become too sensitive? Or are relationships between people always like this?* Ma-ri moistens her lips.

The guard comes up and knocks on the window. "You forgot to lock the doors of the office and turn out the lights. Want me to do it?"

"No, I'm not going home yet. Mr. Kim's car battery died, so I'm going to jump it for him," Ma-ri explains.

"Ohh," the guard sighs, relieved, and nods, moves aside, and helps her back out. She drives down the alley and into the pay lot. I-yop rolls down his window and yells at the attendant that Ma-ri shouldn't be charged because she's here to jump-start his car. She pulls up in front of I-yop's car. The two cars are face to face, as if greeting each other. With the car running, she takes out the cables from the trunk, and connects her car battery's + to I-yop's +, and her − to his. Her cast keeps banging against various car parts, and each time that happens, I-yop yelps on her behalf as he hovers nearby, staring down at the exposed innards of the cars.

"Get in," Ma-ri orders.

He gets into his car, as if he's never done this before.

"Try it," Ma-ri calls.

The car starts. He steps on the gas a couple of times to test it then gets out, looking happier. "Wow, that was amazing."

She smiles listlessly. She unclips the cables from each car as he watches. He lowers the hoods of both cars.

"Keep it on for at least twenty minutes," she advises.

"Okay, thanks! I'll see you tomorrow. Oh, when's the cast coming off?"

"I don't know. Hopefully soon."

He nods like a good little boy and gets back in his car. She gets in hers, backs away, and leaves the lot. He leaves too, behind her. She parks in front of the showroom again. She tells the guard that he should just leave it there, that she's going to come back for it later. She looks at her watch; it's 6:35. It's almost time for her to meet Song-uk. She goes back inside, locks her desk, and turns off all the lights except for the lamp in the showroom. She washes her hands in the bathroom and touches up her makeup. Her lipstick has faded away. She reapplies it carefully, making sure everything else looks good, then finishes up and wipes her hands with a paper towel. She wants a cigarette badly, but doesn't want to smell like smoke the first time she meets Song-uk's friend. And her youthful lover hates it when she smokes. She nods at the guard as he wishes her good evening, and waits for the light to change at the crosswalk.

The light turns green, and she crosses the street along with the other pedestrians, her footsteps falling in time to theirs. She gets into a cab.

"Kangnam station, please."

The cabbie starts the car without a word.

WHEN MA-RI SUDDENLY pops out of her office and drives behind the building with I-yop, Chol-su thinks she's with Ki-yong. He hurriedly maneuvers a U-turn to follow them, but she's already in the pay lot behind the building. Chol-su realizes the man with her isn't Ki-yong when he sees that they're connecting jumper cables to the cars. Ma-ri goes back to her office and Chol-su returns to his spot on the opposite side of the street and parks, waiting for her to leave. She does shortly, but this time she leaves her car behind, crossing the street on foot. Why is she leaving her car? Is she going to grab a bite to eat somewhere close? Is she working late? But as soon as she crosses the street, she hops into a cab, which bolts forward, passing him. Caught off guard, he zooms after the cab moving slowly southbound. Kangnam during rush hour is always chaotic, with cars fighting over every available inch of the road. Chol-su dials Jong to report the current situation, that Ma-ri has abandoned her car and, based on the fact that she's entering an area with a lot of people, she's probably meeting up with her husband. He requests backup assistance. Jong is a little skeptical of his theory. He thinks this tactic is too obvious, and admonishes Chol-su to be careful, since this could be a ploy to distract him. He adds that it might be a while before the backup officers arrive.

The cab comes to a stop at the entrance of Kangnam station. Ma-ri hops out and strides into an alley behind the New York Bakery. Chol-su parks his car in a no-parking zone, sticking a label that says "Official Duty" on the dash, and follows her on foot. She doesn't seem to be at all aware of the tail, instead appearing more concerned with pushing through the crowd and not bumping into anyone. She stops at her destination, takes out a small mirror from her purse, and checks her reflection. She puts away the mirror. She's standing in front of a red sign that says WINE-AGED PORK BELLY. Exhaust fans pointing toward the street pump out the smoke from burning fat.

Chol-su stopped eating meat five years ago, after reading a book called *Simple Food for the Good Life* by Helen Nearing, the wife of Scott Nearing. The book informed him that Scott died at age one hundred, and Helen at ninety-two. Chol-su wants to live a long life. If he told people that this is his life's wish, they would think he's insane, so he's never revealed it to anyone. But he believes that several decades from now, life expectancies will be lengthened to a degree unfathomable today. He wants to maintain his health until then, so he can take advantage of the pending medical revolution. He looks around. How many of these hundreds of young people will live for a long time? A few decades ago, a seventieth birthday party was reason for celebration, but now it has become ordinary, an unexciting milestone. A voice deep within him asks what he expects to accomplish by living that long. His goal is to lead a long life, to achieve old age for its own sake. Some want to be Casanova, others want to be Napoleon. A few want to conquer all the Himalayan peaks taller than twenty-five thousand feet. Still others want to walk around the world, while some people want to break the world record for the fastest one-hundred-meter dash. All Chol-su wants is to live a very long time, so he will watch those men—who brag about their successful careers or have a ton of women flocking to their sides—die helplessly. Every person enters this theater called Earth with the same ticket. Doesn't it make sense that you want to watch as much as you can before you have to leave?

Helen Nearing said that eating meat was unnatural for humans. It makes sense if you think about it. If an apple tree grows in the street, we would pluck an apple off a branch and eat it without guilt. But nobody would rip a leg off a chicken passing by. Chol-su agrees with that basic premise. Eating meat is cruel. To boot, human intestines evolved specifically to digest vegetables, making it longer than that of carnivorous animals. That means that meat ends up rotting as it slides down each intestinal curve. He thinks that makes sense, too. He always felt heavier the day after he consumed a lot of meat. But it's hard to avoid meat in this society, especially since he works in such a macho environment at the Company. When his department goes out for dinner, he orders bean paste soup and rice as soon as they get to the restaurant, saying he's starving. He fills up on lettuce wraps of rice and hot peppers. Within the first year, the chronic sensation of a full stomach disappeared and his complexion cleared up. His breath no longer stank and he stopped burping. Every morning, he gets up at dawn and runs along the river, and he lifts weights at night. Now, whenever he smells meat cooking, he feels nauseated.

Chol-su also read *Beyond Beef: The Rise and Fall of the Cat-*

tle Culture by Jeremy Rifkin, the writer of *Entropy: A New World View.* His beliefs grew firmer. He carefully read the detailed descriptions in the book that revealed the terrible living conditions of cattle, pigs, and chickens, raised solely to be killed. He couldn't comprehend the cruelty of humans. He decided to quietly lead a vegetarian life. Well, it wasn't really vegetarianism, since he refrained only from eating beef, pork, and poultry. He didn't think there was any reason to avoid wild seafood, since it wouldn't have been injected with antibiotics or fed genetically engineered crops, and there wouldn't be the additional problem of animal cruelty.

But something strange started to happen after he shunned meat. Before, he'd go on dates, to see movies or to have dinner. He didn't meet anyone he thought he could marry, but he believed it was just a matter of time. He believed he would eventually meet his future wife, and didn't think much about it. But women disappeared from his life completely once he stopped eating meat. For whatever reason, he lost touch with the women he used to see, and he grew apart from his former girlfriends. They all got married or fell in love with other men. He couldn't get a second date with the women he did go out with. He bored them, and they'd be yawning by 10:00 P.M. The only difference between then and now was that he had stopped eating meat, but he didn't go around confessing that fact. He even wondered whether meat had pheromones in it. Or maybe the women detected something in him that was a turn-off, perhaps the sluggishness of someone who has given up all competition. Most women might be into aggressive men who weren't picky about food and preferred to live a fuller but shorter life. But he doesn't really dwell on the problem. Helen was twenty years younger than Scott, he reassures himself, and there's no reason he wouldn't be able to find someone like Helen, someone who loves that he's a vegetarian. Anyway, despite everything, he's proud of himself, proud of the way he was able to reverse a habit he maintained for thirty years. This shows that he can change many other aspects of his life. And his body is clean, not weighed down with toxins and waste.

Ma-ri walks straight into the pork belly restaurant, without an ounce of hesitation despite the foul odor it is emitting. She quickly becomes less attractive to him. It isn't a pretty picture to imagine the hot, rancid cooked fat passing through her mouth, stomach, and intestines. He can't easily shake the image. He peers into the restaurant through the gap between WINE-AG and ED PORK BELLY on the window. It's dark inside. The interior is decorated in a Zen style, pretty nice for a pork belly restaurant. She's sitting in a corner. He squints, trying to see the man she's facing. It isn't Ki-yong. The guy looks to be in his early twenties, probably still in college, and it doesn't seem like he's a client or a member of her family. His shaggy hair covers his forehead and eyes, and he's wearing big baggy jeans with frayed hems. Another young man comes out of the bathroom and joins them, and they start pouring soju into one another's glasses.

KI-YONG EXITS THE subway at the Uljiro entrance and walks past Lotte Department Store. It's rush hour—the buildings surrounding the street are vomiting a mass of people. It's nearly impossible not to bump into someone. The Westin Chosun is located behind the department store. He circles the hotel first before going into the lobby. He pauses at the Wongudan Shrine, the final display of vainglory of the waning Choson Kingdom, which lasted until the Japanese occupation in 1910, and glances at the cars parked in the valet lot. That would be where the authorities would park a fully rigged surveillance van. But he doesn't see any windowless vans. He studies the people on couches in the lobby. Nobody is acting suspiciously. Soji is sitting beyond the concierge desk, reading a book.

This hotel is a good place to hide out in case he needs to bolt. He could disappear among the shoppers if he goes toward Lotte, and the Sogong-dong underpass in front of the hotel stretches all the way to Namdaemun Market. He could hide in the numerous tunnels that make up the shopping centers under the streets that lead to Myongdong or to City Hall, or dash down the nearby dark alleys. Even the Westin's underground garage is perfect for escape, as it's connected to the parking lot of the President Hotel.

He looks at his watch. It's 6:15. He places a call from a phone booth. In the place of a standard ring, he hears the tune of "Russia Romance."

Soji picks up. "Hello?"

"Hey, it's me."

"Hi. Why are you calling from this random number?"

"Oh, my phone battery died. I'm in a phone booth. I'm running a little late. Sorry."

"That's okay."

He listens carefully to see if she sounds unnatural. They hang up, and he walks out of the booth, continuing to watch her through the glass. Nobody approaches her and she doesn't get a call. He waits for ten minutes. She's just sitting there, reading. Still, he waits a little longer. It can't hurt to be careful. He walks toward Myongdong, but spots a line of cops standing guard. What's going on? Is a diplomat or a high-ranking official coming through? Is there going to be a protest? He doesn't feel like going through a tunnel of cops. He stops and, pretending that he's getting a phone call, presses his cell to his ear, and doubles back toward the hotel. He pauses at the entrance of the hotel and looks around again.

If one goes swimming or plays tennis after a long hiatus, one's disappointed in one's stiffened muscles and frequent mistakes, but surprised that one's body hasn't forgotten the basic moves. This is how Ki-yong feels. In the last couple of hours, he has reengaged mental muscles he hasn't used in a long time. His senses have become more acute, his visual field has expanded. The images that hit his retina are transformed instantly into words and stored in his brain. Three burly men in suits, a woman in sunglasses, two drivers in their cars, two bellhops, no suspicious cars—this is the way he's processing his surroundings, the way he was trained to do years ago.

He circles the hotel again and uses the back entrance to get to the lobby. A couple of men are unloading a refrigerated truck. He can hear Mary Hopkin's "Those Were the Days" through the open door of the truck. *Oh, my friend, we're older but no wiser.*

He comes to a halt in front of Soji, who raises her head. "Oh, here you are."

"Did you wait a long time?"

"No, I got here right before you called."

"Let's go eat," he suggests.

They take the stairs down to the basement. At the Japanese restaurant, the manager, a model of hospitality and decorum, shows them to their table. They sit down and are handed warm towels. He looks at her hand. "Soji, what happened to your hand?"

A red gash, tinted pink because of the medicine she slathered on, adorns the back of her hand. "Oh, I hurt myself." She smiles bashfully, like a student acknowledging a mistake.

"I don't remember that from earlier today."

"No, it happened later, in the afternoon."

"You beat up the kids?"

"No!" She waves her hands, startled.

"I'm joking," Ki-yong reassures her. He orders sushi. She wants braised cod head, but it's sold out, so she orders sushi as well. Ki-yong adds shrimp tempura to their order, worried the sushi won't be enough.

"How about some hot sake?" he asks.

"Sure."

Ki-yong orders the drinks and stands up. "Excuse me, I have to go to the bathroom." Ki-yong goes outside and looks around. Nobody is loitering in the corridor. He notes that there are three different exits, and checks each quickly, darting down each path. He glimpses a door that leads to the kitchens of both the Japanese and Western restaurants. They probably have side doors for food deliveries, which probably lead to the street. He also double-checks the passage to the parking garage before heading back.

"So," Ki-yong says as he sits down, "did you bring it?"

"Can I ask you something?"

"You didn't bring it?"

"Can I just ask you something?"

"Okay," Ki-yong says, and nods reluctantly.

"What's in the bag anyway? Is it really a novel?"

"Why're you suddenly so curious?"

"Well." Soji smiles, embarrassed. "I just feel like it's mine, since I've kept it for so long. You know what I mean?"

"Yeah, I guess. But it's mine. I just asked you to look after it for a while."

"Yeah, but because I had it for so long, I feel like I should get to find out what I've been keeping safe for five whole years. You know that short story by Lee Seung-woo titled 'People Don't Know What Is in Their Houses'?"

The waitress, her hair pulled into a bun, brings them cha-wan mushi and two sake cups. He sinks his spoon into the soft egg custard. "Some things are better left unknown."

The chawan mushi is fragrant, but it feels scratchy as it slides down his throat.

"I don't think ignorance has ever helped mankind. Not knowing has always been the basis of meaningless violence," Soji insists.

Ki-yong puts his spoon down in his empty bowl. The clank resonates unusually loudly. "Soji, this doesn't have anything to do with mankind, it has to do with my personal life. It's completely private. It has to do with my future."

She spoons the chawan mushi silently. "Ki-yong, can't you share a personal problem with me? Why can't I be in your future?" Her voice is low and soft, but he winces at the desperation laced in her words.

"What are you talking about?"

"You've never been like this before," Soji explains. "Why wouldn't I think it's odd?"

"What do you mean 'odd'?"

"You suddenly appear at my school to ask me to bring you the thing you gave me for safekeeping five years ago, you buy me dinner at a fancy Japanese restaurant in a hotel. It's all a little strange, like you're about to leave and go somewhere far away."

Ki-yong picks up a sliver of ginger with his chopsticks and puts it in his mouth. "Do you like ginger?"

"No." Soji shakes her head, taken off guard.

"What about honey?"

"Don't change the subject."

"No, I'm really genuinely curious."

"I don't really like either. I eat them sometimes but I don't seek them out."

Ki-yong swallows the ginger and takes a sip of the hot sake. "I guess that's fairly normal. Everyone eats it once in a while, when they go to a Japanese restaurant or if they drank too much the night before."

"That's true."

"Soji, I might have to go to a place where honey and ginger are prized items. Where, when women give birth, they are given a few spoonfuls of honey stirred into a glass of water, and they're so grateful for that because it's so expensive."

She frowns. "Where are you going? Somewhere like Laos?"

He looks deep into her eyes. "If it were you, would you go?"

"I don't know. For how long?"

"Not for a short trip. If I go I don't know if I'll be able to come back."

The waitress brings their tempura and sushi, interrupting their conversation. Soji plucks a piece of ginger and slips it in her mouth, and he sips his sake, his leg trembling uncontrollably.

"I knew something like this would happen at some point," Soji confesses. "It always seemed you weren't really from here. Maybe it's because you're an orphan, but you always seemed lost."

"I did?"

"I slept with you, remember?"

"That was only once, though."

Soji laughs. "You can't sleep with a woman without her knowing everything about you."

"I've never heard that before."

"Tell me, Ki-yong, where exactly are you going?"

Ki-yong pushes a piece of sushi in his mouth. He isn't sure what kind it is, only that it's a lean white fish. "It's better if I don't tell you."

"Why do you say that?"

"Eat," Ki-yong urges, pointing at her food with his chopsticks.

Soji picks up a piece of shrimp sushi. Ki-yong drinks some miso soup; it tastes nutty and silky.

"I never thought I was going to die a teacher, even when I was younger. I always thought I would live a wonderfully tragic and dramatic life. My dream was to leave home and write in a faraway place, like Hemingway or Joyce. Is Ma-ri going with you?"

"I haven't told her."

"What?" Soji can't believe it. She wonders what that means. "You haven't told her yet, or you won't?"

"I'm not going to tell her."

"Why not?"

"She wouldn't come with me. And I don't have the right to make her unhappy."

"But you're married!"

"Well, we were, until now."

"Wow, Ki-yong, you're really cold. I never thought you were this detached."

"Do you want to come with me?"

"Yeah, but you have to give me some time. I have to collect my retirement pay and I want to get my security deposit from my landlord."

Ki-yong laughs, the heartiest since this morning.

"What's so funny?"

"Nothing." He shakes his head. "You really have no idea where I'm going, do you?"

"No. How would I know?"

"Can I have the bag now?" Ki-yong holds his hand out.

Soji takes the black bag out of the shopping bag she brought it in and hands it over to Ki-yong. He takes it and feels it with his hands, trying to gauge if everything inside is intact. The lock is still intact, too. "Thanks for taking good care of it." They raise their sake cups and clink.

"I had a hard time finding it," Soji says, and presses her lips together.

"So people really don't know what they have in their houses."

"I couldn't remember where I'd put it, since it isn't something I ever used."

"So where did you find it?"

"In a big clay jar outside."

"Really?" He sniffs it. It smells faintly like dry earth a split second before rain.

"It shouldn't smell bad; it's a rice jar. Doesn't it smell like rice?"

"Maybe," Ki-yong says.

"I broke the lid while I was taking it out."

"Oh, that's how you hurt your hand?"

"Yeah, I was trying to catch the falling lid. Jeez, what kind of idiot tries to grab a heavy, falling jar lid?"

They are quiet for a while. Their sushi plates become emptier.

Ki-yong says, "Soji, as a writer . . ."

"Yeah?"

"Do you believe that you will accept whatever life gives you, happily?"

She thinks for a moment, and nods. "I think so. I was just thinking that I've been living so placidly for the past few years. Hemingway fought in the Spanish Civil War, and André Malraux participated in Mao's Long March. But when I look around, I realize there's no possibility of a revolution or danger anywhere here, except maybe adultery—but I don't want to go on such an ordinary adventure. Do you know what I mean?"

"Do you really think that any experience helps with the creative process?"

"I'm sure it's better than having none. A blind man can probably draw well, maybe even amazingly well. But if he could see, and experience the world with his eyes, I'm sure he would be an even better illustrator."

"But if you had been blind and suddenly you could see, wouldn't you be overwhelmed by what you saw and lose your instincts?"

"Are you talking about Yonam? There's a story in one of Yonam's collections about a blind man who can suddenly see. He goes out into the streets and promptly gets lost. And he pleads with people, saying, I can't figure out how to get home, can someone help me? So a passerby tells him, Just close your eyes."

Ki-yong has never been a big fan of adages. He doesn't enjoy fancy words and clever or paradoxical expressions. He doesn't think they contain the true meaning of life. This time, he says the same thing he says every time someone tells him something like this: "That's an interesting story."

"But I think it just shows Yonam's ignorance. Sure, you could get lost during the first few minutes, but once you reconcile sight with the other senses you developed while you were blind, it would be even easier for you."

Ki-yong remembers hearing about someone like this. Aldous Huxley lost his vision in his youth but he recovered it in his late twenties through surgery, and went on to write passionately. He, for one, didn't close his eyes again. "Dialectical development?"

"Exactly! Relying only on your senses and revering ignorance only does you a disservice." Her eyes sparkle.

Ki-yong is reminded of Soji in college. He closes his eyes. People often feel sad on returning home and running into someone they haven't seen in a long time, because the encounter reminds them that they have grown old, although in their minds they are still their young selves. A boy doesn't become an old man, but an old boy. Similarly, a girl grows up into an old girl.

"Ki-yong?"

"Yeah?" He opens his eyes.

"Tired?"

"No, my eyes hurt." He presses his eyes with his fingers.

"When are you leaving?"

He removes his fingers. Although his eyes are open, his eyesight isn't bright. "Tomorrow."

"That soon? Are you ready?"

"No."

"Are you thinking about doing something awful?" Soji looks at him suspiciously.

"What do you mean?"

"Are you depressed?"

"No."

"It seems like you are."

"If I were depressed I'd be lying in bed. I wouldn't be out and about like this."

"Well, I'm glad."

"Thanks. I guess it's good at least one person's worried that I'm suicidal."

"What about Ma-ri?" Soji reminds him.

"Ma-ri's basically a roommate."

"If this is an attempt to get me to go with you up there, it's not working," Soji jokes, pointing above her head toward the white, clean-sheeted guestrooms on the higher floors.

"I don't think Ma-ri feels any lust anymore. I wonder if she's already at that age where her supply of female hormones is starting to dwindle?"

"Can I tell you the truth?" Soji asks.

"Yeah."

"It's just that she doesn't like you. You didn't know that?"

"Then she'd still be lustful, even if she didn't like me. She doesn't have lust."

"How do you know?"

"I know."

"How?"

Their conversation jumps back and forth like a Ping-Pong ball bouncing over a net.

"I'm telling you, I know."

"Well, how?"

"I was trained to know."

"What?"

"I was trained to listen in on conversations and spy on people, to discern truth and lies from someone's words."

"What, were you in some kind of special task unit?"

"Soji."

"Yeah?"

"You know where I was born?"

"Where?"

He smiles awkwardly and writes "Pyongyang" in Chinese characters on a napkin.

Soji glances over, squinting, then her head shoots up quickly, shocked. "What? Is this true?"

"Calm down. Lower your voice," Ki-yong orders. He eats the last piece of sushi and drinks some soup. "It's true."

"It can't be. I've known you forever! Since college!"

"I came down before that."

Soji puts her hand to her forehead, something she always does when she's taken by surprise.

"I'm older than you think I am."

"Oh, I . . . I see. So . . . yeah . . . oh, no wonder, yeah . . . okay. So, you . . . no really, Mr. Kim . . . no, I guess that's not . . . even your name. So really, why . . ."

"Calm down, Soji. I came down because I was ordered to come down. I've never told anyone."

"Ma-ri?"

"She doesn't know."

Soji's features contort, panic appearing on her face. "Why are you telling me any of this?" Soji asks, her eyes bulging.

"You . . ." Ki-yong hesitates. "You're a writer. You use whatever life happens to throw at you . . ."

Soji's expression stiffens. "That's it?"

"Well . . ."

"Are you telling me you've given me something to write about? Am I supposed to thank you or something?"

"No, that's not it. You have to understand, I just got my return order this morning, and I have to go back tomorrow. It's so cruel, don't you think? I've been chased the whole day, and I've only just managed to evade them. Now I'm here, and I'm able to relax for the first time today."

"You do know that under the National Security Law it's a crime to not report North Korean spies, right?"

He nods.

"You know I'm committing a crime just by sitting here looking at you?"

"Yeah."

"I always thought it was an interesting crime: you're breaking the law not by doing something, but precisely because you're not doing something. I always thought people who get caught for this must feel so frustrated. Helpless."

"Look, I'm sorry."

"I take back whatever I said earlier about how ignorance doesn't help mankind. I was being flippant in my own ignorance. Now here I am, committing a crime for just knowing something about you."

Ki-yong lowers his head and eats another sliver of ginger and a clove of marinated garlic. He wonders how strongly he would smell of garlic if he were caught now and interrogated.

"Ki-yong."

"Yeah."

"Don't go."

"Then what should I do?"

"Give yourself up."

"Aren't you scared of me? I'm an agent and a member of the Party. I've sworn allegiance to the Party and the Dear Leader."

"You've changed. I mean, you must have changed. I know you. You like hirasake, sushi, Heinekens, and movies by Sam Peckinpah and Wim Wenders. You like the story of Meursault shooting the Arab and you underline the elegant prose of a far right-wing pundit, Yukio Mishima. You eat seafood pasta at Sunday brunch. You drink scotch at a bar near Hongik University on Friday nights. Right? I think you just told me because you don't want to go. You secretly want me to talk you out of it, isn't that right?"

"Don't you think all of those preferences were merely a part of my disguise?"

"Why would you do that? To make me feel comfortable with you so you could recruit me to the other side?"

"Maybe."

She closes her eyes, as if to gather her thoughts. "You know the plays that are on extended runs, for ten or twenty years? You're like those actors who have been in the play for so long that they don't remember who they were before the play. You live that same role every night, no matter how you live during the day. So then you find yourself confused, since the Ki-yong at night has more continuity than the Ki-yong during the day. You know how the portrait of Dorian Gray ages instead of the man himself? I don't know who you were before, but you've become so good at this particular role that it's come to a point where it's hard to tell which part is you and which part is the character. Like Dorian Gray's portrait being the real Dorian and Dorian Gray the man being fake, I think this is the real you. Forget about your original self."

"The authorities up there don't think that. They think that this Ki-yong is the fake one. They forgot about me for over ten years, but now someone's found me and is trying to make the agent in the file and the real me become one and the same. It's like, everyone's clapping, the show's over, and I've come back to the changing room."

She reaches across the table and grabs his hand. Her tears drop onto it. "Don't go, Ki-yong."

"If I don't, they're going to send someone to kill me." Plus, he would be arrested by the South's public security authorities and charged with murder. But he doesn't say that.

"You won't be safe even if you go back," Soji insists.

"But if I go back I'll have a fifty-fifty chance to live. If I don't . . ."

"You always have a fifty-fifty chance to live. If you die, that's it. Those odds mean nothing. The odds when you're playing Russian roulette are one out of six, but every time the trigger's pulled, the odds are always fifty-fifty. You live or you die. Don't you think that's true?"

He doesn't say anything. She cries, silently. He wonders why she's crying, but he's oddly comforted by her tears. The waitress comes over and pours them tea. Soji takes her hand away to wipe her eyes. The tea is warm and soothing.

LIKE THE FIRST TIME

MA-RI PICKS up the soju bottle. The brand name, "Like the First Time," is printed in a font that resembles a wood carving, under the wings of a bird in flight. She reads out loud the sentence at the bottom of the label: "Soju made from all-natural mineral alkali water."

Song-uk holds out his cup. She pours some soju in it, and toasts, "Like the first time!" Though she says it without much thought, she feels like she's begging.

He smiles mysteriously and repeats after her. "Like the first time."

They clink cups. Song-uk's friend grabs his cup, too, looking a little left out. His Von Dutch hat is pushed low over his eyes, making it harder for Ma-ri to read him. She forgets his name as soon as she's introduced to him. Song-uk refers to him as Panda, which he says is because of the dark circles under his eyes. If Song-uk hadn't told her that Panda is the top student in their class, she wouldn't have been able to deduce it from his appearance.

Their three cups come together in a whirl as they clink, and each drinks. The twenty-proof alcohol is bland, not too strong and not too weak, and it coats their tongues as it trickles down their throats.

"So, going back to what I was saying," Song-uk addresses Panda. The heavy beat of dance music in the restaurant muffles his words. "That's nihilism."

Panda smirks. "Wha . . . wha . . . what's nihilism?" he stutters.

"What I'm saying is that even though people wear T-shirts with Che's face on it when they go on vacation, it doesn't mean that his vision was meaningless. Basically what I'm trying to say is that the Che souvenirs are something separate from revolution. Where do you think the Cuban people would be right now if there hadn't been a Cuban revolution? Cuba would have been turned into another Haiti, with political instability, coups d'état, endless confusion . . ."

"How . . . how . . . how would you know that?" Panda rebuts.

Ma-ri, toying with her cup, wonders whether you can still become a great judge if you have a stutter.

"All the other countries in Latin America are like Haiti."

"Not Chi . . . Chi . . . Chile," Panda says.

Song-uk, revealing his annoyance, retorts, "Are you telling me that you support that dictator Pinochet?"

"Wh . . . wh . . . what I mean is, some countries' governments are stable. Whether it's because of Pinochet or not."

"Are you saying you're condoning terrible torture, kidnapping, massacres, coups d'état?"

"Well, what about the massacres ordered by Mao in the name of the Cultural Revolution? Millions died in China. He was worse than Stalin," Panda shoots back, not even stuttering this time.

"So you're saying Pinochet and Mao are the same?" Song-uk doesn't let it go.

"Look, guys, the meat's burning," Ma-ri jumps in.

The two look down at the grill, at the smoke curling up from yellowish pieces of pork belly.

"I'm leaving if you guys keep fighting," Ma-ri adds.

Song-uk glares at Panda and tries to appease Ma-ri. "I'm sorry, but we're not fighting, we're just having a political discussion. We're just on different sides of the debate."

She scratches her left wrist. *So you can differ in political opinions and can have sex in the same bed.* "Okay, whatever. But all this meat's burning to a crisp while you guys go on and on. What about a discussion on vegetarianism? Why not talk about how the poor animals are painfully exploited?"

The mood turns somber. Song-uk slides over toward her and whispers, "What's wrong? Are you pissed that we've been talking among ourselves?"

Ma-ri shakes her head. Her left arm itches like crazy. "Pissed? No, I was just curious."

Song-uk looks over at Panda and indicates with his head that they should leave. Panda picks up his bag. "Should we go?"

She looks around the restaurant. The air is smoky with the burning fat and cigarettes, as if a fog had settled indoors. She wants a cigarette badly. If she could smoke one, just one, she'd be able to suffer through this uncomfortable situation. "Let's stay just a little longer."

It's unbearable inside, but she doesn't want to leave. If they go outside, they will take her, triumphantly, like males of the Stone Age, to some darkened motel room.

"Why? We're basically done eating. Should we go get a drink?" Song-uk suggests. He turns off the exhaust fan and stuffs the few remaining bits of meat resting on the grill into his mouth. The hot air, which has been warming the back of her neck, vanishes, as if someone has yanked her scarf off from behind. She gets up, slinging her purse over her arm. The two young men follow her. She goes to the cashier and hands over her credit card.

"It's forty-five thousand won," the smiling owner says, and holds out a spray deodorizer. Ma-ri hands it to Song-uk, who sprays it on her back. The artificial lilac scent assaults her nose. Ma-ri explains, "If I don't do this, the smell of the meat will be overpowering . . ."

The owner holds out the credit card slip. She signs it, takes the carbon copy, and pushes the door open.

"Thanks for dinner," Panda says.

Song-uk pats his friend on the back proudly, as if he had paid for dinner, and Panda puts his hand on Song-uk's arm in a friendly gesture. To Ma-ri, they look like good-natured chimps.

It's only pasta in tomato sauce, but Hyon-mi thinks it tastes great. It's hard to believe that a boy of fourteen made it. The noodles are silky but chewy, cooked perfectly al dente.

"Jin-guk, where did you learn to make this?"

"My mom. Why, you like it?"

"Yeah, it's awesome."

"It's really easy. Although it would've been better if I put more stuff in it. Have some pizza, too," Jin-guk offers, indicating the large Pizza Hut box next to the small dish of pickles.

"I'm getting full already," Hyon-mi says, and picks up a piece of mozzarella-laden pizza. She washes down a mouthful of pizza with some Coke. She's feeling better. She didn't feel that great when she arrived at Jin-guk's because of her fight with A-yong, but the smell of tomato sauce and Jin-guk's warm welcome lifted her mood. And spaghetti and pizza are two of her favorite foods.

"Where's everyone else? Are they at cram school?" Hyon-mi asks.

"Oh, Chol? He just went out for a sec."

"Oh, he was here already? Is he the one who doesn't go to school?" she asks, looking around.

"Yeah."

"Where'd he go? To the store?" Maybe he went out to get beer or cigarettes. A straight-A student, she's never participated in anything illicit, but she knows her peers drink and smoke.

"Nah, he's just a little shy."

"Oh, so he left because of me?"

Jin-guk waves his hands around, flustered. "No, no, he's coming back. He said he needed some fresh air. He collects guns—oh, not real guns, just fake ones—and they have some good models at the flea market today, so he decided to go take a look. He said he was meeting the seller at the subway station."

"Oh, okay. Is he the only one who's coming? What about the others?"

"Yeah, the other guys couldn't come because of cram school."

She nods and puts her Coke down.

His eyes sparkle. "Chol, though, he's mad funny. He studies with a gun strapped on him. When he gets home, he puts his gun on, and plays computer games or reads. Isn't that crazy?"

"Yeah, totally."

"Sometimes he'll like, take it out of the holster and shoot it and put it back in."

"What does he shoot at?"

"Just the ceiling or something. I don't know. He's just really into guns."

"What's his name again?" Hyon-mi asks.

"Chol."

"Why doesn't he go to school?"

"He doesn't need to."

"Huh?"

"He knows everything. He just goes to the library if he needs to look something up, or he goes online."

"His parents seem kinda crazy," Hyon-mi remarks. "A-yong's parents are sorta weird, too."

"They are?"

"Yeah, they believe in some weird religion. Like, they think they can live forever or something."

"Huh."

There's a short silence.

Hyon-mi speaks first. "Jin-guk, do you think people can live forever?"

"I dunno, what do you think?"

"I think there has to be an afterlife of some sort. Otherwise life's meaningless. Oh, did you see that article in the paper yesterday?"

"What article?" Jin-guk tilts his head, curious.

"Some guy who owns a video store killed an eight-year-old girl, and like, threw the body into a field and burned it, and his son helped him do it. You didn't see it?"

"Oh, that."

"It'd be so unfair if there's no afterlife for a kid like that, you know? All she was doing was returning a video for her mom, and it's like, so pointless if your life is over, just like that."

"Maybe."

"Do you think that's why there are ghosts?"

Jin-guk laughs. "Hey, there's no such thing as ghosts!" He picks up his empty plate and gets up, taking hers in hand.

Hyon-mi says, "Y'know, I think that there's more out there than what we can see."

Jin-guk puts the dishes in the sink and turns on the water. "What's that supposed to mean?" he asks, turning around.

Hyon-mi wiggles her toes. "When you're playing Go—remember I used to play? Anyway, when you do, the empty points are like, way more important. It's called a liberty, when there's nothing on the point. So you win when you have a lot of liberties, when there are a lot of empty points. So maybe it's important for there to be more unseen stuff in our lives. I don't know. What the hell am I trying to say?"

Jin-guk wipes down the table. "Yeah, I have no idea what you're talking about. Wanna go hang out on the couch? The chairs in here are so uncomfortable."

She gets up and the chair makes a screeching noise.

"Oops," Jin-guk says, shrinking a little.

"What?"

"The lady who lives downstairs is a total psycho. All she does is like, listen to see if we're making any noise. She's like glued to the ceiling. She probably heard that."

The intercom starts ringing—the ring tone is Dvorak's "Humoresque." Jin-guk picks up the handset in the living room, rolling his eyes. The music stops. "Yes, yes, yes, okay. Sorry. Oh, my mom? She's not home. Okay. Sorry."

He hangs up, shaking his head, and rotates his finger next to his ear. Hyon-mi giggles.

Jin-guk raises his finger to his lips and whispers, "The

family downstairs had a daughter in high school, and she jumped off the eighteenth floor."

"Oh my God, when?"

"She was crazy good in school, too. She was like, at the top of her class."

She widens her eyes. "So is that lady her mom?"

"No, after that they sold it and left. But the real estate people didn't tell the lady downstairs about it, so she bought it without knowing about that girl. It's not really their fault either, I guess. It's not like it happened in the apartment. Anyway, so she found out afterwards, and like, went crazy or something. That's what my mom says, anyway."

"Oh."

"Anyway, sit down. I'll go bring the cake. My mom bought it for my birthday."

"Want me to help?"

"Nah, I got it."

Shortly, he brings back two slices of cake. Cheesecake. It isn't half bad. If she weren't so full, she would enjoy it more. They eat quietly, licking their forks.

"So where's Chol?" She looks at her watch. It's already 7:40.

"Oh, I dunno. He'll be here soon," he replies nonchalantly. He gets up and goes into his room and comes out with a photo album.

"So where does he live?" she asks.

"Huh? Why do you ask?" He rubs the album cover with his hand.

"Oh, sorry. I was just curious."

"No, it's okay," he says, shaking his head. "It's just . . . well, he lives here."

"Here? With you?"

"Yeah."

She looks around again. It's a typical three-room apartment. It isn't so tiny that another kid couldn't live there. She points to the room next to the bathroom. "So is that his room?"

"No." He looks a little deflated. It's clear that he doesn't like to talk about it.

She wonders if she should stop asking questions, but thinks it would be awkward if she suddenly changes the subject. "So do you guys share a room?"

"Yeah." He keeps fingering the album.

Hyon-mi is more interested in this kid Chol, who shares a room with Jin-guk, than flipping through some photo album. But she figures she will meet him soon enough, since he's bound to come home. Maybe he is a relative of Jin-guk's, which makes her feel more at ease. Until she got here, she was a little wary at the prospect of meeting his friends who don't go to school. What do they do all day? Are they delinquent pickpockets? She worries even though she figures she doesn't need to if Jin-guk is friends with them, but she also knows that you can never really know.

"So does Chol work at your parents' karaoke bar? Is that why he doesn't go to school?"

His face freezes. "My parents don't know about him."

She frowns. "What? How's that possible?" She looks around again. The apartment is small enough that it would be impossible for anyone to live there without the rest of the family finding out. Even if his parents run a karaoke club and come back dead tired at dawn, how can they not notice another boy living in their home? It doesn't make any sense, even if they don't pay any attention to their son.

"I've never told anyone about him. You can't tell anyone, okay?"

"Okay, sure."

He looks at her, gauging her reaction. "He's a good guy. His parents died when he was really young. He was in an orphanage but he was only there for a little bit, and he's been living here ever since."

"Without your parents knowing?"

"Yeah. They wouldn't have allowed it."

She opens the album. "Is he in this album too?"

He closes it. "No, he doesn't like to get his picture taken."

"Why not?"

"He doesn't like to be in front of people."

"So you're like his only friend?"

"I guess so. He likes the Internet and guns. He's crazy good with computers; he's a hacker, too."

"Really?"

"Yeah. If he wants to he can even hack into the site of the Office of the President. But if he did, they might be able to trace it and he would be investigated. Then they would find out he's living here, and he doesn't want to do that to me. He uses other people's citizen ID numbers and can even download porn. He can do anything."

"Wow."

Jin-guk keeps talking, getting excited. "He reads a lot, too, so he scores with girls when he's chatting online."

"What does that have to do with chatting?"

"Doesn't it make sense? Girls love that stuff. He even chats with college girls."

"Seriously?"

"Yeah, and he makes money selling in-game items. He hacks into the games and sells 'em to other players. He's really busy when I'm in school."

"Are you guys friends from elementary school?"

He shakes his head. "No, from before. We met at the playground in front of the apartment complex. We played together all the time and became best friends. We used to go play computer games at Internet cafés and go to baseball games."

"So you guys have known each other for a long time, huh?"

"Yeah. But why do we keep talking about him?"

"Oh, yeah, that's true. It's your birthday! Happy birthday, by the way."

"Thanks."

They sit there silently. The TV isn't on and the album is still unopened. Jin-guk jiggles his leg a little. Hyon-mi places her hand lightly on his knee, as gently as if a pair of butterflies landed on it. "My dad says it's unlucky if you do that."

It's the first time they've touched. He puts his arms around her. His lips touch hers. She's surprised, but doesn't make a big deal out of it. Her hands are raised in the air, floundering, not holding him but not pushing him away either. He rubs his lips against hers a little awkwardly, then cautiously slips in his tongue. His tongue flicks her front teeth, then pushes through. Her tongue comes forward to meet his, slowly, and slips around his. Like snails who crawled a long way and were checking each other out with their antennae, their tongues greet each other carefully. Each time their tongues touch, they automatically retreat a little, shyly. Finally, their tongues are intertwined passionately and fill their mouths, and she opens a little wider to enable his tongue to move a little freely. Spit pools in her mouth and drips down to her thigh.

Her hand now on his back, she pulls him to her. His hand fumbles near her waist, burrowing into her shirt. Shocked, she pushes him away. Their eyes meet. He looks down. She gets up and goes into the bathroom. She sits on the toilet and retraces what has happened. Her heart is pounding. It isn't her first kiss—in elementary school, she once French kissed a boy in the hallway of their apartment complex, but that was child's play. This time it felt different. She feels like her whole body is damp, almost as if she's angry at someone. She feels hot. Her face is flushed. She doesn't know what to say, and she can't begin to forgive herself for what just happened. But she also wants to call a friend and tell her about what she's feeling. She wants to read a book that really understands and addresses this feeling she has, and she wants to listen to music that makes her feel this way.

Jin-guk knocks on the door.

"Yeah?" Hyon-mi calls.

"Are you okay?"

"Yeah."

"Are you mad at me?"

"No, I'm coming out." She flushes. The water is sucked down to the bottom, free-falling into the depths of the plumbing system. She straightens her clothes, checks her face, and walks out. He's standing outside the door, looking guilty. His face is flushed. She reassures him as if she were his mother. "Jin-guk, I'm fine. It's okay. Let's go look at the pictures in the album."

He follows her to the sofa without a word. They sit a bit further from each other than before and flip through the pictures together. He looks just like he used to as a baby. His one-hundredth-day commemorative picture shows him with his penis exposed, smiling. He looks surprised on his first birthday. He ages quickly in the picture album. He goes to kindergarten in white knee socks, then quickly becomes a

Boy Scout in uniform. The little boy who rides on the carousel in his mother's arms turns into a student going to cram school, waving from the bus. She suddenly wonders what it must be like to be a mother. She wonders whether it will happen to her. She assumes it will be terrifying, but isn't that the same with kisses? Life is a continuous cycle of once-terrifying things becoming normal.

NESTLED IN A dark corner of an Internet café, Ki-yong glances around. The room is filled with teens, smoking and immersed in StarCraft, Lineage, and CartRider, and unemployed men killing time. There are a couple of girls talking into webcams, earphones covering their ears. People are focused only on the monitor in front of them—nobody cares about anything else. He looks over at the monitor of a high school kid next to him, who's immersed in playing StarCraft. The war zone is a dry, barren land. The enemy rushes forward as bullets shower down, but no matter how many bullets they fire, Confederacy marines are falling fast. There is only one point to the game: survive. The marines in the bunker don't retreat even after it's taken, returning intense fire at the Zerglings who come at them, but the Zerglings are cruel and uncaring, tearing them to pieces. The adrenaline-pumped Zerglings, trampling the bunker, attack the command center, while the hydrolisk reinforcements go straight for the SCVs. Two broodlings burst out from a Firebat's body, and the queen, flying over, infests the command center with toxins right before it's destroyed, claiming it as her own. From the command center, the Zerg pumps infested Terrans and sends the walking suicide bomb toward the Terrans' siege tanks. The marines, who surrounded tanks on the hill in a last, protective stand, will have no chance against such force. The boy's nineteen-inch LCD screen flows with blood. The situation is dire. But from twenty inches away, the desperation of the game fails to be conveyed.

Ki-yong opens the bag Soji returned to him and finds the passport. The front page of the passport indicates one Lee Man-hee, not Kim Ki-yong. He sticks his hand in the bag and takes out the English edition of the Old Testament. It's hefty. He opens it. The Colt is still there, in the nook he cut out five years ago to hide the gun. The bullet that burrowed into Jong Ji-hun's head burst from that gun. Ki-yong closes the book and puts it back in the bag. The bundle of one-hundred-dollar bills is still there too. If he remembers correctly, it totals thirty thousand dollars. With that much, he can survive in Manila for a while.

With the bag resting in his lap, Ki-yong grabs the mouse. He opens a search window and types, "Discount airplane tickets." A long list of Internet travel sites comes up. He clicks on one. He chooses Manila as the destination, but then switches to Bangkok. Then he decides to continue on to Paris. Of course, he wouldn't really go all the way to Paris; he would get off in Bangkok and vanish. He types in the name Lee Man-hee and gets his reservation number. He writes down that number and the name of a customer service agent in his notebook. It's an e-ticket, so he can print it once he gets to the airport.

Only after he finalizes the reservation and purchases the ticket does he notice a small warning at the bottom of the screen. It reminds travelers to check their passports' expiration date. He takes out his passport again, opening it to the front page. The expiration date passed ten months ago. He stares at the passport, now as valuable as a piece of toilet paper. He flips ahead to look at the back page, hoping beyond hope that he has an extension, but it has already reached the maximum number of extensions allowed. He slides it back in the bag. He takes out the prepaid cell phone he bought today. He can't remember his wife's cell number because he always uses speed dial. After concentrating for a long time, he finally remembers it. His fingers fumble, his heart races. He calls the wrong number twice. He breathes in deeply, and manages to press the correct eleven numbers.

MOTEL BOHEMIAN

M A-RI STOPS in her tracks and tries to open her purse. Since she can use only her right hand, she has a difficult time getting it to open. The zipper is stuck on something. Song-uk holds her purse for her. She pushes her hand in and pulls out her vibrating phone. She doesn't recognize the number. Song-uk and Panda stand with their backs to her, looking around, as if they are bodyguards. Ma-ri doesn't answer her phone and instead slips it back in her purse.

"Who is it?"

"I don't know. I've never seen the number before."

She closes her bag with Song-uk's help and looks up. A small, upscale motel, built of black marble, stands in front of them.

"This is the place I was talking about. I found it online," Song-uk explains, and heads up the stairs first. She looks behind her for a second, as if she wants someone to rescue her, but nobody is paying any attention to their little group. She feels like a college freshman again, limping along the streets of Apgujong-dong with a sprained ankle.

The three go through the automatic doors, but there's no-body in the lobby. In its place there is a touchscreen about twenty-five inches wide. A sentence floats on the screen: "Welcome, please choose your room." Ma-ri presses "Mediterranean Theme." A picture of the Mediterranean room whooshes into view from the right. They look at the scroll-ing images of imitation limestone wallpaper, bright lights, and a whirlpool bathtub. The room looks nice and large, the photo probably taken with a wide-angle lens. She looks at the guys, wondering if this is what they want. They nod in excitement. They are impatient. She feels in charge, domi-nating them like a showgirl onstage. When it was just one guy persuading her to do this, she thought of it as if she were being dragged to the motel against her will, but it feels dif-ferent when there are two.

She presses "Confirm" and the screen orders, "Please swipe your card."

Song-uk hurriedly takes out his wallet. "I'll do it."

Ma-ri quietly stops him.

He waves his credit card around, the one that was given to him by his architect father. "No, I'll pay for it."

"No, no, let me."

"Song-uk, you do it," Panda urges from behind.

She announces, somewhat firmly, "If I don't pay I'm leaving."

A hush descends over the boys as they step back. She gently swipes her card along the long black groove in front of the screen. The computer of the unmanned room-by-the-hour motel sends her information to the credit card com-pany over the Internet. Visa checks her credit and returns the okay signal. Finally, she is given the go-ahead to have as much sex as she wants with these two young guys in the motel room. When the card goes through, the computer informs them of their room number. They head to the elevator without speaking. Ma-ri isn't worried about what is about to happen. She can't figure out why she insisted so adamantly that she would be the one to pay for the room. She could have let the guys pay for it, which would have been fair. Why didn't she let them?

Her phone starts buzzing again. This time she's able to take it out more easily than before, but it's the same unknown number. Annoyed, she shakes her head and turns her phone off. A long time seems to pass before the power turns off. When the doors open, they enter the elevator. The inside of the elevator smells faintly rancid, but also like dried roses. The tiny elevator shoots up to the fifth floor so quickly that, when the doors open, she's worried that they have opened so soon because of faulty wiring in the door mechanism.

Their room is 503. The knob turns easily and the door opens. They go inside. She places her purse on the vanity and the boys toss their bags on the floor, marking their territory.

"Go wash up," she tells the two guys, who are standing around awkwardly, not knowing what to do.

"Okay," they say, and go into the bathroom together, at ease as if they were brothers. She can hear the water running, them snickering, something falling on the floor. She sits on the bed and looks around. She remembers stories about Nazi concentration camps, Buchenwald and Auschwitz. She read about them a long time ago, about how Jews stood in a line in front of the gas chambers. Jewish leaders pointed fingers at those who were not standing in line in an orderly fashion. "This is why we are called dirty Jews!" They took off their clothes neatly and put them in baskets inscribed with their names. If they bathed, were deloused, and shaved, they would become clean Jews. Without balking at the orders, they walked into the gas chambers docilely. Apparently rumors about executions abounded, but they tried not to believe them and followed the Nazis' orders.

Ma-ri faced a range of options before she reached this bed. She could have run away, she could have pretended to go to the bathroom at the restaurant and disappeared. Even now, she can get up and leave. But one thing led to another. A small decision led to another small decision, and finally turned into a decision that couldn't be reversed. They were all linked together. She can't remember why she agreed to this at Napoli, but in any case she agreed to it, and because of that she went to the wine-aged pork belly restaurant, bought them food and drink, came to an unmanned room-by-the-hour hotel with them and even paid for the room. At this point the only thing that's keeping her in this room is that stupid credit card. If only she hadn't paid! She's already been charged sixty thousand won for this room.

But she couldn't have left even if the boys had paid for the room. Getting up and leaving after they paid would have been unfair; she would have been betraying their agreement. She regrets her foolish decision to charge the room on her card. It's true that it gave her pleasure to do it. Soon, she will spread her legs for the two guys, at their mercy. But since she paid for it, the acts looming ahead become the product of her free choice. The guys are merely hired gigolos. Ma-ri thinks that it isn't true that men are the seducers. She tries to convince herself that it's actually the opposite.

The water is turned off in the bathroom. She holds her breath. She can't deny it—she isn't comfortable here, no matter how she frames it, how ardently she believes it, or how she imagined it would be. In a few minutes, she will have to reveal her body to two twenty-year-old college students with wrinkle-free skin. Her stomach, which pooches a little, still retains stretch marks from her pregnancy with Hyon-mi. She suffers from eczema, and her groin is discolored as a result, a shade darker than the rest of her body. And her thighs are big lumps of fat. She feels as if she is waiting for a gynecological exam. She definitely isn't in that excited state that usually comes right before sex. She wipes her sweaty palms on the sheets. She gets up. She doesn't want to be sitting on the bed when the guys come out of the bathroom. She doesn't want them to think she's desperate. She gazes at the small balcony garden, composed of pots of sanseveria and cacti. The balcony is walled in by translucent glass and brightly lit, making it hard to tell whether it's day or night. She looks at her watch. It's after 8:00 P.M., but it looks as if it's only two in the afternoon.

Song-uk and Panda come out of the bathroom, each with a towel wrapped around his waist.

"You, you, your turn," Panda stutters.

She takes out a pouch from her purse and walks into the bathroom. Song-uk pokes his head in just as she's about to shut the door. "How are you going to wash yourself with your cast?"

She looks down at her arm. "Oh, right."

"Can we help you?" asks Song-uk, glancing at Panda.

She thinks for a moment. "Just you, Song-uk."

Song-uk comes into the bathroom triumphantly. He unfastens the buttons of her blouse, raises her arms above her head, and pulls it off. He unhooks her bra and tugs off her skirt, opening the bathroom door slightly to toss it outside. Ma-ri takes off her underwear herself, bunches it up and puts it on the grill of the radiator. She steps into the tub and raises her left arm high to keep the cast dry. Song-uk grabs the showerhead and turns on the water. A stream of water splashes her feet and travels up her body, slowly. It's cold at first, but it soon warms. Song-uk, having undone his towel, turns off the shower and nuzzles her nipple. She shakes her head. He squeezes some body wash onto his hand and soaps her groin. She closes her eyes. He slides the foam all over her body, the suds warm and soft, tickling her.

"That's enough," she says.

Song-uk rubs the valley between her buttocks. His slippery hand grazes over her anus and moves down further. She bends forward slightly. He slides his hands, covered in bubbles, over her breasts in a circular motion.

"You know why men like breasts?" he asks suddenly.

"Why?"

"Because they look like women's asses. It's basically your ass attached to the front of your body. Otherwise they wouldn't need to be so big, it would be enough just to have nipples. Men look at women's tits and think about asses."

"That makes no sense."

"I read it somewhere."

She looks down. His hard penis nods along as he soaps her, aimed at her breasts. Song-uk turns on the shower again. Water rains down on them. Ma-ri looks down at her body. The foam being washed off makes it look as if someone spat on her. During her first time, at eighteen, the guy spat on her because she was bone-dry. He rubbed the spit on the head of his dick and pushed into her. Ma-ri closes her eyes. Where the hell did that motherfucker learn to do that? Song-uk sprays the foam off with the showerhead.

"Turn around," he orders.

She turns, showing him her back. The water pounds the crevices of her body she can't see. He carefully pats every inch of her just-washed body dry with a towel. It's an intimate gesture she'd expect from a husband. Though Song-uk is still holding the towel, she hugs him, her body still damp. His dick presses into her stomach. She kneels and takes him in her mouth, sucking hard. She stops after a minute and looks up. "You know I love you, and only you, right?"

"Of course I do."

"I want you to know that I never wanted this."

"I know. I'm the one who wanted you to do it," Song-uk reassures her.

"Think about it for a minute. Do you really want me to be with another guy? Is it going to be okay for you?"

"You won't be doing it with another guy, it'll be just you and me. He's there to aid us, like a dildo."

"You love me, right?" Ma-ri asks.

"Of course! I'm more in love with you right now because I know you're doing this for me. I'm never going to forget it."

"So . . . how . . . with him . . . No, never mind."

"What? Just say it."

"So, how far do you want me to go . . . with him?"

He grins, as if wondering why she's bothering to ask. He lowers his arms and holds her head down. She puts her mouth around him again.

"All the way. I want to watch someone else do you. Just think that you're doing it with me. It's all just fun. Let's not think too hard about it."

The head of his hard dick rubs against the top of her mouth and pushes into a deeper place.

CHOL-SU SITS IN his car, gazing at the sign that says MOTEL BOHEMIAN.

"Bohemian, my ass," he mumbles, stretching out in the small space. Wistfully, he recalls the Volkswagen Passat he test drove in the morning with Ma-ri and the way the leather seat nestled his body. He reaches over to the passenger seat and picks up his phone, then changes his mind and tosses it back down. With both hands, he sweeps up the hair that has fallen into his eyes. It's damp from the humidity. He wants to wash his hands. He gets out and walks into the motel. From the ceiling, two surveillance cameras stare down at him, resembling a fly's double eye, and the only thing Chol-su finds on the other side of the sliding doors is an LCD screen. He swivels around. It doesn't look like there's a bathroom. He really needs to wash his hands.

"How can I help you?" a deep voice rings out from above.

Chol-su reflexively looks up at the small speaker attached to the ceiling. "So it's not really an unmanned hotel," he remarks.

The voice asks again, uninterested, "How can I help you? Are you looking for someone?"

He replies to the ceiling, "No, I just needed to use the bathroom."

"If you go out the door and turn left, there's a subway station about nine hundred feet away."

"Thank you," he calls out, and leaves. Outside, he looks around. There's a construction site next door, perhaps for another motel, as well as a faucet that was installed to wash the wheels of the dump trucks that go in and out of the site. It's dark at the construction site and nobody's around. He turns on the faucet. Water gushes out, the pressure higher than he expects, splashing his suit. He adjusts the water pressure and washes his hands. He wants soap. He returns to his car and dries his hands with a tissue. He looks at Motel Bohemian again. He went through all sorts of situations working for the Company, but this is the first time he finds himself waiting outside an hourly motel. Ma-ri entered the motel triumphantly, like a queen, dragging two young men with her. They were standing behind her like servants. They would now be in the throes of passion somewhere up there. Does she do this often? In any case, it's obvious to Chol-su that she has no idea what's going on with her husband. If she did, she wouldn't be engaged in this kind of activity right now.

He dials a number. "It's me, sir."

"You're still there?"

"Yes."

"Chol-su, I don't think that motel's the spot."

"Could it be that this is all part of Kim Ki-yong's plan?"

"You sure it's not just you dying to join them?" Jong jokes.

Chol-su frowns, takes his ear off the phone, and swears, so quietly that only a master lip reader would understand, "Motherfucker, you think that's a fucking joke?"

"So what should I . . ." Chol-su starts speaking into the phone again, but spies a young man looking around, appearing to be lost, then walking into the motel. He's walking rather quickly, and he looks like a typical college kid, a canvas bag slung over his shoulder and wearing sneakers. "Wait, someone just turned up."

"Who? Ki-yong?"

"No, looks like a college kid."

"What about him?"

"He looks like the two guys who went in with Ma-ri. They must be friends."

"He could have an appointment with another bitch."

"I guess that's true, huh?" Chol-su replies, but then feels uneasy—he thinks he might have sounded overly disappointed.

Jong doesn't let that change in tone slip by. "You wish, Park, you wish."

Chol-su doesn't say anything.

"Okay, pull out now," orders Jong.

Chol-su hangs up and curses. He looks toward the motel, but the young man is already gone.

THE INSIDE OF the small tent is stuffy. Ki-yong still hasn't decided. Should he stay? Go back? In the past twenty years, he never prepared for the possibility of this dilemma. Was it carelessness toward fate, or denial? He never went in for a physical either. He doesn't know his own blood pressure or blood sugar levels. He never believed that it would make a difference, that he would meet death peacefully, in bed, surrounded by family.

After Gabriel García Márquez was diagnosed with lymphoma, he spoke about the reason he smoked so assiduously throughout his life. He explained that, as an intellectual-cum-antigovernment journalist living in Colombia, in a system that was close to anarchy, he never believed that he would end up living to such an old age. His homeland was the kind of country where, in broad daylight, someone would shoot a goalie who accidentally kicked the ball into his own goal post during the World Cup. Living in Bogotá, a city bombarded by assassinations and drugs, the smoke coming from the end of a Cuban cigar represented beauty. And he evaded lynchings, confinement, exile, and bullets, only to experience cancer.

Guns. Ki-yong imagines a small, gold, shining bullet exploding into his skull and covering it with gunpowder. It makes him feel like a young girl fearing and longing for her first sexual experience, the way Yukio Mishima felt about knives. Once he thinks of this, he can't shake the image; it sticks to him like a leech. He recalls how he aimed the Colt at Ji-hun's temple. His imagination tangles with what actually happened and his sense of reality quickly flies away. He feels a short, electric burst of clarity, as if he swabbed rubbing alcohol on his skin.

Once, he read a story about a man, Évariste Galois, who was permitted a single day of freedom before his demise, just like Ki-yong. Like a classic Stendhal or Balzac story, it opened with Napoleon. Galois was the son of a radical republican politician in the early nineteenth century. Emperor Napoleon had been banished to Elba, and Louis XVIII had come to power. At one point, Napoleon escaped Elba and marched to Paris, but was arrested and exiled to an isolated island in the Atlantic, St. Helena. Galois's father, who had been elected mayor when Napoleon returned to Paris, suffered a political ousting, following in the steps of the emperor. His father then committed suicide. As a result, the younger Galois became a sensitive antigovernment radical. Galois fought with the royalists, joined the National Guard, and walked the path of a professional radical. He was imprisoned. When he was released, he attended protests daily and became an alcoholic.

At the time, the mathematics world was trying to solve the proof of the general quintic equations. Galois, having shown a latent talent for mathematics at a young age, immersed himself in that problem, and finally submitted a paper to the Académie des Sciences. But his paper wasn't even judged, because the judge assigned to evaluate it abruptly died. Galois believed it was the result of a political conspiracy and was rightfully angry. He fell in love with a woman called Stéphanie-Félice du Motel, who already was engaged to one d'Herbinville, France's most renowned marksman. D'Herbinville, deeply dismayed by his betrothed's betrayal, suggested a duel with Galois. The young genius tried all he could to avoid the fight, but nothing worked. The night before the duel, he sat at his desk, opened a notebook, and started solving the general quintic equation, as intently as if his life depended on it. Scribbles, evocative of desperate cries, covered the margins of the barely legible and disorganized notebook—"I do not have the time!" and "Oh, Stéphanie, my love." That night, after he finished the calculations and the proofs, he wrote a letter to his friend Auguste Chevalier, asking him to send the notebook to the greatest mathematicians in Europe if he were to perish in the duel the following morning.

The next day was Wednesday, May 30, 1832. Galois and d'Herbinville met at a field and aimed their guns at each other. The ace shooter calmly fired and the young genius was hit in the stomach. He left the wounded, bloodied Galois lying on the ground and walked off. Galois was transported to a hospital a few hours later. The next day, he died from extreme blood loss and infection. The mathematician who had solved the quintic equation, an important contribution to the evolution of the history of mathematics, was only twenty-one years old.

Ruing his lack of time, Ki-yong thinks about the last day accorded to Galois, that young man who struggled to solve an abstract idea. At least Galois had something to occupy himself with all night, something to leave behind. Maybe that is a better way to go.

Ki-yong wonders what he has accomplished at the age of forty-two. He has lived in stability, without making too many mistakes, working a slightly more dangerous job than is normal, having avoided any major failures. The first twenty-one years of his life were spent in the North, the latter twenty-one in the South—his life is divided between the two cleanly, exactly in half. The two halves—the student who studied

English at Pyongyang University of Foreign Studies and believed he owned the world, and the illegal immigrant who lived quietly as an orphan—are disparate and float around separately, much like puzzle pieces that don't fit together. He didn't expect this to happen to him. Ever since he started living his current life, he was forced to forget about his past. He wonders if this is how it would feel to discover what you were in a previous lifetime. His past, which he thought could be forgotten, has really been lying dormant like a virus, awakening itself at the most inopportune moment.

He's reminded of one of his films; he purchased the distribution rights at the Cannes Film Festival but has never been able to release it here. It's called *Shout*, directed by Hans Schwanitz. This German film is about a man who recovers from amnesia after undergoing treatment by his doctors. Lying on a hospital bed, the man waits for his memory to come back to him. He tosses and turns, chasing memories that are on the verge of appearing, on the brink of being caught, and desperately wonders who he is and where he's from. Finally, through the fog, a memory comes back to him: a few weeks before, he was diagnosed with a terminal illness. He wandered the streets in shock, got in a car accident, and became an amnesiac. With drugs and electroshocks, the doctors revived the memory of the death sentence. He gets up from bed and says, "Thank you, Doctor! I just remembered that I'm going to die soon."

Ki-yong looks around the tent he's sitting in, feeling cramped and short of breath. The old man across from him is wearing thick glasses, as if he is embracing the stereotype of an old man. He flips through the yellowed pages of a book, scribbling Chinese characters only he can read on a piece of white paper, kept in place by a paperweight. "Your parents passed away early, and you had a difficult childhood," he announces.

"When I was still young, my mother—"

"Yes, that's exactly what happened," the fortune-teller cuts him off. "You don't have much luck in terms of riches, and you don't have luck with your spouse, so I see that you will get married twice."

"Is that right?"

The old man looks over his glasses at Ki-yong. "I can see everything."

"What do you mean?"

"I can see what your problem is, even though you look perfectly normal."

"What are you talking about?"

"Your problem is worrying. You have a lot of worries." The fortune-teller lights a cigarette.

"Why would I come here if I weren't worried about something?" Ki-yong asks.

"Were you cut?"

"I'm sorry?"

"Were you cut from work? If not, why are you out and about at this hour, instead of going home?"

"I'm feeling frustrated," Ki-yong explains.

The old man looks at his fortune again, and starts explaining the results somewhat mechanically, as if he is reading a book. "Your middle age fortune is as follows. You don't have self-confidence, so you are very aware of others. You think of others all the time and try to make things pleasant. You're always smiling, but you're doing this to get other people's attention. You are nice to everyone so as to not make enemies, and you try to be generous, but you don't like yourself when you act that way. You're considerate and peace-loving, but you're overly indecisive and have a hard time making decisions."

"How's my luck this year?"

The old man peruses the fortune again. "Let's see, let's see, let's see. This year you're very lucky. Life has been very hard for you even until last year. You had a parting and you suffered a monetary loss. But this year, things are looking up. Everything you touch turns out good for you. Everything you've done so far for others is coming back to you as good fortune. People will value you and treat you well. But you have to be wary of moving. It's better to stay put and gather what you've been working for all these years."

"I don't think that's true. Can you look at it again?"

"No, that's it."

"I think I have to go somewhere far," confesses Ki-yong.

"You mean you're moving somewhere? You shouldn't move this year. But if you must, go east."

"East?"

"Yes."

"What about north?"

"North?" The old man tilts his head, looking bewildered. "What's up north?"

"Oh, nothing," Ki-yong stammers. "I was thinking about all the directions—east, west, north, south."

"No," the old man concludes. "If you must move it should be east, or southeast."

"Thank you." Ki-yong gets up from the rickety folding chair.

The old man calls out, "Listen. Who doesn't have a hard time with what life throws at them when they're young? It's the toughest when you're young. Just persevere. That will bring luck to you later."

Ki-yong doesn't reply and leaves. Ki-yong is taller than the tent, but from the outside, one might think it's cozy. On one flap is written "Fate is the rock that comes flying at you from the front. If you know it's coming, you can duck, but that knowledge will exhaust your body and soul." He smiles bitterly. *What? I don't have self-confidence, so I am always worrying about what others think?* He has a sudden impulse to pull the tent apart, but as always, he restrains himself. "You are nice to everyone so as to not make enemies . . ."

He takes out his phone again and presses the talk button, dialing the last number he tried. He hears the message that his wife's phone is powered off. His headache starts up again. Or maybe it was there all day and he just stopped noticing it. In any case, it doesn't matter when his headache started. He massages the back of his neck. *Should I be listening to Yuki Kuramoto, like Hyon-mi was saying?* He starts walking down the darkened street, rubbing his neck, as drunken people straggle out from bars, one by one, bobbing and weaving like poisoned cockroaches.

9:00 P.M.

PRO WRESTLING

MA-RI, HER legs spread open, thinks that having sex with two guys at the same time is like a blockbuster action flick—it's good only for the first half. You're hooked by the explosive preview and action scenes, but after a while, when you take a good look, you realize that the same scenes keep repeating. As time passes, the action sequences intensify, but the initial surprise and excitement dull. She's already come twice. Usually by this time, her nerves are beyond relaxed, having reached a point where she doesn't need any more stimulation. But the twenty-year-old boys have different ideas. They position Ma-ri on her stomach, then flip her on her back, and then, unsatisfied, they put her on her side and push into her. One of them approaches her head and pushes his long, limp penis in her face. As she wrestles with the two boys in the big rotating bed, she suddenly hears her dead father's voice ring out, as if a message from God: "You have to live just like you sing a song." The last words he insisted he heard from his spiritual brother, Rikidozan.

Startled, Ma-ri's eyes fly open, but there is no one but them in the room. Ma-ri pushes her ass into the air. One boy is trying to push into her from behind, and the other is sucking her nipple, his head mashed under her chest. It's hard to maintain the position because of her cast, but after striking various poses during the past hour, she has managed to figure out what works. She doesn't feel as lost as she did initially. Sweat drips off her chin and onto her cast. *Rikidozan probably felt like this,* she thinks. *When he got in the ring, he must have had moments where, in the middle of being tangled with opponents who were actually his friends, he wished that time would pass quickly. There are things in life you can't do anything about, and you can't always just do things you want to do. He would have consoled himself like I'm doing now, striking this or that pose according to the script and suffering through one round after another.* Sex is like pro wrestling. Only a game, but at the same time, a struggle. You have to be considerate of the other party while you attack, and you have to be somewhat aggressive to make it work.

She moans every time he thrusts.

"You like it? Like it? Yeah, you like it?"

"Yeah, yeah, yeah."

"Talk dirty to me," Song-uk moans.

"No."

"Please."

"I can't. I've never done it before."

"Do it, you fucking bitch, you fucking whore," Song-uk says, pulling her head up.

"You assholes, you motherfuckers, you fucking assholes, ahh, ahh, fuck." With Ma-ri's every word, the guys become more turned on, and they press up against her more aggressively. Even dirtier words pour out of her onto the bed. Suddenly, someone's phone rings. "Toreador Song." Everyone pauses.

"Isn't that yours?" Song-uk turns to Panda, annoyed.

Panda gets up and slips his phone out of his pants, which were flung onto the floor. "Hell . . . hello? Oh, hey. Are, are you here?"

"What's up?" Song-uk asks.

"It's Tae . . . Tae . . . Tae . . . Tae-su," Panda says, looking panicked.

"And?" Song-uk urges.

"He called when we were at the restaurant . . ."

"You told him?"

Panda nods sheepishly.

"You idiot, why did you tell him? Just tell him no," Song-uk orders.

"He says he's right outside . . ."

Song-uk untangles himself from Ma-ri and takes a step toward Panda, but it doesn't look like he's going to take a swing at him. "How does he know we're here?"

"He texted me a while ago, but I didn't think he'd actually come . . ."

Song-uk turns to Ma-ri. "I don't know what I should do. He's a really close friend of ours . . . He's trustworthy. We're in the same study group," he wheedles.

Ma-ri raises herself up on the bed, slowly. She puts a pillow against the wall and leans back. "Song-uk, can you bring me my purse?"

Song-uk hurries over with her bag. She's about to rummage through it, but stops. She turns to Panda. "Can I have a cigarette?"

Panda takes out a cigarette from his pocket, fumbling, and rushes it to her. She sticks it in her mouth, and Panda lights it for her. Song-uk frowns momentarily. She blows out a stream of smoke. "What the hell is this? Do you think I'm some whore?"

Both of their dicks are now flaccid, pointing down at the ground.

"How can you be a whore when you didn't even get paid for it?" Song-uk protests. "Isn't that right? I'm sorry if this sounds harsh, but what I'm trying to say is, things have already come to this point—wouldn't it be okay if just one more joined us?"

"I'm sore. I'm not doing this anymore."

The doorbell rings, at first gently, and then more and more energetically.

"You've already told him the room number, too?" Ma-ri shoots an accusatory glare at Panda, who hangs his head.

The bell stops ringing and this time the person outside starts banging on the door, another horny guy standing in front of room 503. Song-uk looks at Ma-ri, nervous, but doesn't do anything. She knows right then that this is the last time she will see him. *Isn't it too early for me to arrive at a dead end on the street of life? This is so unfair. It's too early. What did I do wrong? I worked hard, I was, for the most part, faithful to my family, and I lived life to the fullest. I made donations to charities every month and I've been there for every major event in my friends' lives, celebrating happy occasions and commiserating for sad ones. What did I do wrong, other than get old?*

"Tell him to come in," Ma-ri decides.

Song-uk brightens, like a kid who has received a present. Panda regains his cheer as well.

"I did it with two already, so one more shouldn't be a big deal," Ma-ri mumbles to herself. She instantly feels ten years older. This is it. In a few days, the cast will be taken off, she'll forget about Song-uk, and she will go back to her boring old life. She'll sell cars during the day and watch television on the sofa at night. She'll take vacations with her family, maybe go on a camping trip, and on some nights she'll even accompany Ki-yong to the premiere of some film he imported. *I'll go back to that life. This is it after today. Anything more is impossible.*

The door opens to reveal a man too old to be a college student. His hair is wavy and shot with gray, and he's wearing unbecoming gold-rimmed glasses. Panda and Song-uk, who open the door with sheets wrapped around their waists, step back. "Who are you?"

The man steps into the room. "I'm sorry, but you can't do this."

"What are you talking about?" Song-uk says.

"We received a tip that someone was using this room for group sex," the man explains, looking around the room with a glimmer of a smile on his face. But he doesn't hide his disgust. "So I guess it's true."

Ma-ri covers her face with a sheet.

"I'll give you five minutes. Take your belongings and get out."

"I have to shower first . . ."

"Sorry, it's a violation of the rules. Just get your things and leave, before the cops get here."

"Okay."

"Hurry," the man says, and slams the door behind him.

Song-uk, annoyed, addresses Panda. "You dumbass, you said it was Tae-su! What the hell is this?"

Panda checks his phone and finds a new text. "He says he got caught at the entrance."

Song-uk kicks his bag. "What kind of an unmanned hotel is this? Fuck."

Ma-ri gathers her clothes from around the room and goes into the bathroom ahead of the guys, locking the door. She puts her clothes on and smoothes her hair. She washes her face, then perches on the bidet while she freshens up her makeup. She turns the water to cold, and the throbbing in her groin subsides a bit. She wants to shower but she doesn't think she can without Song-uk's help. She hears the guys knocking on the bathroom door but doesn't reply until she's satisfied with the way she looks. She opens the door and goes into the room, looking as demure as she did when she left work. The guys are already dressed.

"I . . . I . . . I had a good time," Panda stutters. "And so . . . so . . . sorry."

"It's fine," she replies curtly and goes out to the hall. Someone is peeking at them from the maid's room. She figures a maid is waiting for them to leave so she can change the sheets.

She addresses Song-uk. "Bye. It's been fun."

"Are you mad at me?" Song-uk asks, deflated.

"No," she says, shaking her head. She tries to compose an expression that exudes equanimity but she isn't certain if it is conveyed to the boy. "We'll say goodbye here."

"Yeah, see you later."

"No, I mean it's over. Bye," she says, her voice faint.

"Wait." Song-uk grabs her arm.

She feels something new, something she's never felt in the time she's been seeing Song-uk. Annoyance. She frowns involuntarily and jerks her arm away.

"What about me?" Song-uk protests.

"What about you?"

"Have you been playing with me? Is that what this was all about?"

Panda tugs at his sleeve. "Come on, Song-uk. Let's go."

She smiles almost imperceptibly. Her annoyance disappears. She reassures him in a friendly but businesslike way, like a late-night radio personality. "I'm sorry if that's how you feel. I'm sorry, okay? I loved you once. You know that, don't you? You couldn't have not known, because you're smart. But that's it. Bye, okay? We'll go our separate ways here. I'm tired."

She walks down the stairs, stopping a couple of times because of her aching pelvis. The guys don't follow her, but take the elevator down. By the time she gets to the ground floor, they are already gone. She walks through the automatic doors. The flashing neon signs rush toward her. Why didn't she notice those on her way in? She walks out into the street. A heavy and poisonous fatigue, the kind she has never encountered before, weighs down her body. Her head hurts, as it sometimes does when she eats sweet white chocolate too quickly, and she feels dizzy.

10:00 P.M.

AN OLD LOYAL DOG
NAMED NIGHTMARE

ALL THE CARS entering the apartment complex stop at the security booth. When a resident's car affixed with an electronic tag approaches, the gate goes up automatically. But if it's a visitor's car or a taxi, they have to receive permission from the security guard before going in. Ki-yong sits in the shadows behind the security booth, in the nook where residents stack Styrofoam boxes for recycling. It's dark enough that the guard, who just finished the rounds, can't see him. The security booth's bright lights make the corner look even darker than it really is. From there, Ki-yong is able to see the cars entering the complex without revealing himself.

Ma-ri hasn't come home yet. He is worried that someone might have taken her away. He hasn't been able to reach her all night. If someone got to her, it's probably the NIS. She might not have been that surprised to learn the truth about him. He imagines her expression as she says, "Oh, I see. I always thought there was something a little odd about him."

He shifts around. Behind him, he hears boxes falling over. He turns his head. A tan cat is hunched on some boxes, eyes glistening.

Ten minutes before ten, a taxi stops at the gate. Ki-yong recognizes Ma-ri sitting in the back seat. He almost missed her. Why did she take a cab, instead of her car? Ki-yong hesitates for a moment. If he pauses any longer, the cab will go straight into the complex. Thankfully, she's alone. He bolts toward the bright booth and jerks open the passenger door. She recoils, shocked.

"Ma-ri," he calls.

"What's going on?" asks the driver, turning around in surprise.

Ki-yong checks the fare on the meter and hands the driver fifteen thousand won. "Keep the change," he tells him, and pulls Ma-ri's wrist. "Get out for a second. I have to talk to you."

"Can't we talk about it at home?" she protests.

"It's important. Why would I do this if we could? Please get out," Ki-yong pleads.

"No, I'm tired."

"Look, have you ever seen me do something like this?"

"No, what's going on? You're scaring me. I want to go home, I really am tired."

"Please, Ma-ri."

The driver stops the meter. Behind them another car pulls up, waiting for them to move. Having no choice in the matter, Ma-ri is led out of the car unwillingly, as if she is a stubborn radish he plucks from the ground.

Ki-yong and Ma-ri pass the dry fountain and go toward

the bench under the wisteria vines, where it's dark. It's cold. Ma-ri sits down, then gets up. Finally, she slowly sits back down again.

"Ma-ri," Ki-yong says.

"What?"

He hesitates. "Do you know which one word you say to me most often?"

"What?"

"'What.' You always ask 'what.' Even when I just call your name, you say 'what.' Isn't that right?"

"Did you just drag me out of the cab to pick a fight? What the hell is wrong with men? Why do they think they can do whatever they want? Do you think I'm some toy?" Ma-ri's voice gets louder.

"Fine, fine. I'm not about to ask you to change the way you speak to me."

"What do you want?"

"I was going to do it over the phone but I couldn't reach you."

She takes out her phone and opens it. The blue light shines on her chin and bridge of her nose.

"You're not in my missed calls list. When did you call?"

"I called a couple of times. I got a new phone."

"Why didn't you text me?"

"It wasn't the kind of thing I could tell you by text."

Ma-ri is quiet.

"Did anything out of the ordinary happen today?" Ki-yong asks.

Thousands of images spiral in Ma-ri's head—yelling at the driver of the SUV, fighting with the cop, lying tangled with the two guys. The montage sparks several emotions, exploding in her brain like fireworks. What is the "anything out of the ordinary" he's referring to? How can he possibly know everything that happened to her today? Does he really know? Her heart pounds. This is why he has accosted her like this, she thinks, instead of confronting her at home in front of Hyon-mi. But then it must definitely be about the Motel Bohemian. But how did he already know about this? Did he get a private investigator to follow her?

"No, what do you mean?" she says cagily, on edge.

"Really, nothing happened?"

"I'm telling you, no."

"Then where are you coming from right now?"

"I had dinner with my coworkers. Why are you interrogating me? Are you accusing me of something? Did you do something? What's going on?"

"You didn't tell me you were having dinner with people from work," Ki-yong points out.

"You left before I had a chance to tell you," Ma-ri retorts. She raises her right sleeve, inviting him to sniff it. He gets a faint whiff of cooked protein and fat. Ma-ri regrets spraying herself with the deodorizer earlier.

"I have to tell you something," Ki-yong says again.

"Can't you tell me at home?"

"Please, please just listen to me."

She nods reluctantly. Heavy fatigue washes over her, but she struggles to keep her eyes open and look at her husband. There's something about him that makes her uneasy, something unfamiliar. "Okay, go ahead."

"If nothing's happened yet, we might get lucky. We might have nothing to worry about. But I doubt that's the case. We're definitely going to go through something. But before that happens, I have to—I mean, you—you have to hear it from me not from someone else—well, I think it's better if you hear it from me."

Until that moment, Ma-ri was still under the magnetic power of sex. But now she senses something in Ki-yong's demeanor, something she has never witnessed in fifteen years of marriage. She understands he's about to reveal a secret that will neutralize her affair, right here in the dark under the wisteria vines. Even though she knows it is useless, that she will be told soon enough, she starts guessing his secret in her head. Did he cheat on her? It couldn't be any old affair, from the way he's talking, so maybe he slept with her best friend, or with someone she's very close to? Did something happen at work? Was he involved in a hit-and-run? No, has the hit-and-run he committed years ago been revealed? Her guesses jump from one to another speedily, but nothing seems quite right.

"Don't be surprised, okay? First of all, I wasn't born in 1967."

Ma-ri always thought he looked old for his age. "So your birth certificate's wrong?" she asks.

"I suppose you could say that. Anyway, I was born in 1963. And my name isn't Kim Ki-yong." Ki-yong is hurrying through the facts, as if he's decided to reveal all of his secrets at once. "My real name is Kim Song-hun. I was born in Pyongyang and came to Seoul in 1984. I got into college, and you know everything from then."

She smirks. This isn't the reaction Ki-yong expected.

"I don't believe it. It's all lies," she says.

"No, it's all true."

"Can't be. No way. Don't worry, I'm not in shock or anything. I just don't think any of that's possible."

A dump truck clanks by on the road beyond the apartment complex, thumping over a speed bump.

"It is possible," Ki-yong insists.

"No, no way." She tries to put conviction behind her words, but her voice is shaking.

"Why not?"

"There's no way I would have been in the dark for so long. I'm your wife, and you know how perceptive I am!"

Ki-yong once heard that all the famous spies in history were failed spies. The best of the best were never discovered, so they retired quietly and died anonymously, having enjoyed their retirement. Failed spies became known because they couldn't keep their secret anymore and had to confide in someone, or leaked their identities by not being very careful, or were seduced by money or women. These men became famous for their lack of success. On the other hand, some spies are like decades-long employees of big Japanese conglomerates, guaranteed employment for life. They don't stand out, they work without drawing attention to themselves, and they don't leak company secrets. To compensate them for their discretion, they are given good retirement and pension plans, and are allowed to enjoy their old age in peace. They are not privy to top-priority information that can be sold, so they aren't ever tempted. You can even say there's no such thing as a completely incorruptible human; anyone who hasn't gone astray just hasn't been seduced by something that can win him over.

Ki-yong has now become a failed spy. All that's left is his quiet removal from this world. One day has changed everything. Nothing has changed in the world; he's the only thing that has changed. For the past twenty years he hasn't succumbed to temptation—or maybe he's just never faced a truly tempting alternative—and wasn't in possession of interesting information that would be in high demand, and he followed all the orders sent down from the North. But his life has veered from its comfortable path and is careening into the unknown. Whether you're a spy or something else, it's deflating to be a failure. He looks at his wife sitting next to him, now the wife of a failure.

Ma-ri asks, her voice trembling and low, "Are you . . . really a spy?"

He doesn't deny or concede the fact. They remain in silence. A black plastic bag floats in the air, past the flower garden. The bag twirls at the edge of the road and drifts back up into the air.

"What's really going on? Are you seeing someone? Is the company bankrupt? Do you want a divorce? Is that what it is? What's going on? Tell me. I'm having a hard time believing what you just told me, so help me understand," Ma-ri insists.

He takes out the fake passport from the suitcase and hands it to her, without a word. She reads it under the faint light, taking in the fake name printed under his picture. "Unbelievable," she says in a low voice, as if uttering a Buddhist chant. She drops the passport on the ground. She's dizzy. She isn't sure if it's because of her fatigue or because of this sudden disclosure. He picks up the passport.

"I'm sorry I couldn't tell you before," Ki-yong explains.

She doesn't say anything.

"Ma-ri," Ki-yong says.

She still doesn't say anything. They sit there, side by side, without saying a word for a while. The black plastic bag reappears, dragged back by a funnel of wind, dizzily whirls around, then disappears again.

Ma-ri buries her face in her hands. She looks up at him. "Why are you telling me this now?"

"I got an order this morning."

"What order?"

"To go back north by dawn."

Ma-ri is shocked into silence again.

"I don't want to go," he says, his voice shaking slightly.

She opens her arms. He bends over and buries his face in her embrace, holding on to her. She smells like barbecued pork belly, disinfectant, and cigarettes.

"At first I lied to you," Ki-yong continues. "But you have to understand that the real me is the one you've known since college. I lost touch with the North and I worked hard to survive and I tried my best to live here, without anyone to lean on. I've even forgotten that I'm originally from up there."

"What happens if you refuse?" Ma-ri asks.

"They'll know for sure that I've betrayed them."

He feels her nod.

"I still can't forgive you," Ma-ri declares.

He raises his head from her chest. "I'm sorry I lied to you."

"That's not why I can't forgive you," Ma-ri explains. "Listen. People make all sorts of choices in life. It's the same with me, too. You recognize several junctures where you're forced to make a choice. I've become myself today because of those choices. Do you know what I mean? That's why people shouldn't travel through time. If we could go back and change even the most trivial thing, this world, this reality that we see, none of it would exist. So what I'm trying to say is—basically, you asshole, if I hadn't met you fifteen years ago, or even if I'd met you but known the truth, I would have made a different choice. I would have gone on to make another choice based on that, and I might be living a completely different life right now. Even this morning, I didn't regret anything in my life because it was all a product of my choices; I knew I had created my own life. Of course, I sometimes chose wrong or made mistakes, but I was fine with that. I'm most terrified of my own foolishness. I was stupid before and today—yeah, even today. Now I get it, my stupidity is a chronic illness. I'm unchangeable. Wait," she says, when Ki-yong tries to soothe her, "I'm not done yet.

"I know what you're thinking, what you want to tell me. I'm not crying. I don't have the right to do that. I'm pathetic. I'm a pathetic piece of shit. I shouldn't be here. I'm stupid, but I didn't even know it. I thought I had it all. I always thought it was my fault that you didn't open up to me, so I tried really hard. I did, I really did. But at some point I realized that there was a limit to that kind of effort, so I gave up. But that's not where it ends, because it wasn't enough to just give up on you or communicate with you. During all of this, I was closed off to other people because I was hurt, because I couldn't even communicate with the person I was closest to. Do you understand what that did to my self-confidence? I shrank into myself and avoided people and was cowed, and that's how I spent my twenties. Oh, you really are an asshole. You knew what you were doing all along, and you were never on my side even when you knew I was having a hard time with everything. You didn't even think to comfort me. I always thought that was just the way you were, so I'd tell myself, Okay, I'm going to try to understand, because that's what he's like—there was no way I could change you. But if I had been able to build a really intimate relationship with you, if I had succeeded, I might have become a different person. Don't you think so?

"What really pisses me off right now is that you knew how much pain I was in, but you were comparing it with your own and dismissing mine. Isn't that what went on in your mind? Whenever I complained that I was having such a hard time, you must have jeered at me secretly, thinking, That's nothing. I'm a spy, I have a secret I can't tell a single soul. What Ma-ri is going through is nothing compared to that kind of pain. Isn't that what you thought? I get it now. You have that damn superiority about pain—you arrogantly think your pain is the absolute worst, and you judge others' pain against it. You're an egotist, a self-righteous pig. An egotist thinks he's the only one who's going through difficult times, laughing at other people's hardships, and believes that because of his unique pain, he can do whatever he wants. You always have that expression on your face. You walk around like life's beaten you, like you're depressed, but really, you're looking down at everything and everyone, superior and arrogant. Sure, I knew that about you, but I was compassionate. I thought it was understandable that you ended up like that, because you were an orphan, because you had to raise yourself. I figured I just didn't know what it was like for you because I had a fairly easy life.

"Shit, I really was stupid, really fucking stupid. I can't even think of another word to describe myself. How can you be so calm right now, after all of this? Did I ask you to tell me everything? No! What about me? What's going to happen to me? I'm practically forty and I can't do anything with my life at this point. I always thought this was the best I could do, and so I was fine with having less, with achieving less, but now you're telling me I could have been living a much better life? That all of this is because of your deception? What the hell am I supposed to do? Say something."

Ki-yong just listens quietly.

She breathes in deeply. She continues her rant. "I always thought people got upset when someone betrayed them because they were angry at being lied to, at having the wool pulled over their eyes. But now I see it isn't true. Betrayal dismantles your confidence. That's why it's so upsetting. Now I can't believe in anything. I can't tell if I enjoyed my life until now, or if I'm doing the right thing, or what. How can someone this stupid do anything well? How can I do anything well in the future? I'm probably just going to get used by everyone. Don't you think so?"

"Calm down," Ki-yong says.

"Just stop acting so cool and collected. This really isn't the time," she snaps.

"Okay, I'm sorry."

She sighs loudly, and he rubs his face with his hands. His hands feel rough against his skin.

Ma-ri opens her mouth again, but she sounds calmer this time. "What are you going to do?"

"I don't know," Ki-yong confesses.

"You must have thought of this possibility during the fifteen years you were lying to me," she says.

"I didn't think anything one way or another. I never actually thought this day would come."

"Are you going to go back?"

Ki-yong remains silent.

She shakes her head slowly. "No, if you were going back you wouldn't have waited for me like this. You would have just gone back without saying anything to me. Right?"

"Yeah." It's only then that he realizes why he waited to accost her like that.

"You don't want to go, do you? You think of Seoul as your home, since you've lived here for twenty years, right? Does this mean you have to turn yourself in?"

"Yeah."

She sniffles. "Don't take this the wrong way. I'm calm now, okay? I understand what you told me, and I know why you did all of that to me. I mean, you were young, too. You couldn't have said no when the higher-ups told you what to do."

"The Party didn't order me to marry you. I chose you," Ki-yong emphasizes.

"Well, you must have had their permission," Ma-ri points out.

He nods.

Ma-ri probes deeper. "It's because I was in the Juche Ideology faction, right? You probably thought, If I play this correctly, I might even be able to bring her over to our side."

"That might have been what I was thinking," Ki-yong concedes.

"I just want you to know one thing," Ma-ri says. "I'm saying this from a really calm place now. I'm rational again. I'm not angry and I'm not looking at this pessimistically. This sniffling is from crying earlier on. Right now I'm totally fine, okay?"

"Yeah, it seems like you are."

"Whenever I'm in a situation where I don't know what to do, I wonder what my father would have done. He always knew what to do in any given situation. Maybe because of his animalistic instinct, which helped him survive in that kind of world."

"He did always know what was going on," Ki-yong says, remembering his father-in-law, who never warmed to him. Ki-yong tried and tried to get on his good side, but the elderly liquor wholesaler seemed to know something about Ki-yong that nobody else could sense. He died without ever approving of him. He was unhappy with his daughter's decision to marry him, and even after the wedding there wasn't much chance for Ki-yong to get close to him. Ma-ri knew that, too, so she didn't bring up her father often with Ki-yong.

She gets up and throws away the tissues she used to mop up her tears. She sits back down. "Go back."

"What?" Ki-yong can't believe his ears.

"Go back. That's what I want. I'm sorry, but I like my life as it is. If you don't go back, they might send someone to take care of you."

"It's not like I'm a close relative of Kim Jong Il," he protests. "I'm not important enough to have my own assassin sent from the North."

"So then why are you being recalled?"

"I have no idea. I'm sure someone's just come across my file."

She scratches her cast. "Ugh, it's so itchy it's driving me crazy. Unless you go back, you'll never know why they're ordering you to return, right?"

He nods.

"And, don't take this the wrong way, but I don't want to change my name and live as a totally different person in a strange neighborhood."

"What are you talking about?"

"If you give yourself up, wouldn't the government move us somewhere else? What about Hyon-mi? Have you even thought about what's best for her? She's just started to enjoy school after quitting Go. What are we going to tell her if we have to move? I want to keep her safe. Think about it. If you go, we're all fine. They're going to relax and they might even send you back for some other mission. Then you can pop back in our lives as if you were abroad on business. If you do that, they're not going to send down an assassination team, and we don't have to be in hiding, living under assumed identities in some sleepy regional city somewhere. Don't you read the paper? All the fathers in the world gladly sacrifice everything for their families. You hear about all those Korean fathers working hard, making money, while they send their families abroad for the kids' education. They eat ramen and wire all their money to the kids. It's not even going to be that bad for you—you're from there! Your parents are still up there, aren't they?"

"My father's still there."

"And you have friends, right? Why do we have to be afraid for our lives because of your goddamn situation? We shouldn't have to change our names and address for that. I really had a difficult time making my way in the world, you know. Do you remember when I tried to find a job after having Hyon-mi? I got rejected from every job I applied to and I had to start from the bottom from managing insurance policies bought with pennies saved by housewives, and now I've worked my way up almost to where I want to be. I'm nearly there. But you just want to—"

"Okay, okay. I get it," he acquiesces, dejected.

"Look, I'm sorry, okay? But you have to think about your daughter. Think about her future, about what she'll have to go through, okay?"

"Okay. But I have to say I thought you'd tell me to stay, even if you were just being polite, even just once."

Ma-ri puts her hand over Ki-yong's freezing hand.

"I'm sorry, but this is what it means to be a mother. I'm not just a woman, I'm a mother first."

"Yeah, that's true," he says, nodding. "But I'm not going back."

She drops his hand, stunned. "What? Are you insane?"

"I thought about a lot of things today, wandering the streets. I really did. I even went to see a fortune-teller. You know I don't believe in that stuff. I'm scared. It will have changed a lot back there. It's going to be different. My father will be there, but he will be old, and if I go back, people who don't even know why I was sent down in the first place are going to decide my fate. Even if I live, I might spend the rest of my life in a dark underground tunnel, training young agents about to be sent to Seoul. It's really a terrifying idea. You don't know what it's like, to live your entire life on a set that looks exactly like Seoul. I've seen it. And the thing is, that may be one of the better scenarios. Something worse could happen to me. All I'm asking is for you to help me. We've been married for fifteen years no matter what happens, and it's not like we can turn back time," Ki-yong pleads.

"No, I can't help you, Ki-yong. You can hate me for it, but you have to go. That's what's going to happen. Think about it rationally, Ki-yong. If you really didn't do anything wrong, like you're telling me, there's no reason for the Party to punish you."

"You're really cruel," Ki-yong shoots back.

"I'd really love it if I could tell you all sorts of nice things, but we don't have the time," Ma-ri snaps.

"Is this payback for me lying to you?"

"No, I'm just thinking about the best solution for everyone. Don't get so upset. We had fifteen good years. And I know you weren't one hundred percent happy with me; I'm not a perfect wife, and I'm not good at being supportive. Why are you balking at this when you can make a whole new life for yourself?" Ma-ri asks.

"Okay, I'm going to ask you one last time. Why can't you sacrifice just a little bit? Please? I'll make it up to you. After I give myself up to the authorities and all of that's done—well, I'm sure I'll have to go to prison for a few years. But after that, after I get out, I'll be the best husband, the best father," Ki-yong tries to convince her.

"No, I told you. That's not possible. Why are you making it so difficult?"

"Even if you don't like it, I have the right to live with you in that apartment," Ki-yong announces.

She exhales and throws down her ace. "Okay, I'll tell you

why you can't do that. I'll tell you all about where I was and who I was with today. There's no way you can bear to live with me after you hear about it."

Ki-yong hears from Ma-ri, from Ma-ri's mouth, from Ma-ri's tongue and lips, in too much detail, about the young man who reveres Mao and Che Guevara, the stuttering Panda, the third guy who wasn't able to get into the room at the Motel Bohemian. He has to hear it. But as he hears it, he feels like he's listening to a twisted version of a Brothers Grimm fairytale. It's unreal and fantastical. It sounds like a story from one of Freud's patients. He's hearing this story from Ma-ri, but he can't believe that it's something she's experienced. A woman meets a boy and falls for him. She's then kidnapped, locked up in a tall tower, and waits to be rescued. But the situation becomes worse and worse . . .

He asks, despondently, "You think I'm going to believe that?"

"It's up to you whether you believe it or not. But right now, I'm not the same woman as the one you woke up next to this morning. I've learned that in life, there's a moment where you have to say no. This is precisely that moment."

"This is all very easy for you," Ki-yong says, dejected.

"It's not," Ma-ri says.

He gathers his thoughts. Even if everything Ma-ri told him is a lie, even if she just made it all up to hurt him, there's one thing he can't ignore—she doesn't want to be with him anymore. That much is true.

"Fine," Ki-yong says.

Ma-ri looks into his eyes.

"I'll go. I'll go back," Ki-yong says glumly.

"Good, I'm glad you made the right decision. I know it's hard for you. But you should go. That's the only decision that makes sense."

"Fine. But on one condition."

"What?"

"I'm taking Hyon-mi."

"What?" Ma-ri bolts up from the bench. From far away, a dog barks incessantly. "Are you crazy?"

"No."

"You can't take her to that hellhole!"

"You know, people live there, too," Ki-yong points out.

"People are starving up there! They don't even have gruel to eat. You know all of this better than I do."

"No, it's not that bad. It's just that there isn't any fast food or computer games. Oh, and none of this pressure to succeed in school, the tutoring, the grueling college entrance system, the drugs, the underage sex."

"You can't take her."

"You used to believe that NK was the solution to all of our problems, too, once upon a time. Right? Don't you remember? You used to be so jealous of Lim Su-kyong, who got to go to Pyongyang."

Ma-ri tries to control her mounting panic. She bites off her words. "Back then. I was young. Now, the political landscape is different."

"Fine, let's assume you're right. Let's say that the North is worse off than it was before. But I think we need to give Hyon-mi the chance to decide. I'm not talking about choosing an ideology; I'm talking about choosing a parent. She should get a say in who she wants to live with."

"Why does Hyon-mi have to be responsible for your mistakes?" Ma-ri seethes. "You're the one who hid your true identity and lied to us. Why does Hyon-mi have to make such a difficult decision?"

"This is a cheap shot, I guess, but you've brought it on yourself. You think you have the right to be a mother when you're out screwing twenty-year-olds, and a spy doesn't have the right to be a father? Do you think that makes any sense?" Ki-yong snarls, his voice rising.

"Oh, so now the gloves come off? Were you always this much of a coward, you asshole?" Ma-ri doesn't stand down.

"Why don't I have even the tiniest right to my own kid?"

Ma-ri takes out her cell. Her hand trembles. "I'm going to call the cops on you. I'm going to call 112 and report that you're a spy. I'm completely serious. Go away."

"You can't do it. Don't do it."

"There's no reason why I can't. After I call the cops and you go to prison, I'm going to file for a divorce, no, an annulment. Kim Ki-yong doesn't even exist, he never did, so I'm going to win hands down. I know I will. Don't come near me," Ma-ri warns. "Seriously, I'm going to scream."

She presses 1 twice, and glares at Ki-yong, her thumb on the 2. "I really don't want to have to do this," she says, her voice icy.

"Fine, fine. Okay. You win."

She moves her finger away from the keypad, whips around, and starts to walk away, but then stops and looks back. "Bye. Be careful." Her voice is small, trembling, barely reaching Ki-yong's ears.

He takes a deep breath. He says, quietly, "Go ahead, go inside. Hyon-mi's probably waiting for you."

She walks toward their apartment building. As she does, she realizes that the fatigue that was draped heavily around her shoulders earlier that evening has vanished. A new energy courses through her veins. She gets farther and farther away from Ki-yong and disappears into the darkness.

KI-YONG WATCHES HER stalk away. He sits back down on the bench. A strong feeling of dejection rips through him, shaking his body and spirit like a powerful tornado. All of the feelings he was suppressing throughout the day burst forth, as if a dam has caved in. He cries, silently. He silences his painful, visceral sobs by clamping his mouth shut. It's the first time he has cried since coming down south. He remembers being in the hospital when Hyon-mi was born. He thinks back to his wedding day, too. Both were oppressively hot days. Both times, he was on pins and needles, worried that someone would appear, reveal his true identity, and wrest his wife or child away from him. He suffered from nightmares for days prior to the wedding and the birth. Nightmares were like an old, loyal pet dog for Ki-yong. He couldn't get rid of them, but he couldn't keep them with him all the time. His dreams were filled with the vanishing faces of his wife and daughter. Sometimes the wedding guests turned and attacked him, like zombies. Once he dreamed that his newborn daughter bared her teeth at him, enraged. But at some point, his old pet dog nightmare went away. And he started to feel comfortable in his staid life. Like any middle-aged man, he could look back and think, Ah, those difficult, lonely younger days. But that nostalgia was merely a product of Ki-yong's delusion, his arrogance toward his fate.

He wipes his eyes, blows his nose, and clears his throat. He takes out his phone. He presses the numbers slowly, very slowly. The phone rings for a long time but nobody picks up. He sits there with the phone to his ear, patiently. Finally, she answers.

"Hello?"

"Soji?"

"Oh, Ki-yong. Where are you?"

"I'm just out."

"Are you okay?"

"Yeah, why?"

"You sound like you have a cold. It's cold outside, right?"

"Yeah, it's a little chilly."

There is a silence.

He swallows hard. "Soji," he starts.

"Yeah?"

"Can I ask you something?"

"Sure."

"The thing you said back at the Westin Chosun—you still mean it?"

"Still mean what?"

"That you don't think you're going to be a teacher forever. Do you still mean it, that you want to leave for someplace like Hemingway or Joyce and write?"

She doesn't say anything for a long time.

He waits for her to answer, patiently. It feels like eons.

"Ki-yong, you've never seen my house, right?"

"No."

"When I got home—I left a huge mess trying to find your bag—I felt unsettled. So I cleaned my house, a large-scale cleaning, which I haven't done in a long time. In the middle of the night. But now that I did that, the house is too clean. It's an old house, although it's going to be redeveloped at some point."

"I see."

"Do you ever get the feeling that the ghosts in your house are welcoming you when you walk through the door? Even though nobody's here, when I walk in it feels like someone's talking to me."

"Yeah. I know what you're talking about." The wind grows chillier. He shivers. He wonders if your body temperature drops when you shed tears.

"The kids are amazing," Soji continues.

"What kids? Oh, your students?"

"Yeah, some of them have a real gift for language. When I'm teaching kids like that, I feel like I've achieved something great. Hyon-mi's one of those kids."

"But you're a writer first and foremost."

"I'm not sure if that's true, though. I've been satisfied a number of times as a teacher, but I've never been happy with myself or my work as an author. Doesn't that mean I can't call myself a writer?"

"Well, a teacher and a writer are pursuing different objectives."

"Exactly."

They share another lengthy silence.

"Ki-yong," Soji says, "you're really a great guy. I know that."

"Do you? Really? Then why don't I know it?"

"What do you mean?"

"It's just, well, I don't have any interest in knowing whether I'm a good guy or not."

"So?"

"I realized something today. I think I always believed that people were worried about very abstract things. Like life, fate, politics, that kind of thing. You know I like math," Ki-yong tries to explain.

"You always said that it was the purest abstract world."

"Exactly. Time flies so fast when I'm working on an equation. I always thought everyone had that side to them. But now, today, everyone's . . ."

"Everyone's what?" Soji asks.

"Everyone's just struggling to survive. They're doing everything they can to survive. Why was I the only one who didn't realize that?"

A few high school students coming home from cram school pass Ki-yong's bench. He pauses for a moment.

"Ki-yong, you know Henry David Thoreau, right? He said that most men lead lives of quiet desperation."

Another bout of silence hangs in the air. The students' voices recede. Ki-yong's mouth is dry. It's unbelievable that this moment is so vivid, this very moment at which his life is coming to an end, as he's falling out of the sky without a parachute.

"I think . . ." He changes his mind. "Never mind."

She doesn't say anything.

"Take care. I just wanted to call before leaving."

"I know what you're thinking," Soji blurts.

"You do?" He laughs, then realizes that Soji would have heard him through the phone. She might think he's laughing at her. "I talked to Ma-ri just now. A minute ago."

"Oh . . ."

"I talked to Ma-ri . . ." He pauses, his emotions taking hold of him again.

Another short silence resonates in his ear. Soji doesn't ask what he and Ma-ri decided—her way of informing him what she decided to do, without uttering a word. He understands that she doesn't want to interfere in his life anymore, that she isn't going with him on such a dangerous excursion. He changes the subject. He has to grow up a little, be a little wiser, even if it's at the very end. "Never mind. I almost said something I shouldn't. Okay then, take care."

"Okay, I should go to bed anyway. Let's talk again tomorrow."

"I'm going to throw this phone away soon. I don't think we'll be able to talk for a while. But I know you'll write something great."

"Safe travels," Soji says.

He closes his phone, and notices that someone is standing next to him. Someone very familiar.

"Hello, sir, here you are. I've been looking for you."

HYON-MI PLAYS WITH the phone, huddled in her bed. The house is quiet. Only the cat is there, sleeping next to her peacefully. She stretches out and taps the cat's leg. The cat tucks her leg under her body, but doesn't bother to open her eyes. Hyon-mi pets the cat's other leg. She presses down on the cushiony pink pads of her feet, too. She starts to feel better. Hyon-mi decides she should call, and starts dialing.

"Hello? Hi, it's me. I'm home now . . . Thanks, I had a lot of fun. Is Chol home now? . . . Yeah? I wish I got to meet him. I guess he got there right after I left, huh? . . . Oh, here, at home? Nobody's here yet. My parents are like, always late . . . Oh me? I don't know, I'm just gonna watch some Go on TV . . . No, it's so much fun! . . . What do you mean, I'm like an old lady? It's 'cause you don't know how to play. It's really a lot of fun, I'm totally not kidding . . . A-yong? What about her? Oh, she had something to do today . . . I don't know, why are you asking me? . . . Sorry, sorry, I'm not mad at you . . . Yeah? So what did Chol say? . . . Really? That's hilarious . . . Really? Oh my God, really? . . . Yeah . . . Yeah, yeah . . . Huh? What do you mean, before—before when? Oh, you mean what we did before? Oh whatever, I don't know. Well, how do you feel about it? . . . Huh? Just say it . . . Well, I felt a little weird . . . I don't know. Is Chol right there next to you? Isn't it weird talking about this stuff with him there? . . . Really? Still . . . Children's Go? Yeah, I know how to play. It's hard if you play with people who are good . . . Of course there are rankings . . . Yeah, if you go online there's a ton of pros. It's different from Go but it's pretty much the same concept. It's basically who can see further ahead . . .

My mom? Oh, she hurt her arm a while ago . . . Yeah. Exactly. But she's still a good driver . . . She lets me do basically whatever I want . . . It's not that great, are you kidding? Oh, but my dad came to school today . . . Yeah . . . Yeah. But Soji went out to see him . . . What? I'm good at Korean lit . . . huh? . . . Soji? Oh, I guess she's around my dad's age? . . . What, an affair? No way. My dad's not the kind of person who would cheat like that. Hey, don't joke about stuff like that! . . . Okay. Yeah . . . What's Chol doing? . . . Oh, okay. So he really likes to spend time by himself, huh. He doesn't get bored? . . . Yeah, I guess you're right. There's a ton of things these days you can do by yourself . . . Oh, really? Oh wait, I think my mom's home. I gotta go. Bye, good night!"

Hyon-mi pads out to open the front door. She's right—it's her mother, her limp hair dangling against her cheeks. "You're not in bed yet?" Ma-ri asks, stroking her daughter's hair.

"No, it's still early!"

"How was your day?"

"Fine."

"Did you eat dinner?"

"Yeah, it was a friend's birthday today so I ate at the party."

She takes off her heels and puts them away. "Which friend?"

"Just a friend."

"Who?"

"Jin-guk. It's A-yong's friend."

"Oh, that boy who does ham radio?"

"Yeah."

Ma-ri takes off her clothes and throws them over a chair. She'll have to get them dry-cleaned tomorrow.

"Mom," Hyon-mi says.

"Yeah?" Ma-ri goes into the bathroom and turns on the water.

"Jin-guk lives in the same room as this kid named Chol."

"His older brother?"

"No, they're just friends."

"I guess it's a big room."

"No, it's just as big as mine. But the funnier thing is his parents don't know Chol's there."

Ma-ri rubs face wash over her face and rinses it off with one hand, which isn't easy. She pats her face dry with a towel. "Okay. Go to bed. You have school tomorrow," she says carelessly and drags herself into the bedroom. Her earlier invigoration is gone and the deadly fatigue has come over her again. She wants to lose consciousness, now.

"Mom, you know what?" Hyon-mi says, grabbing her sleeve.

Ma-ri cuts her off coldly. "Hyon-mi, Mom's really tired right now, okay? Let's talk tomorrow."

Hyon-mi storms into her room and slams the door. Ma-ri doesn't have any energy to deal with Hyon-mi. Still, she takes the time to shut all the windows tightly and to double-check that the latch to the front door is fastened. She draws the curtains and manages to crawl into bed. She tries to think about something but she's instantly sucked into sleep.

While her mother is wandering dizzily among various dreams, Hyon-mi thinks over the events of the day. Suddenly, as if cold water burst out of a showerhead, she understands something.

Chol doesn't exist.

He exists only in Jin-guk's head. Everything that doesn't make sense can be explained by this: Jin-guk's strange behavior and the tiny bedroom that couldn't possibly be shared by two boys. She closes her eyes. She thinks of Jin-guk, who is lying in the dark in his bed, chatting with an imaginary friend named Chol. Instead of being afraid, she feels sad for him, and she imagines holding him tightly. She decides that she will have to get rid of Chol, erase him from Jin-guk's imagination, and take his place. No, it won't be that hard to do that, she thinks, and pulls the blankets up to her chin.

PISTACHIO

So this is what's been going on," Ki-yong says, sitting next to Song-gon, handcuffed. Song-gon is like an actor who just stepped off the stage after a performance. The disguise is still there but he's acting completely differently from his stage persona. His inarticulate bumbling mannerisms are gone, and his bad posture is nowhere to be seen. He's still bald but now it looks like the symbol of a confident winner.

"No wonder. I had no idea you were behind it. I just thought that everything happened really easily for me. There's no way that banks would be that lenient in real life. I thought it was because I was good, smart, and adapted really well to capitalism. I can't even begin to imagine what you guys would have been saying about me, jeering behind my back." Ki-yong is calm.

Song-gon reassures him. "It wasn't exactly like that. You did well for yourself too, sir. A couple of our movies managed to draw a big audience. You didn't have any big hits, but you did have a few medium hits."

"No, no. Capitalism isn't that easy. Right? But good job with the acting, Song-gon. I really didn't catch on."

"No, it wasn't acting. This persona you're seeing right now, this is an act. At the office, I just acted the way I do when I'm at home, watching porn and picking my nose and napping. I was in a theater group for a little while in college, and they used to say that when you act, you're not creating something that doesn't exist, you're really discovering something within yourself."

Ki-yong isn't in the mood to sit there as if nothing is happening to him, listening to stories of Song-gon's brave exploits. He feels as if a snake were crawling up his throat. "You asshole."

"What?"

"You're an asshole."

Song-gon doesn't say anything.

"Admit it!"

The muscles in Song-gon's face stiffen. "I was just doing my job."

"That's why you're an asshole. You just do your job without thinking about what the consequences are. That's exactly what an asshole is," Ki-yong retorts, staring straight into his eyes. Sitting there in the dark, he can sense every tiny movement, the tension rippling through Song-gon's muscles. "I can't believe you guys were working behind the scenes all these years and I didn't suspect a thing . . ."

"I really am sorry about that," Song-gon says, in a way that doesn't sound like he is sorry at all. He sounds like a government official dealing with an annoying, complaining citizen. In this formal, polite man, Ki-yong is unable to glimpse the

Song-gon he has known for years—the Song-gon with bad credit and the porn addiction.

"You know you would have done the same thing if you were in my shoes, sir."

"Yeah, I guess so."

Only now does Ki-yong start to understand why Order 4 was issued. He thought the order came down because a workaholic successor of Lee Sang-hyok had come across his file. A successor with a strong loyalty to Party ideology and obsessive-compulsive disorder. Stumbling across Ki-yong's file, he would have wondered why Ki-yong was stranded in Seoul, and ordered his return. But maybe, for the past few years, the North and the South have engaged in an intense but frighteningly silent tug of war with him in the middle. He's like a trap for roaches—stuck deep in the corner under the sink, believing he's isolated from everything, but all the while emitting a scent into the world, signaling his presence. He was neither harmful nor harmless, but at some point, though he didn't notice it, the subtle balance of power between the North and the South that had been maintained for years was destroyed.

Of course, these guesses could be completely wrong. All he knows for sure is that he didn't know anything, and the fact is that he still doesn't know anything.

Another voice rings out from behind Ki-yong. Song-gon gets up and awkwardly greets the man. Song-gon doesn't sit back down, and the man motions with his chin, signaling that he should go away. Song-gon leaves the bench shaded by the wisteria vines.

"Hello, it's nice to meet you. My name is Jong. My men call me Supervisor Jong." Jong introduces himself and settles down next to Ki-yong. He takes out a bag of pistachios from his pocket and holds it out. "Would you like some?"

"No thanks."

"Please, try one. They're from California; they're especially tasty if they grow in dry climates. They have to be hard and firm on the outside but moist on the inside."

"Okay then." Ki-yong takes some pistachios in his hands, shells them, and tosses a few into his mouth.

"You've lived in this neighborhood for a while now, right?"

"About five years."

"You must have enjoyed the rising property values in this neighborhood."

"Well, a little. Not as much as in Kangnam, of course."

"I bought a house in Chunggye-dong four years ago. It's about forty pyong, and prices have risen quite a bit because the neighborhood's known for its good cram schools."

Silence envelops them, broken only by the crumpling of the pistachio bag and the sound of Jong biting into the nuts. Several more students walk past them.

"I understand you have a daughter?" Jong inquires politely.

"Yes."

"Is she a good student?"

Ki-yong drops the pistachio shells on the ground near his feet. "Yes, she's pretty good. She's like her mom, smart."

"I have a son, and he's so crazy about basketball that he won't sit still with books. It's a big source of worry for me," Jong confides.

"Well, if he's talented at it . . ."

"If he had some talent it would be ideal, but that's not really the case. By the way, your wife is quite a beauty."

Ki-yong looks at him, puzzled.

"Oh, no, don't take it the wrong way. We were waiting near your wife's work because we thought maybe you'd come see her there. She probably didn't even notice that we were there."

Ki-yong closes his eyes and thinks about Ma-ri, lying on her back, legs spread open, two guys having their way with her. He opens his eyes. He wonders if those scenes were broadcast live to an unknown place, like a reality program. "If I were to turn myself in . . . ?"

"We'll arrange it so that you do it with the two others."

"The two others?"

"Oh, please don't pretend you don't know what I'm talking about. This kind of thing is a lot like filing your taxes. You can file by yourself, but that's not as advantageous as it could be. You know what I mean, since you're a businessman, right? You just have to think of us as the accountant. If you leave it up to us, we'll take care of you. You just have to understand that you will have to pay a fee."

"A fee?"

"But it's win-win for everyone. You know how they talk about revealed comparative advantage in international trade? That's the kind of thing I'm talking about. You give us what we need, and in return we'll protect you, our client. That's the kind of thing we're good at."

"Is that really true?"

"If we work together and help each other out, everything will be fine. Even if they were to send people down south—which they may or may not do because they're running out of American dollars—or if the prosecutors' office senses something. Especially since, as you know, this isn't a standard criminal case."

If anyone were to overhear them, they would think this is a conversation between a corrupt corporation and an accountant, scheming about cooking the books.

"So is Han Jong-hun with you too?"

Jong grins and bites down on a pistachio shell, emitting a loud crack. "Of course. It's not like he's so special that he doesn't need us."

"So nobody's gone back?"

"Not that we know of. You never know, though, because this world's always shrouded in fog," Jong explains.

Two men wearing black jackets come forward and whisper to Jong, who nods and orders, "Okay, tell them to stay in their places. We're not done yet."

The two men bow and walk away.

"I guess the boys are a little cold," Jong explains.

"What's going to happen to me?" Ki-yong asks, looking down at his handcuffs.

"It depends on what you decide to do. If you decide to do the right thing, it's all going to be over quickly."

"So if you investigate and discover that I've done a lot of bad things, what happens?"

"We're not a church."

"What do you mean?"

"I mean that we're not the kind of place that will absolve you of the crimes we didn't know about."

"So what will happen to me?"

"First, if you have committed any crimes we have to know about them. Then we move on to the next step."

Ki-yong raises his head. "Why aren't you taking me into custody? Why are we still sitting on this bench?"

Jong smiles. "There's still something you have to do. The show must go on, as they say."

Song-gon and Jong speak in identical theater analogies. Why are they acting like this? Are they making fun of him with stupid jokes about college theater troupes? Is this their entertainment, or is it a tool to whittle away his wariness? Or are they just trying to convince him that all of this is only a play? Why are they doing this? Maybe they are actually afraid of Ki-yong, the victim. Like the chief priest in ancient times who performed sacrifices, they might be terrified about empathizing with the being that is to be sacrificed, worried that they will become emotionally damaged. They might be distancing themselves from this situation where a man's life is dangling by a thread, by making idiotic jokes and awkward analogies, wearing forced smiles. When Ki-yong thinks of it that way, he pities them, and feels freer, though only a little bit. For the first time since this morning, he can step away from the torrent that has swamped him and look down at the situation from a different, detached place. *How could anyone be free of fear, just because he works for the government? It must be stressful for you guys, too, to have to deal with this crap.*

"What do I have to do?"

Jong takes out a black digital watch from the inner pocket of his jacket. "You should wear this watch. It's an electronic bracelet. Once you put it on, it's hard to take it off, and in any case, it'll send us a signal the instant you try to remove it. See, it looks exactly like a watch. It's really light, too, so you shouldn't have any problems on a day-to-day basis. Of course, it also works as a watch and has an alarm function."

The watch has CASIO written on its face.

"Why aren't you taking me in right now and interrogating me?" Ki-yong asks.

"Oh, there's no reason to rush into it. We can tackle it slowly, step by step. After tonight, you can just go back home and act like you usually do. That's it," Jong explains.

Ki-yong bolts to his feet, and hears a sudden flurry of rustling in the flowerbeds, the sound of tree branches brushing against clothing. A few more men must be hiding there. "I can't do that," Ki-yong exclaims.

"Why not? Your family must be wanting you to come home."

"I already spoke with my wife. I told her everything," Ki-yong says firmly. He can't go home.

Jong tosses some pistachios into his mouth. "Yes, I know. I'm sorry, but we heard a part of your conversation."

Ki-yong flushes. "Then how can you ask me to go home after hearing all of that? I can't."

"You must. Don't you think you need to be there for your daughter?"

Ki-yong is quiet for a moment. Does Hyon-mi really need him? "My wife will do a good job raising her."

"Yes, but it's still a very important time in her childhood."

Ki-yong sinks down on the bench. "My wife wants me to go back north. You heard what she said."

"I'm sure she just said that because she was mad, and as you can see it's impossible for you to go back north."

"Well, she's not your wife, is she? I know her better than anyone," Ki-yong says, getting angry.

"Of course, of course," Jong says in a conciliatory tone. "But think about it from her perspective. She didn't know this about you for fifteen years. It's an understandable reaction. But you're married. Like they say, a fight between a married couple is like slicing through water with a sword."

Ki-yong doesn't reply. Jong sits there without saying anything for a while. He throws away the empty pistachio bag. The ground is covered with pistachio shells. He takes a cream-filled pastry out from his pocket and rips open the plastic wrapper. "Excuse me. They cut out a part of my stomach because of cancer, and now I have to eat constantly like a starving man," he explains.

"No, go ahead," Ki-yong says.

Jong bites off a chunk of the pastry and chews. Ki-yong tosses in his mouth the remainder of the pistachios Jong gave him, the nuts having turned damp in his sweaty palms. It doesn't taste like much of anything. "Supervisor Jong, I don't think you understand what kind of man Kim Ki-yong is," Ki-yong says.

"What do you mean?" Jong asks.

"When I was in junior high, when I was sixteen years old —I was Hyon-mi's age—I came home to find my mother had committed suicide. After that I had a hard time going home . . . You probably don't know what that feels like. Your house feeling like a prison, that really is a terrifying thing. I don't know why I'm telling you this, but even now, sometimes I wake up in the middle of the night, thinking that I'm in the Pyongyang apartment I grew up in. In my dreams I'm still sixteen."

"That must be very difficult."

"There's no need for you to be sarcastic. I think the most important part of being a parent is to create as many beautiful memories as possible for your children. But I haven't been able to give that many to Hyon-mi—maybe I haven't been the best dad. I think that the even more important thing about being a parent is not to give any horrible memories to a child. This is why I don't want to do it. I don't want to hurt my daughter by going home, digging into my wife's affair, arguing and attacking her, which would lead to her attacking me—revealing everything—and end with our hating each other. Do you understand? My wife's right. If I'm the only one who gets sacrificed, everything will be fine."

"I do know what you mean. But it all depends on how you do it. You have to go back home."

"Look, I'm telling you I can't!" Ki-yong shouts, frustrated.

Jong looks uncomfortable. "Okay, okay, calm down, Mr. Kim. I'm already convinced, really. Believe me. But I'm just the low man on the totem pole at the Company. Do you know what I mean? I'm just the messenger."

Ki-yong is momentarily taken over by a fantasy of all the blood in his veins flowing slowly, like thick porridge. A pervasive sense of powerlessness sticks to his skin like wet clothes. He can't figure out how to fight, with whom to argue, or even discern where the end to all this may be. Perhaps this is the beginning of the end. If he acquiesces to these demands, he has the feeling that he will, like Kafka's characters, busily and repetitively wander through a complicated maze, experiencing events that are tragedies for him but ridiculous comedies for everyone else. These men will observe him and his every act in a detached way, like biologists studying animal behavior, watching him mate, raise his young, work, and play. "So you're saying that I have no choice in the matter," Ki-yong says.

"Yes, exactly. For now, you should just go home. I mean, married life has its good parts and bad parts, right? Marriage is all about living together despite knowing each other's faults, overlooking them and understanding each other. So you should go back, work on the problem, and just live like you always have."

"Like I always have? Do you really think that's possible after this?" Ki-yong's voice betrays bitterness.

Jong isn't moved. "Of course it is. This is a bit embarrassing, but at the beginning of my marriage, when my wife got pregnant—you know, you can't really sleep with your wife when she's pregnant—I was sleeping with another woman and got caught. Well, I was actually sleeping with my sister-in-law, my wife's sister. It just happened, somehow, I don't know. These things happen, you know? Obviously it was a huge deal. Even now I have no idea how my wife found out. She went crazy, screaming at me that she'd get rid of the baby. But now, you'd never know that happened. I'd like to tell you, as someone who's lived a few more years than you have, it all tends to work out in the end."

"What happened to your sister-in-law?"

For the first time since Ki-yong met Jong, he hesitates, opening then closing his mouth without saying anything. But he starts speaking again. "She committed suicide. Oh, no, don't get me wrong, it wasn't because of that. Her husband ran a business, manufacturing parts like bike pedals and seats, but it went under so their whole family took poison and killed themselves in a motel room. The kids were really cute . . ." He stops talking and sits in silence.

It's late—the noise of the cars whizzing by on the big thoroughfare adjacent to the apartment complex is no longer discernible. The sound of the TV in a nearby apartment is now louder than the cars.

Ki-yong breaks the silence. "Okay."

"What?"

"Give . . . give me the watch," Ki-yong replies, calmly.

"Oh, that? Oh, good. Let me tell you, you made the right choice." Jong signals behind him and Chol-su appears and uncuffs Ki-yong.

Jong says apologetically, "It will be much more comfortable than the cuffs." He hands the electronic bracelet to Chol-su, who presses a couple of buttons and hands it back.

"It's ready," Chol-su announces.

"Oh, great. So we don't have to reset it?"

"No."

Ki-yong holds out his left arm and Jong presses the bracelet to his wrist. The device instantly clamps around his wrist.

It feels like a cold-blooded animal, like a snake, against his skin. Ki-yong shivers despite himself.

Jong smiles, more relaxed, relieved. "Now that you've put that on, there's one last thing you have to do before you go home."

Ki-yong doesn't reply, staring down at his left wrist.

EMPIRE OF LIGHT

K I-YONG SEES the levee stretching straight out toward the lighthouse far away, like a piece of bamboo, but the middle of it is bent, curving toward the artillery of the inner harbor at a fifteen-degree angle, as if children horsing around damaged it. The harbor lies two and a half miles away from where Ki-yong is standing, dotted with a few lights that probably belong to restaurants still open for business. The faint light flickering in the harbor is reflected in the dark sea, dancing among the waves. It's a dark night, the moon and the stars hidden out of sight. Crouched behind a rock, Ki-yong looks at his watch. The lighthouse is shooting a ray toward the open ocean, and on the shore, far from the harbor, searchlights sweep the ground where sea and land meet, aimlessly drawing irregular arcs.

Ki-yong knows that in the dark ocean far away, someone is watching the black shore through binoculars. He knows that the crew—whose nerves are on edge because they have spent days in the cramped midget submarine, sustained only by bits of raw ramen—will be waiting inside, fighting the urge to go to the bathroom and fingering in their pockets the poison-filled capsules to swallow in an emergency. The lead unit will be waiting for the hatch to open, wearing flippers.

At 3:00 on the dot, Ki-yong takes a small Maglite from his pocket and turns it on and off toward the pitch-black sea, as if he were signaling into the depths of the universe. A little later, a somewhat incomplete response bounces over the peaks of waves. This communication makes his heart pound—they've come to get him, risking their lives. They are waiting for him below the surface of the water. They've come from far away, certain of the righteousness of their mission. Well-trained comrades are only a stone's throw away. Nostalgia unexpectedly envelops him. Regardless of whatever Liaison Office 130 has done to his life, he spent his youth there. He was twenty years old, missing his family and the girl he left behind in Pyongyang, uncertain of his own future. He was perpetually covered in sweat and his uniform always stank. He was hungry all the time, but was confident in his toned muscles and alert instincts. He believed that he had found comrades he would gladly die for, that he was working toward revolution, immersed in a lifetime of work they would achieve together. He believed, though briefly, that one man could change another, and that changed people could transform the world. Huddled behind a rock on the Taean peninsula, he realizes once again how far he's come from all of that, how different he is today. How different he is now, compared to twenty years ago, when he swam onto this very shore. The Maglite signal puts him face-to-face with his twenty-year-old self, separated by only a shoreline.

The members of the lead unit are swimming toward the beach by now, pushing against the current with their shoulders, kicking with all their might. Or maybe they are using a propeller with an electric motor. Ki-yong listens. He thinks he can sense the faint vibration of a machine cutting through the rhythmic waves. He trembles. The wind is getting stronger and its dampness chills the tip of his nose. He rubs his nose with the hand that isn't holding the light.

At that moment, the searchlights all begin to focus on one particular point, instead of lazily sweeping the shore. At first, it looks like it's a random accident, but soon the columns of light swing along the curving shore to meet on the imaginary arc that links Ki-yong to the submarine. Then flares shoot up from behind dunes with a swoosh. The flares, bursting up to the sky, brighten the area like it's daytime. Gunfire concentrates on the spot where all the searchlights meet. Bullets from automatic rifles fly through the waves toward the submarine. The shore, illuminated by the flares, looks surreal. The sky is black but the world below is bright. Like René Magritte's *Empire of Light*. There are no shadows on the sandy dunes, which shine brightly. Bullets spray into the sea from the bunker behind the dunes, and the searchlight on top of the rocky hill throws a dazzling brightness on everything, refracting off the surface of the dark ocean. Ki-yong looks away from the fight erupting on the water and reflects on his long day. From far away, he hears the rat-tat-tat of machine guns, but it doesn't sound threatening at all. Soon he doesn't even hear that. Only the flares shoot up again and again toward the dark sky and fall back to Earth, leaving behind gorgeous trails.

Ki-yong hears Jong through his earpiece. "Okay, I think that's enough. You can come back now."

Ki-yong gets up and walks through the shadows, avoiding the slope of the rock, away from the shore.

"The midget submarine has probably gone back safely. I doubt they'll suspect you of betrayal after all of the gunfire," Jong says.

A searchlight spots Ki-yong, still walking, and illuminates his figure. He stops, trapped in a strong beam. His expression is peaceful and gentle, that of a man who has finally accepted his fate. But if one looks closely, one might catch something like tears coursing down, following the grooves in his face. He looks like a ghost, the shadows on his face erased. The searchlight glides away, back toward the dark sea.

PERVERT

CHOL-SU GETS out of his car and walks toward Motel Bohemian. The heavy, humid air still hangs low in the dark of the early morning. He enters the lobby and walks to the end of the hall without stopping. The speaker mounted on the ceiling blares something at him, but he ignores it. At the end of the hall, he pushes what looks like a wall with his foot, and it opens. The room behind it is shabby and sparsely decorated, unlike the ornately designed vestibule outside. A man in his sixties, wearing gold-rimmed glasses, is sleeping inside the room. He bolts up and grabs his remote control, yelling, "Who the hell are you?"

Chol-su wrests the remote away from him. Nine 14-inch monitors fill one wall. The man, fumbling, now grabs his wallet. Chol-su slides his ID out of his own wallet and flashes it at the man.

"Give me everything you've recorded since nine P.M. We need it for investigative purposes."

"We don't record anything," the man stammers, looking at Chol-su suspiciously. Chol-su steps into the room with his shoes still on and scans the wires attached to the monitors. He quickly finds several tapes. He silences the man with a glare and examines the tapes.

"You fucking pervert," Chol-su spits.

"I'm going to report you!"

"Do it, you bastard," Chol-su snaps, and sweeps the tapes into his bag. He walks out of the hallway, through the doors, and gets into his car. He tosses the bag onto the passenger seat, the tapes clattering inside. One falls out. He picks it up and puts it back in the bag. He starts the car and steps on the gas.

A NEW DAY

HYON-MI'S ROOM faces east. Bright sunlight shimmers through the open curtains, stabbing her eyes. She gets up, squinting, and ventures into the living room. Ki-yong is sitting on the sofa with the paper.

"Did you sleep well?" she asks.

"Yeah, what about you?"

"You look tired, Dad," she comments.

"Do I?"

"Yeah."

"I had a lot of work to do."

"You pulled an all-nighter?" Hyon-mi asks sleepily, plopping down on a stool next to the couch. "Oh, Dad, did you come to school yesterday?"

"No," Ki-yong says, forgetting that he did.

"Really?"

"Why?"

"This guy looked exactly like you, and drove the same car, too."

"Sonatas are very popular cars."

Hyon-mi scratches the back of her neck, leaving behind a red mark. "Oh, no wonder."

"What?"

"I figured you'd stop by and see me if you came, right?"

"Of course."

"Mom's not up yet?"

"No, don't wake her up. I think she's tired."

"Yeah, but she still has to go to work." Hyon-mi suspects that something happened between her parents last night. Did they have some serious sex last night? She could always detect a special mood hanging in the air in the morning after a night like that. Dad always looked a little depressed; Mom was bright and softer. Mom would sleep in while Dad got up early to make breakfast or read the paper. They would talk less than usual, but she would catch them giving each other flirty glances or being more playful, and everything would seem at peace. But today it feels a little different. She can't put her finger on it, but today isn't like yesterday or, actually, like any other day.

Hyon-mi picks up the cat rubbing against her feet, and notices the wool blanket folded neatly on one end of the couch. Her dad spent the night on the couch. She notices a new black watch on his wrist, too. She's curious about a few things but she doesn't ask. If she keeps dawdling she'll be late for school. She goes into the bathroom and locks the door. As she shoves her toothbrush in her mouth, she remembers Jin-guk's rough tongue pushing gently into her mouth. She blushes and shakes her head, hard. But the more she tries to forget it, the more acute the sensation is, causing her to tremble. She sticks her tongue out and brushes it with her toothbrush vigorously. She heaves, tensing her neck and shoulders, blood rushing to her head. She rinses her tooth-brush and her mouth. She gargles, the water rinsing everything down to her tonsils, then spits into the sink. She rinses again with cool water and wipes her mouth dry. She feels better. She wonders what awaits her today.

Her mom is standing in the middle of the room, pale, staring at her dad sitting on the sofa. Hyon-mi opens the fridge door and calls out to her mother. "Hi, Mom. Did you sleep well?"

"Hi," Ma-ri replies absentmindedly, then goes back into the master bedroom.

Hyon-mi figures they got into a big fight again. She pours some milk in a cup and drinks it. It's become too cold in the fridge overnight, and doesn't taste as good as usual. She puts down the cup and stretches, twisting her body. She feels more awake and invigorated. She senses a strength building up from deep inside her. Everything is going to turn out fine. She goes into her room, takes out her school uniform from her closet, and closes her bedroom door. A new day.